EXHUME

ALSO BY DANIELLE GIRARD

Savage Art

Ruthless Game

Chasing Darkness

Cold Silence

Dead Center

One Clean Shot

Dark Passage

Interference

Everything to Lose

EXHUME

A NOVEL

DANIELLE GIRARD

This is a work of fiction. Names, characters, organizations, places, events, and incidents are either products of the author's imagination or are used fictitiously.

Published by Thomas & Mercer, Seattle

www.apub.com

ISBN-13: 9781503939301
ISBN-10: 1503939308

Cover design by Mecob Design Ltd

Printed in the United States of America

For Randle—first reader, story navigator, rock star

1

San Francisco, California

Dr. Annabelle Schwartzman threaded her half-circle number-five suture needle, the kind normally used in orthopedic surgery. Pinching together the edges of the Y-incision she'd made an hour earlier, she began the process of closing the victim's chest.

The chest and torso had been badly burned, and the fire left the skin fragile. Since there wasn't going to be an open casket, the standard protocol was to use staples to close the incision. Schwartzman preferred sutures. Staples were effective but seemed too industrial. The sutures were slower, and she enjoyed these last minutes with the victim, the time to fully process the death before contacting the investigator.

Both the intensity and the reward of the medical examiner's job were in being the final voice for a victim. Schwartzman was the last person to have access to the body, the one who decided if death was from natural causes or at the hand of another. It was intense and quiet work, the hours spent studying each piece in a puzzle that needed to be worked out.

In medical school, many of her peers chose specialties in order to interact with patients—gynecology for the joys of birth, or pediatrics for the children.

But those jobs came with sadness, too. Fetuses didn't always make it to full term. Children developed diseases and died.

As an ME, Schwartzman interacted with patients in the most intimate way—limitless in the depths she could go to diagnose a death. For many, forensic pathology would seem like an impossible choice. For her, it was the only one. People chose medicine for the heroics—to cure disease, save lives. In forensic pathology, there were no heroics. Just unanswered questions.

The overhead light shut off. She waved her arm in the air to trigger the motion sensor. After 7:00 p.m., the lights automatically turned off after ten minutes. The halogen in the corner crackled angrily as it flickered on and off before settling into a solid glow. The hallways were dark, the room silent.

Some of the department's other medical examiners worked with loud music, but Schwartzman appreciated the silence. One reason she enjoyed being in the morgue at odd hours.

She had been heading home from a dinner with some women from the police force when the morgue called her, leaving her energized, ready for work.

She didn't go to the morgue because there was work—the work was always there. What she loved about the morgue was the space. The smell of the grapefruit lotion she used after she'd washed up and before she donned gloves, the vinegar scent of the clean instruments and table.

She always smelled these before the body.

The girls' night out with her coworkers on the force had given her a chance to talk to Homicide Inspector Hailey Wyatt, to get to know her away from the crime scenes they had worked together. Schwartzman had surprised herself by opening up about Spencer.

How long since she had done that?

Melanie in the last year of medical school—six and a half years ago—that was the last time she'd allowed herself to get close to someone.

Her phone buzzed. A text from Hailey. `Glad u came tonight. See u tmrrw.`

Schwartzman smiled. She had felt a growing closeness. They might become friends.

Spencer kept her isolated, certainly while they were married but even after she'd escaped. He had planted the notion that he was always close—confiding in someone was offering a key that might be used against her.

Dinner hadn't felt that way at all. It was a relief to get her truth out there—a man she hadn't seen in more than seven years was stalking her. He'd made her believe her mother was in the hospital. Had managed to elude building security at her apartment and deliver a bouquet of yellow flowers. A color Spencer loved and she despised.

But he was a fool to think he could get to her.

She was with the police department. That bouquet of flowers was being processed by Roger Sampers—the head of the Crime Scene Unit himself. In only six months, San Francisco had started to feel like home. Here, for the first time, she had her own space. She was in charge of her own work, which gave her the opportunity to give it the focus it deserved and to excel at something she loved.

Because she was good, she was appreciated. She had the support of her peers. She had . . . friends. A ridiculous thought for a thirty-six-year-old woman, but there it was. She liked it here.

Seattle had always been temporary. The first city away from Spencer, a place to regroup, finish her training. Seattle was perfect for that period of her life.

She was a doctor now, ready to begin her career, put down roots. She had spent long enough looking over one shoulder. She was determined to stay in San Francisco, even more so after the evening with those women.

She made her final notes and signed off on the work. Her phone buzzed in her pocket as she was sliding the body back into the drawer. She snapped off her gloves and pulled the phone from her lab coat. *Hal.*

"You're psychic," she said in lieu of hello.

"Oh yeah?" Homicide Inspector Hal Harris said. In the six months they had worked together, she and Hal had created a comfortable banter that made cases with him her favorites.

"How's that?"

"I just finished our burn victim."

"And?" Hal asked.

"Autopsy showed massive bilateral pulmonary thromboembolism with pulmonary infarction."

Hal groaned. "English, Schwartzman."

"Natural causes," she said. "He died of massive blood clots in his lungs."

"Guy dies of natural causes, then drops a cigarette in bed and torches his own house." Hal had a knack for pointing out the ironies of their job, but they were always relieved when the autopsy revealed a death was due to natural causes.

"Yep. You want me to call Hailey?"

"No. I'll tell her," Hal said. "You ready for another one?"

"Sure," Schwartzman said. She was always game for another case. Lost in a case at the morgue, home alone with a book or occasionally an old black-and-white movie—usually one her father had loved—those were her best moments.

The distractions were all the more important now that Spencer had found her again. The phone calls, the creepy bouquet of yellow flowers that had appeared outside her apartment door. Worse was the fact that no one in the heavily secured building could explain how the deliveryman gained access to her floor. Seven years and five months since she'd left, and he would not give up.

"I'll text the address and send over a picture from Dispatch," Hal said. "I'm about five minutes out."

"I'll try to leave here in the next ten."

"Great," Hal said. "See you then."

She was ready to end the call when he said, "Hey, Schwartzman?"

"Yeah?"

"Nice work on that last one."

She smiled. Hal was good at praising his peers—herself, the crime scene techs, the patrol officers. It was another of his endearing qualities. "Thanks, Hal."

She ended the call and removed her lab coat, hanging it in her narrow locker. After exchanging the orange Crocs she wore in the lab for her street shoes, she packed up her case for the scene. Her phone buzzed with the address Hal had sent. She double-clicked on the attached image. Waited as it loaded.

The image came into focus.

A woman. About Schwartzman's age. Wavy, brunette hair. Laid out on her bed. Shivers rippled across Schwartzman's skin like aftershocks. Someone had already put a sheet over her legs and stomach, as though she'd been found nude, but a thin stripe of her clothing was visible above her waist. Other than the pale color of her skin, she might have been sleeping.

In her hands was a small bouquet of yellow flowers.

2

San Francisco, California

Schwartzman studied the flashing lights of the patrol car parked on the curb. In between the rotating bursts of blue, her vision was stained the color of blooming daffodils. She couldn't shake the image of the flowers she'd found outside her door. No call from the front desk to tell her she had a delivery. The sole alert had been the sound of the bell right outside her door. Through the peephole, she'd seen an empty hallway. Then she'd opened the door and found the huge bouquet beside the door. Pale- and bright-yellow roses, calla lilies, freesia, mums.

She clenched her fists, fought off the fear.

On the street, the lights painted shadows across the front of the stucco building and washed the undersides of leaves on the small oak trees that lined the boulevard, giving everything the appearance of being underwater.

Neighbors stood along the sidewalk, jackets closed over pajamas or sweats to ward off the chill in the San Francisco night air. They huddled in small groups, arms crossed, watching. Waiting for answers. This was not the kind of neighborhood where people were murdered. They looked cold and frightened. Schwartzman felt the same.

She would not give in to it. She didn't know that Spencer was behind this death. Rule one of forensic pathology: never expect an outcome. Something she appreciated about the job. Shortcuts didn't work.

She emerged from the car and popped the trunk to remove a hard-sided black case. Focused, she crossed the sidewalk to the building, showed her credentials at the door, and stepped over the threshold.

Ken Macy was the patrol officer at the door. "Evening, Doc."

Schwartzman smiled at the friendly face. "Evening, Ken. I didn't expect to see you on tonight." She removed her short black boots and slid into the pair of navy Crocs she used for indoor scenes.

"Traded a shift for Hardy. He got tickets to the Warriors tonight, taking the family."

"Lucky him," she said, enjoying the moment of banter.

"I know, right?"

Schwartzman stretched blue booties over the Crocs. "Any new restaurants to add to my list?"

"Did you try that Lebanese place I recommended?" he asked.

"Mazzat," she confirmed. "Yes. I did. Last week. I meant to e-mail you. I had the kafta. It was amazing."

Ken smiled. "That's one of my favorites, too. That and the bamia."

Ken had a seemingly endless list of the best spots for ethnic takeout in the city. "I'm ready for a new one."

"Absolutely," he said. "I'll have something for you when you come back out."

"Perfect. I'm sure I'll be starving." One of the things she'd noticed about her new life in San Francisco was how her appetite had grown. Seattle had amazing restaurants, but her time there had been intense and focused. Stressed by Spencer and by school, she'd rarely eaten out, and the food she did pick up had been for sustenance rather than enjoyment.

Now, living in a new city, out from under some of that weight, her appetite was rejuvenated. It wasn't unusual for her to have a second dinner after a late crime scene. She picked up her bag and turned her attention to the building, shifting into work mode. She glanced into the foyer, unsure where she was headed.

"Oh right," Ken said, shaking his head. "Sorry. Take the elevator on up to four. It's real clean. No blood at all."

"Thanks, Ken," Schwartzman said, carrying her case into the foyer.

The building was probably built in the 1940s. Narrow entry, large marble tiles in the pinkish salmon that was popular then. She passed a woman in pajamas and stepped into the empty elevator just as the doors were closing. The elevator bumped and shook slightly as it rose. Schwartzman was grateful for the lift anyway. She was not a fan of stairs, especially not with the case.

The interior of the victim's apartment had been recently remodeled. Wide-plank hardwood floors throughout. Walls finished in a concrete-like texture that she recognized as American Clay. Sage green. Two large oils hung on the biggest walls. Both rustic scenes, one of a river and a mill, the other an old barn. A tasteful chenille couch with silk floral throw pillows.

Despite the decor, dark undertones were palpable. The room was too bright. Too perfect. Pictures framed on the table, set at perfect angles to one another. Nothing out of place.

Someone used to controlling things.

Or making it look that way.

Her first thought was domestic murder. People assumed domestic murders were committed by alcoholics and druggies, but a perfect home was as clear a sign of dysfunction as a slovenly one.

Under all the illusion of perfection, something ugly was often at play.

In Spencer's house, everything had its place. Down to the white porcelain cup where the toothbrush lived when it wasn't being used. The way the towels were folded in the towel rings, the direction in which the toilet paper unrolled. Her towels were never folded now. Not in more than seven years. She wondered which way the roll in her bathroom faced. She hadn't noticed. Progress.

Hailey Wyatt was on the far side of the living room with one of the crime scene analysts, working intently. Like herself, Hailey still wore the clothes she'd had on at dinner. Not wanting to interrupt, Schwartzman passed the kitchen. A single wineglass with an inch of red wine sat on the counter next to a dark-wood cutting board with an inlaid bamboo center. A thin knife lay across its edge, the blade jutting off the side as though, at any moment, it might fall. Crumbs. Dinner perhaps. Wine and cheese with bread. Schwartzman's favorite meal.

Three doors opened off a short hallway. The rooms were tidy and feminine, similar in style to the living room. No sign of a second inhabitant. She paused at the office door. Nothing out of place there either. A desk with an open book. A yellow bookmark lay between the two pages. No computer, no papers. Tidy. Too tidy. She moved on.

The body would be in the next room.

The dead did not spook her. Skin slippage, blistering, the blackness of putrefaction—those were all natural parts of death. Even the smell had lost its sharp edges and grown manageable. Especially when the body was discovered early, as it had been here.

The room smelled faintly of a candle that had been lit. Something earthy with a slight spice. Perhaps sandalwood.

Homicide Inspector Hal Harris stood by the bed, staring down at the victim as Schwartzman entered the room. Detectives in San Francisco were still referred to as inspectors, though she had yet to find someone who knew exactly why.

Even in the large room, he took up a sizable chunk of real estate. An imposing figure at six four and somewhere north of 220, Hal had flawless dark skin that made his hazel eyes look green, especially in bright light. His expression stern, he gave off the impression of being someone not to mess with. Behind the facade, Hal was both easygoing and extremely kind.

She was particularly glad that he and Hailey had caught this case. She had seen them solve a couple of tough cases since her arrival in San Francisco. A combination of smarts and determination. Those flowers unnerved her, and she felt calmer knowing that they were here.

He didn't bombard her when she walked into the scene. As usual, he didn't say a word.

It was a grand bedroom, particularly for an apartment in a city whose square feet sold for a multiple of hundreds of dollars each. As she did in every case, Schwartzman studied the space before the body. Often the surroundings gave context to the body. What she saw here was more of the same. A single, generic painting on the wall of a meadow, tall wheat bent in the wind.

There were several photographs in small frames on the coffee table in the living room, but none in the bedroom. Nothing personal at all.

The body was arranged on the neatly made-up bed. The sheet that had covered her in the image from Dispatch had been removed. She was not nude. The victim wore a lightly patterned yellow dress.

Schwartzman was reminded of the matching outfits from Lilly Pulitzer that Spencer so loved. Christmas, Easter, even the Fourth of July were occasions marked with a new dress for her and a matching button-down for him. Like they were children dressed by a wealthy housewife.

There wasn't a spot of yellow in her closet. In her house.

The victim's yellow dress had been fanned out and smoothed across the duvet. Gold flats. Tory Burch. Schwartzman could see the familiar emblem on the soles.

And the yellow flowers.

They were not the same as in the bouquet she had received from Spencer. That had been formal, almost a wedding-style bouquet, while these were more like wildflowers, long greens with tiny blossoms, the bunch held together by a piece of white string like cooking twine. Altogether different. Two different bouquets of yellow flowers. A coincidence.

Not everything tied to Spencer.

He only wanted her to think that.

She set her bag on the ground and opened it up for a fresh Tyvek suit, reining in her thoughts.

The victim had been found in her bedroom. Affluent, white, early to midthirties. In a secured building.

Schwartzman stepped into the suit and raised the plastic-like fabric up over her dark slacks. It was warm in the apartment. With the suit at her waist, she unbuttoned her gray cashmere sweater, removed it, and placed it in her scene kit beside the box of gloves before pulling the suit up over her tank top. She hated the feeling of the fabric on her arms, but the room was too hot. Sweating under the Tyvek was distracting. She needed to be comfortable enough to give the scene her full attention.

She checked that her kit was open, made a mental note of her thermometer and the notebook where she would record her initial findings.

"What do we know?" she asked, snapping on her gloves as she crossed to the victim.

"The sister called it in," Hal said. "Came for a visit from Southern California and found her like this."

Schwartzman pressed her fingers into the skin. Lividity was apparent on the right side of her arm. "She's been moved."

"I agree. It's too clean to be the original crime scene."

Schwartzman examined the skin for early signs of bruising, checked the eyes for petechiae and found none. She fingered the victim's rib cage, then her neck. "Not strangled. No obvious trauma. I'll have to get her to the morgue to find cause of death."

"I figured," Hal said. "What about drugs?"

With a penlight, Schwartzman checked the victim's nose and mouth. The passages were clear. She leaned in to smell the victim's mouth. A little halitosis but no hint of drugs. "It's possible. But I wouldn't guess overdose. I don't see any residue in the nose and mouth." She pulled off one of her gloves. "There's a wineglass in the kitchen."

"I've asked Roger's team to collect it." Head of the Crime Scene Unit, Roger Sampers was extremely thorough. Somehow Hal managed to have Roger at most of his scenes, a testament to how much people respected the inspector. Roger was meticulous, comfortable with his own intelligence. Humor came easily to him, and, while he was often self-deprecating, he was careful not to make jokes at the expense of others.

"Good." Her skin was hot and her hands cold and clammy. Coming down with something maybe. "What do we know about her?"

"Victoria Stein. Lived alone. The sister wasn't aware of a current boyfriend. According to the sister, Stein divorced a couple of years ago. Moved to San Francisco and bought this place."

Schwartzman replaced the gloves with fresh ones and raised the victim's top, pointed to the lividity. "Appears she died on her side. Makes the overdose possibility less likely. OD tends to result in death by aspiration."

"Could she aspirate if she was on her side?"

"They can," she said. "But it's not common." She examined the victim's scalp for signs of contusion. "You said she's not from California?"

"From somewhere down south."

"Oh yeah? You know where?" The skull was normal. No trauma to indicate cause of death there either.

He checked his notebook. "Here it is . . . Spartanburg. The victim's sister said it's close to—"

"Greenville," Schwartzman finished for him. One town over from her own hometown.

"You know it?" Hal asked, surprised.

The victim's earlobes were pierced, but she was not wearing earrings. No jewelry visible on the dresser. "The sister mention if there was any jewelry missing?"

"No. Stein didn't wear any, I guess."

A bit unusual. In her experience, most women wore jewelry. The more affluent the woman, the nicer the jewelry. There were exceptions, of course. She herself was one. Schwartzman had gone so long without earrings, her holes had closed up.

Spencer didn't like earrings. Lobes were to be bare.

One of his rules. Something always reminded her of him. Maybe one day it wouldn't. She hoped.

Schwartzman raised the victim's hands, studying the palms for defensive wounds.

"You seeing anything?"

"Not yet," she admitted. "Victim's nails are pretty short, so it's possible we wouldn't see breakage with defensive wounds." She studied the underside of the nails. "But I don't see any tissue underneath." She flipped the hand back over and studied the fingers for the telltale indentation or sun mark that would indicate a ring. None.

No earrings, no ring. Could be skin allergies.

She shifted the neckline of the victim's dress and found a thin gold chain. She pulled it free of the dress to see the pendant. A gold cross. On the right side was a small hole, about the size of a pinhead. Like the kind jewelers used to let light through to gems. After laying the cross in her gloved palm, Schwartzman used her free hand to flip it over.

Embedded in the gold of the right cross beam was a Star of David.

"Oh, God." She dropped the pendant, pedaled away from the body. Snapped the gloves off and let them fall to the floor.

"What is it?" Hal said, crossing to her.

His hands gripped her shoulders. The pressure was reassuring, settling the waves of panic that made it hard to stand. It couldn't be a coincidence.

"Schwartzman," he said firmly. "Talk to me. Are you okay?"

She leaned into his hands, shook her head slowly.

"What happened?" Hailey Wyatt appeared in the doorway.

Just hours earlier they had been talking about Spencer. She had opened up to Hailey and the others about Spencer. She'd told Hailey about being trapped in that marriage. And now . . . Schwartzman hugged herself to fight the shaking.

"My God, you look like you've seen a ghost, Schwartzman," Hailey said. "Are you okay?"

If only Spencer were a ghost. But he was all too real. The victim's dress was yellow. She wore no jewelry. These were just coincidences.

"Shit. Did you know her?"

"No. It's not her—" She pressed her palm to her chest. Hers was there. She felt suddenly exposed. As though by speaking of Spencer at dinner, she had conjured him into being right here. She had allowed herself to open up about him, and here he was.

"Why would you think she'd know the victim?" Hal asked.

"I don't know, but they look alike," Hailey said. "The wavy hair, the shape of the face, the nose. It must have freaked her out."

They did look alike. God, how had he managed to find a woman who looked like her? She wasn't imagining it. The lack of jewelry, the dress, the flowers. It was all him.

"No," Hal said. "She didn't freak out until she saw the necklace."

Schwartzman remained against the wall. Her bare hands pressed to the skin on her neck. It was icy cold and also slick, like a body coming out of the morgue refrigeration unit after being washed down.

"It's a cross with the Star of David on it," Hailey said. "And a little gemstone in the star."

Would they think she was crazy when she showed them? She had spent months building up their trust. It took so little to break it.

What choice did she have? She couldn't hide the pendant from them.

Schwartzman forced herself to lower her hands. "It's a Christian cross with a Star of David on it," she said, struggling to get the words out. "The Star of David is placed exactly where the heart would be if the cross were a woman. A tiny diamond in the center of the star."

Schwartzman fingered the chain on her neck, located the pendant under her tank. To celebrate their first wedding anniversary, her father had designed a pendant for her mother.

The room tipped, and Schwartzman closed her eyes.

A pendant identical to the one on the dead woman.

3

San Francisco, California

"Schwartzman!" The voice was urgent and female. Schwartzman had to pull herself back to focus on where she was. She saw beige carpet, a green duvet at eye level. Above her, Hailey and Hal were staring down. She was on the floor, her back to the wall.

"Help me get her up," Hailey told Hal.

She flinched at Hal's huge hands on her shoulder and back, but she was on her feet quickly. *Compose yourself.* She wasn't some distraught female. She was a doctor, a scientist.

"Can someone get me a bottle of water?" Hailey shouted into the hallway.

Hailey and Hal. She could tell them. They needed to know. "I'm fine." Schwartzman cleared her throat. "Really. It was startling is all."

They would think she was crazy. That was always her mother's response—that she was overreacting or making something of nothing.

This was not *nothing*. Or maybe it was. She was overreacting. She needed time to calm herself, to think about it before she spoke up. Never predict an outcome, a lesson of her field. She was a scientist. Follow the evidence. The body would provide the answers.

"The necklace?" Hailey asked.

"It's unusual."

Hal and Hailey exchanged a glance. It was a necklace. Just a necklace. And of course there would be others like it. That she had never seen another one herself meant nothing.

One of the crime scene techs, Naomi Muir, entered the room, carrying a bottle of water. She gave it to Hal.

He cracked the top and pressed the bottle into Schwartzman's hands. "Drink this."

She lifted the water to her lips, took a sip. The cold jolted her, bringing her focus back to the room, the case. She handed it back. "I'm better." She unzipped the Tyvek suit, released the hot air. "I just overheated a little."

Hailey watched her with a suspicious gaze. Schwartzman felt herself shrink. She needed them to believe her. What would she do if they didn't? San Francisco was supposed to be her fresh start, her clean slate. How she wanted to just start over. But she knew better.

She shook the Tyvek suit at the zipper to force in some fresh air, then zipped it back up.

Donning a fresh pair of gloves, she returned to the body. She studied the slight bump in the victim's nasal bridge and ran her fingers across the cartilage for signs of a break. There was none. Like Schwartzman, Victoria Stein was born with rounded septal cartilage that gave her a traditional Jewish-looking nose.

Schwartzman's mother had offered her a nose job on her sixteenth birthday, hoping her daughter might decide on something straighter and more patrician, more like her own.

"Find something?" Hal asked.

Shaking her head, Schwartzman moved on from the nose to probe the jaw and cheekbones. Nothing to explain cause of death. Finally, she opened the victim's mouth and peered into the teeth. Regularly whitened, straight.

Nothing to suggest trauma.

Schwartzman stood back and inspected the area around the victim, then studied the victim head to toe for contusions or signs of trauma, measured the core temperature, and bagged the hands to preserve evidence. "I can't give you cause of death without an autopsy," she said as she removed her gloves. "No obvious lacerations or contusions, no evident injuries at all to suggest what killed her."

"Well, it certainly wasn't natural," Hal added.

"No. Definitely not."

Schwartzman found Hailey looking back and forth between her and the victim. Hailey was comparing them. The dark hair, the length, their height . . . they might have been sisters. "So there's no reason to draw any connections between you and the victim?"

"Not without being paranoid." The comment was as much, or more, for her as for them. She would not be paranoid. That was what he wanted, to remain at the front of her mind, where every little thing reminded her of him. She would not do that. San Francisco was a fresh break, a real start. "The victim does look like me. She is holding a bouquet of yellow flowers . . ."

"They look familiar?" Hal asked, and she felt the weight of his stare.

Of course Hal knew about the flowers. Roger would have shared that with him.

They had talked about her. It felt like an intrusion, but it shouldn't have. They were protecting her. As colleagues. She would do the same for them. "The flowers are different. The ones I got were more formal." She wondered if Roger was still working on them. "Is Roger here? I was going to ask him if he found anything on the ones I received."

"I haven't seen him yet, but I'll check in with him when I do," Hal said.

No doubt the lab was overwhelmed with real cases, but Schwartzman had hoped they would expedite the flowers. "These are more like wildflowers than the bouquet that came to my apartment."

The dress is something he would have picked. She couldn't force herself to say the words aloud.

That was not evidence, and conjecture was not useful.

"She's from the town next to the one you grew up in," Hal went on.

"There are more than sixty thousand people in Greenville and probably another forty thousand in Spartanburg. It's not like we all know each other, and I have no idea who this woman is."

"Okay," he conceded.

"Anything else you want to add to this, Schwartzman?" Hailey asked.

Schwartzman straightened her back and touched the hollow of her neck. It was as though Hailey could see she was holding something back.

Hailey would be connecting their conversation to Schwartzman's admission that she was still afraid of Spencer. As an investigator, this line of thinking would come naturally.

Schwartzman freed her necklace from under her tank top. Meeting Hailey's gaze, she made the decision to trust them. "There's this. My father designed it for my mother on their first anniversary."

Hal leaned in. "I'll be damned."

Before anyone could comment further, she went to pack up her case. "I'll do the autopsy first thing."

Hailey put a hand on her shoulder. The touch gentle, a reassurance that they were friends. "You mind if we take your necklace?" she asked. Hailey was on her side. They were all on the same side. Finally she had allies against Spencer. "To compare them?" Hailey pressed.

Schwartzman fingered the pendant that had hung on her neck since her father's death. "How would that help?"

"It might not," Hailey said. "But we might be able to get something from yours that we can't from hers."

Schwartzman felt sick about taking it off. She'd worn that necklace every day, the one physical thing that connected her to her father.

It was only a thing. An object. They needed it to catch him.

She didn't see how she could refuse, so when Hailey offered up an evidence bag, she unfastened the chain and let it drop into the plastic sack.

"I'll make sure you get it back as soon as possible," Hailey promised.

After handing over the necklace, she was eager to leave, to get some distance from the scene. She forced herself to slow down, removed her Tyvek suit, and returned it to its plastic sack to be entered into evidence.

The floor vibrated beneath her feet as Schwartzman made her way through the house.

Her house with Spencer had been like this. Flowers and soft tones. Everything always in its place. A chameleon, her ex-husband could change on a dime. He was charming, sensitive, the kind of man who walked on the street side so that if a car splashed through a puddle, the water would hit him rather than her. The kind of man who chose expensive throw pillows that matched the drapes.

At the same time, he was the kind of man to throw his pregnant wife across the room if things weren't kept just so.

He's not your ex.

He was still contesting the divorce. South Carolina was protective of the institution of marriage.

Good Southern women did not leave their husbands.

Back in street shoes, she left the building, anxious for cool air. Her bag was too heavy, her heels too high. She was both cold and hot at once.

She wanted desperately to be home but also didn't want to be alone anywhere. She pressed her arm across her stomach, held it tight so her ulna was against her diaphragm. Took slow breaths and fought against the memories.

The way he had manipulated her from the start. How easily she'd played into his hands.

Arriving on their first date in seersucker pants and a navy blazer, he'd brought her mother flowers. A bright bouquet of yellow flowers. Not something so large as to be gauche. Just the right touch of respect and something to brighten her day.

During dinner at his country club, Schwartzman had felt like some sort of celebrity. The way he'd reached out to touch her hand, she was the centerpiece of the entire room. The envy in the eyes of the women who passed their table had been obvious. Spencer MacDonald was sought after. Wealthy, gorgeous, powerful, he was Greenville's prize bachelor.

That night, when Spencer suggested a nightcap, she'd accepted. There had been champagne and wine at the club, but the real buzz came from him.

Back in his home, he'd poured a second nightcap only minutes before he pinned her down and raped her on the expensive Persian rug in his den.

The sex, her first, was painful and rough as she had struggled against him for its duration. But as soon as he had finished, he'd smiled and cupped her face for a kiss as though the act had been loving and consensual. Then he'd led her, bleeding and crying, to the bathroom and ran her a bath. He had insisted she soak, lit a candle, brought her ice water and Advil, which she did not take.

Afterward, he'd delivered her home, clean as new.

"Doc? Hey, Doc?"

Schwartzman turned her head and saw Ken. The ugly reality of Spencer softened into Ken's kind face.

She was safe. Spencer was not here.

But she couldn't shake him. He had never felt this close.

"Are you okay?" he asked.

She forced herself to swallow, nod.

"You're a little pale."

"I feel a little sick," she said honestly. Exhausted most likely. It had been a long night. It was late. A little sleep and she'd feel fine.

"You want me to drive you home?"

"No." Relying on others had stopped feeling safe. The only true comfort was in being alone. She walked slowly toward the street. "Thank you," she added, not wanting him to worry. "I'll feel better with a little air." The fog gave each breath the sensation of chewing on something light and cool.

Ken said something about a Mediterranean place. She caught *dolma.*

She thought of *dolor*, the Spanish word for "pain." *Qué dolor.* A homeless woman used to frequent the clinic where Schwartzman worked during medical school.

"Qué dolor," she would say, cradling her head. The head. Dorsal funiculus. Composed of two ascending fasciculi—gracilis and cuneatus, one descending fasciculus, the comma fasciculus. Then there was one more . . .

"Doc?" Ken shook her firmly.

She started. Blinked hard. Focused. Taking in his face, she had the overwhelming urge to yawn.

Yawning was linked to stress. Athletes yawned before competition, paratroopers before a drop. Part of the flight or fight, linked to the hypothalamus.

It was part of the fear.

"I think I should drive you home," Ken said.

"Absolutely not," she told him, fighting the physiological reactions. Fear was preferable to dependence. She took care of herself. "I'll be fine." Her eyes rattled in their sockets, making it difficult to meet the intensity of Ken's gaze.

"Okay, but only if you call as soon as you're home and let me know you're okay." He held up her phone. "I'm going to program my number in your phone." She recognized the black-and-white-checkered case, though she had no idea how he'd come to possess her phone. He passed it back to her, clinging to one end. "I'm listed under Ken Macy. But you can search under Ken, too. You really—"

The rest of his words slid over her as her mind wandered back to the scene. She fingered the place where her necklace always lay flat against her manubrium.

Identical. The two necklaces weren't just similar; they were the same.

When he stopped talking, Schwartzman put the phone in her jacket pocket. She clasped her case in front of her, gripping the handle with both hands. Her legs resisted motion, and it felt like breaking through a barrier to propel herself forward.

Then she was at the car. It was open.

Ken lifted the case in the trunk and opened the driver's side door for her. Leaned in. "You sure you're okay?"

She nodded again, not trusting her voice.

He stepped back and closed the door for her. He stayed beside the car for several seconds before turning back to the scene. Watching over her. But he did walk away. *Good.* She waited until he was gone. Her fingers fumbled to slide the key into the ignition, but she didn't turn over the engine.

She was afraid to go home.

She should leave before her colleagues noticed. She was not someone to sit around. She was efficient, professional. A scene was not a place to have a meltdown.

And yet she didn't want to leave. There was something soothing about a crime scene—the banter, the group all working around one another. It made her feel safe.

At her apartment, there was only silence.

She gripped the wheel with one hand. Fingered the pulse in her neck with the other. Throbbing. Like an extra heartbeat, like the volume of her blood had doubled and was at the same time coursing through her body at twice its normal speed. Her cheeks were flushed from the constriction of peripheral blood vessels, her muscles constricted. Ready for flight. The reaction was her sympathetic nervous system kicking into gear.

This is just panic. Physiological fear. An instinct. You can control it. Breathe. He's not here. He can't be here.

Adrenaline washed through her veins in another flood of heat.

Get home, where you can manage your emotions in private. She turned the key in the ignition. Flipped on the defrost, the AC, and the heat. Without the AC, the heat merely fogged the glass. She buckled her seat belt and put the car in drive. Her breath raspy and loud. As if she'd been running. As if it was the first time she'd ever driven.

Schwartzman drove slowly, something that infuriated everyone else on the road. Along Van Ness, cars honked and sped by. Someone shouted, "Get a driver, Miss Daisy!" A minute or so passed, and there was no one behind her.

She turned the heat down, cracked the window. *Your house is secure.* After the delivery of the flowers, the building had added cameras to every entrance. Four new guards patrolled the floors and stairwells, while a second front desk clerk had been added so that the lobby was never unmanned. *More than secure. It's practically fortified.* Schwartzman experienced the slightest release of pressure.

She took a right on Jackson. A car turned in behind her. This was a crowded city. Not the suburbs of Greenville. There was always a car behind her. She eyed her tail as the car followed her through one stop sign then another.

Okay, she told herself. *Turn.*

She took a left.

The car followed.

She cranked the air to cold and glanced back, but the headlights were too bright to see the driver. The shadows made it look as though someone was in the passenger seat, as well. She studied the rearview mirror, trying to make out the features of the driver. She would know Spencer's rounded jaw, his tight mouth. She nearly swerved into a parked car. As she jerked the wheel back to the left, a scream caught in her throat.

"Get a grip," she said aloud.

In the six months since she moved to San Francisco for the ME job, she'd felt safe. There was no indication that Spencer was trying to contact her or that he even knew where she was.

Not until the phone call to the morgue, when he told Schwartzman that her mother was in the hospital.

Then the delivery of the yellow flowers.

In the years she'd lived in Seattle for medical school, Spencer had never once shown his face.

At least not that she could prove.

Somehow, despite that, he had shadowed her all that time. Notes in her locker in the hospital. Typewritten, of course. Vague.

> Good luck on the orals.
> You handled the patient in 3107 like a pro.

All signed YSG. Your Southern Gentleman. A joke from a lighter time in their marriage. Never documented.

Two notes might appear in a single week, or months might pass in silence. She never knew what to expect. Or when.

Once she was at a bar with a group of med school students. Halfway into the night, her server stopped at the table to announce that her husband was on the line and he needed to speak with her urgently. When she denied the possibility, the server had pressed. "You are Annabelle Schwartzman?" She had been forced to take his call. Even though it lasted only seconds, the sound of his low, satisfied chuckle still plagued her nightmares. Later she'd discovered that he had tracked her by her credit card.

She'd come home from school one night to find a bar of her favorite honeysuckle soap, made locally in Greenville, sitting on her pillow, wrapped in a little yellow bow.

She had bagged it and taken it to an attorney in Seattle, one who specialized in domestic abuse cases. He'd helped her hire a private investigator to investigate Spencer. The experience had cost thousands of dollars that she didn't have. To pay, she'd taken an orderly job at another hospital in Seattle, worked her days off for three months.

The investigator hadn't turned up a single thing to demonstrate that Spencer was anything other than an upstanding citizen and successful businessman.

The attorney told her to drop it. "You can never prove anything with a man like that," he told her. "It'll only make it worse for you."

She never asked what he'd meant by, "a man like that." She already knew. Ruthless, dangerous. Unrelenting. Since she'd left South Carolina, Spencer had never taken the threats further than notes and phone calls.

This wasn't notes and phone calls. This was murder. Spencer's involvement in this would mean an incredible escalation.

It had to be a coincidence. She was safe here.

There are people everywhere in this city. You are not alone.

To confirm her theory, she drove slowly and scanned the street. There. A couple walking with a large dog. Something wolf-like. A husky. But that car was still behind her. She slowed almost to a stop. Let the car pass her or make a move. Surely the driver wouldn't wait. Why didn't he honk?

The car remained close on her tail. She revved the engine and sped to the end of the block. Turned right and followed the street down two blocks until the final turn, which took her to her apartment's garage. The car followed. She didn't turn into her garage. No. She wouldn't lead them there.

Instead she waited until the car was right behind her and picked up her cell phone. She unlocked the screen and found Hal's mobile number. Holding her finger over the “Call” button, she shifted into park and pulled hard on the emergency brake.

But what could Hal do? At best he was ten or fifteen minutes away.

This would be over by then. She cracked the car door and stepped into the street. Courage gathered like a storm cloud. She felt the cool sensation of sweat on her upper lip as her blood was shunted from her body’s viscera to the extremities in preparation for fight or flight. She made her way to the strange car.

The window went down. A man. Unfamiliar.

“Why are you following me?” she asked.

Large hands splayed above the wheel. “Was I too close?”

“What do you want?” she demanded, glancing at the phone to see the reassurance of Hal’s number on the screen.

A woman leaned across. “He doesn’t want to admit we’re lost,” she said, laying a hand on the man’s forearm. “Give her the address, Peter. Maybe she can tell us where it is.”

“We’re looking for Macondray Lane. It’s supposed to be close to Leavenworth and Green. We’re just driving through and staying with some friends tonight.”

Relief swept through her limbs, leaving her knees weak. “It’s there,” she said, pulling herself together and pointing to her own apartment building. “Turn left at the corner and go down a block. Get a parking pass from the night watchman. Or you might find parking on the street.”

“See, Peter,” the woman told him. “I knew we were close. We’re down from Chico on our way to Santa Barbara. For a wedding . . .”

Schwartzman didn’t wait to hear the rest of the explanation. Her parasympathetic nervous system now back in control, her empty stomach ached, leaving her nauseous and exhausted. She returned to her car. With the doors locked and her seat belt fastened, she could breathe again.

The couple drove up beside her. Too close. Their proximity gave her a jolt. The woman waved at her.

Schwartzman waited until they turned at the corner and followed her directions exactly as she'd instructed. She made an illegal U-turn and crossed through the alley to the parking garage.

Using her key card, she entered the garage's secure door and waved at the night watchman.

Everything was how it always was.

Only it wasn't. Or it didn't feel that way. Was she crazy to think that Spencer was behind Victoria Stein's death? Was it insane to think he wasn't?

Notes, gifts, inconvenient calls, those had been disturbing, creepy. When she'd received a certified letter saying that he had filed a lawsuit against her for breaking their marriage contract, she spent $500 in legal fees to determine that he had no case. Amazingly, even in South Carolina, a woman was free to leave her husband. Not that it mattered for Schwartzman. Whether or not the law allowed it, Spencer did not.

The continuous ruses and ploys were frustrating, a constant reminder that she was never quite free.

She had to believe it was all in an effort to get her back to South Carolina. She couldn't imagine where else he expected the antics to lead.

But murder changed everything.

The flowers, the similar-looking victim, the fact that the woman was from Spartanburg. The necklace. The stakes were so much higher, which meant something had changed. What would motivate him to murder?

Unless this has nothing to do with Spencer.

She didn't believe that for a second.

4

San Francisco, California

Standing in Victoria Stein's living room, Hal pulled off the latex gloves and tucked them in his back pocket to dispose of later. He carried his own supply of gloves in his car. The Crime Scene Unit never had anything bigger than large, and he had hands that could cradle a basketball as if it was an Easter egg.

He idly scratched the back of his hand. Dr. Schwartzman was usually tough to read, but it was plain as day that this victim gave her a helluva scare.

And why wouldn't it? The victim might have been her sister, holding that bunch of yellow flowers after Schwartzman got similar ones from her ex.

Then that necklace—how in the hell could they explain the necklace? He'd seen plenty of crosses in his day but never anything like that. And they weren't just similar. The two necklaces were identical.

Schwartzman had realized it immediately. She'd gone totally pale, her eyes hollow. He had never seen her like that.

No. He had. Once before when he came into the morgue after her ex had called to say that her mother was in the hospital. Only she wasn't.

Schwartzman's mother was fine. The bastard was just jerking her chain, some sort of sick prank. Hal wanted to nail that guy for what he had put Schwartzman through. But this—a murder. If he was behind that, then that changed the game totally.

"We need to get ahead of the questions about her on this one."

"I can't see how anyone would peg her as a suspect," Hal said. But Hailey was right. The question of Schwartzman's connection was inevitable.

"No," Hailey said. "But we'll need to look at every angle."

They had to anticipate that the questions would come back to her. And it was better to have answers before the questions got asked. "I'm going to do some digging into her ex. You know his name?"

"She doesn't talk about her past. I didn't even know there was a husband until dinner tonight. First name is Spencer, not that it's helpful."

"We'll need a timeline of events. If he's behind this, there must be some reason why he's chosen now. She got the flowers—what—a week ago?"

"Maybe two now."

There could be some significance to the dates. They needed to know more. Hailey had drawn the conclusion that Spencer was involved, but it was still a leap. The necklace, yellow flowers, a similar victim from a nearby town.

But murder?

Murder wasn't stalking. It was a huge escalation. Hal had seen Schwartzman that day in the morgue, when she thought her mother was in the hospital. She was so frail, so broken—not at all like the woman he had come to know in their work together. It raised every hair on his body, brought out every protective instinct.

He needed to understand everything that possibly connected that victim to her. They needed to talk to Schwartzman.

"Inspector Harris?" A patrol officer stuck his head into the living room from the main hallway. "They've got the neighbor out here if you want to talk to her."

"Thanks. I would." He turned to Hailey. "You want to join?"

"I was going to check in with Roger." She glanced at her phone. "Actually, Dave has an early flight back east tomorrow. I was going to drop by on my way home. I could come back in an hour or so."

Hailey was in a new relationship, and things seemed to be going well. Hal was glad. It had been a tough couple of years for her. She'd lost her husband, John, and was raising two girls.

Dave was the kind of guy Hal would have chosen for her. Solid, kind. Not like John.

Hal had the sense that this case was going to take over their lives. Best for her to get time with Dave now. "Go," he told her. "I'll check in with Roger after I talk to the neighbor."

"And Schwartzman?"

He had been thinking the same. "I'll call her, see if we can meet at the station."

"Or we could go to her."

She wasn't a suspect. She was a victim. A colleague.

A friend.

"Good call."

"You're okay handling the neighbor?"

Hal had nowhere to be. He felt the rush of a new case, the surge of energy.

"Absolutely," he said, rubbing the tops of his hands against his jeans. The gloves always made him itch.

"Thanks, Hal."

"Anytime."

She pointed to his hand, where he was scratching. "I keep telling you, you need the latex-free ones."

Hal stopped scratching. "I know, but I've got a whole box of these."

Hailey shrugged. "Suit yourself, but you might not have any skin left by the time you've gone through that box." She gave him a playful nudge, and the two of them walked back through the apartment and out to the landing.

Each floor had only two apartments. Both front doors were on the west side of the landing. Victoria Stein's door faced north, and the neighbor's faced south. Between them a large potted fern obscured the direct view of one apartment door from the other. Even with the plant, if the neighbor had been coming in or out at the same time as the killer, she might be able to make an ID.

As Hailey headed for the elevator, Hal approached a woman standing with one of the patrol officers.

She wore pajama bottoms featuring gingerbread men and light-blue, fuzzy slippers that had seen a lot of miles. On top it appeared she had on multiple layers of sweaters. A tan one was visible under a black one with a belt that tied in the front. In her hands, she gripped a mug.

The officer stepped back and motioned to Hal. "Ms. Fletcher, this is Inspector Harris."

"Good evening, ma'am." He guessed she was between thirty and forty, but the older he got the less he trusted his ability to judge a woman's age accurately.

"I've got a cold," she said without offering to shake. She was composed, her expression concerned. Her eyes remained on him; she didn't fidget.

Nothing about her stood out as suspicious.

"No worries, ma'am. I would like to ask you a few questions about Ms. Stein if I could."

She pulled the mug a little closer. "We could—" She motioned to her door. "We could sit down in there."

"That would be great." One rule of investigation was always agree to an offer to access the inside of someone's house. People were more comfortable in their own homes, which made them share more. Plus it was harder for them to get up and leave. "Officer, if anyone needs me, I'll be in Ms. Fletcher's apartment."

Even from the entry, Fletcher's apartment felt much more lived in than the victim's had. Along the front hallway were large framed images of the Golden Gate Bridge in different seasons. In the bottom-right corner of each one was the same looped signature. He paused to study one with snow on the bridge. The last time it had snowed in the Bay Area was the early 1970s. "Is this Photoshopped?"

"No. That's snow on the bridge." She leaned confidently against the wall, the mug drawn in close. "It's great, isn't it?"

"When—"

"February 5, 1976."

He eyed her. She was too young to have taken the picture. "You didn't take this."

"No. My mother was an amateur photographer. A lot of my images were hers. It was her passion, and over the years it's sort of become a hobby of mine."

"It's an amazing shot."

"Thank you."

The living room walls were covered with photographs. Most were landmarks he recognized from the Bay Area—Fort Ord, the Presidio, and the Palace of Fine Arts, but he also saw the Eiffel Tower, Stonehenge, and one of a giant redwood. A couple of the images captured churches too old to be in this country.

These were not photographs of just local sites—her mother had traveled extensively. The images were blown up and hung in identical custom frames. It suggested substantial wealth.

"What do you do for work, Ms. Fletcher?"

"Call me Carol. I work for an online gaming company. Project management, but I do a little of everything."

He scanned the room and saw a computer sitting on the dining room table. Stacks of papers. The furniture was sleek, all sharp angles in a way that looked both uncomfortable and expensive. A large blown glass statue stood on a high pedestal behind the couch. A thin line was visible where the pinnacle had broken off and been glued again. A deep gouge marred the side of the lacquered coffee table, about the right height for a vacuum cleaner.

Money but not old money.

Old money, Hal always noticed, meant everything was just so. The appearance of flawlessness mattered as much as—or more than—what was being displayed. "So, you work from home?"

"I've got a proper office in the back, but I work out here, too, sometimes for a change of scenery."

The best witnesses tended to be people who were around without much to do. They paid attention to who came and went.

And if Fletcher worked from home, then maybe she'd seen or heard something that could be useful. Hal motioned to the couch. "Mind if I sit?"

"Sure. Go ahead."

Hal moved a square pillow decorated with geometric shapes in black and brown off to the side and sank into the corner of the couch. It was narrow with a short back that hit him well below the shoulder blades, but the cushions were firm, and the fabric felt expensive. He crossed one foot over the other knee but found the couch was too low to make it comfortable, so he replaced his foot on the rug and balanced his notebook on his knees. At his height, it was unusual to find someone else's furniture comfortable. Almost always, things were too small.

This was especially true of women who lived alone.

Hal flipped open his notebook. "How long have you lived here?"

"Almost fifteen years."

Hal made a note. "That's a long time. Mind if I ask how old you are, Ms. Fletcher? Sorry, Carol."

She smiled. "Thirty-four."

He had guessed about right. He did the math and was surprised. "So you've lived here since you were nineteen."

"My dad bought it for me after my mom died. It was kind of a consolation prize, I guess. He left when I was three, so when she died, he bought me this place."

Hal let a beat pass in a moment of deference to her mother's death, then poised his pen to write. "When did Ms. Stein move in?"

"About four months ago, I think. After the new year."

"Do you know what she did for work?"

"I think she said she worked at a bank." She paused. "I can't even think which one now. It wasn't Wells Fargo, I know. Anyway, the bank moved her out here to start some new division. I don't know exactly what it was."

Although he sensed the answer, Hal asked, "How well did you know her?"

"I'd been over there once or twice for a glass of wine. Mostly we just watched out for each other's places. She checked in on my cat when I was away for a week in March, and I took care of her plants when she was gone a couple of times for work."

"Do you have a key to her apartment?" he asked.

"Not at the moment. She always gave me one when she was traveling or if she needed me to let someone in."

There were no signs of forced entry. Whoever had gotten into the apartment had a key. "When was the last time you let someone into her apartment?"

"There was a plumber here sometime in February. I think that was the last time."

"Did Ms. Stein have many visitors?"

"Not that I saw, but we keep pretty different hours."

"You work at night?" he asked.

"Mornings actually," she corrected. "I'm up about four, and I usually work until two or three in the afternoon. After that, I do errands and meet with friends. I'm usually in bed by seven or eight."

Four until two was a ten-hour day. So, not a trust fund baby. Unusual hours, too. "Really," he commented. "Doesn't quite fit the online gaming stereotype I had in mind."

"I hear that a lot," she said. "But most of the issues with gaming happen in the early hours of the morning—when people have been playing for long stretches."

"It's past your bedtime, then."

"I woke up when Victoria's sister buzzed me. Then when she found her sister—well, I couldn't sleep after that." Her gaze settled on the wall.

"So you didn't have company last night?"

"I rarely have people here. My boyfriend is long-distance, and I am not a big entertainer."

He wondered about the expensive furniture. It didn't really seem to suit her. Perhaps the place had been decorated this way when she moved in. Perhaps it was her father's style. "I hear you." Hal didn't entertain either but mostly because his place was about the size of Ms. Fletcher's galley kitchen. "Any indication that Victoria Stein was worried about something?"

Fletcher pursed her lips and shook her head. "No. Things were going well for her, and I haven't seen anyone around."

"Did you happen to know that all the security cameras in the building were out last night?"

"No, but it's not that unusual," she said with a sigh. "The building is working with a totally antiquated system. It probably goes down a few times a month."

Hal made a note. Even with surveillance down a few times a month, he didn't like the coincidence of the timing. "Is the building managed by an outside company?"

"No. The building employs about five front desk guys. They work some rotation. All of them are part-time, I'm pretty sure. But the guys have all been here awhile. The newest one is the tall redhead. Liam is his name, I think. But no one's here after three. That's why Victoria wanted me to let her sister in."

"So the sister buzzed you?"

"Yes, Terri is her name. She was driving up from Los Angeles. She lives down there somewhere. When she arrived, she buzzed, and I let her into the building."

"But you didn't have a key to Victoria's unit?" Hal asked, skimming his notes.

"No," Fletcher confirmed. "Terri had her own key. I just let her into the building. I was getting back in bed when I heard the screaming. Terri had gone into the bedroom and found her sister." She covered her mouth. "It was awful."

"I'm sure," Hal said. "Let me know if you need a moment."

Fletcher looked down at her tea and shook her head.

"When was Victoria supposed to be home?"

"Not until tomorrow, I think. She was supposed to have training up in Sacramento and be back around midday."

Her attention settled into the carpet again. He knew the look from experience. She was recalling the body. People unaccustomed to death often reacted this way—the distant, unfocused gaze, arms crossed, body closed. He'd probably gotten as much as he could.

Hal stood and pulled his wallet from his back pocket. He handed Fletcher his business card. "I'd appreciate a phone call if you think of anything that might be useful."

She took the card. "Of course. Anything I can do to help."

Hal thanked her for her time and headed back to Victoria Stein's apartment. It had been an average interview. He wasn't surprised. People didn't know their neighbors the way they used to. Witnesses had grown less reliable.

Early in his career, there were more people paying attention to what their neighbors were doing. These days almost everything was recorded somewhere—Facebook or Instagram—but no one really saw anything anymore.

In some instances, the Internet made his job much easier. But not here. This one was going to take the old-fashioned kind of work.

Back in Stein's apartment, Hal found Roger squatting next to the bulky ActionPacker that stored his crime scene kit. The plastic box was maybe three and a half feet wide and two feet tall, its exterior bright orange with black handles that snapped into each end to hold the top in place.

At some point, Roger—more likely one of his kids—had put a large SF Giants sticker on the side. The scratches and wear on the sticker suggested it was from a couple of World Series back.

From where Hal was standing, the overhead light hit the top of Roger's bald head and reflected it like the sun.

Roger had been new in the lab about the same time Hal was taking his inspector's exam. Roger suffered from alopecia universalis—he had no hair on his body. Early on, Hal had heard Roger explain the condition to people who came in and out of the lab while Hal was there, waiting for results on one thing or another.

One day Hal asked if it got annoying. While Roger was generous about it, Hal imagined it had to get old. Hal found a bumper sticker that said, "With a body like this, who needs hair?"

To this day, it hung at Roger's work space in the lab.

"Roger, man," Hal said. "I'm gonna need some shades."

Roger laughed without looking up. "It's the halogen spotlights, man. They reflect the bald well, don't they?"

Hal palmed his own bald head. "I guess so. How do I look?"

"Not as reflective, I'm afraid," Roger told him. "To really make it work, you've got to be both totally bald and pasty white. You're only one of the two."

"I've got some pictures where I shine pretty bright, too." He crossed the room and stopped beside Roger. "Find anything interesting?"

Roger nodded. "Couple things, actually," he said, standing up. "There was only one wineglass out on the counter, but we found a second one up in the cupboard. Rinsed out and put away in a hurry from the looks of it."

"Any prints?"

"Prints on both glasses. Won't know if they're the same or if they belong to the victim until we get them back to the lab."

If the two had wine together, then the killer was someone Stein knew.

Did they wash the glass only to hide their prints, or because they were trying to hide the fact that Stein was killed by someone she would drink wine with, someone she knew? "So maybe she had a guest here."

"You talked to the neighbor?" Roger asked.

"Yeah, but she didn't hear anything."

"These places are pretty solid," Roger noted. "Unless someone was really loud, I doubt you'd hear anything from across the hall."

"Definitely the high-rent district."

"You're not kidding. The way the market is in the city, these places probably go for two or three million."

Hal whistled. That was about what he'd make in his entire career, and someone was paying that on maybe twelve hundred square feet of living space. Without rent control, he wouldn't be living in the city at all.

Rents on places like his were close to four grand. He'd been there sixteen years and paid $1,175.

These days you couldn't rent the shelter of a doorway in an alley for that. "Prices like that, you'd think they could afford a better security system."

"You'd think. The computer squad is checking. They suspect it was a virus that shut down the system. Happened about fifteen minutes before three o'clock, which is when—"

"The front deskman gets off duty," Hal finished for him.

"Right."

"So someone sends a virus, and the whole system is down. Makes it easy to get in and out without being captured on film." That implied planning, but Hal already knew that this murder was not an act of blind rage. It had been carefully choreographed, which would almost certainly make it tougher to solve.

Hal tried to imagine Schwartzman married to a man capable of something like this.

"It may not even be as sophisticated as all that. According to the front deskman, they have virus problems pretty regularly. Something about how they perform the nightly update and some issue with their antivirus software."

Hal palmed his head. "So you're saying this wasn't a planned attack? That's a pretty big coincidence."

"It definitely is," Roger agreed. "It basically happened about fifteen minutes before the end of the shift. The front desk guy says he called tech support and waited on hold, but when he called in to tell his boss that he had to stay, guy told him to take off. Kid said he would have stayed. Could've used the overtime pay."

Hal groaned. "So no surveillance all night."

"The computer guys will see if they can locate the source of the virus and track it. But we might not get anything."

"So besides the wineglass and the security system failure, we find anything else noteworthy?"

"Not yet. We collected the flowers to compare with the ones Dr. Schwartzman received at her house. They were a low priority until now."

Everyone would step up the focus on Schwartzman. Comparing the flowers for any similarities, usable prints, skin cells—epithelials—that could be run for DNA.

Anything to link to a suspect.

"That will take us a few days. We've also got all the trash from the kitchen and bathrooms. We'll run through it for prints and evidence. We're looking for the wine bottle itself. There's evidence of broken glass on the kitchen floor, but no glass in the trash. I've got someone going through the dumpsters."

"We get lucky, might find some usable prints."

"That's the hope," Roger said. "You talk to the victim's sister?"

"Not yet," Hal said. "Stein wasn't supposed to be back until tomorrow at noon, so she had a key to let herself in. The neighbor buzzed her in the front door," he added. "I'll check her out."

The apartment had offered precious little about the victim. He needed a list of friends, her work contacts. Someone knew something. It was a matter of following the trail. He just needed one bread crumb to start.

Roger drew a plastic bag out of his pocket. "Ken collected this and gave it to me."

Hal flipped over the bag and looked at the receipt inside.

"It's a gas receipt. The sister filled up on Vasco Road in Livermore at nine fifty."

Hal pulled out his phone to map the distance from Livermore to Stein's apartment.

"Already Google Mapped it," Roger said.

Hal stopped fiddling with the phone. "And?"

"Purchase was made an hour and twenty-five minutes before we got the call," Roger said. "The drive from there is at least an hour, hour and ten."

Hal pocketed his phone. A solid alibi. "That doesn't leave her time to get here, kill her sister, clean it up, stage her, then leave, get buzzed back in by the neighbor, and call us. Plus—" He remembered the image Ken Macy had shared of the petite woman tucked into a ball on the couch.

"Your gut says no," Roger supplied.

"Something like that."

"Mine, too."

Hal trusted his instincts. Roger's, too. The sister wasn't their killer.

He scanned his memory for anyone else who should have stood out. The victim was staged, which meant there was a chance that the killer stuck around to see the reactions. Naomi had taken pictures of the people on the street, but most were dressed in nightclothes and huddled in small groups. Neighbors most likely. No one looked out of place.

"Any other leads?" Roger asked.

As he handed Roger the bagged receipt, Hal considered the people closest to the scene. The neighbor was one, but the careful staging of the body implied a sexual element to this murder. This just didn't feel like a case of two female neighbors fighting over who had to water the plant that separated their front doors. "I'm going to check the front desk staff. One of them is new. Kid named Liam. Then we'll try to talk to the folks at her job, but, basically, I got nothing."

Hal also had to locate Schwartzman's ex-husband. He couldn't imagine that any man would seek out a woman who looked like his ex-wife, kill her, and pose her with flowers and a necklace, all in the name of rattling his ex. If he wanted to scare the crap out of Schwartzman, why not break into her place? Or at the very least attack someone she knew. Other than looking similar and being from neighboring towns that were across the country, there was no obvious connection between Victoria Stein and Schwartzman.

Yellow flowers and the necklace.

Not enough.

The two bouquets could hardly be considered compelling evidence. As for the pendants, it wasn't impossible to imagine that two of those existed. So Schwartzman thought her dad had designed it for her mom. That was a nice, romantic story. Didn't make it true.

And yet the pendant stuck with him. The design was unique, the two pendants identical. He couldn't believe that the fact that the victim had one identical to Schwartzman's was a coincidence.

Roger loaded his tools into his ActionPacker. "I got the pendant from Hailey. I'll be in touch as soon as I've got any information."

"Let's check the pendants as soon as possible," Hal said. "I'd like to identify where they were made." Before anything else, he wanted to rule out the possibility that the two were made by the same person. If they were, this thing *had* to lead back to Schwartzman's ex. He hoped like hell it didn't. Because if it did, it meant that she had been married to one scary bastard.

"Yes," Roger agreed. "I've marked those priority."

Hal gave him a pat on the back. "Thanks, Roger. Get some sleep, man."

"You, too."

"Yeah, I'll try." But Hal wasn't going to do much sleeping. Schwartzman had him worried.

If Schwartzman's ex wanted to play with her, why make the truth so obvious?

More than that, he felt the wrongness in his teeth. It was an aching electricity that settled into the roots of his molars when he ate too much sugar or when he wanted to deny something on a case.

Was it really just some sort of game for this guy? And if he *was* playing some sick game, then what was coming next?

5

San Francisco, California

Schwartzman shivered in the warm apartment and tightened the belt on her thick wool sweater. The thermostat on the wall read seventy. Still seventy. She had checked it three times. But it felt so much colder than seventy. In the kitchen, she dumped her tea in the sink, poured another mug from the steaming kettle. Pressing her fingertips into the porcelain until they burned.

Why had she chosen to do this here? She might have gone down to the station and taken care of it there. But now Hailey and Hal were coming to her home. To make things easier for her, in consideration of her position.

In her home.

The box sat on the coffee table. A Nike shoe box, the orange dirty from handling, faded. Every bit of evidence she had.

She jumped at the sound of the bell.

"Dr. Schwartzman, it's Alan at the front desk. Inspectors Harris and Wyatt are here to see you."

The police were at her door. What would the front desk think? What rumors would start now?

What did she care? These were strangers, a whole building of them. “Thank you, Alan. Send them up, please.”

Waiting for Hal and Hailey, Schwartzman crossed to the antique buffet table in the living room, where the bottle of Evan Williams bourbon sat beside two crystal glasses. Her father’s glasses. She tried to find some sense of him there with her. God, how she would have loved to have him with her now. She drank from the mug of tea until the bell rang.

She opened the door and stood, feeling awkward. They had never been to her home, and this was not a social call.

She invited them in, offered them tea, which both declined.

It was midnight. The hour had taken its toll on them as much as her. Hailey’s dark curls were pulled into a makeshift bun, strands falling loose around her face. She wore no makeup, but her cheeks were rosy, as though she had recently scrubbed her face. Beneath her eyes were hollow half-moons. Hal’s face showed a shadow far later than five o’clock, salt as well as pepper in the growth. She led them to the living room, sat against the arm of the couch, and tucked her feet up and the sweater around them.

“Sorry to come so late,” Hailey said.

Had they met beforehand? Was that why they’d needed additional time? She tried to read the partners, but they didn’t look at each other. Both sat facing her. Schwartzman shook her head. “It’s fine. I wasn’t asleep.”

“You doing okay?” Hal asked, leaning forward in the chair, elbows on his knees. The oversize chair was dwarfed by his stature.

She didn’t want to exchange pleasantries. She wanted to know what they knew, share the case as colleagues. She was antsy, picking at the blanket that covered her legs. She wanted to ask the questions.

“Schwartzman,” Hal prompted.

“I’m fine. As well as expected,” she said. A company line. She had a lot of those. But, no. She was not doing okay. Not even close. “Let’s get this over with.”

"What can you tell us about him?" Hailey asked.

Schwartzman set her tea on the table. There was no comfort in the conversation they were about to have. There was no comfort when it came to Spencer.

"You're one of us, Schwartzman," Hal said.

How she wanted to believe that this time would be different. That being one of them made a difference.

"We're on your side. This isn't an interview. This is us asking for anything you can offer to help us nail this guy."

"You won't link this to him," Schwartzman said. "No one has ever linked him to any of the things he's done."

"Let us worry about that."

Could she do that? Give Spencer over to someone else to handle?

No one had ever asked her to.

How she would love to pass off that burden, or even share it. But she was terrified, too. What if she told them, and they didn't believe her? What if the evidence pointed to something else? How could she work with them day in, day out, after sharing the darkest piece of her history?

Of her life?

"Tell us how you met him, how it started," Hailey probed.

Rip the Band-Aid off. Be done with it. "I was twenty-three, just finishing my third year of medical school."

"You were twenty-three at the end of your *third* year?" Hal repeated.

As a young college student, her every focus had been on getting through school. Undergraduate in three years, med school in three years. People did it. She could do it. The sooner she was through, the sooner she could practice. Her whole life had been preparation. She had wanted to launch herself from the South, start a life somewhere real. "I was in an accelerated program." Two of them actually.

"Was he in school with you?" Hailey asked.

"No. He was working in Greenville when I was at Duke. He was only three years older but already very well established in the bank."

He had told her they were meant for each other. *Think of how smart our children will be.* How appealing that sounded.

"Go on," Hal said. Softly, coaxing.

Get it out. Tell them and be done with it. "My father died May of that year. Suddenly." The words were like weight on her chest. She would never have married Spencer if her father was alive. How could she impress on them the weight of that loss? What her father had meant to her. Did it matter? The familiar ache of loss was in her chest again. Press forward. "I stayed with my mother. She was—" How to describe her? Schwartzman hadn't thought her mother even cared much for her father. She was so standoffish and short with him. But she broke in his absence. "It was very difficult for her."

And for me. Her father was her idol, her closest friend. It was devastating.

"My mother ran into Spencer in the bank, when she was dealing with my father's accounts. Somehow Spencer ended up at the house one evening. Our house." Her mother insisted she dress up to receive one of her father's banking colleagues. That was what her mother had called him. Schwartzman hadn't argued. She argued with so little that her mother asked in those days. Arguing meant an onslaught of emotion from her mother that left Schwartzman exhausted. "We went out for the first time the next week."

"What was he like?" Hailey asked.

A monster.

Talking about him was like pulling on a strip of skin and exposing the dermis below. Raw and red, the truth burned when exposed.

"Charming," she admitted. "So charming. To everyone. People stopped at the table constantly, and he engaged with them. Then he would ask them to excuse him so he could get back to his date. It was so flattering." Images of the club, of her navy button-down dress. "He invited me back to his house and raped me."

"Oh, God," Hailey whispered.

Hal rubbed his face. "Jesus, Schwartzman."

She drew a shaky breath, clenched the blanket in her fist.

"Did you report it?" Hailey asked.

Schwartzman laughed. A hard, sharp laugh that stung her ears.

Hal started at the noise.

"I was a virgin, stunned. I can't even recall that I felt angry about it, although I know I told him to stop. I fought him. That is the magical thing about Spencer. He could rape you or beat you and convince you that it was for your own good."

"When did you see him again?" Hailey asked.

"I didn't hear from him for ten days. My mother was in a panic, sure I'd messed up my chances. Of course, I never told her what he had done. When he finally called, I don't know who was more relieved—my mother or me."

"And how long were you married?" Hailey asked.

"Just over five years." She had once known the number of days and months.

"And did he harm you during your marriage?" Hailey asked.

She nodded.

Hal laid his huge hand on hers, effectively covering them completely. The small gesture made her feel safe, protected. "Did you ever call the police?" he asked.

"Not once."

Disappointment in his face. He couldn't understand what it was like—the pressure to stay. From her mother, from him, and beyond them. She was a Southern woman, carrying his child. It didn't feel as if she'd had any choice at all.

"Why did you leave?" he asked.

"I was pregnant. Four months and—" The hard slab of marble rammed against her belly, the terrific pressure of the baby's form against her spine. "I lost the baby when he threw me into a bureau."

"God, that's awful," Hailey said, her eyes glassy. "Did you tell the doctors what caused the miscarriage?"

"Spencer talked to the doctors. Spencer handled everything. The longer into the marriage we got, the more isolated I became."

"Was it the miscarriage that made you realize you had to leave?" Hal asked.

"Not exactly." Schwartzman recalled that girl. *Kaitlin.* Her long, red locks, her fair skin. "Around that same time, there was a family at Spencer's country club, the kind that looks perfect. The father was in local government; she came from a ton of money and did all sorts of philanthropy work. Two kids: an older son who was on the football team and the basketball team and a younger daughter who competed in dressage and horse jumping. It was within a week of the miscarriage that the girl—Kaitlin—was thrown from the horse. Broke her back.

"It was all everyone talked about. What was the latest with Kaitlin. The doctors didn't think there was any chance she would walk again. But someone's doctor suggested they go down to Georgia for some new experimental surgery. I can't even remember the details of the procedure—if I ever knew—but it had to do with immobilizing the spine and using stem cells to regenerate the area that had been damaged. The whole town rallied behind the family. They were big in the church, and for weeks part of every Sunday focused on Kaitlin's recovery.

"I'll get to the relevant part," she said, sensing the bodies shifting across the room from her. "A few weeks after the accident, Kaitlin's family brought her out. She was in a wheelchair with head support, but she was dressed beautifully—like a doll. Gorgeous dress, her skin and hair. She was truly a remarkable young woman." Schwartzman reached for the teacup and stopped herself. *Get it out.* "Spencer became obsessed with her."

"With this Kaitlin? And she was how old?" Hal was poised to write.

She remembered the way he had looked at Kaitlin, the jealousy it had evoked in her. She didn't want him, and yet that look of longing was so intense; she felt naked that it was aimed at someone else. But his obsession wasn't with Kaitlin. She soon discovered it was much worse than that.

"She was early twenties, maybe. Spencer was never inappropriate with her, but he became obsessed with the idea of her—this perfect woman in that chair. It appealed to him that someone had to care for her twenty-four hours a day, that she was totally helpless. I think it was an incredible rush for him. Spencer started to research the condition and the surgery."

"I don't understand," Hal said. "How does this relate to you?"

She could imagine how it sounded to him. How bizarre, how unrealistic. She'd come too far now. Maybe they wouldn't believe her. She searched Hal's face, but it was intense, unreadable. "For a few weeks, nothing. But then Spencer started to drop hints about the pain I had as a result of the miscarriage. When I fell against the bureau, the baby—" She stopped. "It hurt my back, but Spencer wanted to believe that I had some serious injury."

"Because he wanted you to be like this woman? In a wheelchair?" Hailey asked. Her voice was a whisper. The words too awful to speak in a normal voice. Beside her, Hal's mouth was propped open.

"I know it sounds crazy, but it was almost like I could see him working through the problem of how to break my back without killing me. To create his own Kaitlin."

"Jesus H," Hal said.

"Did he try anything? To hurt you, I mean?" Hailey asked.

"No." How did he imagine he would take care of her if she was truly in a wheelchair? But he wouldn't. He would find someone else to do it. Then what? Would he have tired of her? Would he have expected some surgeon to be able to perform some miracle so that she could walk again? "The true danger of Spencer is that he is so calculating. And patient. He is endlessly patient. After that, he started working on the problem. It was no longer a matter of whether he would do it, just when. I don't know how far he'd gotten when I got away, but I knew he was planning something.

"I knew I didn't have much time. I needed a few hours to escape, and he rarely went that long without checking in on me. One of his colleagues was running a charity event. She asked me to help. I told her I thought I was needed at home. Spencer didn't like when I made commitments that kept me away from home."

"It sounds like prison," Hailey said.

"It was. Worse." She would gladly go to prison before she'd go back to Spencer. His own set of rules, a limitless supply of cruelty—prison would be easy.

"Of course, she told her husband that it wouldn't be the same without me, he talked to Spencer, and I was on the list." That was always the trick with Spencer. If she said no to one of his colleagues, there was a chance it would get back to him. That he would insist she go. It wasn't foolproof, but it worked that time. "I arrived at the charity location, was assigned a task with a bunch of women I didn't know, and hid my cell phone in one of the couches so it would trace back to the luncheon if he tracked it. Then I paid cash for a taxi to my aunt Ava's house in Charleston. I worried he might go there, but she made sure there were people watching the house." Those days of hiding at Ava's, as terrified as she had been, had felt like the first moments of joy in years. Ava had ordered food in. They'd stayed up late, searching the Internet for medical schools where she could reenroll. Ava had saved her life. If not for her father's sister, she couldn't have imagined leaving. "I stayed for about ten days to figure out what was next; then Ava and I took a limousine to Atlanta and got on a plane there. I haven't seen him since. It's been more than seven years."

"And he hasn't left you alone?" Hailey asked.

"No. There have been periods where it's quieter, but it has never stopped. He's always found me."

"I'm not going to let anything happen to you, Schwartzman." Hal rubbed his face with his hand. "We're going to nail this bastard. Whether or not he killed Victoria Stein." He motioned to the Nike box. "Is this all the stuff he's left over the years?"

"Yes, as well as all the records from the private investigator I hired."

"You mind if I take it?"

She thought about how long she'd been carrying this around, adding to it, working it over. Hiring the investigator.

Hal wanted to take it. He was going to nail Spencer. She had long since stopped believing that was possible. *Maybe. Just maybe,* she thought as she handed the box to Hal. "It's all yours."

"We'll get this to Roger," Hal said.

"I honestly don't think there's anything in there that's useful. Notes, cards . . . no one is going to believe he went from that to murder."

Hal wrapped his free arm around Schwartzman's shoulder and pulled her in. Her father had not been a big man, but for a moment she imagined he was there, watching her. That he had somehow sent Hal and Hailey. With the solid strength of Hal beside her, she even let herself lean in a little. How long had it been since she'd let herself lean on someone?

"You're going to be okay," Hailey said. In those words, Schwartzman heard her father's voice. *You'll be okay, sweet girl.* How often had he said that?

How she wanted to believe it. Hal let go, and the three of them walked to the door in silence.

She wondered about the conversation they'd have in the elevator. Would they ask why she put up with that kind of treatment? Would it make them think differently of her?

That she was weak?

"We'll be in touch in the morning," Hal said.

"Get some rest," Hailey added.

"You guys, too."

Hailey reached out and squeezed her hand before turning down the hallway. She felt the solidarity. They were a team. She was no longer alone with Spencer.

But as soon as the door was closed, she knew that wasn't true.

She poured herself a finger of bourbon, swallowed it in a single long gulp. Coughed into the back of her hand from the burn.

Bringing them here was a mistake. She should have gone to the department. The issue wasn't with Hailey or Hal. She would welcome them into her home. By bringing the conversation to her home, she had let Spencer in, as well.

After years of fighting to keep him out, she had just opened the door and welcomed him in.

6

Charleston, South Carolina

Still in uniform from a court appearance earlier in the day, Detective Harper Leighton was butterflying chicken breasts while oil heated in the fry pan. The window above the kitchen sink was open, the air outside stagnant and humid. May used to be cooler in Charleston. Her squad car read the temp as high as eighty-five today. Too hot for May. It meant July would be a bear.

Harper moved the knife deftly. She'd been wielding a knife since toddlerhood, or at least a fry pan and a spatula, as one would expect from a girl who grew up in the back room of her parents' restaurant. For her, cooking was as natural as driving. And like driving, while she did it deftly, she did not enjoy it. Not usually and especially not tonight. She had only just walked in the door from work fifteen minutes ago.

It was nearly nine. She'd planned on coming home by six thirty or seven to make dinner and have it ready before Jed picked Lucy up from volleyball practice and arrived home. Nights like this, she had her go-to recipes. First on the list was her father's fried chicken. Fill a Ziploc bag with flour, salt, pepper, paprika, and two shakes of cayenne the way she'd seen him do it a thousand times. He never measured. Half the time he wasn't even watching what he was doing.

Tonight, she wasn't measuring either. Too tired, too hurried, too anxious to have dinner on the table so she could sit down.

Maybe then she could leave behind the two vehicular homicides she was investigating, plus the domestic violence incident that had escalated into a shooting and killed a neighbor through an adjoining wall. Between the back-to-back interviews, follow-up interviews, and two trips to the lab, she'd been at her desk for only about three minutes, enough time to pop two Advil and make one phone call.

She massaged the chicken to break up the last frozen bits, poured buttermilk into a stainless bowl, dunked the breasts one at a time, shook them in the bag until they were coated, and dropped them in the skillet. The oil crackled and hissed, and as it did she recalled the familiar smell of the crowded restaurant, her father's hearty laugh, and the scent of vanilla custard that was one with her mother.

Lucy would be starving, and she would enter the house with typical teenage drama. There'd be the rumble of the garage door, a slam followed by the quieter, gentler driver's-side door closing as Jed also emerged from the car. Four quick breaths later, the kitchen door would burst open and shoes, backpack, gear, lunch box, water bottle would drop to the floor in a heap as she passed and stomped up the stairs.

At fifteen, Lucy was predictable only in her mood swings. Ten years earlier, when their daughter reached school age, Harper and Jed had set out house rules. One was that coats, bags, shoes, and the like had to be hung up or out of the pathway to the garage.

House rules had fallen apart sometime last spring when Lucy turned into—well, whatever this was. It was practically a fire danger the way stuff was strewn around.

As Harper flipped the first breast, oil spit at her. She grabbed the apron off the hook and pulled it on over her blues, wishing she'd had time to change her clothes before cooking. She checked the biscuits in the oven, thankful for the dough her mother had brought by over the weekend and more grateful that they hadn't baked it all for Sunday dinner. Tuesdays and Wednesdays were always a scramble. Harper worked tens, and they were the busiest days at the lab for Jed.

Though she'd resisted Jed's pragmatic response to her wanting another child when Lucy was two or three, she couldn't imagine now how they could have managed two children.

The garage door started with a kick and rumbled open as Harper slid the biscuits out of the oven. She swung open the refrigerator door, found a bottle of beer, and gave the door a bump with her hip to send it closed. The cap fought a little—probably the opener starting to wear down from use—but Harper won, and the cap popped off. She tossed it into the trash and tipped the bottle to her lips as the door opened from the garage.

Jed entered first, scowling.

She lowered the beer. "What's wrong?"

"According to your daughter, everything."

She was always Harper's daughter when she was being moody and difficult. Unless it was Harper talking. Then she was Jed's. "Want a beer?"

"Uh, duh," he said, rolling his eyes.

Harper handed Jed her beer. "Lucy's better at the eye roll."

"I know. I don't have nearly as much practice," he said with an exasperated sigh—another of Lucy's favorite new mannerisms. Harper opened the refrigerator for another one.

The phone rang.

"You think it's Lucy, calling from the car?"

Jed's hand hovered above the wireless receiver. "If it is, she is grounded for a month."

"Hello." The smile vanished as he set down the beer. Harper closed the refrigerator.

"Okay, Kathy. Hang on a sec. She's right here."

Harper crossed to the phone.

Jed covered the mouthpiece. "Frances Pinckney is dead."

Her breath caught in her throat. "Dead?"

"Your mother just found her."

Harper reached for the phone, but before she could speak, the door from the garage slammed against the kitchen wall.

Making a racket, Lucy kicked her shoes off as she entered the house, dropped her backpack and lunch sack onto the floor, and crossed to the kitchen table, where she dropped into a chair.

"I'm absolutely starving," she announced. "What's for dinner?"

7

Charleston, South Carolina

Harper arrived at the home of Frances Pinckney as the coroner's vehicle was parking. Charleston County owned three coroner's vans, but the one on the curb was the oldest by more than a decade. Rusted wheel wells and a rattling that could be heard a block away, the van was nicknamed "Bessie." The fact that it was Bessie parked on the curb meant Burl Delford was on call. He was the only medical examiner who opted for the old van. The driver's side door opened with an earsplitting screech, and Burl descended from the driver's seat, cowboy boots first. "Evening, Detective," he said with a nod.

Burl was nearly six feet tall with a thick head of gray hair that was a little long for Charleston standards. He wore a mustache with full chops that he'd supposedly had since he could grow facial hair.

Burl had been with the coroner's office for thirty-five years.

Never married, no kids, Burl spent his time off riding with a Baptist motorcycle club called the Holy Rollers. Harper was glad he was here. The coroner's office had a good team, but Burl was old-school. For Frances Pinckney, he felt like the right match.

"Evening, Burl."

"You up again?" he asked.

"No. I called in and said I'd take it since we knew her," she told him. She had grown up with Frances's son, David. She would have to call him. Notifications were the toughest part—somehow even worse on the phone when she couldn't touch their shoulders or hands, offer some physical contact with the news.

"Heard your mama found her," he said.

"Harper!" came her mother's voice as she rushed across the sidewalk toward her daughter. There was an awkwardness to her mother's movements—stiff and slow. They made her seem much older than sixty-eight.

Kleenex clasped to her mouth, Kathy Leighton hugged Harper tight, pressing her face into her daughter's shoulder. She smelled of onions and shrimp in Cajun seasoning. Beyond that, Harper smelled fresh-baked biscuits and vanilla custard. In her arms, her mother was soft and vulnerable in a way that was unsettling.

"I can't believe it's Frances," her mother said. "I just saw her at church on Sunday. Sat in the row behind her."

Harper had missed church to drive Lucy to a volleyball tournament in Myrtle Beach. "I'm so sorry, Mama. You should go home. Is Dad here?"

She pulled away from her daughter and tugged her cotton shirt down over her ample hips as though to pull herself together. "No," she said with a sigh. "I can't reach him. He went over to the bar. Tuesdays, you know."

"Right." Since retirement, her father joined three other retirees on Tuesdays to play Hearts and drink whiskey. "Okay. I'll get someone to take you to pick up Daddy." Harper kept one arm around her mother. She rubbed her shoulder the same way her mama used to rub hers. Months had passed since Lucy let Harper give her a hug. Now she was mothering her mother. Maybe that was just the natural way things shifted.

Her mother shuddered with a cry, and new tears tracked paths down her cheeks. Harper took the Kleenex from her mother and wiped her cheeks. "Tell me what happened."

"I got a call from her neighbor Kimberly Walker. You know, the one who worked at the diner on and off 'round about when you were in high school. Always friendly and upbeat but always had her nose in someone else's pie, if you get my meaning. She ended up marrying that widower Teddy Davies who lives right behind Frances. You remember her?"

Harper shook her head.

"Well, she's been telling me how Frances's dog barks all evening while she and Teddy are enjoying dinner and their evening TV programs. 'Course it doesn't bother Teddy because he can't hear a thing. She was going on about the dog so much, I told her to call me when he started barking.

"So, she calls about eight forty," her mother went on. "Says Cooper—that's the dog—was making a terrible ruckus. I told her to go ring the bell, and she said she already did, but Frances wasn't answering. I don't know why on God's green earth she didn't just look into the window. She'd have seen Frances right there on the floor by the stairs." She fought back tears. "I'll never forget her lying on the floor. The angle of her neck, dear God."

Harper released her mother's arm with a pat and took out her notebook. "You're doing great, Mama. Just a few more questions."

"Of course."

"Did you come straight over after Kimberly called?"

"No. I tried calling Frances first. Tried her home a couple of times, then her mobile. She never has that thing on, so the call went straight to voicemail. But she usually answers her home line when I call. When she didn't, I decided to come over and check on her."

"When did you arrive?"

"I was here by ten to nine. Saw her straightaway and called the police. They called you."

Harper scratched a few notes, then waved one of the patrol officers over. "I've got to work, Mama. Andy will take you home." To the officer, she said, "On the way, will you swing by the Tattooed Moose? Daddy is there playing cards, and I don't want Mama at home alone."

"Sure thing, Detective. I'll do it straightaway."

"Thanks." Harper gave her mother a tight hug. "I'll call to check on you a little later."

Her mother glanced back up at Frances Pinckney's house. "I can't believe you have to go in there and see her like that, Harper."

"It's my job, Mama. I'll be okay."

"Dear Lord, I don't know how you do this job."

Harper kissed her mother and headed inside to the body. On the way in, she used her flashlight to study the lock on the door. There were no fresh marks, no scrapes to suggest someone had broken in. Windows lined the porch. There would be a lot of ways to get in. The crime scene analysts should be there soon. They could do a more thorough search of possible entry spots.

In the foyer, Burl knelt next to Frances. As her mother had said, the dead woman's neck was twisted from her shoulders at an unnatural angle.

Harper had to take a breath before moving forward. This wasn't the first victim she had known. Over the years, she had investigated the deaths of a few of her classmates and plenty of folks who used to frequent her parents' diner. Some of the deaths had less impact than others.

Seeing Frances Pinckney was heartbreaking.

A petite lady with a sweet disposition, she lay dead in her velour jogging suit, eyes wide-open, fists clenched tight, and neck broken. The little dog she loved so much—a gift from her son—whimpered beside her. Frances's expression was both desperate and angry.

"What do you think?" Harper asked.

"She's been dead less than two hours," Burl reported. "It might have been a cardiac event or stroke. If she was alive when she fell, hitting the banister would have been cause of death. Not hard to see that she broke her neck. The break might have been peri- or postmortem." He paused to touch Mrs. Pinckney's neck. "If it was cause of death, it's a clean fracture. Would have been real quick. Painless."

"Small blessings," Harper said.

"Amen," he agreed. "I'll perform the autopsy in the morning. Take a look at her heart and brain for signs of some event. I'll call when I've got some answers."

Harper stood again. "Thanks, Burl. I'm going to head over and talk to the neighbor."

Burl reached up to Frances's face and used his thumb and forefinger to close her eyes.

Tears stung as Harper walked out the front door. The tears were not because of Frances. It was her mother who upset her. Her mother refused to read scary books, wouldn't watch detective shows. Now she had the image of her friend lying dead in her head.

Harper checked which rooms were visible from the porch. Mostly she just needed the air. *You're human,* she told herself. *It's okay to be human.* When she came back around to the front of the house, she found the other patrol officer, Sam Pearson, on the front porch. And there she was crying. *Perfect.* She should have been there to comfort him, as this was his first dead body. Instead she moved awkwardly past without saying anything.

Schoolmates from the time they were just out of diapers, Sam and Harper were also high school sweethearts. Sam had been the biggest catch in high school. He'd lettered in football, baseball, and basketball. Harper had been a track star, but she'd had none of the star appeal that Sam did. Despite the frequent attempts by one or another of the cheerleading squad to break them up, they'd stayed together through high school graduation.

"I need to talk to Kimberly Walker. You want to come?"

Sam cocked an eyebrow high the way he used to do in high school when he was teasing her about being bossy.

She smiled in spite of herself. "Come on, Pearson. It'll be fun."

The porch creaked as Sam followed her down the alley. He had almost five years with the department to her sixteen. Most of his peers in patrol were ten or twelve years his junior. Technically speaking, Harper was his superior, but she did her best not to act it. She supposed they had found a sort of comfortable awkwardness. It was just so different from the way they'd been in high school, and she had to force herself not to try for that old, easy banter.

Harper rounded the house and walked about fifteen yards down the alley before stopping in front of a traditional Charleston single, painted white with green shutters. The large metal disk on the side of the house indicated that it was built prior to the earthquake of 1886.

Because much of historic Charleston was built on landfill, the earthquake had caused houses to sink into the quicksand-like dirt they were built on. The ones that survived the earthquake were fixed with bolts, which could be tightened over time to pull the houses back together, inch by inch. The disks merely created a pleasing aesthetic to cover the bolts.

Before starting up the stairs, Harper checked her notes to confirm the address she had for Kimberly Walker. Sam crossed to the other set of stairs and moved up them quickly. As it wasn't proper for men to see women walking up the stairs, where they might accidentally catch the view of her ankle or, heaven forbid, her calf, many of Charleston's older homes were built with two sets of stairs.

Etiquette dictated that the man be waiting when the woman arrived at the top of the stairs. Though he no longer looked like her high school sweetheart, there were parts of him there. Sam was always there, at the top, waiting. Even if he never met her eye.

Strange what bitterness did. All over the fact that she had gone to UNC and he had stayed behind.

Harper rang the bell while Sam stood back, hands clasped in front of him. Walker was home. At least that was what she'd told Harper's mom.

She reached for the bell again when Sam grabbed her hand. Their eyes met, and Sam dropped his hold. "She's coming," he said, nodding to the door.

The front door cracked, and Harper displayed her badge. "Mrs. Walker, I'm—"

"It's Davies now. Mrs. Davies. And I know who you are," she said, the frown running into the creases around her lips. "I worked for your parents for almost four years."

"I understand you heard noise coming from Mrs. Pinckney's house this evening. We'd like to ask you a few questions if we could."

Kimberly Walker Davies unlocked the chain, opening the door with a flourish. She stood in a nightgown and matching robe in a color Harper would call salmon. Sam closed the door behind them. As Harper stepped inside, Mrs. Davies's gown blended into the apricot-painted walls of the front room. Peach carpet and a chandelier that hung from the ceiling twenty or thirty feet above, with its heavy cut crystal leaves and cantaloupe accents. This was clearly her color.

"Please. Join me in the sitting room." Davies swayed across the foyer like a belle at a ball. Davies was using Frances's death as an opportunity to place herself center stage.

Harper held back a series of not-so-nice thoughts. Growing up in Charleston hadn't armed Harper with any tolerance for wealthy Southern women. They got under her skin like no other type of folk. Always competing to be the center of every darn thing. Davies was certainly playing the role.

When Davies had settled into an upholstered chair in another shade of apricot, Harper sat on the cream-colored couch, grateful that at least she wasn't cast in the glow of peach. She placed the small digital recorder down on the glass-top table and pressed the "Record" button.

"Mrs. Davies, I'm going to record this conversation for the purposes of our investigation. Is that all right with you?"

"Of course," she responded, leaning out from her chair and yelling toward the table as though the recording device was as hard of hearing as her husband.

"Can you please tell me exactly what happened this evening? Start with when you first heard the dog and continue until you called Mrs. Leighton."

Davies twisted her lips. "Mrs. Leighton?"

"My mother," Harper said.

Kimberly Davies stared past her and waved her hand. "Please, do come in, Officer. Join us."

"I'm fine. Thank you, ma'am," Sam responded from the foyer.

"Oh no," Davies said, rising from the chair. "I insist."

Sam sat at the far end of the couch.

Davies spent a couple of moments watching Sam as though to ascertain whether he was truly comfortable. It reminded Harper that—at least in the South—a man in uniform commanded more respect than a woman. She wanted to blame Davies, but it happened way too often.

"Mrs. Davies, when did you first hear the dog?" Harper asked.

"I hear that dog every single day. That thing barks about absolutely everything—"

"I mean, when did you first hear the dog this evening?" Harper was eager to identify a timeline and get on with the investigation.

"My husband, Teddy, was heading upstairs, and I was straightening the kitchen. It was seven or thereabouts. We normally retire about eight to read or watch television unless we're entertaining, which we do several times a week."

Harper noted the time. "And what time did you go over to Frances Pinckney's home?"

"Not for a while. You see, the barking stopped and started quite a bit."

"Is that normal?"

Davies billowed her nightgown out beside her, smoothing the silk against the matching sofa. "Well, yes and no. There's quite a bit of that kind of stop and start during the day, but thinking on it, the barking is slightly more unusual for the evening. Usually Frances can get the dog to quiet down."

"Can you be more specific about when you went over to Ms. Pinckney's home?"

She focused on her nightgown, running long French-manicured nails across the fabric.

Harper tapped her foot on the floor, hoping to refocus Davies's attention. This needed to move more quickly.

"Just about eight."

"Eight," Harper repeated.

She nodded.

"And you rang the bell?"

"Several times."

"Was the dog barking then?"

"Oddly, no." Her eyes widened. "That is strange. The dog completely stopped barking when I rang." She looked between Harper and Sam. "What do you suppose that means?"

"I'm not certain," Harper said as she wrote. But it did make her wonder, too. If the dog normally barked, why suddenly go quiet? "And about how many times did you ring the bell?"

"Two, maybe three. But I waited some minutes for Frances to come to the door. Her hearing is quite good, considering her age. Not like Teddy's at all," she said loudly, with a wave toward the upstairs.

"And when she didn't come to the door, you looked inside?"

Her lips formed a small O as she pressed her palm to her chest. "Of course, I would never look into someone else's home under normal circumstances. But with the dog barking so insistently and Frances not coming to the door, I was concerned for her well-being. It was my civic responsibility to check."

"And at this point, the dog had stopped barking? He was quiet?" Harper clarified.

"Yes. Definitely." Davies shifted her attention to a loose thread on the sleeve of her gown. Some witnesses fidgeted as an outlet to being nervous. Davies, on the other hand, seemed merely self-centered as though the loose thread was of real concern.

Davies had told her mother that she hadn't looked into the house, but Harper knew that wasn't true. Looking inside would be human nature—and especially tempting for someone who enjoyed gossip as much as Davies did. "I assume you looked inside, to be sure Frances hadn't slipped and fallen," Harper said, giving Davies an out.

"Well, of course I was worried."

"Which windows did you look in?" Harper asked.

"The front window beside the door," she began sheepishly. "And I also walked around the porch so I could see into the dining room."

Harper pictured the Pinckney home. "The dining room opens to the front room, doesn't it?"

"Yes. I believe I could even see a bit of the front room from there, but I didn't see either Frances or that dreadful little dog."

It meant that Frances Pinckney wasn't lying at the bottom of the stairs when Kimberly Davies looked in. "You're certain of the time? Can you recall what was on TV?"

"It was definitely eight o'clock because Teddy loves to watch the old black-and-white movies, and they start at eight. When I returned home, the movie was just beginning. The film was *Sierra Madre*."

Harper nodded but said nothing.

"You know, with Humphrey Bogart," Davies added.

Harper didn't know the film. "And did you notice anything unusual? Something that might suggest there was someone else in the home with her? A coat or bag? Anything at all?"

Davies stared at the ceiling, and Harper waited patiently. Finally, she shook her head. "No. Everything was like it always was. Frances is quite tidy."

Harper would bet Davies had taken a good look through that window, and she was the type to notice if something was off. If someone had been in the house with Frances Pinckney, he or she had been careful. Which implied planning. If the death was from natural causes, then something had set the dog off initially but then quieted it when Davies was at the house. Something about that theory didn't sit with Harper. "And after that? You came back home?"

Davies hitched her chin up. "I came back to be with Teddy."

"And when did the dog begin barking again?"

"Eight thirty or just after."

If someone was in the house and had gone to the trouble of quieting the dog, then the barking would have started after he left. By that time, Frances Pinckney was probably at the base of the stairs. "But you didn't go back over there?"

Davies waved to herself with a flourish. "By then I was in my nightclothes. I certainly wasn't about to go out in this."

"So that was when you called my mom?"

"Yes," Davies said.

Harper laid one of her business cards on the table as she retrieved her recorder. "Please call me if you think of anything else. We would certainly appreciate anything you could add."

Davies leaned forward. "Someone said that she fell down the stairs, and I wondered if she tripped on the dreadful dog."

Harper had seen Frances Pinckney with her sweet dog. Frances adored him, and it was lovely to see the companionship the little dog brought her.

Kimberly Walker Davies was the dreadful one.

"We appreciate your help," Harper told her, rising from the couch.

Davies stood, too, in a cloud of salmon, and led them to the front door, promising she would be in touch if she remembered any little thing that might be helpful.

Harper was certain they would hear from her again. She thanked Davies as she jogged down one side of the stairs.

"I don't get it," Sam said. "If she looked in the house, why didn't she see the body?"

"It has to mean that the body wasn't there yet," Harper said.

"So, what—she had a heart attack upstairs and then fell down the stairs later?" Sam asked. It was the most he'd said to her all night.

The timeline didn't make sense to him either. *Good.* The deeper the case pulled him in, the more focused they would be on finding out what happened to Frances Pinckney.

"Yes," Harper said, dread settling heavy in her gut.

8

San Francisco, California

Deep in the covers, Annabelle Schwartzman pressed her face into the yellow silk sheets. Gauzy curtains billowed in the wind. Not yellow. Cornmeal, the decorator had called the color and matched it with cornflower blue. Cornmeal and cornflower. Ridiculous, but she pretended to care. Women were supposed to care about the names of their drape and pillow colors. Successful ones knew the differences between cornmeal and daffodil and hay, the accent colors in the fabrics of the headboard and throw pillows.

Spencer had a thing for yellow, or maybe the choice had been hers. Even if the decision had been hers, it was still his. That was his magic. His charm.

Somehow those things had become more important than medical school, though she was head of her class at Duke for the three years she was there.

Smart like her father, people always said.

Beautiful like her mother. It wasn't as true. Her nose had a small bend that matched her father's larger one. But she had her mother's bright-blue eyes and her slim build, her father's long legs. She was beautiful.

That had been important in her youth. Only later did Schwartzman realize that her mother worried about beauty. A lot. And then it was decided. If she was beautiful enough for Spencer Henry MacDonald, then she was beautiful.

Things might have been different if her father hadn't died. But in the wake of his death, Spencer MacDonald gave her mother confidence that her daughter would be cared for. And Spencer made her mother smile as nothing else had since her husband's death. What choice, then, did Schwartzman have but to embrace him, too?

And so she had dropped out of school and had become the perfect wife. She joined the Rotary Club, among others, to get involved, careful not to overcommit. Her home responsibilities came first.

That night there was a fund-raiser for the children's library, followed by a meeting of the women's auxiliary board.

At the start of their marriage, she imagined being on the board, achieving great things for the less fortunate. She wouldn't have a career herself, of course, but surely she could take on a leadership role in one of the important local charity organizations. But Spencer discouraged leadership positions. Nothing that would require too much—too much time, too much attention, too much of her. After all, there would be a family to think about and his needs.

That night she tipped the precarious balance. She should have chosen to attend one function or the other. Not both. If she had, she would have noticed that the sheets hadn't been changed.

She would not have felt so exhausted that she'd gone to her dressing room and peeled out of the yellow blouse that now barely fit over her extended belly and the bright skirt that her mother had bought her at some exorbitant maternity store.

She would have had time to do her face washing and her eye and hand cream before the blood in her swollen feet made every step feel as if she were weighted down with sandbags.

She vaguely remembered the sheets had felt good, cool against the heat in her feet and back. The baby was active, as was often the case when she settled into bed. Like she missed her mother's movement. *She.* A girl, although they hadn't known it at the time.

Spencer didn't want to know, and she had been utterly incapable of even that small act of defiance. She told herself that she was afraid she might slip. But that was far from the truth. By that time, she had become incredibly adept at keeping secrets.

Spencer had already discovered plenty to use against her, and she had long since seen how he gathered every morsel for later use as ammunition. His skill in this was impressive; he might not even be paying attention, and still, somehow, he absorbed details she shared. The most mundane, irrelevant facts were corrupted in his grip.

Her dislike for brussels sprouts meant they turned up in meals, at his instruction, when he felt she'd misbehaved. That he threw away strawberries that came fresh from the neighbor's yard because he knew how she loved their bright color and succulent flavor.

"Trudy must have tossed them," he would say, referring to the housekeeper. "Maybe they were rotten."

She never once asked Trudy. She knew from the way he delivered the news that their disposal had been his choice. And they wouldn't have been given to someone else—although Trudy would have gratefully taken them for her own sons.

No, Spencer would have instructed that they be discarded, and any other action would have been grounds for severe discipline.

She remembered how impressed she'd been by Spencer's staff. He had the same cook and housekeeper, the same groundskeeper and driver since he'd bought his home at twenty-one. Spencer didn't fire people for insubordination. Nothing that kind. He punished them by making it impossible to leave.

Being his wife was no different.

That night, she was sleeping soundly. The baby, too, had settled into sleep, nestled so that neither feet nor elbows pressed against any tender organs. She slept with an arm over her belly as she had been doing since the third month of pregnancy. Even Spencer seemed to calm with her pregnancy. He was out less often; they ate in more than out and designed the baby's room together. He, too, seemed to be settling into the idea of fatherhood.

Surely, then, he might become the man that everyone outside the home saw. Loving, charismatic. His success was already proven. His intellect and passion and aptitude for strategy. He'd achieved so much already at the bank.

That very night he was out, celebrating some merger or partnership, she wasn't sure which. She would have liked to know. She had a mind for that sort of venture, but, as he often reminded her, she hadn't even finished college and was, therefore, more suited to paint colors than P&Ls.

Sometime in the night, the front door slammed, waking her. Windowpanes in every room shuddered, and Schwartzman along with them.

So much of that night was clear, but after the rattling of glass, the memories became disjointed snapshots rather than a running film. The most memorable were pressing her palms against Spencer's chest, struggling against him. His face scarlet, spit flying from his lips as he turned her and launched her across the room.

She slammed belly-first into his dressing table, shattering a bottle of Gucci Pour Homme cologne, a smell that would forever more remind her of death. She remembered the feel of blood and amniotic fluid as it flowed down her legs like a thick, warm soup. She could see it pooling on her feet and into the pale-yellow carpet.

She tried to let the images of *that* night fall away. She had already lived it too many times.

The pain of striking the dressing table, the incredible pressure of the marble driving into her. The sense of everything inside slamming against her spine. She knew with absolute certainty that it was that third blow to the abdomen that killed her unborn daughter.

The image of the blood stayed with her.

She blinked and fisted her charcoal-gray cotton sheets.

Safe.

"You are safe," she said out loud, and her voice was hoarse, her throat dry, as though she'd been screaming.

Sitting up against the hardwood headboard, she took even, deep breaths and pressed him away as she looked at the four corners of her bedroom. To her left, the corner where the two gray walls met. On one wall a black-and-white silhouette drawing of a woman that she'd bought at an art walk in Seattle. The second corner with the dark door to the walk-in closet. A beautiful six-panel door she'd had stained black, the wood grain like swirls of gray sand. The knots were like pools of tar. The third corner with its windows drawn in black shades, then, to her right, the ashen wood of the bedside table with its metallic light and off-white lamp shade.

He is not here, she told herself. *He is not here.*

You are safe.

The familiar routine in the fight against the memories. The room was silent. Her room. Spencer MacDonald wouldn't come here.

She settled herself back down in the bed, pulled a pillow into her arms, and held it tight against the emptiness of her belly, but there was no going back to sleep. Instead, she lay in bed and stared at the ceiling until the sun rose over the horizon and light filled the room.

—

Schwartzman arrived at the morgue just after eight. It was particularly cold as she entered through the doors, tying her gown behind her waist. The thermostat, when she checked it, was set at sixty-seven as always.

As she made her way across the room, her fingers automatically went to the place where her necklace normally lay, against the flat, bony surface of her manubrium, several inches below T2. Only skin.

People said they felt naked without a wedding ring. She understood.

She worked to push images of the scene from her mind. They would only be a distraction. Her job was in this room, lying on that steel table. Everything she could discover about this woman from the physical details of her body would help the police find her killer. She would have to be satisfied with that.

She fingered the implements on the metal tray. Her scalpels, bone saw, a camera for documenting injuries, the trimming shears she used to cut through the ribs. It was all there. Same as every other time. She ran her fingers across the tools again with the sense that something was missing.

Whatever she might have been missing did not make itself known. The metal wheels clacked on the cement floor as she wheeled the tray to the body. She tied her hair in a bun at the nape of her neck and checked for loose pieces before donning a pair of latex gloves.

She wouldn't guess how long the autopsy would take. She'd start with the clothes. Hailey and Hal had taken the only piece of jewelry. She bagged the Tory Burch flats, an eight and a half—the same size she wore. Next she checked the two small square pockets on the front of the yellow dress. Finding them empty, she carefully removed the dress and bagged it to go to evidence. Under the dress, Victoria Stein wore a simple white lace bra and matching underwear.

The bra was underwire, surprising since Spencer disliked underwire bras. The panties were a traditional cut rather than a thong. Spencer also disliked thongs.

She bagged the two pieces separately, checked that everything was labeled correctly, and set the stack of evidence on the counter by the door to take to the lab later.

With Victoria Stein undressed, Schwartzman started the recorder and announced the victim's details. "Name: Victoria Stein. Age: thirty-three. Height: five-seven." An inch shorter than Schwartzman. "Weight: one thirty-five. Race: Caucasian. Hair color: brunette." She studied the victim's hair at the roots. The hair was dyed, recently. The color job looked expensive. She bagged several strands for evidence.

The expensive hair matched the expensive apartment. Her nails had been recently buffed and were painted an almost nude pink. Spencer would approve.

Schwartzman drove him from her mind. Returned her focus to the victim.

There was something about her overall appearance that didn't quite add up. She noted that the skin on her hands and face showed more signs of skin damage than Schwartzman usually saw on wealthy women her age. She noted the inconsistency.

Before searching for evidence to determine cause of death, Schwartzman examined the body for signs of external injury, as well as any markings on the skin. While Stein had no tattoos, which were useful for confirming identity, she did have several distinct markings. On the backside of her left forearm was a small nevus, or birthmark, and there were several noteworthy moles on her chest and shoulders. Schwartzman documented each one individually, using a small ruler to show its size.

Behind Stein's right knee was another birthmark, this one a hemangioma. The hemangioma—sometimes called a raspberry—was the result of blood vessels that clustered in utero and never fully dissipated. Schwartzman documented several small scars, mostly on Stein's right hand. Along with the scars, the victim's right hand was slightly larger; both suggested she was likely right-hand dominant. People tended to cut and scrape the dominant hand more often than the nondominant.

One other scar was just inside her right pelvic bone. An appendectomy scar should have been lower and more centrally located. The jagged edge suggested some sort of trauma, but the scar appeared to be at least a decade old. She documented it with film, then made a final check for anything else she might have missed.

"Eyes: blue-gray. No signs of petechiae." She had not been strangled. Even though she had done it at the scene, Schwartzman checked the mouth and nose for injury or obstruction again, using a small penlight covered in a plastic sleeve. "Nasal and tracheal passages are clear and unobstructed."

She lifted the camera off the table and took a series of pictures of the face and head, then flipped through the images. The camera was designed to pick up any signs of perimortem bruising, but the images showed no evidence of injury or struggle. Next she fingered the skull for any sign of contusion. Again nothing.

Schwartzman completed her external exam and performed a rape kit, although there was no evidence of recent intercourse and even less to suggest that she'd been raped.

She drew blood for toxicology, collected fingernail scrapings, and inspected the victim's mouth for signs of anything that might be caught between the victim's teeth.

Schwartzman had solved a case in Seattle the previous fall by using a piece of tissue found lodged between a victim's lower central and lateral incisors. They were able to match the DNA to a rapist recently paroled. The power she'd felt when she got that call was indescribable, the flash of invincibility like a drug.

She was born for this job.

Now, using a small prod with a camera on the end, Schwartzman explored farther up the victim's nose into the sinuses. Once there, the camera projected onto the screen beside the autopsy table.

Schwartzman used a keyboard command to capture the images for her file. Victoria Stein's sinuses showed evidence of bleeding. Schwartzman stared at the screen, studying the image.

Drowning.

Victoria Stein had been trying to breathe. The effort built up the pressure in her sinuses, making them bleed.

Schwartzman gently palpated the victim's stomach. The muscle was slightly enlarged, the liquid contents gurgling beneath Schwartzman's touch. Another indication of drowning. She pulled off a glove and lifted the digital recorder. "Evidence of bleeding in the sinuses suggests victim may have drowned." She paused. "External exam now complete." Schwartzman set the recorder down and replaced the glove she'd removed with a fresh one.

Just another case, she told herself. The fact that the victim looked like her was irrelevant. There were plenty of victims who shared her coloring—brunettes with light eyes. Plenty who were tall and thin as she was, even some with an aquiline nose like her own and others who had been born with a nose like hers and then had the hump surgically removed.

These were merely coincidences, a game of odds.

The more victims she processed, the more likely she was to run into ones who shared her attributes. The key was to treat Stein like any other victim. She drew the camera out of the sinuses and discarded the disposable protective cover.

Schwartzman proceeded with the Y-incision, cutting from the edge of the collarbone to the breastbone, pressing the scalpel through the skin, fat, and muscle of the chest. Once the two diagonals were cut, she ran the scalpel down the abdomen to the pelvic bone. This allowed her to open Stein's chest like a heavy textbook, using the scalpel to slice away the connective tissue and remove the flesh to expose the victim's peritoneum.

Other than the stomach itself, which was distended and full, Stein's chest cavity was normal. She would remove the stomach to collect its contents, but first she wanted to see the lungs and heart.

The morgue had a pair of metal rib cutters, but they were difficult to use. The handles were uncomfortable and small, requiring too much torque to cut through bone. One of her first outings in San Francisco had been to buy a pair of red-handled pruning shears at the garden store. Using them now, Schwartzman snapped through the outside edge of the ribs until they were a single piece she could lift up and remove to expose the chest organs. Her focus was on the lungs, which were enlarged and distended like the stomach, again consistent with drowning. Using a large bore needle, Schwartzman collected several samples of the fluid from the lungs to be sent to the lab for testing.

As she injected the fluid samples into the evidence vial, she detected the faintest smell of lavender emanating from the contents of the lungs. She stepped back from the table as she fought her gag reflex.

Lavender was the scent Spencer loved for their home. It had been in every drawer, every closet, every bathroom. Soothing. Peaceful.

She, too, had liked the smell of lavender early in their marriage. She had used a lavender spray to help fall asleep. But then the smell became pervasive, a reminder of feeling trapped, and she found it kept her awake rather than helped her sleep.

When had that happened? She couldn't recall when she had started to dislike the scent.

Schwartzman removed her gloves and retreated to the metal desk and chair across the room. She rarely stopped mid-exam, but at that moment, she couldn't bring herself to continue. She pulled a bottle of Pellegrino from the refrigerator and twisted off the top. She took three or four long drinks and willed her stomach to settle.

It's just a smell.

A dead body was full of them.

She didn't recall smelling lavender at the victim's home. She made a note of it, then lathered her hands with grapefruit lotion, taking a couple of minutes to inhale the clean citrus scent.

With a fresh set of gloves, Schwartzman returned to the body. With the major cavities opened and cleared of fluids, it was time to remove the organs. She weighed each one and took samples.

The heart was normal, weighing just over nine ounces, within the averages for a healthy woman her size. The kidney, glands, pancreas, spleen, also normal. An examination of the uterus showed that Victoria Stein had never had children and was not pregnant.

Finally, Schwartzman collected the contents of the stomach into a clean container. The red wine was identifiable by its vinegar smell and the pinkish tint it gave to the rest of the contents. There was some greenery that suggested a salad, small red pieces that were too firm to be tomatoes, so probably red pepper, and maybe a dozen very small seeds similar to lavender.

The contents were less diluted than Schwartzman had expected—Stein had ingested more wine and less water. If Victoria Stein had been conscious during her drowning, she would likely have swallowed a great deal of water during her struggle.

Stein had been intoxicated, and possibly also drugged, and then drowned.

With her examination complete, Schwartzman rinsed the body with water so it would be ready to go to the funeral home and stared at what remained. The quiet, pensive face above the angry Y Schwartzman herself had created. The wall clock showed it was close to six. Fatigue from lack of sleep had settled its talons into her neck and shoulders. She would call Hal with the results on the way home.

Her cell phone rang from her pocket. Schwartzman removed her gloves and pulled out the phone. "Schwartzman."

"Is this Annabelle Schwartzman?" asked a cheery voice.

Schwartzman wished she hadn't answered. "It is."

"This is Cassie calling from Dr. Khan's office. We received the results from radiology on your most recent mammogram."

The word *radiology* got her attention. "Yes?"

"They would just like to take another look. Are you available to come in tomorrow morning? We have availability at eight forty-five if that works."

They wanted her to come back. Tomorrow. "What were the findings?"

"Pardon me?"

"What did radiology find that makes them want to take another look?"

"Oh," Cassie said, as if she was trying to sound upbeat. "There was some asymmetry in the scans."

"Asymmetry," Schwartzman repeated.

"That only means that the tissue is different from last time."

Her oncology experience was limited to med school and residency. Too long ago. "Does this happen often?"

"It does happen," the nurse said, and Schwartzman sensed the forced cheer on the other end.

"They'll do another mammogram, then?"

"Yes. And probably an ultrasound, as well. So the eight forty-five appointment will work, Ms. Schwartzman?"

"Yes. I'll be there."

"Perfect. And remember—no deodorant as it can interfere with the scans."

"Right." As she replaced the receiver, her gaze returned to Victoria Stein, lying on the autopsy table.

Lavender. Why drown her with lavender water?

The thought was quickly swept aside by another.

Her doctor wanted to do another mammogram. *It was nothing,* she told herself. *Asymmetry.*

She would put this all aside for the night. Have a hot bath and sleep hard. Sleep for twelve or fourteen hours. Or twenty. Maybe a day.

With or without her early morning doctor's appointment, she would not sleep past seven o'clock, no matter how tired she was. Her body always woke her.

Waking first was a tactic she'd employed to keep the peace with Spencer. Although he'd rejected any idea she had about working, he was bitter and angry when he rose before her. She slept with the alarm clock under her pillow, muffled so it wouldn't wake him, rising so she could be dressed and make coffee before he got up at seven thirty. Even weekends, when he often slept past nine, she was up, terrified that the one day she would sleep in would be the one when he woke early.

The idea that she could choose to stay in bed for twelve hours used to feel like real freedom.

Nothing felt free now.

9

San Francisco, California

Hal arrived back at the victim's apartment Thursday morning with two cups of black coffee and a box of Krispy Kreme doughnuts. Roger had called him an hour before to say he was coming back to the scene with some of his techs to do another sweep.

Hailey was working a gang-related shooting, so they had split up with plans to meet back at the station in the afternoon to compare notes.

Hal had failed to catch up with Terri Stein yesterday other than receiving a text to say she was getting in touch with their family and dealing with funeral arrangements. She had said she'd meet him at the station later today. There were a lot of gaps he hoped she could help him understand.

As it was, they knew very little about the victim. The apartment offered no clues about where Victoria worked, who she spent time with. Most pressing in Hal's mind was the question of where they'd grown up. If the town where Stein was from was so close to the place where Schwartzman's ex was, did Terri or her sister know Spencer MacDonald?

Hal parked in the red, threw his department pass on the dash, and got out of the car with two coffees in one hand and the doughnut box in the other. The coffee burned through the cups as he walked, so he moved quickly to the apartment building door and used the "Handicap" button to open it automatically.

He'd been up much of the night—two nights, actually—thinking about this murder. Stein was found Tuesday evening, and he still hadn't been able to interview the sister.

It was more than the link to Schwartzman that was bugging Hal about Victoria Stein's murder. As much as movies liked to make murder out to be random, it wasn't. At least not the vast majority of the time.

Sure, victims got caught in the crossfire of gang wars. Those deaths were almost always random—people in the wrong place at the wrong time. But the kind of death that Victoria Stein died was almost always personal. If Schwartzman was right, the death was a warning to her.

What kind of warning was it meant to be? That he would do the same to her? If what? If she didn't come back? If she did? There was no clear message in Stein's death. But the staging, the care with the victim, these details spoke to an organized killer. How had Spencer found himself a partner willing to kill on his behalf?

Or were they looking at the Schwartzman connection too closely? Maybe the connection was somehow looser. Either way, it did not feel random.

In his time in Homicide, Hal had worked only a few murders that were truly random. One of those was still unsolved. In five months of intense investigation, Hailey and Hal had turned over every rock around the victim. On nights he couldn't sleep, Hal poked around the Facebook pages of the victim's family and friends, always hoping something would jump out at him. In seven years, nothing had.

Hailey and Hal had dozens of cold cases between them, but that one stuck with him because it was impossible to understand why someone had shot the victim. You live a high-risk life—gangster, thug—you can expect a bad outcome. Hal liked to believe in karma that way, although he'd seen plenty of examples where karma fell short.

That victim hadn't had any risk factors. He was ordinary. Hal felt ordinary, too. Of course, he wasn't. Being a cop bumped him into a high-risk category. Homicide inspector, higher. With guns available to every hoodlum with a few hundred bucks, it was amazing they didn't get shot more often.

Other than being a cop, though, Hal was a normal guy. He liked sports; he liked beer. He enjoyed the company of his girlfriend, who was also a cop, and he didn't like the idea that normal guys got killed. Worse, he really didn't like the idea that they got killed and the killer got away.

Victoria Stein's murder was starting to feel like that.

She, too, seemed pretty normal. She didn't fall into any obvious risk categories. For one, she was affluent. No obvious signs of drug use. An abusive relationship almost always came with telltale signs—old bruising, scars. He'd spoken to Schwartzman the night before, and Stein had none of the telltale marks. The one unusual scar Schwartzman found in the autopsy was on her pelvis. It was more than a decade old. That didn't fit with a pattern of abuse. He thought of Schwartzman. Had she shown the signs of her abusive marriage? Perhaps Spencer had controlled Schwartzman in other ways.

But Victoria Stein wasn't killed by Spencer. Hal had confirmed yesterday that Spencer hadn't left South Carolina in months. Whatever had happened to her, the violent death appeared at odds with her life.

Appeared. Which meant there was something he didn't yet know about her life.

After signing in with a patrol officer at the front desk, Hal rode the elevator to Stein's floor. Hal found Roger in the kitchen, arms crossed, staring at the cupboards.

Hal set Roger's coffee on the protective paper that covered the counter and placed his own down beside it.

"Thanks." Roger lifted the coffee and popped the top off. He raised the cup and blew on the hot liquid before taking a small sip. "Hot."

"I know, right? They must get that stuff to boiling before they pour it."

Roger raised a brow at him. "Okay, smart-ass."

Roger was one of the most earnest people Hal knew. During the time after Hailey's husband was killed, Roger had seen Hal at his worst—angry, under too much pressure. But Roger was always there. Steady and affable, serious and reflective when the situation called for it.

He didn't let emotions or demands from the brass affect how he did his job. He was objective, careful, kind. Always. One day, over beers, Hal would have to tell Roger how much he appreciated him. For now he was grateful for their familiar banter.

Some days, messing with Roger was the only levity in Hal's day. "What are you staring at in here?" Hal asked.

"Trying to imagine where there might be prints I haven't found."

"Any luck finding that wine bottle?" Hal asked.

"Yes. We found it in the dumpster. It was in a paper bag and dropped down the garbage chute. Not surprising," Roger said. "Get the glass out of the house so you don't accidentally cut yourself later."

"Prints?" Hal asked hopefully.

"Only the victim's."

No surprise. He didn't allow himself to react. This was just the start. There were lots of opportunities. Whoever had been here had made a mistake.

Schwartzman said Spencer never made a mistake. Hal didn't believe that, but even if he did, Spencer wasn't here. He had never left South Carolina. This killer had made a mistake. There was something he hadn't thought of, some place he'd touched inadvertently. They just had to find it. "And on the other wineglass?" he asked. "The one in the cupboard?"

"Wiped clean."

That meant whoever killed her drank wine with her. "How about DNA?" Hal asked.

"None."

"And we've got the victim's prints in the house. How about others?"

"Victim's and several that belong to the neighbor, but those were only found on two of the houseplants."

"She said she takes care of Stein's plants when she's gone."

"I figured," Roger said. "We've got one other set on the front door and bedroom knobs, as well as on the bedroom wall by the light switch. We assume those are the sister's, but we'll need the comparison to be sure."

"Anything on the bouquet of flowers?" Hal asked.

"It's a tough surface for prints, but we'll check. As far as the flowers themselves, there was nothing exotic and no packaging, so it's going to be difficult to track where they came from. They're too similar to the kind sold at every grocery store. But," Roger said, moving to his computer, "I did cross-reference this bouquet with the one Schwartzman received. Both included calla lilies and Gerbera daisies. But they're different species, so the bouquets aren't from the same source."

"Not from the same source," Hal repeated.

"The lab is compiling a list of growers, so we can try to track where they were sold. It's not going to be a short list."

Now Hal was frustrated. No way to narrow in on the flowers that came from Spencer. Nothing to help them locate the place where this bouquet came from. "So we don't have anything yet."

"Precisely why I'm staring at every surface in the house. There have to be prints here somewhere."

"I thought we determined the perp was wearing gloves," Hal said.

"He was, but I doubt he would walk into her house in gloves. Seems like she'd notice."

Hal agreed, thinking through the killer's steps. He would have come through the door without gloves. She would have opened it for him. "Doorbell?"

"Clean," Roger confirmed.

Okay, not the door. They'd had wine. The lab had already collected the glasses and the bottle. Then, somehow, he'd incapacitated her and gotten her to the bath. "You heard cause of death, right?"

"I got a call from Schwartzman. Drowning."

"So what about that? Awkward to drown someone wearing gloves. Did you try the areas around the bathtub?"

"Clean."

"Linen closet?"

"Just hers."

Hal took two gloves from Roger's box and pulled them on, ignoring how they cut into his wrists.

The cabinet doors were open above the oven and dishwasher. Four aqua-colored dinner plates, four matching salad plates, mugs, and bowls. In the next cabinet, four lowballs, four highballs, two wineglasses. With the one that had been on the counter and the one that was wiped clean, it made a set of four. Hal lifted one of the plates and studied it. No scratches. No nicks. No water damage. He turned it over.

"Looks new, right?"

Hal motioned to the cabinets. He thought about the mismatched bar glasses in his own cabinet. Maybe a half-dozen plates, all but one chipped. Fine cracks from going through the microwave. "All of it. New and basic. Who lives with only four plates?"

"Someone not planning to stay long."

"Right. I'm going to talk to her sister today. I'll ask her." Hal pulled open the silverware drawer and found it as sparsely stocked as the cabinets. He opened drawers. A corkscrew, which he showed Roger.

"Good thought," Roger said, retrieving an evidence bag from his case.

Other than the corkscrew, the victim had a single spatula, a salad serving set, a ladle, and a large serving spoon. The food cupboard contained only a few cans of soup, trail mix, granola bars, crackers, and a small box of cereal. Another bottle of the same wine. In the refrigerator were some vegetables and a couple of takeout boxes, yogurts, Diet Coke, and water.

Hal pushed the refrigerator door closed. It was as if someone had walked down the housewares aisle at Target and bought the first twenty items that came to mind. Maybe she ate most meals at work. But it was more than that. The house felt impersonal, like an extended-stay hotel room rather than a place where someone lived.

She'd been here for months, not for a couple of weeks. Where was the wear and tear? It felt wrong. "Huh."

"Maybe they had her working all the time. She ate at work."

Naomi Muir, one of the crime scene techs, emerged from the back of the apartment. She said hello to Hal.

"Find anything?" Roger asked.

"Nothing. No personal papers. No pictures other than the ones that are displayed. The desk drawers are literally empty."

"Maybe someone removed things?" But Hal had a strange feeling that this wasn't what it appeared to be.

Victoria Stein didn't live here, not in the sense that most people lived in their homes. The more he looked at it, the more certain he felt. There wasn't even enough dirt. Maybe she kept this place as some sort of facade.

He wanted to circle back to the neighbor and ask how often she actually saw Stein.

"No," Naomi said. "The dust has settled evenly on the surfaces. No voids to suggest anything was removed."

"So maybe the job thing wasn't a permanent transfer," Roger said, thinking aloud. "Or maybe she didn't want to move everything until she was sure the job would work out. Hedging her bets."

"Maybe so," Naomi said. "but if I was moving across country, I'd pack my iPad and my computer."

If Stein was living here, then he would expect to find more of her personal things. Certainly a computer. "You didn't find a computer?"

"No. And not just no computer," Naomi continued. "There's no box or case, no extra cords, no modem, or Internet hookup. There is no evidence that she had a computer here at all."

"How about her phone?" Hal asked.

"Can't find that either," Naomi said. She lifted a plastic bag. "I found a wallet. Social Security card, driver's license from South Carolina, and one credit card."

Everyone knew you didn't carry your Social Security card in your wallet. He thought about his own wallet. He'd learned the hard way out of college that he couldn't afford credit card debt. He never carried a balance, but he still had three different cards. Plus the debit card for his bank. "One credit card," Hal repeated.

"Bank of America."

"Even I've got more than one credit card," Hal said.

"Right. I've been through the whole place. There's nothing else. No secret hiding places, no wall safe."

"You mind if I take that?" Hal asked, motioning to the bagged wallet. "I'd like to run her through the system and see if I can find out anything else about her."

Naomi glanced at Roger, who nodded.

"Thanks," Hal said. "I'll get them back to you for fingerprinting." He opened his notebook and made a note.

"There's more," Naomi said.

"Such as?" Hal asked.

"All the furniture matches."

Hal studied the dining room table with its curved legs and rounded edges. The wood stained the color of molasses. The same curves and stain were on the coffee table and the end table. "Huh." Hal set down the notebook and crossed to the dining room table. There, he got down on his knees and crawled under.

Hal studied the underside for some sort of sticker but found none. He crawled back out and proceeded to the living room. He turned the coffee table over and searched beneath it. Nothing there either.

"Maybe she bought it as a set," Roger suggested. "You looking for the manufacturer?"

"No." The signature in the lower-right corner of the painting in the dining room was a *C* followed by a series of letters that were so flattened into a line, he couldn't make them out. Then a large sweeping *W* followed by more indecipherable letters. He pointed to it. "Who's the artist on that painting?"

Both Naomi and Roger turned toward it.

"I'm afraid my art history is a bit rusty," Roger said. "I'm really best with the Renaissance period."

Hal waved at him. "Read me the signature already."

Roger chuckled and moved to the painting, where he squinted at the corner.

"Capital *C*, then stuff you can't read followed by capital *W* and more illegible letters?" Hal asked.

"Yes," Roger confirmed. "That's exactly it."

"Naomi, help me get this off the wall, would you?"

Together, Hal and the tech took the painting off the wall. "Where now?" Naomi asked.

"Let's turn it around," Hal directed, backing into the living room. "And set it against this wall." When the painting was down, Hal scanned the back of the canvas. There, on the lower-left corner was a small gold plaque that read **K&Z Interiors**.

"What is it?" Roger asked.

"K&Z Interiors," Naomi read to him. "You're interested in the interior designer?"

The bedroom furniture had the same bland consistency, each piece part of a set you might find in an upscale hotel. "I don't think it's an interior decorator." Using his iPhone, he Googled the company.

"What is it?"

He read aloud from the website, "K&Z Interiors, the nation's premier staging company, helping you sell your home faster, at a higher price."

"A staging company?" Roger repeated.

"I've heard of those," Naomi said. "They decorate houses before they go on the market."

"But maybe in this case, it's not for sale," Hal said, taking down the contact number for the company.

"So, you think Victoria Stein rented the furniture?" Roger asked.

"I'm wondering if she didn't rent the whole place," Hal said. "It's like Naomi said. Look around—there's nothing personal. No books or knickknacks from work or trips. No family photos except for the ones of her and her sister."

"Which is sort of weird, too," Naomi added.

"Right. No friends or parents."

"No boyfriend," Roger added.

"That makes sense with what I'm finding in the rest of the place," Naomi confirmed. "Come look at this."

Hal and Roger followed her back to the bedroom, where she pulled open the top drawer of the dresser. It was nearly empty.

"Underwear?" Hal asked.

"Six pairs of underwear?" Naomi said. "Assuming some dirty laundry, maybe seven to ten pairs. Enough for a week." Next she lifted one bra from the drawer. "Two bras," she said. "Assuming the victim was wearing one."

Hal and Roger said nothing.

Naomi laughed. "Guys, no woman owns only ten pairs of underwear and two bras." She waited, and when neither spoke, she added, "Especially two bras."

"Maybe this isn't her primary address," Hal said. "Like she wanted it to look like she lived here, but she didn't. I'll ask the sister." He made notes on the questions he had for Terri, then turned back to Naomi. "What did we find on her employer? Maybe they can shed some light on what she was doing out here."

"Uh . . . ," Naomi said, looking apologetic.

Hal had a sinking feeling. "What?"

“There are no pay stubs either, and her key ring only has two keys on it. The one to the building door and the one to her front door.”

“No key card to her work?” Hal asked.

Naomi shook her head.

“So maybe she wasn’t here for work,” Roger suggested.

Nothing in the condo was what it had originally seemed. Hal rolled off the latex gloves and shoved them into his back pocket. “I’ll make some calls.”

“We’ll finish our sweep here and let you know if we find anything else,” Roger told him.

Hal called Hailey, but the call went straight to voicemail. “Something’s up with Victoria Stein. I’m going to get the sister to come into the station as soon as possible. Call me.”

From the car, Hal dialed Terri Stein again. That call, too, went straight to voicemail.

He thought of Schwartzman, of her ties to South Carolina. She didn’t recognize either of the sisters—not their faces or their names.

That, too, was a dead end without more information. With nothing left to do, Hal drove in the direction of the department, hoping he could dig up something to shed some light on this case.

As it was, Hal was sitting in a dark closet, and he didn’t like it one bit.

Maybe Victoria Stein wasn’t who she said she was.

What kind of person lived with only the thinnest veneer of a life? She supposedly had a job but no computer, no Internet, no personal files, not even any identification other than a driver’s license and a Social Security card.

It made Hal wonder if they’d somehow stumbled into another agency’s turf. Hal found the number for his contact at the bureau and gave him a call.

10

San Francisco, California

Midday Thursday, Schwartzman returned to her office from the morgue in search of a bandage for the nasty paper cut she'd managed to give herself opening a suture kit.

She almost never worked in the office but instead used the little metal desk in the autopsy room.

She was startled to see a strange woman in the chair across from her desk. Although the room was warm enough, she looked cold in a dark-orange wool coat with the hood up. It was a sort of peacoat with large wooden buttons that made her seem more like a large child than an adult.

Schwartzman rifled through a drawer for a Band-Aid. "Can I help you?"

The woman looked up at Schwartzman, her eyes wide, and pressed the back of her hand to her red nose. Fresh tears trailed down her face.

"Let me get someone to help you." Schwartzman had work to finish up. A victim of a gang shooting had been in the drawer two days, and last night had brought her a stabbing victim, as well.

She moved to the hallway, looking for someone who might show the lost woman out. The woman began to cry, big, silent, rocking sobs.

When she came back into the room, Schwartzman noticed her slouched white boots and a pair of dark-yellow tights.

The ensemble made her look like a piece of candy corn, propped upside down.

The woman dried her eyes. "I'm waiting for the medical examiner."

Schwartzman ripped open the Band-Aid and wrapped the stretchy fabric around her index finger. "I'm the medical examiner."

"Oh . . ." The woman sat upright, and the hood slid off her head. Her straight dark hair was cut above her shoulders in uneven layers that made the damaged hair look like dark-colored straw.

"But if you're inquiring about a case, you need to talk to the investigators. Homicide is on the fifth floor." She turned to leave when the woman called after her.

"Did you do the—"

Schwartzman looked back.

The woman pulled the handkerchief away. "I'm Terri Stein. Victoria is my sister."

Schwartzman froze in the doorway, studied the woman more closely. Her hair was darker than it had been in the photos at the victim's house. Shorter. She was not familiar. The realization seemed both obvious and surprising. Even if Spencer had sent Terri, she wouldn't have been someone Schwartzman knew.

But more than that. She looked wrong. He would have hated the hooded coat, the odd layering of her hair, the flashy dangling earrings. Victoria was Spencer's type, not Terri.

Spencer wouldn't have chosen her.

Schwartzman realized she hadn't spoken. "I'm so sorry for your loss."

"Can you talk about it?"

She didn't want to be there alone with Victoria's sister. She didn't know what questions to ask, what to say. "I'm afraid not," Schwartzman said. "The lead inspector is Hal Harris. I can call him."

Terri sat forward on the chair. "They said she drowned."

Schwartzman had left that information with Hal yesterday, but since then they had been trading voicemails and had yet to connect.

"Drowned? In her own bathtub," Terri said, pressing her fist against her teeth.

"So you spoke to Inspector Harris." Had Hal sent her here? To see if she was familiar in some way? Had she missed his call? She reached into her pocket for her cell phone.

"In lavender water," Terri went on. Her gaze seemed to look right through Schwartzman.

Schwartzman wasn't used to the relatives, but she understood grief. "I am very sorry."

Terri watched her.

Schwartzman felt uncomfortable under her scrutiny, as though the woman was waiting for some other type of confession. Something about Spencer? She couldn't think. "We should be able to release the body for burial soon. Within a couple of days, I would think." Schwartzman leaned down and pulled out a form. "If you'd like to complete this paperwork, I can call you when we can transfer the remains." She slid the form across the desk, but Terri made no move for it. "We need information on which funeral home you've selected. If the remains are going out of state, you'll need to make arrangements for that ahead of time."

"How did he drown her with lavender water?"

He. It was a mistake to assume gender. Victoria Stein could have been drowned by another female. Schwartzman tapped the paper on the desk. "I'm afraid I can't speculate—"

"Was she drugged?"

Schwartzman closed her mouth and said nothing. She had gotten the tox results back less than an hour before. Diazepam, the generic form of Valium, had been used in addition to wine.

"You know, don't you?" Terri pressed.

"Ms. Stein, I'm not at liberty to speak about any ongoing investigation. I'm sorry. If you'd like to fill out this paperwork, I'll make sure everything is ready for you, but I'm afraid I've got to get back to work." Schwartzman inched the form a little closer to Terri Stein and set a pen on top. Then, offering an encouraging smile, she walked out the door.

"You look like her," Terri called after her.

Like a punch to the gut. Schwartzman closed her eyes and stopped moving.

Maybe Terri Stein knew something about the connection between Spencer and her sister.

Hal had promised to follow up. He must have learned something. But he hadn't called. Was he pursuing a lead? Had he found something to link Stein's death to Spencer?

"That's why I started to cry when I saw you," Terri added. "Because you look so much like her."

Schwartzman breathed a deep sigh and turned back around. Hal would be in contact. He would reach out when he could. Something had come up. It must have. "Yes. We have similar coloring."

"It's more than that," Terri said. "The shape of your nose. Even your gestures. You two are much more alike than she and I are."

And how is that possible? Schwartzman wanted to ask. Looking at the victim's sister, she saw almost no similarities. Perhaps a little in the mouth. "Do you have other siblings?"

"It was just us."

"And your parents? Are they living?"

Her eyes welled up again. "No. They both passed."

"I'm sorry. I noticed a lot of pictures of the two of you in her house."

"Yes." Terri's face flexed into a smile, a little too fast, too happy. Grief made people strange. She studied the faint freckles on Terri Stein's face, the single dimple on her left side that added to the air of youth about her.

Schwartzman felt calmer, taking charge of the conversation again. "I didn't see any images of your parents."

"No," she said as though accepting some criticism. "I don't know that she had any."

The images began to surface in Schwartzman's mind. "In one of the pictures, you two were in front of an aircraft carrier."

Terri nodded. "I think that's right."

"Was that taken near the ferry to Fort Sumter? At Patriots Point?"

Her expression was blank. "I don't remember."

"I wondered because it's down near where you guys grew up."

"Why would someone kill her?" Terri asked.

Schwartzman was startled by the question, which came out of nowhere. *Because she looked like me.*

"She had a boring job," Terri went on. "She hardly ever dated. Why would someone go into her home and kill her?"

Schwartzman wanted to ask more about Victoria. What she did, who she spent time with.

And yet that wasn't her job. Her job was the remains.

Her job was done.

"I have no idea," she told the victim's sister. "I'm sure the inspectors are doing everything they can to find out who did this to your sister. Have you spoken to Inspector Harris?"

"I'd like to see her."

Schwartzman was not going to show the body without Hal. She didn't even want to see it again. "We should make arrangements with Inspector Harris."

"You can't just take me to her?"

Schwartzman lifted the phone and dialed the extension for Homicide.

"Never mind. It's okay," Terri said, sounding disappointed. "I just wanted to talk to someone. I'm going a little stir-crazy."

Schwartzman held out the phone. "You don't want me to call?"

"No. I'm sure Inspector Harris will call me if there is any news."

Schwartzman replaced the receiver in its cradle. Terri stood and dug her hands into her pockets but remained rooted in place, silent.

Schwartzman let several seconds pass. Finally she said, "Is there something else I can do for you, Ms. Stein?"

"I heard someone had a pendant like Vicky's. The cross with the Star of David."

Schwartzman felt her mouth drop open and closed it quickly in an attempt to hide her surprise. How would the victims know about Schwartzman's necklace? The details of a case were never shared with the family, not during an active investigation. Plus, that necklace was not just a detail of the case.

It was about her personally.

"It was you, wasn't it?" Terri asked. "You had a necklace like hers?"

"You heard that?"

"The officers were talking about it."

Schwartzman said nothing. That she and the victim had matching necklaces was odd, worthy of gossip. But it made her angry. At the case, at herself. For sharing her past with Hailey and Hal.

That information was sensitive. The leak could be damaging to the case. But more than the case, the information felt deeply personal.

That it was shared felt like a betrayal.

"When I was waiting to talk to the inspector," Terri added.

"Which officers?"

"I don't know. They wore uniforms. A couple of men." Terri paused. "I was eavesdropping when I probably shouldn't have been," she admitted.

Schwartzman tried to imagine who would have been talking about evidence from a murder scene in front of the victim's sister.

"It just seems like you knew her somehow, that you two were connected."

"No," Schwartzman said firmly. "I didn't know your sister at all." There was an edge in her voice, but she let it sit.

"It was really nice to get a chance to meet you, Dr. Schwartzman." With that, Terri Stein walked out of her office.

The woman knew her name.

The office was too hot, too small. She had to leave. She lifted her coat off the hook on her door, her eye on the chair where the victim's sister had sat. Some realization fluttered at the edge of her mind. Something strange about Terri Stein, but she couldn't quite place it. Her phone rang, and she lifted the receiver. "Schwartzman."

"Oh good. I'm glad I caught you in the office."

Schwartzman couldn't place the voice. "I'm sorry. Who—"

"Sorry, it's Renu Khan."

Her gynecologist. "Dr. Khan." She glanced at the clock on the wall. She'd been in the doctor's office only five hours earlier. They'd already read her scans, and the doctor was calling back. For a fleeting moment, Schwartzman missed the cheerful nurse who'd called before. "That was fast. I assume you are calling with news about the second mammogram and the ultrasound."

"Yes."

Schwartzman remained standing, frozen as though she could control the doctor's next words by sheer power of will.

"I just got off the phone with the radiologist," Dr. Khan said.

"The radiologist," Schwartzman repeated.

"Yes. I wanted to get back to you as quickly as possible because I know you often have a lot on your plate."

Radiology meant cancer. "What did the radiologist find?"

"There are several microcalcifications—I'm sorry, several calcium deposits that we believe warrant biopsy."

Cancer. They were talking about breast cancer. "In my breast."

"Yes. Both breasts," Dr. Khan corrected.

Schwartzman sank into the chair, the coat caught under her so that it felt like the added weight of a person on her back. "Breast cancer."

"We need to do a biopsy to be certain. We can't confirm the lesions are cancerous until then. They may be benign."

"Of course." Schwartzman's reply felt empty. *Of course.* There was no reason to assume the worst.

"You're young to have mammograms, but I notice that this isn't your first. You must have familial risk factors."

Schwartzman didn't have an answer. She didn't much remember the first mammogram other than that it was done in Seattle as part of her medical training. It was some component of a course she took on genetics when testing for the BRCA gene was growing more common.

That period was a blur, all of it happening only weeks after Spencer had found her in Seattle. She'd had more than a year of reprieve from him, and then, somehow, he had tracked her down. She suspected her mother was the leak, but the timing was terrible. His calls came in at all hours, on her cell phone and—when she stopped answering that—on the landline in her apartment, in the anatomy lab at school, even once on rounds at the hospital. Just six weeks before her orals.

The mammogram had come back clean. That was in her file.

She'd hand-delivered that file to Dr. Khan herself. But she hadn't read it. Somewhere in there it must have indicated that she was at risk. Otherwise, why would she have another mammogram before she was forty? How could she not know this? But she knew how.

The pressure of preparing for her oral exams, Spencer. In that period, she hadn't slept, barely ate. She didn't take care of herself at all, so how would she remember the results of a test no one was concerned about?

"Dr. Schwartzman?"

"Yes," she said quickly. "I was trying to recall, but to be honest, I'm not sure. I'm not aware of any family history. I think that first mammogram was done as part of a medical school course."

"Hmm," Dr. Khan said. "I recommend Dr. Norman Fraser. He's very good. I took the liberty of calling ahead to let him know he might hear from you. He's a friend. He can fit you in as early as tomorrow afternoon if you can be available."

"Tomorrow afternoon," Schwartzman repeated. That was soon. If the microcalcifications were benign, why the rush?

They didn't think they were benign.

They thought she had cancer. *Breast cancer. Breast. Cancer.* She squeezed her eyes closed. It couldn't be. She thought of her father. He always said God only gave you what you could handle. How did God think she could handle this? She couldn't.

"Yes. Tomorrow at four fifteen."

It wasn't a diagnosis. It was a test result. *Maybe* she had cancer. She wanted to ask what the odds were. How often did they get the diagnosis wrong? What chance did she have to be the false positive? The one with some weird benign calcium deposits.

"Dr. Schwartzman?" Dr. Khan interrupted her thoughts. "Can I call someone for you?"

"No," she said firmly. *Hailey? Hal?*

No.

Ava.

Ava would know what to do. But how long since she'd talked to her aunt? It didn't matter. Of course it didn't. Ava would be there. Ava was her first call when everything with Spencer happened. Schwartzman had retreated to her aunt's home and slept for two days straight. Ava fed her and shielded her from the barrage of phone calls from her mother and Spencer. Schwartzman stayed in Charleston for ten days, mapping out her next moves, her plan.

Ava wrote her a check for $30,000 to help her move to Seattle and covered her living expenses to get her back to school. She put Schwartzman in touch with a woman in the medical school admissions office, someone who helped her apply for scholarships to cover her tuition.

Ava made all that happen.

Yes, she would call Ava. Once she knew the diagnosis. There was no reason to worry anyone prematurely.

It would be okay.

She drew a slow, even breath. "Thank you, Dr. Khan. I will be in touch with Dr. Fraser."

"They're holding the spot for you," Dr. Khan said, sounding relieved. "Just call in the morning to confirm."

"I'll do that."

"Good." A pause. "There is a chance that the deposits are not cancerous. We just need to check to be sure," the doctor offered in a small gesture of kindness. Empty of promise. Almost void of hope.

"Of course," Schwartzman agreed.

She hung up the phone. As she stood straight again, the blood rushed to her head, filling her vision with stars. Schwartzman moved to the door and pulled it open.

Standing in the entry was Inspector Hal Harris.

She reeled backward, releasing a guttural cry.

"Sorry," he said quickly, raising his hands in the air. "I didn't mean to startle you."

Schwartzman backed into her chair and sat down. She hadn't seen Hal since he and Hailey were in her apartment. She worked to gather her nerves again.

Push aside the thoughts of cancer. Focus on Stein.

When she glanced up, Hal was seated in the chair opposite her, doing his best to make his substantial size appear small and nonthreatening. It might have been comical if not for the adrenaline flooding her nervous system.

"You okay?" he asked.

It was all she could do to shake her head.

11

Charleston, South Carolina

Harper stood at her desk, shuffling piles of papers, waiting for Burl. She was anxious for the results of the autopsy. Her gut was divided on this one. There was plenty about it that felt like an accidental death. It was a little off that Kimberly Davies hadn't seen the body when she'd come around the porch, but it was possible that the victim fell after Davies looked. Perhaps the dog was barking because Mrs. Pinckney had fallen or suffered a heart attack or a stroke. Then she tripped, trying to get downstairs. But why go downstairs? Why not call for help from upstairs? And why did the dog go quiet?

Burl entered from the back stairwell. "You got something for me?" she called.

"Yep," he said. "Let me grab coffee."

She followed Burl into the break room. He tasted the coffee and made an exaggerated smacking sound. "Hmm. Mmm," he said. "Delicious."

"I'm glad you're so easily pleased." Burl reminded her of her father, who could never understand all the fuss about an espresso or a latte or a cappuccino. Used to drive him crazy when "city folk"—as he called them—came into the diner asking if they made espresso drinks.

Like Burl, her father enjoyed his coffee even when it might be considered mediocre, which was probably a stretch for the coffee offered at the department.

"I'm a man of simple pleasures, Detective. What I can't figure out is why the coffee up here is better than the coffee two floors down."

"Because there are dead people down there," Harper said flatly.

"Well, we don't stir them into the coffee." Burl raised his mug and took a long drink. "At least not on purpose."

Harper had been raising her mug to her own lips when the image of little pieces of human flesh floating in coffee entered her mind. "Burl." She groaned and set the coffee down.

"You want to come down and see what I've got?"

"You're done with the body?"

"Yep." He lifted the mug into the air. "Just came up for my celebratory cup of joe. Come on," he said, hitching his chin toward the stairs. "I'll show you."

In almost sixteen years on the force, Harper had grown accustomed to dead bodies. It was hard to work Homicide if you didn't. The charcoal-lined masks were effective at eliminating most of the smells. Add a couple drops of lavender or peppermint oil on the inside, as she did, and even the summer's worst bloaters were almost sufferable.

What she had never quite gotten accustomed to was the process of carving the body apart, examining it in pieces, and weighing and measuring the components before shoving it all back in again, zipping it up with a staple gun, and sending it off for burial or cremation. The sight of the closed-up Y-incision was the thing that made her most uncomfortable.

Jed always teased that it was because Lucy had been born by Cesarean section so Harper had her own version of the scar.

Maybe eighty years ago C-section scars looked like Y-incisions, but hers was only three or four inches long, hidden below the bikini line. The scar was more recent than her last bikini.

Burl held the door open, and Harper stepped into the morgue. As always, the room smelled of bleach and death. Like the rest of the building, the morgue was old, and little had been done in the way of updates.

At least upstairs the walls were covered with the latest most-wanted lists and campaign posters about spousal abuse, drunk driving, and the one Harper found the eeriest, an image of a young meth user, teeth missing, face covered in sores, and track marks up and down her scrawny arms. The caption read, "I wanted to be prom queen. Meth changed that."

Down in the morgue, though, nothing hung on the walls. Instead the south wall was covered with an orange-yellow water stain from a pipe that had broken a few years back. The water had ruined hundreds of case files. Had the pipe burst on the north side of the morgue, it would have filled the cold storage, where the bodies were kept. According to Burl, the morgue had five "guests" at the time, so the loss of the files was preferable to the alternative.

Today Frances Pinckney was laid out on the autopsy table. Her face and shoulders were uncovered, but Burl had draped a white sheet over the rest of her. As always, Harper kept herself at a firm six or seven feet from the victim. She would have taken the autopsy results over the phone, but Burl tended to be more detailed when he was standing over the victim, and she didn't want to miss anything that could be important.

"I ruled out natural causes first."

Harper exhaled. "So, she was murdered?"

Burl crossed to the file cabinet without answering. He enjoyed the process of unveiling the cause of death, and Harper tried to remind herself that this part was his show. His cowboy boots made loud clacking sounds on the floor despite the blue booties he had pulled over them. He returned with a file and flipped it open.

Another of Burl's little quirks.

Most of the other medical examiners talked from memory, especially when the victim was as recent as this one. Burl liked to hold the folder open in one hand while pointing out relevant markings with the other.

"Heart was healthy," he said, pointing to her chest. "No obstructions and the brain showed no signs of a stroke."

"She could have slipped on the stairs."

"I considered it."

Harper didn't like where this was going.

"Let me show you the X-rays."

The one thing the morgue had updated in the last decade was its computers. It was now outfitted with a state-of-the-art computer system, but Harper wasn't surprised when Burl led her to the light screen. Burl preferred X-rays the old-fashioned way. She watched him work and wondered how many more years he'd be around. She would miss the way Burl did things.

When he found the slide he wanted, he turned the knob on the old machine and cranked on the lamp. The light flickered twice before illuminating. Burl slid the X-ray under the clips and pointed to Frances Pinckney's vertebrae. "From the fracturing, we can see that she landed on her sternum first." He pointed to the image. "Basically, she took the brunt of the fall on her chest."

"Okay," Harper said. She pictured Pinckney. "She would have been facing down the stairs."

"Yes. Her arms were at her sides." He switched the slides and showed her a line in one of the wrist bones. "She's got a hairline fracture on her left side, which appears to have happened because the wrist was caught under her. But there are no other breaks on her arms."

Harper imagined the victim falling. Her arms would be out to break the fall. "You're saying the break to the wrist wasn't caused because she had her arm outstretched when she fell?"

"No. The break pattern suggests it was against her like this when she landed." Burl held his arm to his side, elbow against his ribs.

"She didn't put her arms out to break the fall? Isn't that unusual?"

Burl whistled. "Yes, ma'am. In a fall, we almost always see evidence of the victim reaching out to break the fall."

"Her hands weren't bound."

"No," Burl confirmed.

He knew the answer. She could tell from the quick responses, but she wasn't ready to give in yet.

Other reasons a victim wouldn't reach out to break her fall. "What if she was carrying something?" Harper suggested, snapping her fingers. "Like Cooper. The dog."

"Possibly."

"What do you mean? You know the answer."

He nodded smugly.

She came back around to drugs. "What about the tox screen?"

"Clean, but you're on to something."

"So, it's possible she fell and couldn't break her fall. That she was impaired somehow."

Burl nodded.

"Out with it," Harper told him.

He responded with a low chuckle. "I did a lung biopsy."

"A lung biopsy," she repeated. "What for?"

"I noticed a faint odor on her at the scene. I wanted to be certain that I didn't have it wrong."

"And you didn't," she guessed.

"Nope."

"What was it?"

"Chloroform."

Harper studied Pinckney's face. She had been drugged. "So someone knocked her out with chloroform and then sent her down the stairs."

"Yes, ma'am. Those are my findings." Burl rocked back on his heels like the sheriff in an old Western, but the game lost its appeal as Harper recognized the woman whose children she had grown up with.

Frances at their eighth-grade graduations, taking pictures before prom. Drugged and thrown down the stairs. Deaths like this didn't happen in this wealthy pocket of Charleston. People died of old age and cardiac disease. How could she face her parents? What could she tell them? She knew the cause of death, but she still had no explanation for why.

"Who on earth would want to throw an old lady down the stairs?"

"That, my dear, is your job." Burl set his hand gently on her shoulder in encouragement, and Harper nodded, pulling herself away from Pinckney's corpse.

Harper climbed the stairs and returned to her desk, where a plain white coffee cup told her Andy had gone to a French café a couple of blocks away. The Gaulart & Maliclet cup was like a gift.

She took a sip of the drink, disappointed to find it was tepid.

It was tepid, and Frances Pinckney, a lady not very different from her own mother, had been drugged and savagely thrown down a flight of stairs to break her neck. Harper felt as if her skin was crawling. She scratched through her shirt at an itch she couldn't reach.

What she needed was to get out of the building. It was after noon, but she craved breakfast. Callie's served the best biscuits. She dialed her husband's work line. Jed answered on the second ring.

"I'm going over to Callie's for breakfast," she told him.

"Bad news on a case?"

"Yes."

"I'll be there in ten," Jed told her. "Order me some coffee."

Harper hung up and left the coffee cup on her desk. She grabbed her coat off the chair, told the admin that she was going to be out for about an hour, and hit the street, walking in big, fast strides. The itching began to wane. A light breeze cooled her skin as a horse-drawn carriage stopped on the sidewalk, one of Charleston's historical tours en route. This particular guide, an older gentleman wearing a tweed vest and cap, was explaining the earthquake bolt plates on a building along King Street.

Pinckney's house had the disks, too, Harper recalled. Solving Frances Pinckney's death was like putting bolts in one of those old buildings. Somehow Harper just needed to pull the pieces together, bit by bit, to figure out who would have wanted her dead.

In the meantime, she was counting on biscuits and gravy to take her mind off the case.

12

San Francisco, California

"She was right here. In my office."

Hal watched Schwartzman pace a tight semicircle around the backside of her desk. "In that chair." She jabbed her finger toward the empty chair beside him. "She knew about cause of death. She knew about the pendant." Her expression was a mixture of terror and fury. "How could she know about that?"

Motionless, Hal tried to make sense of her rambling. He had missed the entire beginning of her rant because she was talking too fast, and he was hopelessly lost. "'She' who?"

"Stein."

Without offering more, she turned and walked around the desk again. Her fingers were working in and out of fists, her brow furrowed as though she were doing some sort of intricate surgery while she walked. He'd seen her this rattled only once before—when he'd walked into the morgue after Spencer told Schwartzman that her mother was in the hospital. Lied about her mother being in the hospital.

That was Hal's first encounter with Spencer and his sick games. And this had to be another game. After what felt like five minutes spent watching her talking and pacing, Hal was dizzy. "Schwartzman."

She kept moving.

"Hey," he said louder. "Schwartzman."

She halted. She seemed surprised to find him in the room.

"Who knew that Stein drowned in lavender water?" he asked.

"The sister."

"Victoria Stein's sister?"

"Yes. She knew about the lavender, the water. She asked if she'd been drugged." Schwartzman touched her chest as if she was searching for something. "And the pendant. She knew about the pendant."

"When did she leave?"

"She was here five minutes ago."

Damn! He'd missed her. "I've been trying to reach her all day," he said. "If she wants answers, why not call me back?"

Something was up with Terri Stein. By the time he had arrived at the crime scene Tuesday night, she'd been taken to the hospital by one of the patrol officers to be treated for shock.

According to the hospital, she had checked herself out shortly afterward and was put into a cab. She'd agreed to come to the station today in a text message, but he hadn't heard from her. He had no idea where she was staying or for how long. He'd called her three times since then.

"She doesn't need answers," Schwartzman said. "She already knows it all."

"Schwartzman," he shouted to get her attention.

She stopped and stared at him.

"All the moving around is making me dizzy," he said softly. He motioned to the desk. "Maybe you could sit for a couple minutes."

She sat down as Hal opened his notebook. When he looked up, she was seated, her hands folded on her lap as though obeying a schoolmaster.

"How did she end up in your office?" he asked.

"I don't know. I came in for a bandage, and she was sitting there, crying."

Hal wondered about the tears. He'd seen grief enough times to get a good sense for when emotion was real and when it wasn't. Of course, there was no way of being certain. He'd been fooled plenty, too. "Did you ask her?"

She stopped to think. "I did, but she didn't answer. She just started into how Victoria had drowned in lavender water."

Dread was heavy in his gut. "She shouldn't have known that."

"I thought she'd talked to you."

"I haven't told anyone but Hailey." He scanned her office. "There's no way that she read something on your desk? A file?"

"All my files are in the morgue. My computer, too."

Neither spoke for a moment. "If she knew—" Schwartzman said.

"She had to be involved," he finished. Her alibi was the gas station. How quick she had been to provide an alibi. Ken Macy had had the receipt in his hand when Roger showed up at the crime scene. A time-stamped credit card receipt. That was a solid alibi. Which meant someone else was working with her. A boyfriend maybe. But what was the motive?

Hal was already pulling out his cell phone. "I've got to see if we can find her before she gets out of town." Hailey was working the gang-related shooting, so he dialed Dispatch directly. "This is Inspector Harris. I need to get a BOLO out on a suspect in a 187. A female, age approximately—"

"Midthirties," Schwartzman said.

"Midthirties."

Schwartzman kept talking. "Approximately five foot three. A hundred and fifteen pounds. Brown hair, brown eyes. Wearing an orange peacoat and yellow tights. Last seen at 850 Bryant Street."

Hal passed the information on to Dispatch. "Going by the name of Terri Stein, but may be known by another name." The BOLO—be on the lookout for—would cover the state, but the more specific he could be, the better the chances of locating her. Maybe she was heading home to Southern California. She probably didn't have another place to stay. At least, he hoped she didn't. "Suspect may be heading south toward Los Angeles. Pass the description to highway patrol." He tried to imagine her getting on a plane. "Airports, too," he added.

"We have a description of the car?" Dispatch asked.

"Her car?" Hal said out loud.

Schwartzman stood from the desk. "Let me ask at the desk."

"Not yet," Hal said. "Is Officer Ken Macy on patrol today?"

"I'll check," Dispatch answered.

"Get that BOLO going, and I'll see about getting more information."

There was a brief pause as Hal crossed his fingers. He needed someone to help create a composite sketch for the BOLO for Terri Stein. Macy had been first on the scene, which meant that, aside from Schwartzman, he'd had the most interaction with Stein's sister.

"Inspector?" asked Dispatch.

"I'm here," Hal confirmed.

"I'm patching you through to Officer Macy."

There were a series of beeps and two short ringtones followed by Ken Macy's voice. "This is Macy."

"Inspector Harris here. I'm calling about the Stein murder. Did you see the car that Victoria Stein's sister was driving?"

"Her sister?"

"Right. The victim from Tuesday night," Hal said again. "You met the sister at the scene. Her name was Terri Stein."

"Right. Sure," Macy said quickly. "I'm trying to think. No, I met her inside. Fischer took her to the hospital, but I was on the street when they left. She didn't go to her car."

Hal fought off his frustration. It wasn't Macy's fault that he hadn't seen the car. He couldn't be blamed for letting the sister leave the scene. It was his duty to help her get medical care if she needed it. Hal just hated the fact that he hadn't gotten to see the sister himself. "Macy, I need you to come in and help create a composite sketch of Terri Stein."

"Sure. I'm only a couple of blocks from the department. I'll call the captain and let him know."

"The sketch artist will meet you in Homicide. As soon as it's done, it needs to go to Dispatch for the BOLO. Got it?"

"Got it, Inspector."

"Thanks." Hal hung up as Schwartzman was coming back in the door. Something in her had shifted. The dizziness-making woman of a few minutes ago now wore a different expression, something more focused, almost fierce. "Anything?" he asked.

"They didn't see where Terri Stein went when she left the building."

Terri Stein was involved, but why would she admit it? What was she hoping to get from Schwartzman? And if she was involved, what motive did she have for killing her sister?

"I don't think they were sisters," Schwartzman said, as if she could read his mind.

How did she do that? "What? Why?"

"I'll show you." She ran her hands down her arms as if she was cold. She was unnerved but trying to play it off. Hal didn't blame her. If she was convinced that there was something weird about Victoria Stein's death before, the interaction with Terri Stein added merit to the theory.

Schwartzman pulled open the door.

"Where are we going?" Hal asked her.

"The morgue."

13

San Francisco, California

The room was quiet except for the soft humming of the compressor that kept the bodies cold. Schwartzman breathed deeply as they entered, waited until Hal passed to close the door behind him. Entering the morgue brought a familiar sense of elation and also a deep calm. This was where things fell into place for her, where she worked out the puzzles. For years she had waited for some solution to fall into her lap.

For Spencer to simply give up and go away.

The staged victim, the flowers, the pendant—she had to believe the scene was meant for her. Maybe that sounded crazy; maybe it was. But she couldn't believe in the kind of coincidences that would have to exist for this to be anything other than Spencer's doing. His plan to terrify her. He had succeeded. This was not a crime planned by a man ready to give up.

The days of wishing and waiting were done. She had to do something about it now. She had Hal and Hailey, the support of a team.

She was still alone with Spencer—he wanted her and only her. But it was different now. It felt different. She was a stronger force.

She wondered if Spencer had any idea that this had changed in her mind.

"You okay?" Hal asked.

Schwartzman was breathing heavily. "Yes," she said, surprised that it was the truth.

She pulled out a drawer from the wall and folded the sheet back to expose Victoria Stein's head and shoulders.

"You can tell they're not sisters just by looking at her?" Hal asked.

"Not definitively," she answered without pause. "Short of testing DNA samples from both women, I can't confirm the genetic relationship." She might have asked if Hal thought Terri Stein would show up again. If she did, there could be a chance of doing that kind of testing. But Schwartzman already suspected the answer. Spencer would love the idea of sending someone to her office, making something that looked innocuous into a reminder that he was always lurking. She could only imagine how pleased he was.

But he had underestimated her, as well.

"Tell me why they're not sisters."

Schwartzman pulled on a pair of gloves and pushed the hair off the victim's face. "Stein has a small widow's peak," Schwartzman said, pointing to the V on the forehead.

"Okay."

"The widow's peak is a dominant gene," Schwartzman explained.

"And Terri Stein doesn't have a widow's peak?" Hal clarified.

She pictured the woman's high, rounded forehead. "No."

"So, if it's dominant, does that mean everyone gets it?" he asked.

"No," she admitted. "It's not entirely understood how these attributes are passed on. It's likely not as simple as one gene with two alleles, dominant and recessive."

Hal frowned.

"Basically," Schwartzman went on, "it's possible Terri and Victoria Stein are, in fact, sisters. But it's unlikely."

"Because of a widow's peak?" Hal said.

"In part because of the widow's peak," she answered. "Victoria Stein has the widow's peak. Terri does not. Terri, meanwhile, has freckles and also a single dimple on her left side." She returned to the victim. "Victoria has neither."

"Freckles and a dimple? And that means . . . ?"

"Those things are all considered dominant traits in humans," she explained. "Widow's peak, dimples, freckles, along with some other things like the ability to roll the tongue and detached versus attached earlobes. Obviously I can't check for the tongue rolling, and both women have detached earlobes, but the chances of the two women having those three different dominant traits between them is low." The more the words rushed from her tongue, the more certain she was that the two women weren't related.

"You mean having the three between them but not sharing them? Like you'd feel better if they both had widow's peaks?"

"I'm not sure I'd feel better, but the claim that they were sisters would seem more plausible," she told him.

"I hear you." Hal leaned in to study the victim's face. "And are we sure she didn't have a dimple?"

"Positive," Schwartzman confirmed. She lifted the corners of the victim's lips. "We can see the existing lines in her face. The nasolabial folds, for instance, are perfectly clear." She ran her finger along the creases that ran between the victim's chin and nose.

"She has light parentheses lines, as well," Schwartzman added, pointing to the fine semicircles on either side of her lips. "Those lines are extensions of the nasolabial folds. But there are no signs of any dimples." She crossed the room and wheeled back her magnifying scope, raising it so that the height would be more comfortable for Hal. "Here," she told him. "Look."

Hal peered through the glass.

"See these," she said, pointing to the facial lines around the mouth.

He stood back. "Okay. No dimples," he agreed. "But it's possible they're stepsisters or half sisters. Or one of them was married to the other's brother."

"That's technically true," Schwartzman agreed. "But she didn't talk about their relationship that way. She made it sound like they were sisters."

"How so?" he asked.

Schwartzman paused to recall the words. "When I asked her if their parents were still living, she said that they had 'both passed.' Like she was referring to a single set of parents."

"I agree. I would've thought the same. We call that a hunch."

Schwartzman felt a twinge of pride. "I guess that's what it was. She also said that she was glad to have a chance to meet me." She paused, replaying the conversation. "No. Not glad. She said it was 'really nice' to get a 'chance' to meet me. Nice." There was a twinge in her gut as she said the words. Like bad milk.

Spencer.

Hal wrote down the words. "Nice to get a chance to meet you?"

She nodded, watching Hal underline the word *nice* with the quick stroke of his pen. He agreed that it was odd.

"And she called me by name," Schwartzman remembered. How had that woman known her name if it hadn't come from Spencer?

"Maybe she saw the name on the door," Hal said, his pen poised on the page.

"My name's not on the door." Something she had specifically requested, one of the tactics to evade Spencer. She wasn't listed on the department's website either.

Schwartzman had commented on the photographs. Only of the two girls. The one at Fort Sumter. Something flashed through her memory. Another piece dropped into place. "I asked her about one of the pictures from the house."

"Which one?"

"There was one of the two girls standing in front of a ship. Not a ship, an aircraft carrier."

"Sure. I remember." He pulled his phone out of his pocket. "I took a picture of it."

Schwartzman slid Stein's body back into the wall. She pulled off her gloves and dropped them in the trash as Hal searched for the image.

"Here." He handed her the phone.

Schwartzman turned the phone sideways and used her fingers to zoom in on the image.

She was right.

"That's the USS *Yorktown*," she said, breathless again. "I went there a dozen times with my aunt as a child." She tilted the phone so he could see. "In this picture, you can see the entire length of the boat behind the girls."

"Okay."

"In reality, that's impossible. The dock that leads to the boat isn't long enough to allow for a view of the entire boat. You can see maybe two-thirds at best."

Schwartzman studied the edge of the girls for evidence that they were somehow edited into it.

"You're sure?" Hal asked.

"Positive. My aunt took a picture of me and that boat almost every summer from the time I was maybe four until I was in high school. Every picture is me and one end of the boat or the other, never the whole thing."

She handed the phone back to him and watched as he zoomed in on the girls until the image was completely grainy. "So you think it's been Photoshopped?"

"Yes."

Hal was about to say something when his phone buzzed from his pocket. "Harris."

Schwartzman could hear a deep, craggy voice on the other end.

"Did you find anything?" he asked.

The man said something, and Hal's expression said it was bad news. "Hang on. I'm going to put you on speaker. I'm here with my colleague." Hal lowered the phone and nodded to Schwartzman. "You repeat that, Gary?"

"Your Victoria Stein doesn't exist," the craggy voice said.

"Doesn't exist or isn't with the bureau?" Hal asked.

"Doesn't exist. Period."

Hal groaned.

Schwartzman glanced toward the bank of drawers. If that wasn't Victoria Stein, who was it?

"The driver's license is a fake," the voice went on. "The Social Security number belongs to an elderly woman—Victoria Stein—in Pensacola, Florida, and the credit card links to that Victoria Stein's bank account."

"Florida?" Hal asked. "Huh."

Schwartzman watched him, trying to put it together as he did.

"Identity theft," Hal said.

"Technically," the agent agreed. "What's weird is that there are no charges to Stein's bank account. That card was issued in March, delivered to Victoria Stein in Pensacola, and activated through the automated number, but your perp hasn't used it once."

Hal exhaled. "No chance she'd be with another agency?"

"No. I checked."

"The DOJ have anything to add?"

"Nope," he said. "Nothing there. If you get me an image, we can run your victim through recognition software, see if we can come up with a name."

"I'll get one over."

"Probably take us a week, though. Those guys are way backed up."

A week. The body would be a Jane Doe by then.

"What about the other name?" Hal asked. "Terri Stein."

"You get any kind of ID on her?"

Schwartzman exhaled. It hadn't occurred to her to ask for ID. She never saw families. They went to the police station for answers, not the morgue. But this one found her.

"No," Hal said. "And I think she's in the wind."

"I assume you don't know if we're dealing with a Teresa or just Terri?"

Schwartzman shook her head. Of course she hadn't gotten the spelling of her name. She hadn't asked for ID. She hadn't done anything right.

"Okay. I'm running it both ways," the agent said.

"Plus, Teresa could be T-E or T-H-E," Hal said.

"Ah, Christ, Harris. Hang on." There was the sound of the agent hunting and pecking on the keyboard, then a pause. "I've got a hundred and sixty-three variations on the name. You want me to narrow it by age?"

"Yeah," Hal said. "Narrow it to ages twenty-five to forty and send it over."

"Will do, but I'm guessing none of these is your suspect."

Hal sighed. "I know it."

"Sorry, buddy."

"Appreciate the call anyway." He ended the call and returned the phone to his pocket.

"The Stein sisters don't exist," Schwartzman said.

"Doesn't look that way," he conceded.

"So the two women pretended to be sisters," Schwartzman said. "One of them supposedly lives in LA and the other here. Then one of them kills the other."

Hal watched her. "You have a theory about why?"

Because Spencer enjoys scaring me? No. That's too simple. He had something larger in mind, but she had no idea what his plan was. She shook her head.

“Until we know who they are, it’ll be hard to figure out what they were up to.”

There had to be something else they could do. “So what’s the next step?”

“We’ll put together a composite sketch on Terri Stein, and I’ll run Victoria’s image through the database and get it out to Missing Persons. Someone, somewhere will recognize them.”

Schwartzman lined up the tools on her tray, spacing them with a focused precision. That plan was too slow. She wanted something she could do right now. That moment. Something to connect Spencer to the woman lying in the metal drawer.

“Once we know who they are,” said Hal, “we’ll figure out how they connect to Spencer McDonald.”

The scalpel slipped from her fingers and clattered to the floor.

She watched as Hal bent to retrieve it, watched as he set the knife on the tray and slid it into line with the others. The pulse in her carotid thundered inside her eardrums. “You mean ‘if’ they connect to him.”

“Do you believe it’s an ‘if’?” he asked.

Without answering, Schwartzman lifted the scalpel and carried it to the cleaning station. She knew what Spencer was capable of, the lengths he would go to get her back, the time he would devote to a plan. Their careers weren’t long enough to wait him out. She straightened her neck, drew her shoulders back.

“Do you doubt the connection?” he asked again.

She turned toward him. “No, I do not.”

“I don’t either. Not even a little bit.”

She let the words sink in. He believed her. Not just that Spencer was crazy or scary but that he was capable of this.

For the first time, someone was truly on her side.

“We should get to work, then.”

She opened the door and waited as he passed. “Yes,” she whispered.

14

San Francisco, California

There was no word from Hal on Friday. It had been a busy day in the morgue, made worse by the fact that she stopped what she was doing every time her phone made a noise. She completed three autopsies before leaving at three forty-five to make it to Dr. Fraser's on time.

She shouldn't have been surprised that she didn't hear from Hal. There was no reason to be in touch unless there was something to report.

Which meant there was nothing.

No lead on Terri Stein, no news about Victoria's real identity. No link to Spencer. No word from him either.

She couldn't decide if that was a surprise or not. What she did know was that it wouldn't last.

His silences never did.

Dr. Fraser's office was designed to calm, with its ficus trees and fresh-cut yellow tulips. *Yellow.* She rubbed her palms over her shoulders and drew a deep breath to calm her racing heart. For distraction, Schwartzman checked her e-mails and the most recent lab results on her phone.

The origin of the specific lavender seeds found in the victim's lungs couldn't be isolated. She wasn't surprised. Lavender wasn't commonly associated with murder, so the notion of sourcing a specific plant was probably uncommon. She forwarded the information to Hal. Checked for new e-mails every fifteen or thirty seconds and, finally, out of desperation, picked up an issue of *Us Weekly* off the table.

The cover story was about an actress facing cancer. The proud-looking woman smiled for the camera. Her head was shaved entirely bald. She wore a bright-yellow sweater. Yellow was the color of cancer. Of course it was.

Schwartzman was grateful when she was finally called into the exam room. Dr. Fraser was comprehensive in his explanation of the procedure and her odds. "I sit in this room with women whose biopsies come up totally clean and women who will be back the next week to plan treatment," he told her. "Whatever happens after this, Annabelle, I am here to help you get through it."

She shivered.

"It's normal to be nervous." The door opened, and a nurse came in. She introduced herself as Bonnie. Perky. Alert. Positive.

"Bonnie is a breast cancer survivor," Fraser announced.

She wore a pink pin pinned to her surgical top, above her heart. "Nice to meet you, Annabelle," Bonnie said, offering her hand.

Again Schwartzman felt the deep run of cold.

"Please," she said. *Please don't call me that. Annabelle.* "I go by Anna."

"Of course," Bonnie said, making a note.

She wasn't nervous. The idea of breast cancer was terrifying, but one only had so much room for terror, and she was already consumed by something, someone, much more lethal than cancer.

The biopsy itself was quick and not terribly painful. They took a sample from the calcification in her right breast and did a sentinel lymph node biopsy. Bonnie chatted through the entire procedure, explaining in more detail than necessary how long the soreness might last, that she could take ibuprofen, and on and on about procedures and coping with anxiety.

"I'll be fine," Schwartzman said finally, and Bonnie's mouth snapped closed. Perhaps she'd been too short. Distraction techniques were useful. She had plenty of experience there.

And yet there was something calming about the idea of cancer. When thoughts of breast cancer crowded her brain—for as long as her mind raced with images of mastectomy, chemo, and being bald lasted—she wasn't wondering when and where and how Spencer would appear again.

Arriving home that evening, though, she was antsy and frustrated. It was almost six and nothing from Hal. She would probably have to wait until after the weekend to hear anything.

She tried to imagine a way to put work aside for the night. She could go to a movie. She hated being in the theater alone. She was normally so content with a book and a cozy blanket, a glass of Evan Williams bourbon. She was working on the last bottle her father had left when he died. There had been eleven. She wondered if she would buy it herself when the final bottle was gone, or if it would no longer appeal if the bottles hadn't come from him.

She'd successfully been able to push Spencer from her mind before, hadn't she? She just needed to find a way to do it again. Distract herself with work or a book . . . an old movie?

She had almost convinced herself to go to the new exhibit at the de Young Museum when a text message came in from Ken Macy.

New Balinese place you have to try. Only been open 1 week. Was there last night. No delivery for takeout yet. Soon, I hope. Will keep you posted.

She could just go by herself for a quick dinner. Get out of the house. The restaurant was ten blocks away. She entertained the idea of walking. It wasn't raining, but the weather was cool enough to be comfortable in a jacket. She had expected spring to come more quickly in San Francisco, but May was as wet and cold as the winter.

No. She didn't walk. Walking meant crowds, unfamiliar people. She imagined passing people on the streets. Looking at their faces. Would Terri Stein, or whoever she was, be out there somewhere? Would Spencer? She used to love to walk, but these days she didn't allow herself that kind of vulnerability.

She drove only to and from work and once a week to the store, the dry cleaner. If she was at a scene late, she asked one of the officers to escort her to her car. She had meals delivered. She lived like a shut-in.

Because of Spencer.

Since leaving Spencer, she'd rarely ventured far from her routine—school, work, the occasional outing. But since Spencer had found her again in San Francisco, every time she left her building—no, every time she opened her apartment door—it felt as if she was taking a risk.

Hal Harris had left her a voicemail informing her that he'd reached out to the Greenville police. Spencer was there. Or so they said. But she knew better. She'd lived almost seven years certain that Spencer was just behind her while—as far as anyone else could tell—he never left Greenville.

She could stay home, order something else. There were a hundred places in San Francisco that delivered. Takeout and her book. The McCullough book sat closed on the table by the chaise, a slender white bookmark to remind her that she'd read only ten or twenty pages in a week. She could read.

No.

She needed to be out. If only for a few minutes.

Decided. She would drive to the new Balinese place. Be there in ten minutes, wait twenty or so for the food, and be home in another ten. An hour, hour and a half, on the outside. What if . . .

She caught herself.

Enough. Enough of letting Spencer rule your life.

It was a restaurant. There would be people. The restaurant was located in the Marina District. The streets would be packed. In fact, parking would probably be a nightmare. Have an Uber take her? She rejected the idea before it was even fully formed. She simply couldn't imagine getting in a stranger's car. If someone could hear her thoughts, they'd say she was paranoid, crazy even. She couldn't argue.

The truth was that even with something so simple, Spencer ruled.

Pocketing her car keys and a single credit card, her driver's license, and her phone, Schwartzman headed out. Her pulse raced slightly as she emerged from the parking garage and took her first turn. Her hypothalamus sent messages to kick her sympathetic nervous system into action. She was more alert, more tense. She took deep breaths and turned the radio to a 1990s country station. Heard Garth Brooks.

Slowly the music, the familiar roads calmed her. The restaurant, Rumah, was actually a couple of blocks east of the busiest part of the marina. Schwartzman drove past to confirm its location. The door opened, and a couple came out, but it didn't appear to be packed. She found a parking place half a block from the restaurant. Walking toward the restaurant, she was relieved. She could do this.

A couple walked past with two huge dogs, crossing into the street to allow her to pass. "Evening," the man said.

Schwartzman studied his face. He wasn't familiar. He didn't sound Southern. Just someone being polite. It still happened.

She reached the door of the restaurant. Four women sat at one table, dressed up for a night out. A long table surrounded by dark-headed adults and children, a gray-haired man at the head. Couples sprinkled in, but she saw no one alone.

She hesitated. Sitting alone would be so uncomfortable.

She could always order and go wait in her car. Or just walk through the streets. There were plenty of people out.

"Hello."

Schwartzman jumped and spun, catching one foot on the other as she twisted away. She stumbled backward and fell hard on her backside. Rough pavement shredded her palms, and her keys flew from her hand as she tried to break her fall. Her heart hammered in her chest.

The man who squatted in front of her was Ken Macy. "I am so sorry."

Schwartzman wiped her hands tenderly across her pants, the skin raw.

"Let me help you up," Macy offered, reaching for her hands.

She turned on her side and got up on her own. She scanned the sidewalk for her car keys.

"Did you drop something?"

"My keys," she said, getting back on her knees to peer under a black Mercedes SUV parked at the curb.

Macy used the flashlight on his phone to scan the pavement. "Did you hear them land?"

Hot with embarrassment, she wanted to go home.

Macy walked off the curb and into the street to search from the other side.

Standing again, Schwartzman glanced at her palms. The right one was bleeding, and the left had several small pieces of rock embedded in it. She would need to wash them.

"Got 'em." Macy returned the keys, and she winced as the rough edge of her house key touched the abrasion on her palm. "Let me look at that," Macy said, taking her hand before she could tell him no.

She flushed at the touch of his hand. Warm, soothing. She forced herself to pull away. "It's nothing."

He didn't let go. "Ouch. Come on. You can wash up inside. You've got a little gravel in that one."

She was desperate to stay and leave, both at once. "I'm okay. Really," she said, starting to turn for her car.

"You need to get that cleaned out, Doctor." He smiled gently and nodded toward the restaurant. "And the food's really good. I'll order for us."

The air stuck in her throat.

Macy sensed her stiffen. "Hey," he said with a reassuring touch on her arm. "Just two friends having dinner."

She glanced over his shoulder in the direction of her car. Racing past him to make a run for it crossed her mind. "I—"

"Colleagues," he offered. "Honestly, Doctor. Just food. You need food. I can tell. And a nice cold bottle of beer is going to feel great on those hands."

He was right. She could have a meal with a colleague. In a public restaurant. This was what normal people did. For tonight she could be a normal person. What was more, she wanted to have dinner with him.

"Say you'll stay," he said softly.

"I'll stay." She felt a moment of joy. She was out, with a friend. She felt safe and happy. She could do this.

"Good." Macy held the door open, and the noise from the small restaurant flooded out into the street. "Restroom's in that back corner," he told her, pointing over her shoulder.

She made her way around the tables, glancing at the food on the table. Her stomach growled. When was the last time she'd felt hungry? Not even hungry, she was ravenous.

In the bathroom, Schwartzman turned the water on cold and tested it with her fingers before letting it run over her palms. The burn passed quickly, and after a few moments in the cold water, she lathered with soap and gently washed. The scrapes were mild, none reaching below the top layers of the epidermis. They would be healed within a day or two. She let the cold water run over them again, then pressed the backs of her hands to the warmth in her face before patting her skin dry and heading back into the restaurant.

Her stomach gave a little jolt as she spotted Macy, hand raised from a two-top against the far wall of the restaurant.

He was smiling. He had an easy smile. It made her want to smile back.

She was relieved that they were far from the front window. She would not think about needing to hide; for one hour, she would not think. Instead, without allowing herself to hesitate, she walked toward him.

He rose when she arrived at the table and moved out of the seat against the wall to let her take it. Schwartzman appreciated the gesture. Having the view of a room made her more comfortable. She wondered briefly if he'd planned it this way. He was the kind of man who would notice those things.

The waiter returned with two glasses of water and asked if they were ready to order.

"Maybe a drink." Macy looked across at Schwartzman. "I didn't order any drinks because I wasn't sure what you'd want."

Schwartzman opened the menu and scanned the list of beers. "I'll have a Tsingtao," she told the waiter.

"I'll have the same," Macy said before turning to her again. "You okay if I order us a few starters? There are a few things I think you'll like."

"Sure," she told him, wrapping her hands around the cool water glass. This was not a date. She felt both relief and disappointment.

Macy picked out a couple of things she'd never heard of, and the waiter left the table. Now she would have to make conversation. She should have asked more questions before the waiter left. Something to bridge the awkward gap between falling on her butt in the street and being seated across from a man she hardly knew.

Macy, on the other hand, seemed completely at ease. He rubbed his hands together like someone about to partake in something wonderful and took a long drink of water. Then he launched right in. "How long have you been in the city?"

"Just a few months," she told him, then quickly asked about him.

Macy was easygoing and funny, and it took little time to get him talking. Leaning back, he told her about moving down from Klamath Falls, Oregon. His father was a cattle rancher, and Macy was the only boy surrounded by five sisters.

"It's how I got my start in the police department," he told her.

"Ranching? Or being the only boy?"

Macy laughed, and it made her laugh to hear him. "I worked in animal control for the city," he said. "You wouldn't believe how many of those guys are terrified of raccoons. I became the raccoon guy. Was there three years and decided it was time to try something new."

The normalcy of their conversation was so striking. Just two people, eating and talking. Laughing. It was so lovely. She wanted to bask in it, and yet she found herself thinking that this was not her life. It took only seconds for the shadow of her real life to fall back over her.

"What about you?" Macy asked.

Schwartzman took a bite of a risoles and chewed slowly, then lifted her beer glass.

"You don't like to talk about yourself, do you?"

"There's nothing particularly interesting about me," she said. "Tell me more about your family. I can't imagine a house with so many kids."

Macy carried the reins of the conversation through dinner and their second beers. Only when the waiter asked if they cared for dessert did Schwartzman notice the crowd standing on the street, waiting for a table.

"I think just the check," Macy told him.

Schwartzman pulled out her credit card.

"No, you have to let me treat," Macy said. "After all, I did all the talking."

"No," she said firmly.

"Split, then."

"Split," she agreed.

When the check was settled, Macy walked Schwartzman to her car and opened the door for her. She waited for the awkwardness of the end of the evening, but there was none. He simply let her get into the driver's seat and closed the door behind her.

Standing on the curb, he watched her drive away.

Back in her apartment, Schwartzman felt lighter than she had in weeks. It was just a distraction, but an effective one. She didn't realize how badly she'd needed it. Not to mention the reminder of spending time with a nice person—a nice man. She set her keys on the entryway table and shrugged out of her coat. Crossing toward the kitchen, she saw the flashing light on her answering machine. Froze.

Of course. Of course it couldn't last. She turned on the teakettle just to hear the scream. She stared at the flashing red number 1, then jabbed the "Playback" button.

"This is a message from the building superintendent. We will be doing the annual inspection of fire extinguishers a week from Monday. Please leave your fire extinguisher outside your door no later than seven o'clock Monday morning. If you are out of town or need assistance, please contact the building superintendent."

Schwartzman tossed her coat onto the kitchen chair and laughed out loud. It was a message about checking the fire extinguisher. How perfectly boring and mundane.

The kettle whistled the first notes of a song, and Schwartzman could have sung along.

15

San Francisco, California

It was the end of the day when Hal entered the department and spotted Hailey at her desk. He felt a rush of gratitude. They had been partners for almost a decade, and, though he rarely admitted it, working without her was difficult.

His mind functioned in pieces, and he depended on hers to help him pull them together. That and she was probably his closest friend. He had Ryaan, of course, although their relationship was new and came with the complications of romance. He also had plenty of guy friends—the kind he called to play ball or see a game or grab a beer, but few of them talked about anything more personal than their fantasy football leagues.

Over the years, there had been friends who had shared personal hardships. There was a fellow officer whose wife was leaving him for another cop, another inspector whose wife couldn't get pregnant. As those hardships passed, so did whatever had brought the two men together. The result was that the friendships naturally ebbed back into the casual banter of acquaintances.

Hailey never let things go quietly between them. When he tried to avoid a subject, she had a knack for digging deeper without nagging, and, to give her credit, she relented easily when the tables were reversed. Somehow their gender difference had never made things awkward between them. Hal liked to think it was because he had two older sisters who'd beat him up whenever he met a girl and thought of her first as a potential girlfriend. But it was Hailey, too.

They were both married when they'd started as partners: he to a woman with an affinity for putting herself into dangerous situations and she to the son of a congressman. She had children; he vowed he'd never have any. Their relationship had quickly become easy; they bantered like siblings. After her husband's death, Hailey had simultaneously pulled away and depended on him like family. Whatever bond they'd had before that was fixed in stone then.

He thought about Schwartzman.

She reminded him of Hailey in the months after her husband died—both strong and fractured at once. He was drawn to Schwartzman, to the desire to support her. He had seen her competence in her job, her strength in arguing the finer points of an autopsy on the stand in front of a jury. She was great at her job. Recently he had seen moments of humor behind her reserved exterior.

The humor was gone now.

That made him angry, too.

Maybe he had a thing for broken people, but he definitely had a thing against bullies. Though he was six four now, Hal had been a small child, one of the shortest in his class through high school. He had grown more than six inches his first year of college. Spencer MacDonald was just a bully—only he was the very worst kind. He hid behind his status, his job, his social reputation, his money. He thought he could use those things as a wall to stand behind as he committed the worst kind of atrocities. It had been a long time since Hal felt this strongly about a suspect.

He crossed to Hailey's desk without stopping at his own. "Hey."

"Hi, stranger," she responded. "Glad you're here."

"Me, too," he agreed.

"I've got something for you," she said, turning to the stack of papers on her desk.

"Man, I could really use some help on this Stein murder," he admitted, grateful just to say the words.

Hailey stopped digging. "How's Schwartzman?"

Hal rubbed his head. "It's tough to say."

"She's reserved."

That was an understatement. If he had expected her to open up more after their conversation about her marriage, he would have been disappointed. If anything, she seemed more closed.

"Any new leads?" Hailey asked.

Hal exhaled, fighting his frustration. "Nothing since the disappearance of the victim's fake sister."

"That pendant was so eerie. How can that be a coincidence?" Hailey said, speaking softly. "Not to mention that Schwartzman and the victim could be sisters. You have anything new on her ex?"

"I got in touch with a deputy in the Greenville Sheriff's Office on Wednesday. He made a couple of calls. Talked to the ex's assistant. She said she books all his flights, and he hasn't traveled since last December. A four-day trip down to Florida to visit his mother."

"That doesn't mean much," Hailey said. "He could have made his own arrangements."

"Nope. Ran his credit cards, too. Only airline ticket in six months is the one to Florida . . . which is also where the real Victoria Stein lives."

"The real Stein? What do you mean?"

Hal recounted the call he'd had with the FBI contact.

"So you think he went down there to steal an identity?" Hailey asked.

"It's not likely. Pensacola is almost in Alabama. His mother's place is in Palm Bay, on the eastern coast. It's not like he could drive over and pick up Stein's card."

"And there's no other connection between the real Stein and Spencer MacDonald?"

"None," he said, the frustration in his teeth. "Or his mother. I've got a request to search the flight manifests in case he booked using cash or someone else's card, but it's like a needle in a haystack." He sighed. "I've got nothing to go on. Maybe we could go back over to the vic's place? Take another look around?"

"I'm still interviewing witnesses on that gang shooting," she said. "But I should be done today."

"Sure." He tried to hide his disappointment, but he wished she'd finish up already. He would have liked some help with the Victoria Stein case. He needed two heads on this thing. Hell, he needed a dozen of them. He felt as if they were missing something, that they were close, but it was so elusive.

It wasn't uncommon to have dozens of prints to sort through at a scene, but to have nothing was rare. And he didn't like it.

She grinned and gave him a little elbow nudge in the gut. "You're missing me."

"Yeah. I have to cry myself to sleep," he told her.

"Poor Hal. Tomorrow, I promise."

He really did hope she'd be able to rejoin the investigation tomorrow. "You said you had something for me?" he asked to change the subject.

"Yes." She turned back to the pile and shuffled the pages until she found a pink message slip. "You got a response on your missing persons. Sacramento PD called about twenty minutes ago. They've got a woman who came into the station and said your missing person is her daughter, Sarah Feld. Mother, Rebecca Feld, said she last talked to her daughter about two weeks ago." Hailey passed him the slip. "Here's the local sheriff's number. Mom's a real mess, so they're holding her until they can get in touch with you."

Hal flapped the note against his thigh.

A lead.

ID'ing the victim meant gaining access to her friends and family, people who might be able to point the police to who she hung out with and worked for. And Hailey had been hanging on to it. "Why didn't you give me this first?"

"I was having too much fun hearing about how much you were missing me."

He rolled his eyes and crossed back to his own desk, where he dialed the sheriff.

"Sheriff Bowman," came the response on the first ring.

Hal introduced himself.

"Boy I am glad to hear from you," Bowman said.

"I hear you've got someone who recognized our victim."

"Yes. Mrs. Feld came in about an hour ago, and we were able to confirm that your victim is her daughter, Sarah. The mother brought in her passport and her driver's license. Birth certificate." He dropped his voice. "I think she might have a few photo albums in her bag, too."

"Sheriff Bowman, I'm going to need the mother to come down here to make an identification and answer some questions. I assume she's not in any shape to drive."

"No," Bowman said quickly. "Definitely not." There was a brief pause. "I can have an officer bring her down."

Hal exhaled silently, relieved not to have to make the four-hour round-trip. "That would be really helpful. How soon can they be here?"

"Well, it's after six, Inspector. I still need to confirm your victim is Feld's daughter. You send me those pictures, we'll be sure of that, and then we can bring Ms. Feld down first thing tomorrow morning."

"That works. Thanks, Sheriff. Give your officer my cell number. I'll be waiting for the call. I can be here anytime after eight." Hal recited his mobile phone number and hung up. Slapped his thigh. This was how it went. It just took one crack to break something open.

He thought about calling Schwartzman. *Not yet.* He didn't want to get her hopes up. He would talk to the mother first, make sure Victoria Stein was, in fact, her daughter.

When the phone rang a second later, he assumed it was the sheriff calling back. "Yeah?"

"Hey, Hal."

It wasn't the sheriff, and Hal couldn't place the voice. "Yeah?"

"It's Roger."

"Oh, sorry. Thought you were someone else." Hal pulled out a notepad and grabbed his pen. "You got something for me?"

"We found a napkin in the trash, kind of shoved down in there. Evidence of two compounds found on it. The first was red wine, consistent with the bottle we found in the dumpster and the wine in the glass on the kitchen counter."

Hal felt his pulse revving. This was it. The case was cracking. "Not surprising," he said. "And the second?"

"Right," Roger went on. "A dark-red stain, very small. Less than two millimeters. We thought it was blood."

"But it wasn't?"

"No. Some sort of sauce. We're working on what kind exactly."

Hal felt slightly let down. "So we have wine, which we expected, and something else. How does this help us?"

"While we were trying to identify the stain, we found a partial print. We were able to salvage the print and run it through the system."

Adrenaline stirred in his veins. "And?"

"We got a match," Roger said.

"That's great." Hal slapped his desk. "Was it a match to MacDonald?"

"No."

Okay. Not MacDonald but his accomplice. That was one step closer. "Who, then?"

Roger spoke slowly. "Actually, I don't think you're going to like what we found."

Hal swallowed. "Why not?"

"Afraid he's one of ours," Roger said.

Hal closed his eyes and took a slow, deep breath. One of our own. These cases were always the worst.

"Hal?"

"I'm here." He resigned himself to what was coming. This was the job.

"You ready for it?"

"Do I have a choice?" Hal gripped the pen and waited for Roger to give him the name.

16

Charleston, South Carolina

Four days had passed since Frances Pinckney's murder, and they had nothing. The only evidence other than the body was a size eleven tread print found just inside the front door. The print was partially smudged, making it difficult to determine when it had been left. Harper had already checked on the people who worked for Pinckney.

The couple who cared for the house were eliminated based on their alibi—they'd driven down to see her sister near Atlanta. Plus, they had absolutely nothing to gain from Frances Pinckney's death unless they had planned to rob the place. But nothing had been taken.

Not to mention his foot was a size thirteen men's and hers a size six women's.

The gardener was the right shoe size, but he and his wife had been attending their granddaughter's dance recital that night along with approximately eighty other parents and grandparents.

The tread indicated it was some kind of running shoe, and the lab would run it against a database to identify the brand and shoe type. But that would only be helpful if they had a suspect to match it against. There were no tread prints found farther into the house, so the one they'd found might have been a neighbor helping Pinckney carry something heavy in from her car or bringing over a piece of mail that had come to the wrong address and stopping in for a chat.

It could have been from anyone. Which meant she had nothing.

With Jed and Lucy at a volleyball game, Harper spent the afternoon sitting at her desk, reading over tiny print on lab results from the scene and waiting for something to strike her. Eyes burning, she flipped back to her own notes on Frances Pinckney's death.

Employees, family, there was not a single good suspect, and she'd covered every base, checked all the right boxes. Pinckney's children arrived in town the day after her murder, and Harper met with each of them more than once. She took them through their mother's house to confirm that nothing was missing. The art was accounted for, as were the more mundane valuables like electronics.

Pinckney's financial accounts—credit cards, bank and investment accounts—had been checked for any sign of fraudulent activity and had come up clean. Robbery was unlikely as Pinckney's wallet had been sitting in her purse by the door with more than $100 in cash and five or six different credit cards. Plus, Pinckney was found wearing her antique wedding ring and a necklace with a diamond pendant, a gift from her husband for their fortieth wedding anniversary.

With robbery off the table, Harper had moved on to another most likely motive—greed. She hadn't gotten anywhere there either. Frances Pinckney's estate was divided 30 percent to each of her three living children. The remaining 10 percent went to an organization that worked to create stiffer penalties for driving under the influence. Her son Patrick had been struck and killed at eighteen by a drunk driver. Even if Harper could find a motive for one of the children, they all lived in different states. Distance created ironclad alibis. Not that they needed them. It was obvious from their distress that the children were crazy about their mother.

These were the toughest cases. Everyone wanted to know why, and she had absolutely nothing to offer them. She glanced at her watch and saw that only fifteen minutes had passed. Andy had gone out for coffees and offered to pick one up for her.

She needed it.

Harper lifted the receiver off her desk phone to dial Jed about dinner when her captain stuck his head out of his office door.

"When did you get here?" she asked him.

"Forty-five minutes ago, hour maybe. Walked right by you." Barrel-chested and buzz-cut, Captain Brown looked like a typical Southern boy, especially dressed in jeans and a casual button-down as he was now. Add his boisterous voice and he was as stereotypical as they came. In reality Beau Brown was a sweetheart with a soft spot for stray kittens.

"What are you doing in here on a Saturday?"

"Budget's due this week," he told her. "I just got a call on my cell. You know someone named Ava Schwartzman?"

"She's Frances Pinckney's best friend." Maybe Ava had news. "Is she on the phone for me?"

"Nope." Captain Brown scratched along the line of his buttons, the way he did when he had bad news.

"What is it?"

"Cleaning lady just found her."

Harper rose slowly from her seat. "Found her?"

"Afraid she's dead."

17

San Francisco, California

Hal set a box of Kleenex in front of the woman across from him. She pulled out a handful, using one to dry her swollen eyes. Her shoulders shook in the way of women crying. Her eyes pleaded with him to offer her some alternate possibility. *Say it isn't my daughter.*

He remained silent.

He had hoped Hailey would join them, but after five minutes of waiting, he assumed she had been called out on something else. He settled down into his chair, making himself as small as he could, before speaking. "I am very sorry for your loss, Mrs. Feld."

Hearing about Terri Stein crying in Schwartzman's office, Hal had wondered if the grief was real. He'd wanted to see for himself if the crying was part of some act. Sitting across from Rebecca Feld, he had not a shred of doubt that her pain was genuine. He used to think that saying he was very sorry for the pain people were feeling was a worthless gesture, stupid even. That there had to be a way to offer the families something more.

There wasn't. Those seven thin words and his solemn promise that he would do his best on behalf of whatever loved one had been killed, that was all he could offer. Anything else was false, a lie. He felt the deceit, and they did, too.

"I know this is difficult, but I'd like to ask you a few questions." He spoke the words carefully. This first step was like tapping on an eggshell. He wanted to open it up enough to get at what was inside without breaking it completely.

She nodded.

Hal opened his notebook. "When was the last time you saw Sarah?"

Rebecca Feld blotted her eyes and lowered her hands to the table. "The holidays," she said. "Sarah came home for Christmas."

"Where's home, ma'am?"

"Placerville."

"So Sarah didn't live in Placerville."

"No. She was down in Los Angeles." A tiny cast of spit flew from her mouth with the words.

"I take it you're not a fan of LA?"

"I don't have anything against the town," she explained, regaining her composure. "But it was no place for a smart girl like Sarah."

"Had she been down there long?"

"Oh yeah. She went down about five minutes after finishing high school. It's almost fifteen years now."

"And what did Sarah do in LA?"

"Little bit of everything. Bartending, waiting tables, a couple short secretarial-type jobs, but they didn't last long. Got in the way of her auditioning." Again with the spit.

Sarah had gone to LA to pursue acting.

The story was common enough, and he might have jumped past all the background and gotten right to the questions about roommates, boyfriends, and recent jobs, but in his experience, there was a lot to be learned about a child from how her parents spoke of her. "Sarah was an actress?"

"Actor," Rebecca Feld corrected. "She wanted to be called an actor. Said that the word *actress* was sexist. They were all actors. She and her dad used to really get into it over that one."

"Her father," Hal said, making a note. "Does Sarah have a relationship with him?"

"He passed. Last October. Colon cancer. Sarah didn't have any brothers or sisters, so it was just her and me left. Now it's just—" She stopped talking.

He gave her a moment before pressing on. "Do you know what she was working on?"

Mrs. Feld shook her head. "Used to be Sarah would call and tell us about everything. Auditions, of course, but every little detail, like if she met someone in the business or saw a movie that was what she imagined for herself. Or one she hated and thought she coulda done better. Back when she first went down, she called most days." Rebecca Feld stared down at her hands folded in her lap.

"Over time, she did that less." Her expression filled with the excruciating guilt reserved for the parents of victims. "I guess we didn't always take how much she loved acting serious enough. It was hard, too. We wanted her to have a normal life. Like we did. You know, have a husband and a family."

Hal had no idea what it was like to have a normal family, but he understood the mother's desire. His mother had the same one for him.

"But she came home different at Christmas."

He shifted up in his chair. "Different how?"

"She had money, for one. She never had money."

Hal had talked to Sarah Feld's landlord in LA the night before, once the Sacramento sheriff had called back to confirm her identity. Her rent and utilities had been prepaid for six months. Fourteen thousand paid in a single deposit by a holding corporation out of Florida.

Florida again. Victoria Stein from Florida. Spencer's mother in Florida.

The holding company that had paid the rent was in Miami. Forensic accounting was working to follow the paper trail, but the company had been dismantled, which meant it would be difficult to locate the parties involved. He also had someone digging for any possible connections to the holding company and Victoria Stein of Pensacola or Gertrude MacDonald of Palm Bay.

Nothing yet.

There was no connection to the various pieces.

"But she didn't tell you where the money had come from?" Hal asked.

"She sort of pretended that she was the same old Sarah. But she sure wasn't. Her clothes were different—she looked more like someone working in an office than she ever did before. Usually she came home in those tight yoga pants and running shoes. This time she wore nice skirts and blouses. She even had a pair of shoes with red soles. They had some fancy name. You know which ones I'm talking about?"

"Afraid not," he told her. "Women's shoes aren't really my thing."

She cracked a sad smile. "Well, I can't think that Sarah woulda known what they were last summer, but at Christmas she sure did. She took things to be dry-cleaned. She never used a dry cleaner in her life. She was more . . . sophisticated, I guess. Her hair was straightened and a little wavy, even after she washed it. She always had real frizzy hair, like her daddy. But she had something done to tame it down. She said it was a kind of South American treatment. It looked good. She brought Christmas presents—some fancy chocolates and some whiskey she said a friend introduced her to."

There it was. The friend. Was that Spencer? If he had paid for her apartment, there had to be a trail that led back to him. Hal made a note to find out if MacDonald had access to any cash businesses, something that enabled him to move money without it showing up in his accounts. "Did she tell you about the friend?"

"She swore he wasn't a boyfriend. She hadn't even met him in person."

Hal wrote that down. "Did she tell you how she met him?"

"Some online talent search. She was going to be the star of some new reality show."

Had Spencer reached out to Feld by posting an acting job? "Did she mention the name of the show? Or of anyone else who was involved?"

Rebecca Feld pressed the tissues to her eyes as the tears flowed again. "All that was top secret. She said she didn't even know much about the job, but that it was going to be huge. Bigger than *Survivor*."

Hal knew almost nothing about reality TV. He got enough reality in his job, so he opted for sports on TV. "Was the show going to be like that one? Some sort of physical competition?" he asked.

"I have no idea. She wouldn't give any details. Either she didn't know or she didn't want to share."

Hal tried to think of another angle. "You ever hear her on the phone over Christmas?"

"She didn't talk to anyone. Texting. She did a lot of texting."

Hal flipped the page in his notebook. "Would you write down your daughter's phone number for me?"

Rebecca Feld took his pen and wrote down a number with a 310 area code. "But I think she had a new phone, too."

"A new phone for this number?"

"She was texting her friends at home on her old phone. It was nothing fancy, one of those where the top slides up and there's a keyboard underneath so you can text. But she had a new iPhone, too." As her voice drifted off, her gaze settled on the wall behind Hal. "It's like she was some kind of double agent."

Hal couldn't believe that Sarah hadn't left some clue about her new life when she was home for the holidays. It was starting to feel as if what she did on that visit was his only chance to find out who she had become involved with.

Or to confirm it was Spencer MacDonald behind this whole ruse. But not alone.

That didn't seem possible.

Which meant they were still missing another piece.

Who was paying for her rent, buying her new clothes and phones? And for what? What was the purpose of paying for her to live there for six months if the plan was simply to kill and stage her for the police to find? "Did she see any old friends when she was home for Christmas?"

"A few. She went out with some friends from high school a couple of nights."

Okay. Maybe there was something. "I'd like to get their names and numbers so I can talk to them and see if Sarah told them anything else that might be helpful."

"You think this new job is the thing that got her killed?"

"The more I know about what Sarah was doing when she died—her work, her friends—the better the chances that I can find out what happened to her." Hal slid the notebook back again. "Can you write down some names for me?"

Feld wrote three names. "These are maiden names. I'm not sure what names they go by now."

"I should be able to find them." Hal opened the manila folder and pulled out the composite sketch of Terri Stein that they had been circulating. "One last question, Mrs. Feld. Do you recognize this woman?"

"No. I've never seen her before."

Hal did his best to mask his disappointment. He wasn't surprised. It wasn't going to be that easy. "I appreciate you coming in."

She hesitated before standing from the table; then she opened her purse and pulled out a plastic sack, placed it on the table. "Maybe this stuff will help you."

Hal turned the bag in his hands. He saw a passport and California driver's license in the name of Sarah Feld. Behind those was a folded paper, which he drew out and opened. He recognized the blue paper.

Her birth certificate. He returned the paper to the bag. "You can keep these, Mrs. Feld."

Standing from her chair, she shook her head. "I can't. Please take them." She motioned to the bag and started crying again. "She got that passport while she was home. Planned on going to Spain in the fall when the show was done filming." Mrs. Feld adjusted the strap of her purse up on her shoulder. "I don't want any reminder of what my baby girl will never get to do."

Hal understood the torture of parents whose roles were cut short by the death of a child.

A parent was supposed to die first. It was a child's job to look back on her parent's life to appreciate what she had accomplished and even where she had fallen short.

A parent who lost a child never had that kind of peace. The child's life would always feel truncated, opportunities stolen.

Mrs. Feld struggled to maintain her composure, and, when she got control, she said, "If you don't mind getting me a ride to the bus station, I'd like to go home."

18

San Francisco, California

Schwartzman shut off the shower. The phone was ringing. She wasn't working today, so the call was likely from Hal. Or maybe it was Macy, asking her for a date. Or something benign, like the dry cleaner. She dried efficiently, moving gingerly around the site of the breast biopsy. She put vitamin E on the healing wound before pulling on her robe, taking her time.

The phone would be there. She had all day to waste. May as well draw it out.

Though it was Sunday morning, it felt like a second Saturday. Every third Monday she was off to make up for the weekend shift she took every six weeks. It was one of the perks mentioned when she'd applied for the job. People loved having a weekday off. It was a time to go to all the places that were only available while working people worked—the post office, the dentist. Or to be at the grocery store or the gym or Nordstrom without the weekend crowds.

Schwartzman was not one of those people. She didn't mind the sea of people at the Marina Safeway on Sundays or the fact that there were always people on her favorite trails. Those bodies created comfort, safety. She was most comfortable in a crowd as long as she was on the periphery. Schwartzman normally dedicated these days off to the stack of medical journals and forensic pathology reading that piled up when she was working. This morning, though, she was off to a slow start.

In the kitchen, she poured a cup of coffee, then returned to the bedroom. The phone sat silently on the bedside table. She moved to the closet, nudged aside the small vintage brass iron that kept the closet door from opening on its own. Several months before, she had fixed the latch so that the door would stay closed properly, but sometime in the past few weeks, it began to open on its own again. She hadn't mustered the energy to fix it a second time. So the iron resumed its place as a doorstop. She found a comfortable pair of workout pants and a slouchy sweater in the closet and took her coffee back to bed.

The day would go faster if she could sleep longer, but she never had any luck staying asleep past seven. Just one of the scars from her life with Spencer. Who would have called on a Sunday morning before eight?

Hal had been working all weekend. She'd received a brief text from him yesterday about the interview with the victim's mother. The message included three pieces of information, and only one was remotely helpful. Hal said he had a lead but didn't say what it was. He also admitted that he hadn't learned anything more from the victim's mother about why her daughter was living in a barely furnished apartment in San Francisco. But he told her that Victoria Stein's real name was actually Sarah Feld. That last bit, at least, was of interest to Schwartzman.

A Google search of the name revealed a series of head shots and a single commercial credit for Feld.

It made sense that Spencer had hired an actress. She'd been hired to play a part. How much did she know beforehand? Had she signed up to play the part of a victim without realizing how realistic the role would be?

Schwartzman rarely saw the victims before they ended up on her table and found it intriguing to study the woman's images. Her face had been more angular in life, the masseter muscle in her jaw overdeveloped. Stress most likely. The orbicularis oculi muscles around her eyes indicated that she'd recently gotten Botox on her crow's-feet. It wasn't relevant to the case, but Schwartzman made a mental note to tell Hal.

When she reached for her phone, she saw another missed call and a voicemail from a San Francisco number. Not a department number and not Hal's cell phone.

She set the phone down, then picked it up again. There was no good reason to wait. It wasn't like she was avoiding working. She pressed "Play."

"Dr. Schwartzman, this is Renu Khan. I hope I'm not waking you. I saw Dr. Fraser when I was doing rounds yesterday at UCSF and pathology had the results of your biopsy." A beat passed, and Schwartzman used it to suck in a deep breath. "I wanted to get the information to you as soon as possible, so you can determine next steps. The biopsy confirms the presence of invasive lobular cancer in your right breast. I know Dr. Fraser's office will be in touch with you directly, but I wanted to give you my cell phone number as well so that you can contact me. I know it's Sunday, but I'm around today if you would like to talk."

Dr. Khan started to recite her phone number when the phone rang again in Schwartzman's hand.

This time she knew the number. *Hal.* She pushed herself too fast upright in the bed. Dizzy and nauseous, she lay back down. "Schwartzman," she said into the phone.

"It's Hal. Good morning," he said, though it didn't sound like it actually was.

"Good morning," she responded with approximately the same lack of conviction. *Cancer. Invasive cancer. Lobular.* She tried to dredge up memories of med school.

She caught the tail end of something Hal said.

"Sorry, Hal. I think my other line was ringing through. I missed what you said."

"No problem. Do you need to go?"

"No, it's fine," she said quickly, blushing at the lie.

"Was wondering if you're coming in today? I know it's Sunday."

"I can," she told him, sensing the edge in his voice. "What's going on?"

"I'm interviewing a suspect at nine o'clock. You might want to watch, if you're available."

"A suspect? Did you locate the sister?"

"No, and you were right. They're not sisters. Sarah Feld doesn't have any siblings."

She had let that woman go. She'd known something was off, but she hadn't acted on it. Worse, she had actually entertained her questions, let her sit in that chair and watch her, all the while knowing—whatever she knew.

"Who are you interviewing?"

Hal sighed. "Ken Macy."

Schwartzman was upright again. "Macy wouldn't have—"

"I like him, too," he agreed.

She was stunned. "It's not a matter of liking him. It's just—" But then she couldn't say what it was. He was trustworthy, honest. Good. Decent. After Spencer, she was cautious—overly cautious. She had a strong sense of people, and Ken Macy seemed as upstanding as they came. Or maybe Hal was right. She liked him, considered him a friend. "Why?" she said finally.

"They found his prints at the scene. On a napkin in the victim's trash."

Schwartzman pictured Macy's easy smile. "His prints on a napkin? So he accidentally threw something away in her trash. That doesn't mean he killed her . . ."

"The napkin is also stained with the wine she was drinking."

"Isn't it possible that the wine got on the napkin in the trash?"

"By the location of the stain, Roger doesn't think so. The napkin's not enough for a warrant, let alone an arrest, but I've got to bring him in for questioning." The words came out harsh. "He's agreed to come down."

"Does he know about the evidence? The napkin, I mean?"

"No," Hal said. "I thought I'd tell him in person."

"Sure," she said.

"How well do you know him, Doc?"

They'd had dinner the other night. She had bumped into him on the street. How unexpected. She was sick. "I don't know him, but—"

"But what?"

"I did have dinner with him on Friday."

"You had dinner with him Friday night? Like a date?" he asked, curiosity in his voice.

"No," she said quickly. "Not like a date." A date meant they were involved. She was not ready for that. Maybe she would never be. "It's not like that. He's always telling me about good new ethnic restaurants that are opening up. It's one of the things we talk about when I see him at a scene."

"And he invited you to dinner?"

"No . . ." She went through how it had happened. "He sent a text about a new place down in the Marina. It doesn't have takeout yet." The yellow waiting room at Fraser's office. The biopsy. Friday, the cancer had been only a chance. Now it was reality. People waited a week or longer for the results of a biopsy. Hers had been fast-tracked. Because it was serious? Because she needed to act quickly? Or because Dr. Khan's sister-in-law was an inspector in the department's special investigative division on hate crimes?

Whatever it was, a call on a Sunday morning was special treatment.

"Schwartzman?"

"I'm sorry. What did you say?"

"You okay this morning?" Hal asked.

"Still half-asleep I guess. Sorry. Say it one more time?"

"You said that the place didn't have takeout?"

"Right," she agreed.

"So what does that mean?" Hal prompted.

"Well, I don't eat out often," she said. "I usually have something delivered." Even she heard the unspoken part. She was alone. Without friends. Without a partner. "Friday, I needed to get out of the house, so I decided to go down there for dinner."

He didn't ask if it was just her. He understood that she would be alone. "And Macy just happened to be there?" he asked, the skepticism clear.

Schwartzman felt a renewed urge to defend Macy. But how could she? What did she really know about him? Before their dinner, she hadn't known anything other than his name and his job title. "I don't see how he could've known I would go," she said finally.

"Safe to assume you two talked over dinner?"

"Yes. About him mostly. His family, that kind of thing."

"You talk to him about your ex?" Hal asked.

Hal always referred to Spencer as her ex. Technically, they were still married, although she had thought of him as her ex-husband for years. She kept telling herself she would point it out. And then she didn't. It was humiliating that they were still married. And frustrating. And not relevant.

"Schwartzman?"

"No. We didn't talk about him."

"Are you sure?"

"Positive. I don't even think I mentioned where I'm from. I might've told him I'm an only child. That's it." As she spoke, she replayed the evening in her mind. She had been so relaxed. She had actually relaxed in the company of a man—a man she liked—and now he was a suspect in the murder of a woman who could have been her twin. "I didn't tell him anything important," she added.

"It's okay," he told her.

She took a deep breath in response to his words. It wasn't okay, and the panic filled her anyway. "I'll see you at nine." Before he could say anything else, she ended the call. She dropped the phone on the bed and let herself slide onto the floor. Her back pressed to the bed, she watched the shadows of the sun move through the clouds through the dark blinds.

The emptiness was like hunger and indigestion, all tucked up under her lungs. She was reminded of her father's death. The call she had taken that evening in her tiny med school apartment, her mother telling her that he was in the hospital. She had not changed clothes or told anyone she was leaving. Took her purse and keys and drove straight to the hospital.

She was shocked when she entered that room—the sheen of his face, the ashen tint of his skin, his body so much smaller in that bed. The infection raced through his body. The doctors' optimism shifted into tenuous hope and then acceptance that there was nothing they could do.

He died in the night.

The days she had passed at home were a blur, but months later, back in something like normalcy, she had woken one morning with this same pain. At the time, it was like being devoured from the inside out.

Something had shifted in her that morning. The realization that her father was truly gone felt both sudden and complete. She was stunned at how gone he was. *I keep looking for traces of you, and you are just so absolutely gone,* she had written in her journal that day. *There should be more of you lingering. I should feel you, know that you are with me. It's just absolute, stark absence.*

She still felt the anger of that day, the idea that his silence was an affront. She had meant more to him than that. Everywhere she went, she wanted to scream out to him to show himself, but it was all just the normal, silent world staring back at her with no sign of him in it. She was desperate to tell him that she was not going to be okay without him. Not ever again. She was grateful for what he had given her, that he was her father, but with him gone, she was left with this forever hole in her heart because he was so much of her life. And it just didn't make any sense that there was a world without him in it.

It never quite went away, that feeling. She eased herself off the floor and drew the shade just as the sun slipped again behind a gray cloud.

None of this would have happened if you had stayed.

And, as always, she knew it was true.

19

Charleston, South Carolina

Sam was standing outside the victim's bedroom door, his arms crossed, as Harper came up the stairs. She could tell it was bad. He didn't meet her eyes. She suspected this was difficult for him. The first ones were always the hardest. Two in a row, in such quick succession, made it worse.

She wished he'd say something. They could have both used a break from the mood, and she would have liked a little pep talk. Or humor. Something to break up the emptiness she felt.

Those were Andy's traits, not Sam's.

Andy was supposed to be on the scene, too. She would find him later.

First, the body.

She reached the top of the stairs slowly, dreading what was waiting for her. Frances Pinckney was someone she'd known all of her adult life. Ava Schwartzman was not. But she was someone Harper had sat down with, face-to-face, only days before, and that made her death more personal than was comfortable. Not to mention that the word *serial* was starting to get tossed around the department. A serial killer in Charleston. That was downright terrifying.

"Ugly?" she asked Sam.

"Worse than that," he answered.

From inside the room came the flashing lights of the crime scene analyst's camera. Though Harper rarely saw the face hidden behind the cyclops of the camera, the tech was distinctive for the strawberry-blonde ponytail that snapped left and right as she pivoted from shot to shot.

"Almost, Burl," said the tech as Burl inched ever closer to the body. He occasionally complained about the number of photographs the crime scene techs took these days. When Burl started with the department, they took maybe twenty. Film was expensive and not high quality. Digital film was cheap, cost of development, zero.

For some of the inside scenes, techs took as many as seven or eight hundred photographs.

For Harper, clicking through those images was an important part of putting the puzzle together.

Staying out of the tech's way, Harper stepped into the room, which might have been staged from 1920s Charleston. The furniture was dark wood and heavily carved. A large Persian rug occupied the center of the room and ran under the bed and bureau. The wear suggested the rug had been there for some decades. The room was lit only by two bedside lamps. Eyelet window shades let in the sunlight, but the room was especially dark as she moved toward the bed.

Harper fought back the intensity of her own reactions.

The woman lying on the bed was nothing like the Ava Schwartzman who Harper had met. Seated in the police conference room, Ava Schwartzman had been composed. Strong, elegant, even a little intense.

Now she seemed small and terrified and much, much older.

While her eyes remained wide-open, her mouth was tightly closed, the muscles of her jaw bulging in her cheeks. She was a thin woman, but in her sleeveless nightgown she looked emaciated, almost sickly. Her arms were stretched above her head. Each wrist was bound with a red bungee cord, which had been hooked around the bedpost.

"If he wasn't wearing gloves, we might find epithelial cells in the cord," Harper said. It could be that easy.

"Yep," the tech agreed. "We'll test 'em."

The victim's feet had been bound by regular white rope. A square knot. Nothing fancy there. "And—"

"Yep," the tech said, cutting her off. "The rope, too." The young woman continued her arc of the victim, finger depressed on the shutter release.

Finally, she appeared from behind the camera. Narrow brown eyes and brows that were the same pale reddish-blonde as her hair. She scanned the victim and glanced up at Burl. "All yours."

"Thank you, ma'am," Burl said, even though the tech probably wasn't much older than Lucy. His case already open, his hands already gloved, Burl moved right in and inspected the victim's eyes and face. He shined a penlight across the skin, shifting his angle as he searched.

Burl had told her he'd once found a perfect thumbprint on an eyelid. Boy killed his aunt because she wouldn't give him thirty bucks. Afterward, he closed her eyes and left a print. Swore he'd been out all night, but the thumbprint said otherwise. They'd gotten a conviction on that one.

"Petechiae," Burl said, waving her over.

She rounded the bed and stood across from him.

"See it here." He lifted Ava's lower eyelid to display the red dots associated with strangulation. "And also here, around the mouth." He moved the light down her face.

"Some sort of asphyxiation."

"Looks like it."

Without fanfare, Burl unbuttoned the victim's nightgown and exposed her chest.

Harper forced herself to study the body. This wasn't Ava Schwartzman. This was the victim. Just below her breasts were two oval bruises about 50 percent larger than chicken eggs.

"Perimortem," Burl confirmed. "You can tell because the edges are well defined. The injuries did create bruises—that doesn't happen if the victim's already dead—but the blood didn't spread into the surrounding tissue, so she wasn't alive long."

"What caused those?"

"If I were gambling man, I'd say knees."

"Knees?" But as soon as she'd said it, she pictured the victim's killer mounted on top of her small chest.

"She was burked."

Harper had never seen a burking victim, but she was familiar with the term. Normally, burking involved two killers. One to hold his hands over the victim's mouth and nose to prevent breathing while the other sat on the victim's chest to press the air from the lungs.

In this case, the evidence suggested that both parts were accomplished by a single killer. With her hands and feet bound, the killer was able to use his hands to cover her mouth and nose and his knees to prevent her chest from rising to draw in air.

Burl studied the victim's hands. "No defensive wounds."

"You think he surprised her?"

"Can't imagine he could get her tied up without waking her," Burl said.

"Could have threatened her with a gun to get her to comply. Once she was tied up, there wasn't much she could do to fight him. I'll have patrol check with the neighbors and see if they heard anything."

"Not sure she put up much of a fight," Burl said.

"Why do you say that?"

"If she struggled, I'd expect to see more bruising."

Harper hated the idea that Ava didn't fight her attacker but said nothing. But what about Pinckney? What would have kept her from fighting? "Chloroform?"

"Would make sense. I'll test for it." He used the penlight to illuminate the chest bruises and moved his head to see them from different angles. "Hmm."

"What?" she asked.

"You notice anything in those bruises?"

Harper stared at them. "They're oval."

"Maybe I'm just seeing things. Here, take this." He handed her his flashlight.

Harper shone the light across the bruises, left, then right, and back again. There were a series of ridges, slightly lighter than the rest of the bruise. "It's like there are lines running down the bruises."

"So you do see it." Burl used his finger to identify the same three ridges on the opposite side. "Right here?"

"I saw it on the other side first, but yeah, I see that, too." She handed back the flashlight. "What is it from? Was there a design on her nightgown?"

Burl moved the gown back across the victim. Aside from the small row of buttons, which would have been between the two bruises, there was nothing on the gown that would explain the ridges.

"The seam of his pants, maybe?"

"Don't think so. Not in the middle of the knee."

She tried to imagine a pair of pants with seams down the knees. He was right. She couldn't picture it.

"What about a knee pad?" he said.

"You mean for skating or something?"

"I was thinking more for carpentry work."

Harper nodded slowly. "Like the padded ones. Nice work, Burl. If we get that tech back in here to take some images, we could probably identify the brand."

"Don't call the paparazzi," he said. "I can take the photographs myself." He stooped to his bag. Harper expected him to pull out some ancient Kodak, but the camera he brought out was as sleek and modern as the tech's had been.

"Nice," Harper said.

Burl frowned. "Just because I appreciate things that have withstood the tests of time doesn't mean I don't recognize the benefits of modernity."

"Deep," she said and was about to tease him about his attachment to Bessie the van when Andy called her.

"You should come see this, Harper."

She followed him as he jogged down the stairs in a one-two, one-two rhythm like a trotting horse while she tried to keep up without tripping and falling. Andy led her into the kitchen. There, on the counter, was an old-fashioned phone with a long spiral cord. It was light yellow. She hadn't seen one like it in decades. Even the phone in Frances Pinckney's kitchen was cordless.

"Here," Andy announced, stopping beside the tech.

"It's an old phone," Harper said, trying to figure out if the tech was young enough that she'd never seen one.

"Not the phone," Andy said. "Hey, Sylvie, can you move for a second so I can show Detective Leighton what we found?"

The tech lowered the camera and walked away.

A list was tacked up on the wall above the phone. "You have a glove?" she asked Andy.

"Sylvie, we need gloves."

Sylvie returned to pass him a pair of gloves without a comment.

"One pair?" he called after her. "We've each got two hands."

The tech rolled her eyes.

"One will do," Harper said, taking a single glove and pulling it onto her right hand before peeling the list off the wall and setting it on the counter.

Judy

7/2—7/9 wtr lr, ktchn, mstr, Cody am

9/8—9/20 wtr " "

Frances

8/1—8/12 Cooper here, 2x wtr prch

Okay 8/30—9/4, Dallas

Some sort of list. Multiple strips of tape at the top of the page suggested it had been pulled down and posted up a few times, and the writing was in several different colors of ink. "Cooper was Frances Pinckney's dog." She glanced over the words again. "These are arrangements to take care of someone's house. Judy must be another friend."

"And WTR LR?"

"Water. Living room, kitchen. MSTR is master. There must be plants in those rooms."

"Cody is Judy's dog?"

Harper shrugged. "Or a cat. A goldfish? Who knows. Some pet Ava was supposed to take care of in the mornings. We can figure out Judy's last name and contact her."

Andy looked back over the list. "Okay, but pet and plant sitting are hardly motive for murder."

Harper studied the last item on the list. "Okay Dallas" was unlike the others. No description of what she was supposed to take care of. Maybe Ava was the one traveling and Frances was doing the housesitting. It made sense that they would housesit for each other.

Harper reached for the drawer under the phone and found a line of spatulas, a whisk, a garlic press, a grater. She pushed it closed and tried the one to the left. Silverware.

Then on the right. *Bingo.*

One side of the drawer was occupied by a bulky phonebook. On the other side were two rectangular wire baskets, the kind people used to organize drawers. One contained a dozen or so pens. The other held a neat line of keys, a small colored circle with a label on each. "House," "Office," "POB." Her post office box. Spare keys. The drawer stuck, so Harper wiggled until it yielded. Farther back was a small red carabiner with three additional keys. Harper flipped the tags over one at a time. "Judy." "Evelyn." The final one read, "Frances." Harper exhaled loudly.

"She had a key for Frances Pinckney's house," Andy said.

Harper turned to Andy. "I need you to go back over to Pinckney's house and see if you can find Ava's spare key."

"Sure. You think it will be there?"

Harper said nothing.

Andy let it go. "I'll call you when I know."

She didn't expect that Andy would find a key to Ava's house at Frances Pinckney's. She almost hoped he didn't because its absence would explain how the killer got in. More than that, it would be their first real evidence to connect the two crimes. If Frances Pinckney's copy of Ava's key wasn't there, it suggested that getting that key had been the killer's motive to go to Pinckney's house. The fact that he had come with chloroform to knock out Pinckney meant the attack was premeditated.

But killing her? Had that been part of the plan, or had something gone wrong? When the dog wouldn't stop barking? Or when Kimberly Davies showed up? Had he planned to kill Frances Pinckney all along? Were they dealing with someone so comfortable with murder?

Harper set the keys back in the drawer and bumped it closed with her hip. The discovery was something, a small step in the right direction.

But if this was the right direction, it was terrifying to think where these crimes would take her.

20

San Francisco, California

Schwartzman sat in the small viewing room and watched Hal and Hailey interview Ken Macy. The crease in his brow deepened as Hal slid the bagged napkin across the table. "We found this in the victim's trash."

Ken Macy stared at it blankly.

"It's got your prints on it," Hal explained. "And wine from the victim's house."

"Her trash?" Macy repeated.

He looked miserable. Schwartzman felt miserable. It had to be some sort of a trap. Didn't it?

"Did you throw something away in the victim's kitchen?"

"No. I wasn't even in the kitchen." Macy rubbed his face. "Fischer and I arrived together. The sister was standing in the lobby, freaked out. She took us up, and we went into the bedroom. I followed procedure and checked for a pulse while Fischer called for backup. Then the two of us cleared the stairwell and returned to the lobby, where the victim's sister was. Fischer took her to the hospital, and I remained on the street to wait for backup."

Hailey and Hal exchanged a glance. Schwartzman assumed they could read each other, but she couldn't read them. Did they believe him? She did. Eyes wide, mouth dropped open, he appeared to be experiencing a heavy rush of adrenaline. He looked genuinely upset.

Surely if he were guilty, he would be prepared for these questions.

"We pulled your patrol rounds that night, and you and Fischer split up for about an hour that evening."

"Yeah. We did."

"That's kind of unusual, isn't it?" Hailey asked.

"It is. And in the end, it was some kind of screwup."

Schwartzman winced at the words, watching as Macy's shoulders dropped. The rounded slope of his trapezoid muscles appeared genuine. He didn't appear to be faking.

"A screwup?" Hal echoed.

"I got a call from Dispatch that Fischer was needed in the vicinity of Bay and Taylor, where there was an accident with injuries. I was to drop him off and report to a different location. The address was on Vallejo, where it dead-ends before Montgomery."

"The call came in on the radio?" Hal asked.

"No. My cell phone actually."

"But it came from a departmental number?" Hailey pressed.

Again Macy shrank down in his chair. "It came in unknown, which I thought was weird, but it sounded like Dispatch."

"You mean the voice was familiar?" Hailey clarified.

Schwartzman had learned long ago to be wary of unknown numbers. Every call that came in to her phone was suspicious. Ken wasn't like that. He was trusting. It was one of the things she liked most about him. But he was a cop. He was supposed to be aware of the possibility of being deceived. She hated watching him get interrogated like this.

"I don't know if it was familiar. There are a lot of different operators. It seemed right. Nothing about the call seemed weird."

Schwartzman felt him digging himself deeper. She wanted to leave but couldn't pull herself away. *Come on, Ken. Stand up to them.* He was doing his job. Didn't they see that? She had never witnessed an interview, and it made her uncomfortable. Did they feel any guilt that they were interviewing one of their own?

No. Of course not. This was the job. They had to ask the tough questions.

"So you went to this address?" Hal asked.

"Yeah. I dropped Fischer and went straight over there. It's a storefront, so I assumed there had been some sort of break-in. I walked the perimeter, checked the doors and windows for signs of entry. Then I checked the neighboring buildings. I called Dispatch a couple of times during the process, trying to get them to find out what the code was."

"And could they tell you?" Hailey asked.

"The first time, they put a call out to officers responding to that address, asking for a callback for an update."

"I take it no one called?" Hal guessed, his tone sarcastic. Ken had followed directions. Nothing about the call was out of place, so of course he had gone to the address. He was tricked. Surely Hailey and Hal saw it the same way.

"No," Ken admitted.

Schwartzman watched Hal's expression, saw the slight shake of his head. Was he just frustrated or did he think Ken was lying? She couldn't tell.

"So you called Dispatch again?"

"I called three times in total. No one had any information about why I was there. Figured it was just a miscommunication at Dispatch."

Something lodged in Schwartzman's throat. This didn't feel like a screwup or some random mistake. This felt like a plan.

A Spencer plan.

Did that occur to Hailey or Hal? Did they imagine Spencer might be behind this, too?

Why would they?

And why would he frame Macy? She pressed at the tightness in her chest. She thought of running into him on the street, the randomness of it. But that was after the murder. Had Spencer somehow made that happen, as well? It seemed impossible. She had left the apartment of her own free will. He hadn't invited her.

"I confirmed there were no signs of B and E and called Fischer," Macy went on. "He was finishing up, helping out with the accident, so we pulled up the cones and waited for the tow truck to come, and then we went back to the beat."

"Where did you have dinner that night?"

"We didn't. Fischer's wife packed him a sandwich, so I ate a few bites, but we got called to the murder before we could stop."

Again the look between Hailey and Hal. Schwartzman's phone buzzed in her lap. Her mother. Her mother had called earlier. Before Hal called. After Dr. Khan called.

You have cancer. Invasive lobular cancer of your right breast. Invasive. Cancer.

She answered the phone.

Without warning, tears filled her eyes. She had cancer, and her mama called. Her mama knew.

She wasn't alone with cancer.

Schwartzman caught the flood of tears against the back of her hand. How would her mother know? Had the doctor called her? No. It was impossible. She couldn't know. So, why was she calling?

"Mama?"

"Oh, Annabelle. I am so glad it's you. I called earlier, but I didn't hear your voice on the recording," her mother said, her voice breathless.

Schwartzman sat up in the chair. If it wasn't the cancer . . .

"I didn't even know if this is your number," her mother went on. "Oh, Lord, what if it hadn't been your number? You're always changing your phone number."

She had changed her number three times in seven years, and every time Spencer had gotten ahold of the new one within a few months. "It's me, Mama. It's my number." *I have breast cancer, Mama.* She was desperate to say the words, to cry with her mama. To be held and told it would be all right. Everything would be all right.

"Hello," her mother said again.

"It's me, Mama. It's—" But then she didn't want to hear her name out loud. Annabelle Schwartzman had cancer. Annabelle Schwartzman had a husband who wouldn't let her go. Annabelle Schwartzman was weak and gullible, a child who lost her father and married the first man to pay her any attention. She didn't want to be Annabelle Schwartzman.

"Thank God," her mother cried.

"What is it, Mama? What's happened?" She tried to sound confident, but there was fear in her own voice, as well.

"The police just called me. It's Ava, Annabelle."

Annabelle pictured the statuesque woman with her father's eyes. "Aunt Ava?"

"I'm afraid she's—"

Ava. Ava, the smart, together woman Schwartzman wanted to be. Ava, the person Schwartzman modeled herself after. Ava's house, the home where she'd spent weeks each summer until after seventh grade, when her mother refused to let her go for longer than a few days. At that age, girls began to come into society. There were cotillions and parties, weekly lessons at the country club about manners and etiquette, things that, in her mother's view, were crucial to her success. Her father conceded to her mother's wishes.

"What is it, Mama?"

"She's passed, Annabelle."

The air vanished from the room. Her insides pooled into her stomach and lungs. She couldn't draw breath, couldn't speak. *No. No, no, no.* She shook her head, fought to draw in air, tears already streaming down her face. "No!" The word erupted from her chest.

"It happened Friday, but I went down to Savannah for the garden show, and I didn't get the message until I got home this morning. The police came right to the house to tell me."

The tears streamed harder. She'd been thinking of Ava just—was that yesterday? She had planned to call her. What had stopped her? Why hadn't she called? So often she thought of her aunt, wished she could see her, go stay in the house on Meeting Street.

But something always stopped her. Some other voice that said to wait until things with Spencer were resolved, until she could finally go home again. And now it was too late. Ava was gone. "How?"

"Oh, God. I don't even know where to start," her mother continued. "They found my name in her address book. She didn't have any family. We're all she had, Bella."

Schwartzman shuddered at Spencer's nickname. How often did Spencer see her mother? Fill her head with poison?

"How soon can you be in Charleston?"

Schwartzman's hand instinctively clamped onto the base of the chair. "No."

"What do you mean?"

No way. No way was she going out there. "I can't come out, Mama."

"You have to come. She was your family, Annabelle. Your father's sister."

She fought against the desire to shout at her mother. *I have cancer. My husband is evil.*

"Annabelle."

Her mother wouldn't listen about Spencer. She never had. "It's work, Mama. It's too busy."

"You can deal with the deaths of other people's family, but you won't take time off for your own?"

Schwartzman didn't answer.

She would never have missed her father's funeral. Couldn't imagine missing Ava's. But the biggest draw of her father's funeral was Ava, being there with the woman she was closest with in the world, the one woman who loved her father the way she did. Her mother loved her father, but she loved him for taking care of *her*, for loving *her*. Or that was how it felt to Schwartzman.

"How would your father feel if he heard you say you couldn't get away from work to help bury his sister?" her mama said in the same hard how-dare-you-cross-me voice as always.

Schwartzman exhaled. Guilt, too. Her mother's favorite tool. And so effective. Because Schwartzman would never disappoint her father. The fingers that held the phone trembled.

She would not go. Her father knew why she couldn't.

But it was Ava. Dear, sweet Ava.

How could she not go? If only to see her one last time, to touch what remained of her aunt. How was it possible that she would never see Ava again? At least burying her would create some sense of closure.

She was swallowed by a tremendous sense of loss. Ava was gone. Why hadn't she reached back out to Ava? Why hadn't she let herself lean on her aunt? Wasn't that what Ava wanted?

"Annabelle Schwartzman," her mother snapped.

She cleared her throat. "I'm sorry, Mama."

"I cannot believe I have raised a daughter who would miss her aunt's funeral. You're going to have a lot to sort out down here, you know? Who do you think will inherit Ava's house? Her things? What am I supposed to do? That's *your* job."

Inheriting the house? In Charleston? Ava had no one else. Ava holding her tight at her father's funeral. Making her promise to come stay in Charleston. The old house on Meeting Street, the one that had been her grandparents'. The place where she'd hidden out after the miscarriage, while she planned to go finish medical school. How she'd longed to stay longer. If only Spencer weren't so close. But now, without Ava, what would Schwartzman do with a house in Charleston?

Her mother made an uncomfortable noise. There was something else. Something she wasn't saying. "Mama?"

"You should know that she was—" The sound of her mother's voice catching on something. "Her death wasn't natural."

"Wasn't natural?" Schwartzman repeated.

Her mother said nothing. There was a beep as another call came through.

"Mama, are you saying she was murdered?"

"I hate that word."

Murdered. Ava was murdered. Grief pulsed through her like waves of electricity. *Spencer.* The phone pressed to her ear, she pulled her knees to her chest, tried to close herself in a ball. As though she could cut off this new reality. Make it disappear. But it was real. What better way to force her to come back to South Carolina than to kill her favorite person?

"You call me as soon as you book your ticket, Annabelle," her mother said. "The moment you book it."

"Mama, you're not listening. I'm not—"

But the line was dead. Her mother gone. Schwartzman pressed the phone against her chest. Held it there. She had breast cancer. A woman here had died because of her. Ava was dead. Because of her. She had lost Ava. Gone without a second's notice. How desperately she wished that she'd seen her one last time, or called.

Would he just keep killing people until she came home? Would he target anyone who showed concern for her? Was it even worth the fight? She could stop fighting it all. Go home and be with him. Let him handle her cancer and her surgeries. Live in the yellow hell. At least then no one else would get hurt.

For as long as the game lasted. Surely he would tire of her. He would tire of a wife who couldn't be perfect. He just wanted her back. If she gave him that, he won. If she went home, maybe he would just give up. Divorce her. Because what else could he possibly imagine would happen?

Shivers ran through her. She'd spent all these years fighting to get away. She was a doctor. She had a life. She was not going to South Carolina. He could not make her go. Cancer was not a death sentence, not necessarily. Going to South Carolina was a death sentence. Hadn't enough people died?

She wondered who would perform the autopsy on Ava. Had it already been done? She wanted to be there, to watch and make certain nothing was missed. To watch over her.

In the interview room, Macy and the inspectors stood from the table. They were finished. She'd missed the end, but from Macy's expression, maybe it would be okay. She experienced a little pang of regret that either way, she would distance herself. There was no room for anyone in her life.

Cancer and Spencer's shadow were her only companions.

She slipped out of the viewing room and ducked into the bathroom at the end of the hall. She sat in a stall and forced herself to pull it together. She had time to sort things out. She might have gone to the morgue, but she would be worthless there. She would research the cancer and its treatments, call the police department in Charleston and find out what happened to Ava. She would make a game plan.

She would move forward as she always did, but first she would give herself the morning, allow herself to find distraction in the simple tasks of living. There was a pair of slacks at the dry cleaner, supplies to be replenished at the market. She could buy a coffee, read the paper, draw the errands out. If she were lucky, it might last a couple of hours.

Schwartzman moved through the hallways without seeing anyone familiar and was grateful to step outside, where the sun finally shone. The stairs to the department were damp, and the air had the wet, clean smell of rain. But even as she reached the fresh air, what she really wanted was to be back inside, in the comforts of her morgue.

"Schwartzman."

Ken Macy jogged toward her.

"I'm glad I caught you. Hal said you came in to watch the interview." He exhaled.

Seeing his face confirmed what she'd already known—she believed him. It might have been easier if she didn't, but she did. Not that it changed anything. Everything was different now.

"Thank you for being here," Macy said. The intensity in his eyes made her look away.

"Of course," she said, reaching into her purse to find her car keys. "I didn't do anything."

"You did." He reached for her free hand, the one on the strap of her purse. Schwartzman stood, frozen.

"Thank you," he said, squeezing gently. "I hope you will let me buy you dinner as a thank-you."

"That's not necessary."

"I didn't say it was." He let go of her hand. "I'll text you later in the week."

She didn't tell him no. She had enjoyed their dinner. How was that less than two days ago? How had everything changed so dramatically since Friday?

He walked back into the building. Even after being questioned, he moved with ease and confidence, comfortable in his own skin. He turned back and gave her a smile. She liked him.

Alone on the stairs, Schwartzman was cold and filled with the awkward sensation that she'd made a scene and everyone was watching. But as she scanned the crowd, it was just people doing what they did. Walking, texting, talking on the phone, a homeless man asking for money from a group of women who were gathered against the outside of the building, smoking.

She was invisible to them, the woman surrounded in dark shadows.

Schwartzman turned back toward the building. Just thinking of the morgue, the bodies waiting for her, brought a sense of calm. The morgue was the only place she felt calm now.

21

Greenville, South Carolina

The alert on his calendar buzzed Monday morning at ten forty-five, fifteen minutes before their scheduled time. She would be hanging on to her phone, waiting. He spun the Italian leather office chair and stared out the window. The sky was blue. Leaves on the trees that lined the street waved gently. A typical day.

What he liked most about his view wasn't the sky or the city below but the Baptist church. From here, he gazed down on the historic building with its Roman columns and the steps that rivaled Lincoln's memorial. He peered down even on the green spire with its crossed arrows and down on the parishioners who trudged inside each week like ants drawn to honey.

He could have had the corner over the park. His partners thought he was crazy not to choose that one. He had first pick, of course. But he liked this one. Some believed it was his strict Baptist upbringing. His mother, in fact, had commented on that exact reason when she visited.

"Your father would be proud," she'd said.

Although the office building was only eight stories high, their offices occupied the top floor. In his angry moments, the view mollified his fury. In frustration, it calmed him. And in the rare times of fear, the church below infused him with power. How could it not? There he was, peering down on God himself.

As he spun back around to the desk, he unfastened the top button of his dress shirt and pulled his tie loose. He pressed the intercom.

"Jenny?"

"Yes, Mr.—"

"I'm not to be disturbed until I buzz you again," he said, interrupting.

"Of course, sir." He punched the intercom off and stood from his desk. He had come to dread these calls. What had been so invigorating early on was now tiresome. The anticipation, the planning, he always enjoyed that. He was used to leveraging help. He could not, after all, travel to her. So he had others do it for him. But this was the furthest anyone had ever gone on his behalf. The manipulations had to be perfect, intricate but also simple. The challenge was delightful, but this part . . . the aftermath with its cleanup, all the reassurances that had to be made because people inevitably became nauseatingly wobbly-kneed after the deed was done. These things fatigued him immensely.

He bolted the solid oak office door that, along with soundproofing, he had installed when he moved in, then crossed to the large painting that hung above the couch. He pulled it down and set it on the leather to reach the wall safe. With his eyes closed for practice, he punched in his sixteen-digit code and heard the short, soft beep before turning the knob ninety degrees to the right. The door fell open. He retrieved the small nylon sack and closed up the safe, rehung the picture.

Then, instead of sitting at his desk, he dragged one of the guest chairs to the window and sat on it, as he did every time. From the nylon sack, he removed the cheap burner phone and cord, the small black box, and a digital recorder with his required background sounds.

He slid the battery onto the phone and plugged it into the outlet just below the windowsill, giving him enough slack to raise the phone to his mouth to talk while it charged. He did not like to leave charge in the battery, and he certainly never left the battery on the phone. He appreciated that the idea of a burner phone was that it was untraceable, but this recent acquaintance had taught him that very few secure technologies were actually secure.

He set the digital recorder to the appropriate file, slid the black headphones over his head, and set the speaker beside the phone. The voice transformer was a relatively inexpensive gadget that altered his voice, making it sound approximately a half octave lower. He suspected the gadget's target market was something mundane like married men attempting phone sex with their wives or girlfriends. He had tested it out thoroughly. It also succeeded in making him sound in character.

He double-checked all the settings and dialed the number. At the first ring, he pressed the recorder and held it to the phone. The sounds of men shouting filled the air.

"Is that you?"

"Yeah, babe. It's me," he said.

"It's always so loud there," she said. The same thing every time he called. She might have been part of the recording.

"Yeah," he agreed. "Hang on. Let me see if I can find a quiet corner." He pretended to move and instead turned the volume down slightly on the recording.

"It sounds so awful." Again with the same refrain.

"Not long now," he told her. Another redundancy. He had come to think that if he could pinpoint the time required for her inane comments and the big sighs she used to punctuate their conversations, he might have been able to record himself and set up these calls to run themselves. There was no ending the relationship now. He would have to stay the course for another month at least.

"Chuck?"

"Yeah?"

"How did that parole meeting go? I forgot to ask last week."

This was the problem with posing as a real-life prisoner. It made it easy to get the details of what they'd done, to play the part realistically. But every damn thing ended up on the Internet.

"Okay. Don't want to jinx it by talking 'bout it yet." He could sense her pout in the silence. "We're getting closer, babe. That's all that counts, right?"

"When do I get to see you? I could come up there, just for a visit?"

"No." His voice cracked, and he hoped it was less apparent through the modulator. Damn her. "We mustn't let—" He halted. He hated her for making him flustered. He found his character again.

"Chuck?"

"We can't let no one know 'bout us. Blow the whole thing we worked so hard for."

"I know. All the bartering you do to use the guard's burner phone and get the private room to talk. Protecting me."

"Yes." He reiterated all the lies he'd built to gain her trust and help.

"But you're not even on the chat room anymore."

He had already told her that he was afraid the cops were patrolling the room, that it was too dangerous so close to his potential release. He should not have to repeat himself. "You know why." The truth was he didn't like being connected to someone for too long. It raised the risk.

He was not going to get caught because of some pathetic loser.

"I know, but it's so hard not seeing you."

He said nothing. This was just what she had to do. He no longer bothered to try to stop the rant. He was used to the way she talked in circles.

"I'm trying to be patient, Chuck."

"You're doing a good job, babe. I'm torn up about it, too, but it'll all be worth it in the end. You know I couldn't do it without you."

A beat passed. "I did it just like you said," she said proudly. "Every last detail."

She'd given him the details last week. He was hardly interested in hearing them again. The endless questions about lavender and yellow flowers. Some women asked far too many questions.

He hoped he wouldn't be required to find another one to finish up.

"So when do I get to see you?" Her voice was pure whine. A spoiled girl used to pouting her way into getting what she wanted. He'd known loads of them growing up. Despised them all. "Chuck, you promised after it was done."

He exhaled silently, controlled. "Got to watch to see what direction the police investigation goes. No one has made contact with you?"

"No," she said, sounding slightly disappointed. "I saw her, though."

"Saw who?"

"The coroner who got you put away."

He exhaled at the reference to Bella. He had told her to steer clear of Bella.

"I know. I wasn't supposed to talk to her, and I didn't. Not much anyway. You were right, though. Sarah was a dead ringer for her."

He said nothing. He wanted to end the call. Immediately. And at the same time, he wanted to hear every detail. How long had it been since he'd set eyes on Annabelle? Nearly seven years. He had images, of course. They were served to him regularly through different sources.

He longed to see her movements. The length of her stride when she was intent on getting somewhere. The way she touched the hair behind her right ear when she was hesitant. The way she dug her toes into the floor when she was angry. He missed every little detail. He sucked a breath through clenched teeth and let the air out slowly.

"You get the picture I sent?"

"What picture?"

"Of her and that cop she's dating."

"Dating?" he said, his voice slipping. He coughed to cover the rise in his voice, clenched his fist. *Get control, damn it.* That would be too much, too far.

"Yep. Same one we talked about. I sent the picture to your e-mail."

Dating. Speechless, he fumbled with the digital recorder, inadvertently starting up the same noise as the beginning of the call. He jabbed the "Forward" button and found the track with the guard yelling at two prisoners who were fighting. He had recorded it off a YouTube video. He covered the mouthpiece of the phone and whispered, "I got to go, babe. A few more weeks and we're home free."

"Okay, Chuck. I love you. I'll talk to you tomorrow?"

"Probably not, babe. Day after for sure."

She sighed but didn't complain. "'Kay, baby. Bye."

He ended the call and slid the battery off the phone, then snapped the burner phone into two pieces. Time for a new one. He slid the phone into his pants pocket, took the painting down, and opened the safe. He returned the rest of his things to the wall safe, locked it up, and rehung the painting. He forced his hands to keep moving while his brain spun on her words. *The cop she is dating.* Annabelle had never dated anyone. It was impossible. He closed out the thought as he scanned the room, confirming that everything was in its place before he quietly unlocked the office door.

Returning the chair to his desk, he paused to gaze down on the church steeple. His chest rose, and his shoulders straightened. There was nothing to connect him to the woman on the phone. No money trail. The chat room where they'd met and built the relationship was gone. He could stop calling, and she should have no way to track him.

And yet he would be calling again. He had hoped Ava's death would be the final act, but he wasn't sure he was done with her. If Schwartzman left again—returned to Seattle or San Francisco or headed out of South Carolina—then there would be more calls, more plans.

He had done everything right so far, and he was not a man who screwed things up in the last stretch. The church taunted him. His father's voice. A quote from Corinthians.

For our light and momentary troubles are achieving for us an eternal glory that far outweighs them all.

And another of his father's favorites. Rejoice in sufferings. *Repent your sins and rejoice in giving yourself fully to God.* Fury raged inside him, and he turned his back to the church. With the sweep of his hand, he sent the coffee mug on his desk flying into the wall. The ceramic exploded with a satisfying snap.

He took two deep breaths and reached across his desk to hit the intercom. "Jenny, can you please bring some towels. I'm afraid there's a broken coffee cup, and it's a bit of a mess."

"Certainly, Mr. MacDonald. I'll be right in."

22

San Francisco, California

Schwartzman slid the body back into refrigeration bay four and made a note of his placement in the file. With the bodies cleared, she washed up. Normally she would have completed her paperwork at the desk in the morgue, but the deceased was a smoker and the smell lingered. Instead Schwartzman exchanged her lab coat for a sweater and moved into her office.

Beside "Cause of Death," she made a check next to "Natural" and wrote, "Ventricular fibrillation leading to sudden cardiac death." If not for the hefty life insurance policy, the man's death wouldn't have called for autopsy. He had all the risk factors for sudden cardiac death—hypertension, high cholesterol, history of heart disease.

In autopsy, she found clear evidence of both recent and old myocardial infarction, premortem coronary thrombus, plaque rupture, and the presence of 83 percent coronary artery disease.

From what she saw, he was lucky he lived as long as he did.

With the file completed, she shut down her computer and took her coat off the hook beside the door, pulling the wool over her shoulders and feeling the weight of it stretch down her back and neck. A very hot bath. With Epsom salts and a glass of wine.

She was tying the belt when the phone rang on the desk. She debated answering. It was past work hours. But it wasn't in her nature to leave it. If she didn't answer the call now, she would want to check the message from home.

"Schwartzman."

"Bella." He drew the name out.

She shivered, pressing her fist against her gut. A hundred thoughts entered her head at once. Confront him about Victoria Stein. The flowers. The lavender water. Say nothing. Hang up. Scream. Call the police. Hire someone to kill him. That one she'd had before. Instead she took a slow shaky breath, gripped the phone, and said nothing.

"Are you under the weather, Bella?"

Could she trace the call? He hadn't called her office line directly before. She wondered if he had gotten the number from Terri Stein, or whatever her real name was. What else could that woman have learned from being in this office? What good would it do to trace the call?

He laughed lightly as though he could see all the thoughts racing about her mind. Then, after a brief pause, he said, "Be well, sweet Bella."

There was her own quick gasp in the receiver, then the click of the line going dead. A wave of cold was followed by the scalding heat of nausea. She shuddered and fought the desire to be sick. The room was off-kilter. She set her palm on the desk, saw she still held the receiver.

Breathe. She drew a breath, then a second, replaced the receiver on the base, ignoring her trembling hand. He had called before, she told herself. *This is nothing new.* And yet it felt like another step, another intrusion. He'd asked if she was under the weather. Was he implying she was sick? Or was it some sort of clue? Something about Victoria Stein?

Hearing his voice, she knew that she was right. Spencer knew about Victoria Stein. He was behind her death. Which meant he was probably behind Ava's, as well. She could feel the truth like bitter cold in her bones. What would he do? He knew where she lived, where she worked, how to reach her, whom she loved . . . how could she possibly escape him?

She remained frozen in place as though he were an animal that could hunt her if she moved. She had waited too long for that. There would be no waiting in place. She had to leave, didn't she?

Run and hide again?

She knocked the stapler to the ground and let out a small gasp. She glanced around the empty office. She was alone. She pulled out the chair and sat at the desk. Her legs were achy and weak. As though she were, in fact, ill. *No.* That was just him, getting inside her head. She couldn't let that happen. It was so hard to keep the thoughts and memories at bay, but she had to try. If she let him in . . .

"Stop it," she said out loud. "You are fine." She stood. Put her computer bag over her shoulder and found her key to lock up the office. Halfway out the door, her cell phone rang.

She would not answer. Drawing the phone from her pocket, she saw the number was local. Was he here? She stopped in the doorway. Took a breath to steel herself.

"Hello."

"Dr. Schwartzman?"

She didn't recognize the voice. "Yes?"

"This is Dr. Norman Fraser calling. Is now a good time?"

Schwartzman let out the breath she'd been holding. "Sure, Doctor. It's fine."

"Your biopsy came back positive."

Spencer's words. *Are you under the weather, Bella?* "Yes. I heard from Dr. Khan this weekend."

"Yes. She told me she would call you," Fraser said. "You have invasive lobular cancer in your right breast. The cancer is slow-growing and not aggressive. Grade one and less than two centimeters."

A pause. A tightness in her chest.

"Dr. Schwartzman?"

"I'm here."

"I can't tell you what stage it is until after surgery." The word *surgery* rang in her head like a bell. He said something else that she missed. ". . . receptive, which is good. It is HER2, which is also positive. I would like to get you back in to do an ultrasound on your left breast to be certain we haven't missed anything on that side. I have a one o'clock appointment open on Thursday. I know this might seem like a lot."

"Yes," she agreed.

"You don't need to make any decisions tonight. I'll inform Dr. Khan and hold that Thursday appointment for you until you can get back to me. Does that sound okay?"

She didn't know how much time passed before she heard his voice again. "Dr. Schwartzman?"

"Yes," she confirmed. "I will call you back about the appointment . . . the appointment on . . ." She had no idea when the appointment was.

"Thursday. One o'clock. If we don't hear from you, we'll touch base tomorrow afternoon to confirm."

Tomorrow. Cancer. It was too whispery a word. It should have a harsher sound in the middle. Or perhaps the word was fitting. Cancer was like a snake.

"Do you have any questions for me?"

She couldn't think of a single thing to ask.

"It's quite common to experience shock with this kind of news," Fraser said. "The prognosis is positive for this type of cancer. Hopefully some of the websites Bonnie directed your husband to will be helpful for you both."

She flinched. "Husband?" The sound was like a wheeze.

"He called and spoke with Bonnie earlier. Patient confidentiality prohibits us from giving him any specific information on your file, of course. But Bonnie was able to give him some general information on how you two might proceed."

Her *husband*. "I don't have a husband."

The line went silent. "Well, perhaps—"

"Are you certain Bonnie spoke to someone who said he was my husband?"

"I thought the same thing—you're not being married, I mean, but Bonnie looked it up in your chart. And he was able to confirm your date of birth and address. Bonnie mentioned that he was recently added to your emergency contact list." Fraser was breathless, afraid. Breaching patient confidentiality was a serious offense. "In fact, he's the only one listed." The shuffling of papers. "Yes, here it is. He was added to the file yesterday morning."

Schwartzman pressed her palm to her racing heart. "Added how?"

"Via fax, I believe. It will be here somewhere." More paper shuffling. Another voice behind his.

Spencer knew. Somehow he'd found out. She pressed her eyes closed.

"Ah, yes. Here it is," Fraser said with relief in his voice. "It's got your signature right on it."

Spencer would know how to forge her writing. "What name has been added?"

"Henry."

Spencer's middle name.

"Henry Schwartzman. We—"

"Yes," she said, cutting him off. "Remove him immediately. No one is to have access to my files. And I want a copy of that fax sent to my mobile phone. Do you have a pen?"

"Yes. Right here. Go on, then."

She recited her number for him and made him read it back. "I'll be there."

"Be where?" Fraser sounded a little nervous.

"Your office on Thursday. One o'clock."

"Oh good. That is good. And I'll speak with Bonnie and the front office," he added in a rush. "We will take care of your records and eliminate your—"

"Thank you," she said.

She ended the call, her fingers trembling as they hovered over the screen. Stunned, she stared at the wall of the hallway. Spencer knew she was sick. How fast did cancer spread? Was it coursing through her body? She imagined spiky toxic cells killing off healthy ones. How could she know so little about it?

Was that how it worked? And what would Spencer do with the information? What if she died? Would he let her go then?

She wanted her body donated to science. And then to be cremated.

Would Spencer insist on bringing her body back to South Carolina to be buried in his family plot? Torment her even after death?

She faced the ceiling. "God," she whispered. A plea. A question. How could God do this to her? Why? *Please make it go away.* How did she get cancer? She had Spencer. Surely that was bad enough.

Then she pressed her eyes closed.

A minute or perhaps three or ten later, she opened them. She was sitting on the floor just inside the office door. It took her several minutes to pull herself up. *Go home. Go home and take a bath.* Wash away the feel of his voice on her. A glass of wine to ease the fear. If only for the night.

23

San Francisco, California

Yellow pressed against her mouth and nose. Soft amber clouds that wouldn't budge. Her arms pinned, she struggled to turn to one side, to capture a breath. A soft voice whispered to her. Don't struggle. Let go. Slide into the warmth. It pulled from below. Heaviness and weightlessness at once.

Schwartzman fought harder. There was no warmth. It was a trick. Fight. Fight harder. She had barely moved and already her head pounded. It was too strong. Spencer would win. If she couldn't fight it, he would win. All this time, all this distance, and he would beat her.

She screamed out silently and fought against the inability to move. It was as though she were pinned down, yet she couldn't feel the straps.

She focused on moving in the darkness. The yellow faded. Gray tones emerged. Her fingers twitched against the sheets. She gasped and screamed again.

Some small sound emerged. More gray, less yellow.

And then a final scream.

Sound.

Noise. Not mighty but enough to press away the yellow, to bring the gray in deep and safe.

She was free.

She pressed herself onto one side, reached her arms out for the safety of the edge of the bed.

The throbbing in her head was blinding. She pressed her fingers against the bone behind her eyes, trying to recall the night before. She'd made dinner at home. Had a glass of wine in the bath, but only one. Something was wrong. She was sick. Did breast cancer cause headaches?

She put her hand out to push herself up and felt something warm and firm beside her. This time the scream was loud, full, shaking her awake. She fumbled away from the warmth. Legs caught in the sheets, she tumbled off the bed, hands first. Caught herself on the hard floor and slid in something slick. Hit her chin on the floor, bit her tongue, and tasted blood. Smelled it. Warm and alive, it was so foreign.

From the window, pale moonlight shone through the edge of the shades. Disoriented, she found herself on the floor on the far side of her own bed. In her own room.

And yet she'd never been in this spot. She always slept on the other side.

She lifted her hands and saw thick crimson smeared across her palms. More blood. She touched her tongue to the back of her hand, creating a tiny smudge of red. This was too much blood.

She pressed herself up, wiped her hands on her pajama bottoms, and moved to the bed. The bedside light was missing. She jerked up the window shade. Moonlight cast a faint light across the room. In the bed, the covers made a mound in the shape of a body.

A trick of the light.

She moved toward it slowly. Saw a head, dark hair.

Not a trick.

She reached out, stretching until her fingertips touched the wall, and palmed her way to the light switch. The room was flooded in white light. She blinked hard. There was a man facedown in her bed.

"How did you get in here?" she screamed.

No response.

Blood streaked the wall where she'd swiped for the light switch. She checked her body, touched her hands to her chest and belly. It was not her blood.

Her pulse throbbed at the base of her neck as adrenaline sent her own blood speeding to her legs and heart. Dizzy, she forced herself to the bed. She drew a breath, fighting her own flight instincts, and used both hands to turn the body onto its back.

She stared down at Ken Macy.

From the center of his button-down shirt, a bone knife handle lay almost perpendicular to the skin. It was a small paring knife. One from her set. She pulled the shirt away, but the knife held it in place. Hands trembling, she worked one of the buttons loose. Saw the blade was buried in his chest. Wounds across his chest. So much blood. "Oh, God."

Schwartzman scanned the bedside table for her cell phone, but it wasn't there. The white cord, where she plugged the phone in religiously every night, was there, but no phone.

His chest rose slightly, and Schwartzman cried out, "Ken." She pulled the nail scissors from her bedside table and cut away Ken's shirt. Red froth bubbled at the site of the wound. He was still breathing.

She sprinted through the apartment and found the kitchen phone. An antiquated device, attached to the wall by its thin, translucent cord. She almost cried out at the sound of a dial tone. Pressed 9-1-1 with shaky fingers. "Nine-one-one, what is your emergency?"

"This is Dr. Anna Schwartzman. I need an ambulance immediately." She recited her address. "I've got a man with a knife wound to the chest in my—" She stopped speaking. A man with a knife wound to the chest in her bed. She could not speak those words.

"Okay, Doctor. Just hold on the line with me."

"I am going to treat the victim as best I can. Get an ambulance here." She hung up and glanced across the countertops. Two glasses.

The empty bottle of Evan Williams. Her father's last one, the one she'd been saving. But she'd had wine last night. She remembered a bath, going to sleep.

Lost memories, but how?

She dialed the department's main number. "This is Dr. Schwartzman. I need you to call Hal Harris at home and have him meet me."

"I'm afraid Inspector Harris is off duty."

"This is Dr. Schwartzman. I'm the medical examiner. I am instructing you to call Inspector Harris and have him come to this address now. Do you understand?"

"Of course, Dr. Schwartzman. What address?"

Schwartzman recited her home address.

"If you can't reach Inspector Harris, then call Inspector Hailey Wyatt. Do you understand?"

"Yes, ma'am. I'll do it right away."

"This is a matter of life and death," Schwartzman said, hearing the panic in her rising voice.

"I understand, Dr. Schwartzman."

Schwartzman dropped the receiver, which clattered across the counter and landed on the floor. She didn't stop to retrieve it. She turned the water on and slammed through the cupboards for a large metal bowl, a roll of paper towels, her kitchen shears. To make room for the bowl of hot water on the bedside table, she swept a stack of books onto the floor. Ken's body jerked at the noise. He was conscious.

"Ken, it's Anna Schwartzman. You're going to be okay. Help is on the way, Ken. Okay?" She touched his wrist and searched for the pulse. Thready but palpable. *Keep talking.* "It's me. You're injured, but you're going to be okay. Can you open your eyes?"

Schwartzman studied the blood-soaked sheets and tried to calculate how much blood there was. Pressed her fingers to them, came away wet.

Ken's eyes remained closed.

She studied the knife. The handle jutted to the right, indicating a right-handed assailant. But this wasn't a victim. He wasn't dead. *You're a doctor.*

"I'm going to get you fixed up, Ken," she told him and ran to retrieve her medical examiner's bag from beside the front door.

"I'd love to see your eyes, Ken. Can you try to open them for me?" She watched his eyes, saw the slightest twitch as she fumbled to open her case. She opened the top and stared into the contents. There was no blood pressure monitor, no stethoscope to listen for breathing sounds. She was a doctor for the dead. The living were outside her expertise.

The pounding returned to her head. *Drugs.* They'd been drugged.

She put her hand in Ken's. "I want you to squeeze my hand if you can hear me."

His fingers lay motionless against hers. "Come on, Ken. You owe me dinner. You've got to fight, okay?"

Come on, Schwartzman. First step: stop the bleeding. She ran across the room and scooped an armful of T-shirts from her drawer. "We're getting you all fixed up, Ken. Good as new." Talking as she worked, she rolled the T-shirts, then folded them in half to create firm packs she could press on the wounds that were bleeding more actively.

Ken remained motionless. "Come on, Ken. Hang in there, okay?"

She looked at the bundles laid out on his chest. The compressions would only work if she had a way to apply pressure to all of them at once. *Think!* She sprinted back to the closet, grabbed a fistful of black stockings. Straddling Ken's torso, she worked the stockings under his body and tied the legs across the rolled shirts. Listened to his breath. "I hear it, Ken. I hear you breathing. Good. That's so good." She held her hand on his. "Can you wiggle your fingers, Ken? Give me a finger high five."

With her free hand, she reached down for her blood sample kits. His finger moved. Or was it hers? "Again, Ken. Do it again." She pulled the empty vials into her lap and reached down for clean needles.

As she sat back up, she felt movement.

He did it. He could hear her.

"Do you know your blood type, Ken?"

A tiny flutter from his index finger. "I'm going to take a sample of your blood to find out what type you are. Then I can tell the paramedics." If she needed blood from the dead, she drew it from the jugular or the femoral artery. She hadn't drawn blood from a living person since med school. "Hang on, Ken."

She grabbed a pair of the tights and tied them high on Ken's arm and made a fist with his hand. The vein was flat. She used the nail scissors to cut off one of the legs of the stockings and tied it on her own left arm, using her teeth to tighten it over her bicep. "I'm going to take my blood, too, Ken." She was AB positive, a universal recipient but not a good bet for a donor. "We'll both do it. While your vein gets ready, I'm going to take some from mine. Because you know what, Ken? I think we were drugged. I think someone drugged us."

She pumped her fist. Removed the syringe from its packaging and pressed the vial into its base. Then, with her teeth, she removed the orange protective cover on the needle and stuck into the thick blue vein in the crease of her elbow. She had good veins, easy veins. The kind nurses commented on because they were so fat and ready to give.

The vial filled with blood, and she turned her attention to Ken. She had no rubbing alcohol swabs to clean the wound site. The vein was languid and flat. She wondered if she could kill him by drawing blood. She'd been to medical school. She should know the answer to something so basic. The vial from her own arm was full. She pulled the vial off and replaced it with an empty one. How much blood would they need to test? Two vials? Three? She'd give them four.

She fingered his arm. "Okay, here we go," she told him, glancing at the shirt packed around the knife in his chest. She slid the needle into the vein and took a breath as she pushed the vial into the base of the syringe. Blood trickled into the vial. "You're doing great, Ken. You hear me?"

She touched his fingers, but there was no response. His grip loosened. His pulse was palpable but barely. And slow. Too slow. *Damn it.* Where the hell was the—

Just then there was pounding at the door. She sprinted, holding her arm, and studied the peephole. *Paramedics.* She fumbled with the lock. *Men dressed as paramedics. Spencer. How far would he go? Fake paramedics?* She threw open the bolt and pulled the door open.

"Dr. Schwartzman?"

"He's in the bedroom."

She raced across the apartment, the gurney wheels clacking against the hard floor behind her. She stepped aside, and something caught her arm. Saw the syringe in her arm but the vial was gone.

"What drugs has he taken?"

The paramedic was a woman. Thin, Asian, intense. The other paramedic moved to Macy.

"We need to know what drugs are in his system," the woman said.

"I don't know," Schwartzman told her. "I am drawing our blood to find out. I've got two vials of mine." Just then she spotted the second vial on the floor, rolling slowly toward the door. She scooped it up and showed it to the paramedic.

"Ma'am," the female paramedic said. "What kind of drugs did you take?"

"None. I don't even know how he got here. I woke up, and he was here. With the knife."

"Pulse is one ten," the second paramedic reported. "Blood pressure's ninety-six over seventy."

The woman moved past Schwartzman, guiding the gurney to the edge of the bed as the other paramedic set up an IV. "How long since he was stabbed?"

Schwartzman shook her head.

"How long?"

"I don't know," Schwartzman said. But she might have yelled it.

The two paramedics lifted Macy onto the gurney, the fitted sheet still beneath him. Did they believe she had stabbed him?

"If you want to save your friend's life, you need to tell us what happened here," the woman said as they strapped the belt across Macy, avoiding the knife that jutted from his chest.

"You're speaking to the San Francisco medical examiner," came a voice from the hall.

Schwartzman started. Hal Harris stood in the doorway. He looked half-asleep. His shirt on backward. He held his badge open, the brass aimed at the paramedics. "She's a victim here, too, so assume she knows nothing."

"If you say so," the woman said, dubious.

"I do," Harris told her, moving aside as they wheeled Macy out.

Schwartzman started to follow.

Hal took her arm and stopped her. "Hey."

"I've got to go with him."

"Do you have a robe somewhere, Doc?"

For the first time, she glanced down at herself. Her pajamas were covered in blood, her breasts visible through the thin material of the cotton. She wrapped her arms around her chest. "In the closet. By the door."

Hal pulled a navy terry-cloth robe from its hook and handed it to her. He held the closet door open to allow her to put it on without facing the room. As she tied the belt, she realized she was still holding the vial of blood.

She handed it to Hal. "It's my blood. We need to test it for drugs."

Hal took the vial. "What do you remember?"

She shook her head, scanning the room.

Blood. There was so much blood.

"Wait," she cried. "I took his blood. I had a vial of it." Schwartzman palmed the damp top sheet until she located the vial with less than an inch of blood. "This is his." She crouched at her ME bag and found labels. "I'll put our names on them." She dug through the kit for a marker. Normally she had tons of them. Her vision blurred.

"Hold up, Schwartzman."

She tried to stand. The blood rushed to her head. She reached out with the vial of Ken's blood and felt it roll off her fingers. Hal's hand swept through the air. His fingers closed on the vial as the walls moved sideways; the floor rose. Hal's arm around her waist. Her head fell into his chest, and everything went gray just before it was black.

24

San Francisco, California

The hospital room smelled of astringent, plastic, and the musty smell of body odor and urine that could never quite be scrubbed away. Hal stood against a wide metal beam that ran along the inside of the window. It was as far as he could get from the noises and smells of the rest of the hospital. Schwartzman had been brought directly to the ICU. There was no private room, no privacy at all save a thin curtain that divided the ten-by-ten space from the main desk, where phones rang constantly and doctors and nurses conferred about their patients in voices not quite loud enough to understand but too loud to ignore.

Normally he would have assigned a patrol officer to watch her. Like it or not, she was their primary suspect in Macy's attack. Occam's razor—the simplest explanation was usually the correct one. But nothing about this was simple. He wanted to believe, as she did, that her ex-husband was at the center of all of it, that somehow they would be able to tie him to the death of Sarah Feld and now to Macy's attack. Homicide. God, he hoped it wouldn't be that.

The last time he'd seen Macy was in the interrogation room. Confused, deflated, Macy had seemed so genuinely stung by the questions Hal asked. It was the job, but it hadn't made him feel any better.

He stood now in the room of another person who *looked* guilty of a crime. Another colleague. Worse, a friend.

The window behind him was large, the ledge down at his knees, but the room was dark and cold. A single chair with a plastic blue cushion stood against one wall, but he had yet to sit down.

Hours had passed, and still adrenaline pumped through him. Schwartzman had woken twice. The first time she cried out like a child, and in the moment it took him to cross the room to her, she tried to sit up, clawing at her IV. Her expression was pure terror until she saw him. She had calmed slightly just before the room was invaded by nurses. As Hal held her hand, the IV was fixed, a sedative added to the fluids. "To help her sleep," the nurse had said, as if he didn't understand sedation. The second time she woke, she simply whispered the name. "Macy?"

Again, he took her hand. "He's going to pull through," Hal told her, although he had no idea if it was the truth. Macy was in surgery, and it would be hours before they knew what kind of damage was done. Hal had been to his share of scenes where a victim had died by bleeding out. From what he'd witnessed in Schwartzman's apartment, there was enough blood for it.

Macy was out of his control, but he could be here for Schwartzman. There would be a lot of questions when she woke. Difficult ones, and he wanted to be the one to ask them. Where had she gone last night? When did Macy come to her apartment? And what the hell happened after that?

When Hal had arrived at her apartment, she was holding a vial of her blood. Somehow, in the midst of all the chaos, she'd taken samples of their blood. She told Hal to test the blood for drugs. Hal had given the patrol officer strict instructions to wait for Roger's team to arrive and to have them take it directly to the lab. It was there now. They would have results by tomorrow. That was as rushed as they could manage with the current backlog.

He tried to imagine Schwartzman stabbing Macy some dozen times, then waiting before calling 9-1-1. Then, while waiting for the ambulance to arrive, drawing their blood. Why would she do that if she was the one who'd stabbed him? But it might not be so simple. It was possible that the stabbing was her doing. There were plenty of drugs that caused hallucinations. It wasn't difficult to imagine a scenario that would fit. A woman with an abusive ex-husband, alone, confronts a man at the door and mistakes him for that husband. In a drug-altered state, she attacks without thinking. When she wakes, the drug has worn off and she realizes what she's done.

He stared down at Schwartzman sleeping. Blood in her hair and across her forehead.

Macy's blood.

Was that MacDonald's end goal? To manufacture a scenario where Schwartzman stabbed Macy and was arrested for assault? Or worse, for murder?

Had MacDonald realized he wouldn't get her back and decided this was the next best thing? Or was killing Macy his plan from the beginning?

Hal hated that he couldn't send a car to pick up MacDonald, throw him in an interrogation room somewhere, and let him sit for a while. He wanted to face MacDonald when the questions were asked. Instead the most he could do was make long-distance phone calls to a department where he had no clout and ask them to pull in a man who was, by their records, a well-respected citizen.

Damn this.

Hal's phone buzzed with Roger's latest text.

> The security cameras went down at 11:17. The basement alarm went off at 11:39. The desk clerk followed procedure, locked the outer door, and went to check.

Hal frowned. False alarm?

Yes, Roger confirmed.

Hal considered the building where Schwartzman lived. It was modern, new, high-end. The security systems in those places had to be top-of-the-line. Any idea why the sec system went out?

The line of dots on his screen told him Roger was replying.

The company is working on that now. The night guard said everything was working. He saw images on the screens but nothing at all was recorded after 11:17.

And no Macy before that? Hal typed.

Roger wrote back, No.

Roger occasionally complained about inspectors who requested text updates while he was processing a scene. It used to be simply impractical, the constant removing of gloves to type out a text before donning a new pair and going back to work. These days, Roger wore a Bluetooth device that he could voice activate, and he recorded his texts, no fingers required.

Outside communication meant Roger had to shift his focus from the scene, but there was nothing regular about this case.

From the frantic pace of the texts Hal was getting, Roger was working this one like a kidnapping. In those cases, the protocol was all about speed. The scene was preserved so that it could be revisited, but that first sweep had to be done as quickly as humanly possible. The sooner they identified and traced the evidence, the sooner they found the victim.

What about Schwartzman?

Have her coming home just before 7. Nothing after that.

So maybe Macy came over. Maybe they were a couple. It wouldn't be the first time he'd missed signs of an interdepartmental relationship.

Will get traffic cam feeds. Have one pic. Could be her. On corner.
Send pls, Hal texted back.

Coming . . .

An image appeared in a text message. He enlarged the photograph, but what he saw was not especially useful. Dark, wavy hair under a black ball cap. A black trench coat belted at the waist. Black boots with a small heel, black slacks. A large bag, something between an oversize purse and an overnight bag. It might have been Schwartzman, but it just as easily could have been someone else.

Think it's her? Roger texted.

Hal studied the image. He had seen her in slacks and boots, but the baseball cap was odd. Unless she was trying to conceal her identity.

Not sure, Hal wrote back. What time?

11:33.

Almost exactly fifteen minutes after the cameras stopped recording. Just six minutes before the false alarm in the basement. That was no coincidence. No Macy?

Nothing yet.

Thx, R. Keep 'em coming. You send a team to his house?

There was a short delay before a single word popped up on the screen. `Yes.` Then a few seconds later, Roger wrote, `And we're pulling additional footage from surrounding cameras in the area. It'll take us a while.`

Everything was being done. Roger would get him results as quickly as possible, but this wasn't magic. Someone had to pull the traffic cams, run search programs, and hope like hell they got lucky. In the meantime, there was nothing for him to do but wait until Schwartzman woke up and hope she could answer some questions.

He watched the rhythmic beat of her pulse on the monitor. Outside he saw the sky was cast in an orange glow. *Morning?* He glanced at his watch. *Damn.* It was almost seven. Exhaustion cut into his shoulders and neck like heavy straps. He stretched his arms up and laid his palms flat on the ceiling. He could have gone for a walk, but he didn't want to leave her. Instead he convinced himself to settle into the chair.

The top edge of the metal chair dug into his back just below his shoulders. He shifted down and stretched his legs out. Folded his arms across his chest and waited for the vibration of his phone to alert him to news.

25

San Francisco, California

Schwartzman couldn't draw her gaze away from Hal, asleep in the hard hospital chair in her room. His chin tucked to his chest, his arms crossed, his enormously long legs stretched across the floor, he looked distinctly uncomfortable. Touched that he had stayed with her, she could not wake him. She was letting Hal down by leaving.

She had no choice. It was obvious she'd be the primary suspect for Macy's attack.

Moving silently, she slid the lock on the IV to stop the drip. Gritting her teeth, she yanked the lead from her hand. She held her thumb against the skin to stop the bleeding and used her feet to push back the sheet and the thin blanket.

It was temporary, she told herself. Until Macy woke up. Her pulse drummed inside her ears. If he woke up. *God, please let him wake up.* If he didn't survive, she would be charged with his murder. He was found in her bed; she had been covered in his blood. The tox screens might create questions, but without another suspect, she was the obvious choice.

So she would run.

She was the kind of woman who ran. Spencer had made her this person. Always looking over one shoulder, afraid. Who would she have been without him? *No.* The question was, who would she be?

Because she was ready to be done running.

Her feet met the cold linoleum floor, and she crept across the room to the locker where her personal belongings would be. If she had any. *Please let there be something.* She took a deep breath and opened it slowly. The hinge let out a little cry. She froze, but Hal didn't move. She peered inside. Her purse, her trench coat, and a pair of tennis shoes.

She bent down to put her shoes on, slipped the coat over the hospital gown, hitched the purse onto her shoulder, and turned the coat collar up. Then she removed her phone from her purse, held it to her ear, and, with her hair half covering her face, walked out of the hospital room. She kept her head down. "Right, right," she said into the phone when she was far enough away from Hal not to wake him. "I'm on my way." She paused until she was at the door, pushed it open with her hip. "Urgent. Yes, I understand."

She ducked into the stairwell rather than take the elevator and came out the service entrance at the back of the hospital. There, a group of doctors, nurses, and employees was gathered to smoke. Head down, she kept moving. If she looked strange, no one said anything.

At the corner of the building and out of view, Schwartzman sped up to a jog. Spotting a cab at the front curb, she ran. She was woozy and off balance. Her head thundered with every step. She wondered if the hospital had performed a toxicology report. It would be useful to know what drug had been used so she'd have an idea of when the effects would wear off.

As she opened the cab door, her cell phone vibrated. Hal was calling.

She dropped the phone into her pocket without answering as she slid into the back of the cab. *I'm sorry.*

Pulling the door closed, she decided on a plan. "Crunch on Polk Street, please."

The driver's eyes appeared in the rearview mirror. "Crunch?" he repeated.

"It's on Polk between Union and Green."

"A restaurant?"

"A gym," she said.

"You are okay?" he asked, touching his own forehead. "There is a little blood."

"I'm fine," she said quickly. "But I'm running a little late."

With that, the driver started his meter and pulled away from the curb. Schwartzman ducked as the hospital's front doors opened and Hal ran through them. He stopped and scanned the street, rubbing his head. He hadn't seen her. At least she had that.

Schwartzman massaged the tender lump on the back of her hand where the IV had been. For a doctor, she had little experience with IVs, and in her hurry, she'd been rough. She thought about Macy. She had to know if he was—she stopped herself. She searched for the hospital number and asked the receptionist to be connected to ICU.

"Patient name?"

"Ken Macy," Schwartzman said, whispering his name like a prayer. There was a brief hold, and during the wait, it was impossible to move air in or out of her lungs.

"ICU," said a male voice.

Macy had five sisters. "I'm trying to get an update on my brother's condition."

"His name?"

"Ken Macy."

"Hold on, please."

More waiting. Her chest walls hardened again.

"This is Sammie."

"I'm calling to check on my brother, Ken. Ken Macy."

"Oh, hi. Is this Susan?"

"No," she said. She hoped not all of Ken's siblings had already called in. "This is Anna."

"Oh sure, Anna. He is doing okay. He's been stable for a few hours, which is encouraging. Nothing we can do but watch him. Was it Susan who said she was on her way out here?"

"Uh, yes," Schwartzman said. "I think that's right."

"Are you coming, too?" Sammie asked.

"No. I'm afraid I won't be able to make it, but I'll call back a bit later."

"Sure. I'm here until about three thirty. I'll tell him you called, Anna."

"Thank you." She wished she'd asked if she could talk to him. But of course she couldn't. He was barely out of surgery. She wondered when she would be able to talk to him. Or if.

As the cab turned onto Van Ness, Schwartzman found the compact mirror from her purse and checked her reflection. She had nothing to clean the blood from her forehead—Ken's blood—so she pulled her hair to cover the side of her face. The hospital gown hung down below her jacket. She couldn't show up to the gym in a hospital gown. She touched the bottom of her coat, which reached almost to her knees. It was long enough to suggest she might be wearing something other than underwear beneath it. Even if she showed too much leg, it was better than a hospital gown. She reached behind her head and untied the gown, working it down one arm under her coat.

She hadn't been to the gym more than a dozen times, but at the moment, she was extremely grateful that she paid the $125 a month for the membership. With her right arm freed from the gown, she worked on the other side and pulled the whole thing out from under the bottom of her coat. There, she balled up the gown and shoved it as far as she could under the seat with her foot as the driver turned right onto Green. *Almost there.*

Schwartzman opened her wallet and was relieved to see she had a twenty-dollar bill. As the cab stopped at the gym, Schwartzman stared at the front of the building.

"This is the place?"

She scanned the front window. Saw people on the treadmills. *Good.* The gym was open. "This is it," Schwartzman told him, passing the twenty though the bulletproof glass.

She slid out of the cab carefully and took a last glance at the floor. The gown was hidden from view. She crossed the sidewalk and pulled the door open, grateful to see the little display of workout clothes.

"Good morning."

Schwartzman found her membership card and pressed it against the scanner, then moved to the clothes turnstile and searched for the clothes with the most coverage. Settled on a pair of capri workout pants, glad they had her size in black. She was less fortunate with the tops. The only medium top with a built-in bra had wide yellow-and-pink stripes. Yellow. The color of cancer and Spencer. There was the appointment with Dr. Fraser, the appointment she would miss.

Perhaps yellow was a fitting color to wear as she returned to South Carolina. She pulled the jog bra off the rack and chose the least offensive zippered hoodie to go with it. It was cheetah print. At least her coat would cover them. She added two large water bottles to the clothes to help flush the toxins from her system and paid with a credit card. Taking her selections back to the changing room, she found a quiet bench in a corner and searched her phone for flights to Charleston.

26

Charleston, South Carolina

Schwartzman felt as if she'd been on her way to Charleston for days. An extended delay in Minneapolis due to weather was followed by a mechanical issue. By the time the plane was ready to go, the pilots had been on the clock too long, so the flight was canceled. The last thing Schwartzman felt ready to contend with was idle time. She would have liked to walk through the terminal, but her body and head ached, the drugs still working their way out of her system. Even lifting her arms and arching her back felt like trying to shift in drying concrete.

Instead she sat, flooded by a storm of emotions.

Disbelief that Ava was gone followed by waves of cold, hollowing grief. She worried about the cancer, about leaving Hal with no explanation, about Ken, about missing the appointment with Dr. Fraser. Then the fear rose to the surface again. Fear of actually seeing Spencer, confronting him.

The thoughts trampled in circles until they were ruts she couldn't escape.

She managed to catch the last flight from Minneapolis to Atlanta, but there was no way to get to Charleston until the morning. No travel items, no pajamas, she took the shuttle to the Hampton Inn at the airport, where she barely slept. Exhaustion had set into her bones. She'd kept her phone off throughout the trip, calling her mother from a pay phone and then later the hotel in Atlanta with her updated arrival times. She would listen to the messages once she arrived. She just had to get there first.

Closing her eyes to sleep on the short first morning flight to Charleston had brought a stream of memories. She'd last seen Ava at her graduation from medical school. Ava and her mother had both come, leaving her with the awkward role of negotiating whatever unspoken walls were between them and no opportunity to really talk to either. And since then? Occasional calls. Conversations that were loving but brief. Birthday cards. One year missed. Perhaps two.

Her sympathetic nervous system had her body locked into flight mode, leaving her shaky and short of breath. Grief spread like tentacles from her stomach and carved a painful path up into her chest and lungs. Her thinking was dull and foggy.

It was worse than losing her father. Because without Ava, nothing of him was left. Nothing of either of them.

She was haunted by visions of Spencer killing her. Had Ava seen his face? Did she watch Spencer while he did it? Look him in the eye? People always told Schwartzman that she took after her aunt. More so even—one of the reasons she suspected her mother resented Ava. While he was killing Ava, did Spencer imagine killing her instead?

The plane vibrated as the wheels lowered on their descent into Charleston, and Schwartzman focused on the runway just below. She had never flown into the Charleston airport. When she was a child, her father had always driven her up for the weeks she spent with her aunt. Occasionally her mother came, too, though that became less common the older she got. Ava didn't drive. Living as she did in downtown Charleston, she'd never had a need for a car. Her law office was within walking distance, and though she loathed exercise of any kind, Ava was a dedicated walker.

Even in the heaviest of rains, Schwartzman recalled her aunt putting on a long black raincoat and tall yellow rain boots and tying a clear plastic bonnet over her head before stepping out onto the porch and popping open a giant black-and-gray umbrella. The plastic bonnet was the silliest-looking thing in the world. As a young child, it had made her giggle. As a teenager, it made her roll her eyes, but she never swayed Ava from wearing the thing. Ava, like Schwartzman herself, had the kind of hair that would frizz with moisture inside the house, so rain created havoc with the tidy bun that was Ava's preferred hairstyle.

Ava also seemed to have a sixth sense for rain, impressive considering that Charleston's weather was nothing if not unpredictable. In more than a decade of visits, Schwartzman could recall only one time when they had gotten caught without an umbrella. They were visiting the historic city market in the center of downtown, maybe ten or twelve reasonably short blocks from Ava's home. The market, which was always a vibrant display of crafts and jewelry, was one of her favorite things about visiting Charleston as a child. She remembered she'd chosen a small silver bracelet with a turtle charm. It had taken her forever to decide between the turtle and the dolphin.

"The dolphin is quite smart," the saleswoman weighed in.

"But the sea turtle is born on the sand and finds its way back to the sea by the light of the moon," her aunt said, making the choice easy. Then, on what appeared to be a whim, Ava bought herself a silver necklace with a sea turtle pendant.

On the walk back to her house, Ava had said, "Now every time you look at your bracelet, you'll know I'm wearing my turtle, too. It'll be like we're together even when we're not together."

Schwartzman wore that turtle bracelet day and night for months until the silver had worn off and it left a black ring around her wrist. That first day, with her new turtle bracelet, the two of them got caught in a rainstorm. In the distance of only a few blocks, they were drenched. Charleston had few cabs to begin with, and finding one in the rain would have been impossible.

With total confidence, Ava took her niece's wet hand, walked right into the lobby of a fancy hotel, lifted an umbrella from a stand that held ten or twelve for hotel guests, turned around, and walked out again. Schwartzman was certain they were going to be arrested on the way out the door, but Ava had assured her that she had borrowed umbrellas from them before.

On the walk home, the two huddled under the one umbrella. Schwartzman remembered the smell of the rain. Dirt, leaves, seawater, magnolia, hydrangea, every living thing was reaching upward as the rain came down, and the smell of Ava—a mixture of gardenia and something earthy like tea leaves—and the feeling of being tucked in beside her, warm, dry . . . loved. They were almost home when, without any reason that Schwartzman could recall, Ava stopped on the sidewalk and folded the umbrella. They continued down the street slowly, their faces turned up to the sky, and let the rain fall on them in fat droplets. The rain slid down the back of her collar and behind her ear, and when she raised her hands, it rolled off her palms and into her sleeves, then down her arms in a cold, wet tickle.

They arrived at the house drenched. Ava stood on the porch, unpinned her bun, and shook out her wet hair, casting droplets across the front windows and door. She shook and shook, and while Schwartzman watched her, Ava began laughing a low, girlish giggle. Schwartzman joined her, shaking her head and laughing until she was dizzy and her belly ached.

That night, after a hot bath for Schwartzman and a shower for Ava, the two of them sat by the fireplace and drank hot chocolate and made s'mores. "I haven't had so much fun in ages," Ava told her later as she tucked her in. "Or maybe ever."

The next day, her neat bun restored, Ava took Annabelle to return the borrowed umbrella, bringing along with it a box of local artisan chocolates as a thank-you for the front desk clerks.

"Ma'am."

Someone touched her shoulder. She flinched and saw the man seated by the window motioning to the aisle. People were exiting the plane. Schwartzman rose quickly but paused in the aisle before remembering that she didn't have a bag. She hitched her purse onto her shoulder and walked down the aisle. Though the Jetway was covered, she could smell the South even as she stepped off the plane. The scents of overheated coffee, a woman's perfume, the warm plastic of the floor mats, the musty odor of recently cleaned carpet, sweat only partially masked by deodorant.

Humidity increased molecular volatility, meaning odor molecules bounced around more, striking the human nose more often than in dryer climates. Good or bad, everything smelled more in the South.

Inside the terminal, she switched her phone back on and made her way to the street. As she walked, it buzzed in her pocket. Once. Twice. Three times. And then on and on until she lost count. *Hal.* How many times had Hal tried to reach her? Hesitant, she drew it out.

Thumbed through text messages from Hal. Saw the word *Macy* and her knees grew weak.

But her eyes found a text from her mother. `I can't make it to the airport. I will meet you at the funeral home. A. G. Woodward.` The address followed in a separate text.

Her mother was only sixty. Was driving to the airport so overwhelming? Or was she struggling with Ava's death?

Her mother had a weaker constitution than Ava.

And yet she was surprising, too. Her skill in the kitchen; her dedication to her charities with or without the support of the latest trend . . . there was a lot to her mother that Schwartzman didn't know or understand. It was almost as if something a decade ago—or more—had set them off on separate tracks that crossed too rarely to develop any real relationship, any familiarity.

The only thing the two had in common, in her mother's mind at least, was making sure Schwartzman was taken care of . . . by someone like Spencer.

Schwartzman gave the cab driver the address of the funeral home. He tried to make polite small talk on the drive, but Schwartzman focused on her phone. Reading Hal's messages made her feel both guilty and resolved.

There were six messages and two voicemails. All urged her to call him.

`Where r u? We need to get ahead of the questions on last night. We'll sort this out together,` the first text said. `U have to trust me.`

Each was increasingly more threatening, more alarmed. The last one read: `S, running means you're guilty. Even if ur not. It's what everyone's thinking. U gotta help me here.`

Guilty. But she was guilty, wasn't she? Perhaps not of wielding the knife, but certainly of luring Spencer to Macy. She started to power down the phone when another text popped onto the screen.

An unknown caller. `So nice to have you in town.`

A knob in her throat made it difficult to swallow. She started to respond but stopped. That's what he wanted. She navigated back to Hal's messages.

`Not guilty,` she wrote. `In SC.`

Hal must have been watching his phone as the response appeared within a few seconds.

`South Carolina?! What r u doing?`

She was dealing with the problem. She was confronting her demons. Her one demon. Reclaiming her life. Avenging Ava and Ken Macy and Sarah Feld. Hal would say it was not her place. She couldn't be judge and jury. She might get herself killed.

She decided on the one thing to refute any argument from Hal. `My aunt was murdered,` she wrote. And shut off the phone.

27

Charleston, South Carolina

Schwartzman entered a room filled with caskets.

"Oh, there you are," her mother said with a glance in her direction, then turned back to the man in the dark suit who stood beside her. "Mr. Woodward, this is my daughter, Annabelle. Ava's niece."

Woodward crossed the room and offered her a dry, cool handshake. "I'm so sorry for your loss, Annabelle."

Schwartzman thanked him and went to stand beside her mother. "I'm so happy to see you, Mom."

"Oh yes, dear." Her mother touched her daughter's arm and offered her cheek to be kissed. Schwartzman kissed it dutifully and scanned the line of caskets.

"This one is lovely," said her mother, waving at a glossy white casket.

A white casket made her think of the baby. The nurse who had taken her tiny body had promised. "We have to take her now," the nurse said, prying the bundle from her arms. "But you can take her and have her buried; I promise." By the time Schwartzman woke the next morning, her daughter's remains had already been destroyed. At Spencer's orders. She didn't count as a live birth until twenty weeks' gestation. She made it only to sixteen.

Schwartzman wanted to be cremated. But cremation was against the Jewish religion. Her father was buried, as were his parents. Surely Ava would want a burial. Jewish tradition held that the burial should happen in the first twenty-four hours after death. A homicide made that impossible. They would be lucky if they could bury Ava within a week of her death. Schwartzman had been a restless nine-year-old when her father and Ava sat for their mother. There would be no sitting Shiva for Ava. Schwartzman could not stay here any longer than necessary. Ava would understand. Her father would understand.

"Do you like the white?"

The white casket was so Southern, so belle-like; it was a terrible choice for Ava. And yet Schwartzman believed that everything that was truly Ava no longer resided inside the body being stored somewhere in this building or down at the morgue. Ava was gone. Long gone. Which meant the casket was for the family, not the deceased.

"Annabelle?" her mother pressed.

"Sure," she said. "Yes."

Woodward slid in. "So, it's this one, then?"

Schwartzman nodded.

"And for the inside? We can do silk crepe or cotton, velvet, suede."

"Silk would be fine," Schwartzman said.

"Silk crepe it is. And do you have a color in mind? Perhaps a more vibrant shade to accompany the white? Pink or something in the yellow tones?"

Her mother's eyes brightened at the suggestion of color, but Schwartzman only shook her head. "White, please."

"Yes," her mother agreed. "White is very nice."

"Fine, then," Woodward told them. "I'll get the paperwork started."

As Woodward left the room, Schwartzman turned to her mother. A few inches shorter than Schwartzman, she had an ample chest and rounded hips and bottom. She wouldn't be considered heavy although she probably had fifteen pounds on many of the anorexic-looking women who were her friends and contemporaries in Greenville. Schwartzman remembered her father was always very complimentary of her mother's fuller figure, which Schwartzman envied as she herself was built long and boyish like her father and Ava. The weight had always made her mother look younger than her counterparts. Today she was thinner, her cheeks and eyes more hollowed than the last time Schwartzman had seen her. "Are you okay, Mom?"

"Not really, Bella," she said. "I shouldn't have come."

"What do you mean?" Schwartzman asked.

"The travel is very difficult."

The drive from Greenville to Charleston followed Interstate 26 from the outskirts of Greenville all the way to Charleston and took exactly three hours. As a child, she had made the trip a half-dozen times every year. "The drive, you mean?"

"Yes. I think it was a mistake to come." She turned to her daughter. "I'm afraid I need to get back home, Annabelle."

"Of course," Schwartzman said in response to the panic in her mother's voice. "I'll push to get her remains released so that we can hold the services on Sunday. That gives us four days to talk to the attorneys and sort out Ava's affairs."

Her mother's lips closed in the thin, narrow line that meant she had made a decision.

"What is it?" Schwartzman asked. "Are you thinking we should hold the services sooner?"

"I'm driving back home first thing in the morning."

"Tomorrow?"

Her mother waved at the ceiling. "It's too late in the afternoon now. It'll be dark in a few hours. I can't drive in the dark."

"You can't leave tomorrow. You have to be here. We need a couple of days to sort everything out."

"I don't have a choice, Annabelle," she said, and Schwartzman noticed the tremor in her hands. "I need to be at home."

"I want to be home, too. It's just a few days."

Her mother walked to the door.

Schwartzman went after her. "Mama."

Her mother's movements were unsteady as she crossed the threshold.

"I'll drive you back home," Schwartzman told her. "I'll take you first thing after the services."

Her mother was shaking her head.

"It's only a few days, Mama. I need you here. I can't do this alone."

"You should know . . . I'm not well, Annabelle."

Schwartzman took her mother's hand in both of hers. Was she sick? Cancer was her first thought. "What do you mean? What's wrong with you? Cancer?"

"Cancer?" she balked. "No. It's nothing so clean as cancer."

"Clean?"

Her mother lifted her chin in the air. "I've got all sorts of symptoms but no diagnosis. A total mystery."

"You've seen doctors?"

"All I do is see doctors."

"Why didn't you tell me?"

Her mother waved her hand, dismissing the idea that she would share her medical issues with her daughter.

"What sort of symptoms?" Schwartzman eyed the street and saw a bench. "Come. Sit down." She led her mother to the bench. As they walked, her mother leaned heavily on Schwartzman's arm. The biopsy site under her right arm ached as they moved. When they reached the bench, her mother sat slowly, her face in a grimace.

"Tell me about the symptoms."

"Annabelle, it's of no use. The doctors can't sort out what's wrong."

"I'm a doctor, Mama."

"For dead people. I can assure you I haven't been murdered." Her mother extricated her hand from Schwartzman's and gave her daughter a cursory pat on the knee.

Hands in her lap, Schwartzman sat back against the bench. "But you're sure it's not cancer."

"I'm not sure of anything," she said. "But there is no sign of any cancer."

"Have you ever had cancer?"

"No, no."

Nothing as clean as cancer, her mother had said. So Schwartzman had the "clean" disease. The two women sat together on the bench. Her mother had visited Seattle one summer for some big garden show. Was that three years ago? Or four? "Well, humor me, then," she told her mother. "Tell me what is going on. What do the doctors say?"

"They tell me there's absolutely nothing wrong with me. That it's all in my head."

"What's in your head?"

"It changes all the time. I've got vertigo. Some days my vision is blurred. I shake." Her mother raised her hand, and as soon as it was at eye level, it began to tremble.

"Have you seen the eye doctor?"

"Yes. The doctor adjusted my prescription and said my vision is quite good for someone my age. My age." She shuddered.

Schwartzman remembered how her father used to tell her mother how young she looked. "Not a day over twenty," he always said. Her mother reveled in that attention. All these years after his death, who was there to tell her she looked great? And now she was burying Ava.

Were the symptoms just in her mother's head? A person's emotional state had a real impact on her physical health. Schwartzman considered the vertigo. "Are you having headaches? Or nausea?"

"Sometimes," her mother said, nodding, and Schwartzman felt a rush of sympathy. Her mother was young, but she was burying her last contemporary family member. Surely that made her feel uncomfortably mortal, as if she was next in line.

"What are the other symptoms?"

"I've got pain in my knees and back . . ."

Schwartzman waited to hear something that suggested a disease. What her mother was describing were the pains of getting older. "Why don't we go back to Ava's? We'll get you settled in, Mama, and we will talk about what's going on. You can decide in the morning."

"Oh no. You go on. I'm staying at the Embassy Suites."

Schwartzman drew a sharp breath. "What? I thought we were staying at Ava's. Together."

Her mother began digging through her purse. A minute passed, and she pulled out a set of keys, pressed them into her daughter's palm. "You stay there, Annabelle. It's all yours anyway. But I can't. There are too many memories. I'm just not well enough to go to that house."

Schwartzman stared at her mother. Her mother had rarely come to Charleston when she was young. In fact, Schwartzman didn't think she'd come at all after she was in elementary school. Ava had always come up to Greenville for the holidays. It would have been almost thirty years ago. "What memories?"

"Oh, did you know that your grandparents wanted us to have our wedding reception at the house? They wanted the services to be here, at the temple?"

"I thought the service was at our church in Greenville and the reception at Greenville Country Club."

"Oh, it was. I would never have gotten married in any other church, but that was what Ava and your grandparents wanted."

"And that upset you." Schwartzman wondered when her mother had become so frail.

"Of course it upset me. It was awful."

"Is that the reason you don't want to stay there?"

Her mother dismissed the idea with another wave of her hand. "Plus the house will be terribly dusty. It was always so dusty and moist. I never felt comfortable there."

"I don't want to stay there without you," Schwartzman admitted. "I could stay with you, at your hotel, if you would prefer."

"That's silly, Annabelle. You'll be just fine. You can handle yourself."

"Mama, Ava was murdered there."

"But the police are letting us back in. If they aren't worried, then why should we worry?"

Schwartzman stared at her mother. More than anything, she wanted to be mothered. A strong, reassuring hug. The one that said, "I will always be here for you. No matter what. You can always come home to me." But her mother was not that person.

"Oh, Annabelle. I can see you're disappointed in me."

"No," she said quickly, fighting off an uncomfortable rush of emotion and a desire to say yes. "I'm not. I just want to—" *Be your daughter. Be with you. Tell you about my cancer.* "I just want to spend some time together." Schwartzman blinked back the tears that stung her eyes.

"I'm afraid I have so little energy. I need to go lay down for a bit." She patted Schwartzman's leg. "You understand, dear. Don't you?"

"Of course," she said. She had to stop wishing her mother was someone she had never been. Ava had been that person for Schwartzman. Before that, it was her father. *Accept what she can offer,* she told herself. "What if I come to the hotel a little later? We can have dinner together?"

"All right," her mother agreed. "That sounds lovely."

"Six o'clock?"

"That works just fine," she agreed. "But if you make other plans, don't worry about me, dear."

"I won't have other plans. I'll meet you at the hotel restaurant at six o'clock."

"Good, good. That works just fine." Her mother stood from the bench as a taxi pulled to the curb.

"Did you call a cab?"

"Mr. Woolworth called it for me," she said as she made her way across the sidewalk.

Woodward. She was getting old. "I'll see you in a few hours," Schwartzman said.

"That sounds good, dear. See you later."

"I love you, Mama."

"Yes, dear. I know you do, and I love you." Without a backward glance, her mother wrapped her veiny hand on the door handle and pulled it open to slowly lower herself into the cab.

28

Charleston, South Carolina

Harper recognized Ava Schwartzman's niece as soon as she entered Woodward's funeral parlor. Like her aunt, she was thin and tall. Her shoulders held back, wavy, dark hair just barely grazing them. She wore a pair of yoga pants and a zippered hoodie under her trench coat. Travel clothes. Harper guessed she'd come straight from the airport.

Harper stood back while she and an older woman talked over a white casket. When she turned, Harper saw Annabelle Schwartzman also had her aunt's nose but her full mouth and wide, light eyes matched the woman with her. Her mother. She had been told that the niece was an only child.

T. J. Woodward approached. "Ava Schwartzman's sister-in-law and niece. They've made a selection, so feel free to go on over."

Harper hesitated. Although there was plenty she wanted to ask Ava's family, coming to the funeral home was an uncouth way to track them down. Her mother would be appalled. She decided she would simply introduce herself and ask them to call her at their convenience. And then she would hope that it would be convenient soon.

The younger Schwartzman leaned toward her mother. The mother, on the other hand, only stared at the casket while she spoke. The two women didn't touch, but in parts of the South, that was the culture. Not to mention that grief did strange things to people.

T. J. stood next to her, watching them, too. As an undertaker, he'd probably seen it all. A few years older than Harper, T. J. had been a troublemaker in high school. The locker chatter among her peers was filled with stories about T. J. and his friends. Drinking, smoking pot, and occasionally wreaking havoc in his father's mortuary.

There was little about T. J.'s person that was consistent with his profession as a mortician. He was tall and skinny with a mop of wavy blond hair that was just starting to gray. He wore a beard and mustache in an attempt to give himself an older and more mature appearance, which was, at best, only partly successful. When not dealing with a deceased's family, he rarely kept a straight face. He had never settled down and tended to date women who were increasingly younger than he. Harper suspected there was still a good bit of weed involved.

"You want an introduction, Harper? Not like you to be shy," T. J. razzed.

"Just giving them a little time," she told him.

"Suit yourself," T. J. said, heading for his office.

Harper followed as far as the main viewing room and took a seat in the front row. There were no services today, and it was as good a place as any to wait for the right time to approach Ava's family.

In two days, they would fill a room like this for Frances's service. Her parents and Jed. Harper would take a seat toward the back. Her mother would sit on the aisle so she could leave if her crying got to be too much. She was a noisy crier. Harper would wear her funeral clothes, a black skirt and blazer, and Jed would wear the dark-gray suit he wore to court appearances and funerals. The other suit he owned, navy pinstripe, was saved for weddings. There were fewer of those. More and more, Jed and Harper attended funerals.

The room was smaller without a body. At the front hung heavy velvet curtains in a deep purple. Thick ropes in forest green held them to the walls. Tassels hung at their ends. The carpet had the same deep-purple and green hues. T. J. had remodeled the room after his father passed a few years back. His choices suggested a sophistication she wouldn't have expected from him. The curtains were his addition, for what he called a mixed viewing—when some guests wanted to view the deceased while others preferred not to.

A large black cart with gold accents sat in the place where the casket went. The coffin caddy, T. J. called it when he wasn't speaking with a family. Harper listened. She no longer heard voices. She returned to the showroom. The two women were gone.

She hurried out the front door, where a taxicab stopped at the curb.

"Dr. Schwartzman," she called out.

Ava's niece shut the door of the cab and stood back as it pulled away. Only as she turned back toward the building did she notice Harper, who quickly closed the distance between them.

"Dr. Schwartzman," Harper said again as she reached her. "I am Detective Harper Leighton." Harper offered her hand, and Annabelle Schwartzman shook it. "I'm very sorry for your loss, Dr. Schwartzman."

"Call me Anna, please," she said with a glance back toward the street, as if she had remembered something she'd meant to tell her mother.

"That was your mother?" Harper asked.

"I'm afraid she's not well," Dr. Schwartzman said, her hand tight on the strap of her purse.

"I imagine this is very difficult. And you've just come from San Francisco, I understand—"

"I know. I should have told him I was leaving," she said, her gaze sweeping from Harper to the street and back again.

A note of panic in her voice. Something was wrong. Harper waited an extra beat before speaking. "Told him?"

"I'm going to call Inspector Harris right now. I just haven't had a chance."

Inspector Harris. Inspector? There weren't many departments that still called their detectives by the older term.

Anna's eyes narrowed. "Why did you want to talk to me?" She shook her head as the realization came. "Of course. My aunt," she said, answering her own question.

Harper wanted to ask about Inspector Harris, but she couldn't see a way to do it. "Yes. Your aunt. I was hoping to ask you some questions."

"I'm afraid it's been a long time since I've seen her." Regret was evident in her face. The expression was one Harper saw more often than she cared to consider.

Anna's mother had told her how little they saw Ava. "I understand. I'd still like to ask a few questions. There's always a chance that something you say might provide some clue to help catch their killer."

"*Their* killer?" she repeated.

"Yes. Your aunt's friend Frances Pinckney was killed, as well."

Anna's hand swept out, searching for a chair that wasn't there.

Harper grabbed her arm, but Anna Schwartzman had already gotten her legs back under her. She extracted her arm from Harper's hold. "Her friend? She was at the house also?"

Harper motioned to the bench. "Perhaps we should sit?"

"I'm fine. I just didn't know there were two victims."

Harper explained their theory about Frances Pinckney's death and the key to Ava's home, the fact that there was no sign of a break-in there. She offered enough detail to convince Anna of the urgency in the Pinckney case.

The doctor stared at the ground as she listened. Her face gave nothing away. Her shoulders were set back, her spine straight, and yet it was as if she were holding her posture under some tremendous weight. When Harper finished talking, Anna stepped away. She leaned down, pressing her hands into her thighs before standing and arching her back.

When she faced Harper again, her cheeks were damp, but she was composed. "I'll answer all your questions, Detective."

"Thank you."

She hitched her shoulders back again. "But first I'd like to see her."

Harper followed. "Of course. There are some injuries that might be disturbing."

Anna looked back at her, brows raised.

"I know your position, Dr. Schwartzman," she said. "It's different when it's family."

"I appreciate the concern, Detective." Anna paused. "I have to do it."

"Of course," Harper said.

Harper called out to T. J., who emerged from the storeroom. "Dr. Schwartzman would like to see her aunt."

"Of course," he said, the mischievous smile carefully tucked away. "Your aunt is in our prep room. We have a very talented hair and makeup artist who will work on her later today. So I want to warn you, she won't look like herself just yet."

"I understand."

"Most of our families prefer to wait until their loved one has been dressed to see them."

"T. J., Dr. Schwartzman is a medical examiner. In San Francisco."

T. J. pulled open the door to the stairs and let Anna pass. "In that case, follow me."

Harper followed behind Anna as T. J. led them down to the prep room. She'd done this before, many times, with the families of victims. People tended to be nervous before viewing the body. Weepy, hesitant.

Anna Schwartzman followed as though they were heading to a kitchen rather than a morgue. But why wouldn't she? This was her business.

T. J. paused at the door and peered through the small window into the room. Checking to see that other bodies weren't out, no doubt. He pushed the door open, and Anna stepped inside.

T. J. moved to the body and held the top of the sheet, checking with Ava's niece for a nod before lowering the sheet down to her neck and exposing her face. Ava's eyes were closed, and the tightness in her jaw had softened with the passage of rigor mortis.

Likely, T. J. had altered the dead woman's expression. He once told Harper that rearranging the deceased's face was the first thing he did when they arrived. A peaceful expression made it easier to be with them. It worked. Lying on the table, Ava Schwartzman looked at peace. Harper appreciated seeing her this way.

"Annabelle," T. J. said.

"Please. Call me Anna."

Harper wondered why she chose Anna. Perhaps Annabelle Schwartzman was too much of a mouthful or maybe Annabelle sounded too Southern for someone living in San Francisco. Either way, Harper would remember.

Not Annabelle but Anna.

"Right," T. J. said. "Anna, your mother brought over some undergarments, but we don't yet have an outfit selected for the services. Did your mother mention that?"

Anna shook her head.

"Perhaps she was going to do it herself," T. J. suggested.

"I'll select something tonight and bring it to you tomorrow. Will that work?"

"Yes. That would be fine." He moved to the body. "You may want to choose something long-sleeved. It requires less makeup and . . ."

Anna crossed directly to her aunt. People dealt differently with death. Harper waited to see if Ava's niece would take her aunt's hand or lean in to kiss her. Instead she leaned over and studied her face without touching it. Then she rounded the side of the body and folded back the sheet to reveal her aunt's arm.

T. J. glanced at Harper.

Anna lifted the arm and studied the ligature marks on the wrist.

T. J. cleared his throat. "Obviously, long sleeves would cover those, as well."

Anna made no reply as she turned the arm over and studied the underside. With a stoic professionalism, she checked the fingernails and palms, between the fingers, then made her way up the arm. When she was done, she placed the arm back on the table and brought the sheet down. Acting as if she were alone in the room, Anna walked around the gurney and repeated the process on the other side. Harper wondered if she would find something Burl had missed.

"We will also need to discuss the style of her hair and makeup," T. J. said. Harper sensed that watching her was unnerving to him.

"It is easiest," he went on, "if you bring in a photograph of your aunt as you would like her hair and makeup to appear. Or send us one if you've got a digital image."

Anna said nothing.

"I did mention it to your mother, as well, so perhaps she—"

"I'll take care of it," Anna told him, moving down the body and lifting the sheet to examine her aunt's legs.

Harper watched as she studied the body, waiting for her to say something. Make some comment on what she saw.

When she finally raised her head, she said, "Do you have a magnification lamp?"

"A magnification lamp?" T. J. repeated.

"Like a light with a magnifying glass." Anna glanced around the room. "Maybe for doing makeup?"

"I'm afraid not," T. J. said.

Anna finished her exam of the legs and returned to the head of the body. Beside Harper, T. J. seemed to let out a breath. But rather than being finished, Anna Schwartzman drew the sheet down until her aunt's entire upper torso was exposed.

A strangled sound came from T. J.

Anna regarded him momentarily before returning to her work. The bruises on Ava's torso were slightly yellowed at the edges. Anna moved to her aunt's face and lifted her eyelids one at a time before opening her mouth and inspecting her gums.

"Uh," T. J. said.

Anna finished by opening Ava's jaw and staring into her mouth before closing it again and pulling the sheet back up around her aunt's neck. She pulled a single hair off the sheet and let it fall, watching as the hair floated to the floor.

T. J. stared at Anna's hands as she went across to the sink and washed them.

She pulled several paper towels from the dispenser and walked back across the room as she was drying her hands. "He sat on her chest and held her nose and mouth so she couldn't inhale. She would have suffocated quickly." Anna was focused on the body.

"Those bruises were from his knees?" T. J. asked.

"With some sort of knee pad," Anna said.

T. J. stared at her. "How do you know?"

"I've seen a lot of imprints left on skin," Anna told him, her demeanor calm, professional.

Harper was impressed.

"It's an educated guess, of course," Anna continued, "but the placement and symmetry on both sides of her torso, the pattern left in the bruises—some sort of diamond shape—it all indicates some kind of knee pads worn by the killer."

"Our coroner said the same," Harper confirmed. "We took some measurements and images, and we're trying to match the marks to a set of knee pads, maybe track them back to the store."

"He won't have kept those." Anna tossed the paper towels in the trash and returned to her aunt's side. "He wore gloves to hold her mouth and nose," she said, running the back of her hand on her aunt's cheek.

"How do you know that?" T. J. asked.

"If he had used his bare hand, we'd see more defined, smaller perimortem bruising. I've seen documented cases where they've pulled whorls off flesh."

"Whorls?" T. J. asked.

"From fingerprints," Harper explained.

"He probably knew that, too." She lowered her forehead and rested it on her aunt's.

Harper touched T. J.'s arm and nodded toward the door. "We'll give you a few minutes alone with her."

Anna had tears in her eyes. "Thank you."

T. J. held the door open for Harper and closed it behind them, taking a long look through the glass before walking a few feet away from the door. "That's a first," he said. "What a loon."

Harper found it touching. How a medical examiner said good-bye to a loved one. The thing that kept running through her head was the way Anna kept referring to "he." Like she knew exactly who he was, how he thought, how he planned the murder.

Was it the result of working in a big city? Maybe Anna had seen enough murders that she understood how criminal minds worked.

The other option was that somehow Anna Schwartzman knew exactly who had killed her aunt and Frances Pinckney.

29

Charleston, South Carolina

Schwartzman stepped into the shade of Ava's front porch. The smell of gardenias lingered in the air as though Ava herself had just brushed past her. Chilled, Schwartzman zipped her jacket up to her neck despite the hot, stagnant air. From her pocket she pulled out Ava's house key, hanging from a thin silver heart engraved with her initials. A gift to Ava from her father. How many times had she watched Ava slide that key into the door, the little heart dangling? Their arms filled with grocery bags or sacks from the shops, ice cream from the parlor three blocks away. Laughing, talking excitedly as they returned home from their latest adventure.

This house was never empty. Ava never left her alone here. Even when the two of them were home and Ava was in another room—in the kitchen cooking, or in her bedroom—there was always the soft sound of her whistling or singing, the shuffling of her feet on the hardwood, the little noises she made when she tasted something that wasn't quite right or that was exactly as it should be. Even living as a single person in such a big house, Ava had filled the space.

Schwartzman pressed her palm flat to the door and waited, listening. Eyes closed, she searched for an image of her aunt in this house, of her standing on this porch. Instead she saw Ava on the mortuary table. The images were too vivid. The ligature marks on her arms, the perimortem bruising where he knelt on her chest. The house was silent.

She opened her eyes and pounded her fist into the wood door. Cried out. Then pounded again and again until the pain in her hand forced her to stop. She stepped away from the door and swiped angrily at the tears. *Go on, then. There's no use putting it off.* She slid the key into the lock and turned it. The bolt slid smoothly. She twisted the knob. With a sigh, the door was open. The entryway before her. The soft ticking of the grandfather clock, the flowers that Ava had bought freshly cut before she died, their scent musty as they wilted. Ava's smells. Toast and pine-scented hardwood cleaner and flowers. The smells of home.

The police had released the scene. It was hers now. The house and all its contents. Her aunt's life. Her grandparents' lives. All that was left of them were these things that now belonged to her.

She would be the third generation of Schwartzmans to own the home. Her family home. She loved this house. When she and her father came to visit Ava, it was obvious he loved it, too. With all its quirks. The one corner of the living room where the old hardwood floorboards had separated. Ava and her father had chosen that specific corner to play jacks because the uneven surface meant the ball bounced unpredictably, making the game more challenging.

The old china cabinet in the dining room where their grandfather, Schwartzman's great-grandfather, had used some sort of powerful adhesive to permanently attach his wife's teacup collection to the shelves so that they would not be destroyed if there was another earthquake like the one he'd lived through as a young boy in 1886.

The library was her favorite room. Books that had been her father's and his father's and his father's father's before him. One of her greatest regrets was how few books she was able to keep, moving as much as she did. But here, in this house, books were stacked two deep in the library, where shelves stretched ceiling to floor.

Her father loved the house the way you love a person, patting the banister at the base of the stairs like an old friend or carrying his tools around the house to tighten this or adjust that. Its location on Meeting Street in the historic district of Charleston meant it would command a high price if she were to sell it. But the thought was unbearable. Her family roots were here—everything that was left of her father's family. This was home. More home than the one where she'd grown up.

Schwartzman hadn't had a real home since her father died. Now she owned the one he grew up in. His bedroom was a den with a Murphy bed. She could sleep there, surrounded by his childhood books. It was the same room she'd slept in when she visited Ava all those years as a child.

Her father gone. Ava gone. Only she was left.

Alone to deal with Spencer, with cancer.

And all she'd left undone in San Francisco.

Schwartzman took one step across the threshold and set down her purse on the sideboard table. But she couldn't go farther. Being in the house was too much, too daunting. How could she possibly manage everything that was inside? The estate attorney had called to talk about making arrangements. She didn't want to make arrangements.

What she wanted was to sit in front of the fire with Ava and a cup of hot chocolate. She wanted to confide in her aunt, open up about her fears, her guilt. She had let Spencer get to Ava. Spencer would say that Schwartzman had forced his hand. That was exactly how he would say it. "You forced my hand, Bella. What choice did I have?"

Breathless, she stepped out of the house and yanked the front door closed. She had not forced his hand. She had not made him kill Ava or Frances Pinckney or Sarah Feld. She had saved herself, had stood up against his cruelty and walked away. Now she was back. Because he would slip up. Because this time she *would* force his hand. Force him to take a risk and make a mistake. She glanced through the glass panel beside the door. He could be inside.

She clutched the phone in her pocket. He would confess to her. Not even confess. He would brag about what he had done, be proud of it. If she could get him on tape, the confession would be enough. Hal would help her. The local police would launch a full investigation. There would be evidence somewhere. No one could cover every trace. Not even Spencer.

But first she had to confront him. She had to let him get to her. She had to see him and let him touch her, let him close. Her stomach tightened; a deep shudder curved along her spine. She rubbed her arms and stepped away from the door.

Now could be that moment. But she couldn't. Not in Ava's house. Not where he took her aunt's life. She needed to find a way to control the sharp pain of that loss, the debilitating rawness. To face him, she had to be strong, resilient. She needed to be every bit as calculating as he was. With a deep breath, she turned the key. The bolt shot closed.

She crossed the porch to the stairs. She'd take a walk. Give herself time to prepare for him. It was smart not to rush it. For tonight she could stay at the hotel with her mother. Leave for the hotel so she and her mother could share a meal, mostly in silence. They would make polite conversation. Maybe about Ava. Her mother would know so much more about Ava than she did, but she couldn't imagine her sharing that. Sharing anything.

Even if her mother couldn't—or wouldn't—share, she could. She'd start by telling her mother that she had cancer. That she was alone and terrified. She had played that conversation out in her mind a dozen times. In every version, no matter how she put it, the answer always came back to Spencer. "Call Spencer," her mother would say. "Let Spencer help you. Spencer still loves you."

He loves me so much, he killed for me. He killed Ava to bring me down here. That's how much he loves me. No. She could not say that. She had shown her mother the bruises to prove how she'd lost her baby. An accident, her mother had said. To her, Spencer was perfect. The perfect gentleman, the perfect husband.

Would Spencer kill her mother, too? Or did he leave her alone because she was his best ally? And how could she possibly keep her mother safe if she wouldn't believe the threat was real?

Schwartzman sank onto the top stair of the porch, the place where so often she'd sat and begged to stay with Ava—just one more night, one more hour—each time her father announced it was time to go back to Greenville. She dropped her forehead to her knees. From down the street came the sound of a crying baby. Schwartzman stood, not wanting to be seen by a passing mother. Ava always greeted everyone by name when they walked down these streets.

Schwartzman wasn't prepared for the condolences, the questions. She retreated against the wall, sheltered by the porch columns. The sound of a second child. She listened, waiting for the reassuring whispers of mothers, but none came. Only wailing.

She moved to the edge of the porch and peered down the alley behind the house. One of Ava's carriage-style garage doors stood ajar. More screeching. Then a hiss. *Cats.* It was just cats. Ava probably left milk for them in the alley. Quiet, then metal clanked and glass shattered on concrete.

Anxiety brewing, Schwartzman walked down the stairs and rounded the corner of the house. How long had the cats been in there? She hoped it wasn't a total mess. As her feet hit the gravel drive, she froze. *Spencer.* It could be Spencer. Cats. A ruckus. A perfect way to lure her. Her pulse drilled in her neck. This could be her chance.

She inhaled deeply and pulled the phone from her pocket, opened the camera to video, and pressed "Record" before sliding the camera into her back pocket with the microphone facing up. *You can do this.*

Charged with adrenaline, she scanned the side of the house for a weapon. A shovel or a rake would be ideal, but Ava didn't do her own gardening. Along the side of the garage was a metal fence stake, maybe two and a half feet long, the point dug into the dirt. A little heavy but it would do. Schwartzman pulled out the stake and held it point first with both hands as she walked.

At the entrance to the garage, she stopped. The cats were quiet. She imagined Spencer using a recording, standing just inside with a device, waiting for her to step across the threshold. She licked her lips and tightened her grip on the post. *Come on, Schwartzman.* She could turn and run. *No.* She would wait. If Spencer was inside, he'd play the screaming cats recording again. She took a step forward. Nothing.

"Here, kitty," she said. Did that even work on cats? Was that too obvious?

Did Spencer know she was suspicious? Could he hear it in her voice?

The seconds stretched out in silence. She was imagining things. Not every unusual thing that happened was caused by Spencer. Perhaps the cats were real. Like her cancer. Oh, if only Spencer had made that up.

She took a step forward and gave the garage door a little nudge with her foot. A small gray cat sprinted out from behind the door. Schwartzman jumped back. The cat ran partway down the alley and stopped to stare back at her. It was hardly bigger than a kitten. An actual cat. Not a recording.

She exhaled and pushed the garage door, cautious. The sunlight cut a bright pathway across the floor, and in the center was a small tabby cat, sitting on its haunches.

Schwartzman had never owned a cat. Only a series of fish and, for about ten months, a single turtle named Humphrey. Her mother didn't want cats in the house. But Ava had cats over the years—occasionally hers but more often just ones she fed. There was always a bowl of milk out. Schwartzman propped the garage door open with a rock and lifted the metal stake over her shoulder. Ears perked, she took a single step inside. Halted and scanned the corners of the room as she moved slowly toward the tabby. The garage space was open: no large boxes, no equipment, nothing big enough to hide behind. Spencer was not here. The side door was fashioned with a cat door. She lowered the stake onto the floor and reached out her hand.

"Here, kitty kitty," she said in her most soothing voice. "Come on." The cat rose onto all fours, arching its back high in the air as she got close. Schwartzman lowered into a squat, offering a hand. "It's okay. Come here, kitty."

While she waited for the cat to make the first move, she glanced at the damage. Across the garage, a paint can was turned on its side. The top had popped off, and white paint puddled on the cement floor. Beside it, an old lamp lay broken, porcelain shards sitting in the wet paint—she remembered that lamp from the table beside Ava's favorite chair. The crimson silk shade lay just at the edge of the white paint. She eyed the cat, who appeared in no rush at all. When she tried to scoop it up, the cat sprinted past her and out the door.

If they were Ava's cats, surely there was food for them somewhere, even if they were wild. Schwartzman didn't see any litter box or food, only the spilled paint and broken lamp. She stooped down and righted the paint can. The smell emanating from the can was acrid, far more intense than paint.

She used the inside of her elbow to cover her mouth and reached to save the lamp shade. As she came up, she struck something solid behind her. Something human. "No," she cried and launched herself forward. Her palms skimmed the concrete. He yanked her backward, her knees coming off the ground.

She flailed against him and landed on her backside. The impact vibrated in her spine, knocked her wind out. Before she could catch her breath, he had hold of her again. She swung her elbows, struggling to connect with his head. "Let go of me."

He wrenched her closer, pulling her into his lap. Gucci cologne. Spencer's cologne. He pressed a cloth over her face. Another smell.

From the paint can. *No. Not paint. Chloroform.* She tried to pull his hands free, but he was too strong.

Then it was gone, leaving her dizzy and nauseous as his arms closed around her throat. She latched on, tried to pry away his arm. He said nothing. The hold tightened.

She opened her mouth to scream, but no sound came out.

The pressure grew painful. She blinked against the blind spots in her vision. His shirtsleeves and elbows were visible in front of her. He wore some sort of blue denim like a car mechanic. "Spencer," she choked out in a raspy voice.

"You still know me, Bella." The voice in her ear.

Nausea rose in her gut. Fear swelled to fill her ribs.

Think calm thoughts—get him to talk. But the hold was too tight. White spots grew until her vision was blank. She thrashed, trying to connect her elbows to her chest, but she was pinned too tight. She clawed at his arms with every bit of energy she had. Something hard beneath his shirtsleeves protected the skin from her nails. She fought to pitch herself forward, to reach her hands to the floor. His weight was too much.

The pressure loosened ever so slightly on her neck. She stole several breaths, blinked away the flashes of lights.

"Don't fight," he whispered. "You're not well, Bella. You have to take care of yourself."

She froze at the mention of her cancer. A sob caught in her throat.

"I'm going to take care of you, Bella. You need me. You can't go through cancer alone. The chemo, the radiation . . . say you need me, Bella."

She shook her head. Her chest heaved. She couldn't do it. She couldn't say the words, not even to catch him.

"Yes," he said firmly. "This is life or death, Bella. You will die without me. You have cancer. Eating away at you."

But he was wrong. She could survive the cancer. She could fight that.

"You have to stay," he said. An edge in his voice. The way there always was just before he hurt her. "You can't run away. You know I won't let you go again." As quickly as the pressure had eased, it tightened again.

She dug her chin into his arm. Struggled to wedge it between his arm and her neck, to relieve the pressure on her carotid. Not enough oxygen.

"Shh," he whispered. "The more you fight, the worse it will be."

Her lungs burned with the desire to sob. There was no air in her. She forced herself to be still.

The pressure lightened. She took a full breath. Cried out.

The choke tightened. "Bella," he warned.

She clamped her mouth shut. Grabbed hold of his arm again, tried to find the border of the arm protection, some vulnerable spot. Tears streamed down her face. *Let him win. Let him have this. He won't kill you. He doesn't want you dead. He wants you back.* Her stomach heaved in a tide of nausea. She went limp.

"Good girl. That's it."

She willed herself to be motionless. Closed her eyes. Focused on the burning smell of chloroform. Willed away the scent of Spencer. Imagined the morgue. Her tools. Her tray. The cold metal handle of the scalpel. The phone. She was recording him on the phone.

His lips on her temple. The soft kiss like a knife.

She clawed at his arm.

His hold tightened.

She couldn't fight anymore. The fight drained away.

She was strong. But he was stronger.

"I've missed the feel of you, Bella." His fingers on her jaw. Across her cheek. "I've missed your taste." His tongue on her cheek. Then at the corner of her mouth. She gagged, wanted to spit. "How I've missed it."

A whimper escaped her lips. How had she thought she could stand up to him? Trick him to confess? She was naive. Stupid.

He loosened his hold, pressed his lips to her ears. "You've missed me, too. But we'll be together."

She drew a breath against the burning in her throat, felt the sobs break free.

His thumb swept across her tears. "There's no need to cry, Bella. I forgive you. I forgive you for leaving." His lips on the line of her hair. "Because now we can be together. Ava made that happen."

At the sound of Ava's name, Schwartzman bucked against his hold. Again she swung her elbows. But he held her too tight, too close. She reached her hands back and tried to pinch and claw at his face, couldn't reach. She would not give up.

The arm across her throat tightened.

She silenced her body. *Wait. Wait for an opening.* He couldn't hold her forever. *Don't move,* she told herself. *Then you can escape.* She imagined his fingers on her face, his kiss, his tongue. Fingerprints. DNA. Evidence. The recording on her phone. It would all be captured. The only thing to do was wait and get away. Then she could prove what he had done. All of it.

"You should sleep, Bella. We can talk later." His arms clenched across her neck. She bucked against him. The hold cinched tighter. She reached back. Grabbed a pant leg. Tried to scratch, pinch, dig. Bright spots of light crossed her vision. Tingling in her hands and feet.

Wait. She opened her mouth to speak, choked as the word rose in her throat.

He loosened the grip.

"Please. I'll stay," she croaked, the words fire in her throat. "I promise."

"I know you will, Bella."

"Now," she said. "We can be together."

"That's a good girl."

She waited for him to let go, but a beat passed and the pressure was back. Harder. The lights more blinding. A shooting pain in her right eye. *No. No.* But the words didn't come out.

"I've got you," he whispered.

Blacking out.

"Good night, sweet girl."

The lights grew brighter. The fight was lost.

She was alone. With Spencer. She'd never be free. Panic rose in a black wave and swallowed her.

30

Charleston, South Carolina

Harper leaned her forehead against the closed freezer door. It wasn't cold. Not even the slightest bit. She wished it were. She longed for cold air on her face and neck. Lately Charleston was too hot. Too crowded. Too city. She was getting old. Living close to downtown had always appealed to her even though it meant living in a tiny house with a huge mortgage. Only the memory of last month's utility bill kept her from sticking her head in the freezer for ten minutes. Almost $200 for their thirteen-hundred-square-foot place.

She and Jed had always managed. Dual income, one child. They made the numbers work. Bought cars used and drove them into the ground, traveled little if at all. In her fifteen years, Lucy had been on only one plane ride, to bury Jed's grandmother in Illinois when she was three.

Harper turned her cheek to the freezer. As a kid, she loved the small walk-in freezer in her parents' restaurant, which she was largely forbidden from entering. Her mother was convinced that Harper would get locked in and somehow forgotten there. The allure was too strong in the hot weather, and anytime she didn't have a specific task to complete,

Harper disappeared to the back corner and yanked on the metal lever. There was a hissing as the door cracked, the crisp cold rolling over her like a spell. Among the grills and ovens in Charleston in the middle of July or August, that walk-in was the closest thing to heaven on earth.

She gave up on the idea of a frosty fix. Instead she found the last bottle of Dixie beer from the six-pack Jed's brother brought down on his last trip from Durham.

The heavy beer was the kind that might help her sleep. That was what she needed. A deep, dark sleep. The kind of sleep to help her forget this case. Anna Schwartzman knew something that she wasn't saying. But why? If she knew the identity of the killer, why keep that a secret? To protect someone?

It was obvious Schwartzman cared about her aunt. She'd seemed genuinely distraught that there was another murder. So what possible incentive did she have to hold something back?

So desperate for a lead, Harper had Googled the Inspector Harris Schwartzman had mentioned on a lark. There were a ton of Harrises in the California police departments. But when she added *Inspector* as his title and narrowed the search to San Francisco, she came up with only one.

Inspector Hal Harris. Homicide.

Harper left him a long, rambling message. Who knew if he'd even call her back?

She grabbed the beer bottle by the throat, popped the top, and sat in a kitchen chair.

Why the hell couldn't they find a single witness who had seen someone enter Ava Schwartzman's home? Two wealthy women dead in two days. Four blocks apart. Friends, but so very different.

Frances Pinckney had been a stay-at-home mom to her three children, married for forty-two years. She attended church and garden club and played bridge with friends.

Ava Schwartzman, on the other hand, had never married or even had a serious longtime lover. At least not one that anyone knew about. She lived in the house her parents had bought when they came to Charleston to escape religious persecution as German Jews just before the start of World War II. She attended law school and continued to practice until the day she died. Ava was heavily involved in philanthropy and donated primarily to organizations working to protect civil rights.

According to Frances Pinckney's children, the two women became friends when Ava did the Pinckneys' estate planning, before Thomas Pinckney passed. As was natural in that kind of situation, Frances relied heavily on Ava in the months after her husband's death, and the two women had begun a friendship. The children told Harper that their mother and Ava had dinner almost every week. No one knew exactly what they had in common, but both women counted the other as a close confidante.

And now both were dead. As with Frances Pinckney's death, there was no indication that robbery was a motive in Ava's death. No signs of forced entry, although there was the possibility that a key to Ava Schwartzman's house was taken from Pinckney's home.

But there was no way to prove it.

Harper groaned and pulled herself up from the table, draining the last of the beer, then filling a bowl with chips. She had a terrible weakness for sea salt and vinegar chips.

Not the healthiest dinner, but Jed and Lucy would stop for dinner on the way back from the volleyball game in Charlotte, and Harper had no inclination to cook for herself. One bowl. What could it hurt? She used a healthy-size cereal bowl, topped it off, and tucked the bag under her arm in case she wanted a little more, then went back to the bedroom, where she changed into her pajamas and climbed into bed.

Across the room, her phone let out a desperate ping to indicate a voicemail. The call had come from an unfamiliar number with a 415 area code. Missouri maybe. Or was that 414?

She pushed "Play" on the voicemail and pressed the "Speaker" button.

"Detective Leighton, my name is Hal Harris. I'm a homicide inspector in San Francisco."

She sat up. Inspector Harris had returned her call.

"I got your name from Captain Brown," the message continued. "Captain Brown also gave me your home number, so I apologize in advance if I'm interrupting dinner."

"This is probably going to sound a little weird"—he made a sound like a soft chuckle—"sorry. The accent on your voicemail reminds me of my mom's sister. She's from Savannah. She used to call everything bat-shit crazy. That's what made me laugh just now." The voice stopped, and Harper thought he'd disconnected.

A soft sigh. "It's been a long day, Detective, but I hear you've got a homicide victim out there named Ava Schwartzman. I've got one out here, and I think they're connected. And this is going to seem—well, it's going to sound bat-shit crazy, excuse my French. I believe the cases are related to my colleague out here. She's the medical examiner, and her name is Annabelle Schwartzman and—" There was a beep and the message ended.

Harper stared at the machine. It didn't sound as if Inspector Harris had gotten her message at all. She lifted her phone to call Captain Brown when it rang in her hand. The same phone number.

"Detective Leighton," she said.

"Oh, hi," came the same voice from the message. "I was leaving a message and I got cut off." A brief stop. "Actually, if you didn't get it, that would be g—"

"I did. I just heard the message. This is Inspector Harris?"

"Yes. And sorry about that message," he said. "I'm afraid I probably didn't make much sense."

The inspector sounded about her age—late thirties, early forties. A gruff tone but a kind voice. In years of detective work, Harper had learned to tell a lot of information in a very quick time. "I called you earlier today. Did you get my message?"

"You called me?"

"Yes. Maybe three hours ago."

"No. I'm sorry. I'm confused," Hal admitted. "What did you call me about?"

"Same thing you're calling me about, I think. And you ought to be confused. I know I am. None of this makes a lick of sense," Harper told him.

"I'm working this one alone, and it's making me nuts. So you heard about my colleague out here? Annabelle Schwartzman."

"Actually, I met her earlier today."

There was a brief pause on the line. "She did go out there." His voice dropped to a whisper. "Damn."

"She seemed to think she knew something about her aunt's death, as well, but she asked if we could meet tomorrow to talk." Harper sighed audibly. "I sure would appreciate if one of y'all would let me in on what's going on."

"I'm happy to tell you, Detective Leighton."

"Call me Harper, please."

"Okay, Harper. I have to warn you, though—it's kind of a long story. I'm not sure if you've got someplace you need to be."

Offering up information without asking for anything in return was a rare event in police work. Usually "cooperating" meant handing over everything you had on a case and getting out of the way. Harper had a good feeling about Inspector Harris.

"Now is perfect," Harper told him, settling back against the pillows as Hal Harris started the story about a woman who may have been killed by a woman posing as her sister. An obsessed ex-husband. At the center of it, Annabelle Schwartzman. Harper let him talk, interrupting only for clarification, and ate her chips. As he explained that he believed the murder in Charleston might be related, Harper reached for a pen and paper. "His name is Spencer MacDonald, and he's a mean SOB."

"Spencer MacDonald?" she repeated. "He's here in Charleston?"

"Greenville. I've been in touch with a deputy down there, but I've done about all I can do from here. I'm privy to some very nasty details about MacDonald, and after what we've seen out here, I think he's more cunning than I gave him credit for."

"I've got some contacts down there," she told him. "Let me see what I can find out in the morning, and I'll give you a call."

"Be careful, Detective. One of our patrol officers was assaulted last night. Eighteen stab wounds."

Violent crimes in Charleston were rarer than one might think. They had their share of drug- and gang-related murders, some domestic situations that escalated to murder. But deaths like Frances Pinckney's and Ava Schwartzman's, the kind of man who would stab a police officer eighteen times, those were rare. Almost unheard of. She'd certainly never had one in her career. Harper stared at the name she'd scrawled on the notepad. "You think MacDonald did that? So he's in San Francisco now?"

"No," Hal said. "In fact, I confirmed earlier today that he hasn't been out of South Carolina since a visit to his mother in Florida a few months back."

"So, how did he stab a patrol officer—"

"We don't know. In fact, we know almost nothing. Only what Schwartzman told me. That she woke up at approximately one in the morning and found the officer in her bed, fully dressed and bleeding to death."

"And you believe her?"

"I want to," he admitted.

The woman she met today was reserved, stoic. She knew better than to judge Anna Schwartzman by her demeanor in the mortuary. But eighteen stab wounds? "So if she didn't do it—"

"It's possible he set it up," Hal said. "MacDonald."

Harper digested the theory. An accomplice. Two men working together. MacDonald's motivation was related to Anna Schwartzman, but what about the accomplice? Why stab a police officer? For some, it was just for the pleasure. With the Internet, it wasn't even much of a stretch to think MacDonald might have found someone willing to do his dirty work. But why that officer? "The patrol officer and Schwartzman—they're involved?"

"I don't know," Hal said honestly. "No one seems to think so, but . . ."

"But they'd have to be for motive, right? If you go with the idea that MacDonald wanted to off the new boyfriend?" Harper asked.

"Maybe."

Harper wrote, "Stabbed eighteen times." How in the hell was that guy alive? She was afraid to ask. She'd seen enough to know he'd be in rough shape.

"Only problem with that theory is that setting the murder up at her house makes her look good for it," Hal said.

"True," Harper agreed. "Assume there's no motive for her to kill the officer?"

"None."

"You have any evidence at all that there was someone else involved?"

"The strongest piece we've got is the presence of a potent gas in the apartment. A general anesthetic. Lab's calculating the rate of dispersion to identify the concentration at the time of the attack."

"Be hard to stab if you're high on laughing gas."

"Right. The drug wreaks havoc with hand-eye coordination, among other things."

Her thoughts returned to the officer. She had to ask. "How is he? The officer?" A catch in her voice. One of their own. "He going to make it?"

"He's stable."

She imagined him in a hospital room, hooked up to the machines. If he were conscious, the inspector would have more answers. "But you can't talk to him?"

"No," Hal said with a sigh. "He's heavily sedated. Doctors hope tomorrow."

When Harper had met Schwartzman, she'd held her chin up, a show of strength. Nothing in her appearance hinted at what she had been through. The terror of waking in the night to someone she hardly knew. Then to find him bleeding to death. "You ask Anna why she thinks that guy was stabbed?"

"Schwartzman? She was pretty rattled when I saw her. Only thing she could think of is that they had a dinner together. Wasn't planned. They just both happened to be at the same restaurant."

"That seem likely?" Harper asked.

"None of it seems likely, but I've got no reason to think she would lie," he said. "At least not about that."

Harper tried to wrap her head around the kind of man who would orchestrate all of this because his ex had a random dinner. Surely there was more to the relationship than Anna was saying.

"I haven't talked to her since the night the officer was attacked," Hal said. "I don't know if she's heard that the officer—Ken Macy is his name—I don't know if Schwartzman knows that he's going to pull through. Hell, she might even think she's a suspect."

"Is she?"

"Well, until we find someone else, she's the only suspect."

Harper blew out her breath.

"All I know is she left here and went out there. It's a suicide mission. There's a lot she's not saying. She's—" He stopped, and Harper waited, pen poised. She needed to know what Anna was. If this MacDonald was after her, then he was also the best suspect for the two murders on her turf.

"Inspector?"

"I actually don't know exactly what she is. Scared, certainly, but oddly determined, too."

It was obvious from his voice that Hal Harris cared about Schwartzman. He respected her. He was worried for her. "I get the feeling this isn't the first time MacDonald has done something like this," he added.

Harper sat up. "You mean he's killed before?"

"No," he said. "It might be the first for that, but he's been harassing Schwartzman for a lot of years. And he's definitely capable of violence. Some of what I know was shared in confidence, so I can't be specific . . ."

"I understand." It had been an abusive marriage. She had long since stopped being surprised by the strong women who ended up under the thumb of men.

"These latest events suggest some serious escalation," Hal continued, "but it's not really clear what triggered it. Maybe something about Ava Schwartzman's murder could help make sense of it."

"You mention the one murder out here, but you know we've had two."

"Two?" His voice was tight, strangled.

He didn't know. "Yes," she confirmed. "A woman named Frances Pinckney was murdered first—drugged with chloroform and thrown down her stairs. Broke her neck."

"Made to look like an accident?" he asked.

"Yes. If not for the coroner catching the smell of chloroform and the issue of a dog who was inexplicably silent, it might have worked."

"But Captain Brown told me Ava Schwartzman was asphyxiated, correct? Was that set up to look like an accident?"

"Not at all," Harper told him. The image of Ava's rail-thin frame tied to the bed came unbidden, and she tried to force it away. "The murder was rather brutal, actually. She was tied to the bedposts and asphyxiated by someone sitting on her chest and applying pressure over her nose and mouth. Then her body was left tied to the bedposts."

"Staged."

"In some sense," Harper agreed. Harper explained their theory that the two women had exchanged house keys, adding that they had never located Ava's key at Frances Pinckney's house.

"He killed her to get access to Ava," Hal said in a whisper, and Harper felt chills run across her shoulders and back.

"How was your victim killed?" she asked.

"Drowned," he said. "And then staged."

A drowning, a woman thrown down the stairs, an asphyxiation. In quick succession but no obvious pattern or purpose for the type of murder in each case. Harper couldn't make sense of it.

"The other murder out there—what was her name again?" Hal asked.

"Frances Pinckney," Harper repeated. She wondered how long Frances's name would come with the image of her lying on the base of the stairs, her neck at that unnatural angle. It would fade. The images always faded. But they never went away. She still had the first ones in her head.

"The method is less personal than the other two?" Hal asked.

"Much," Harper agreed, happy to focus away from Pinckney. "Ava Schwartzman was asphyxiated. Your victim drowned." She considered the two deaths. "Both focus on breath. He stopped them both from breathing."

"Well, in the case of the victim out here, someone did it for him."

"But you've got no idea who?" Harper asked. She had never had a case of two killers working together in some organized fashion. "Some sort of apprentice?"

"I don't think MacDonald would risk letting himself be known to another criminal. He's arrogant but unbelievably careful. And good. He's too damn good."

If he didn't train someone personally, he might have turned to the Internet for help. Anything and everything was for sale on the Internet.

"Our one potential suspect is gone. We've got a BOLO out, but I'm not holding out a lot of hope on this end. I'll send an artist's sketch."

"You think the same person assaulted the officer?"

"I can't answer that one either."

"Please do send the sketch," Harper said. "I'll get the image out around here, too, and I'll be in touch tomorrow, Inspector."

"Appreciate it." There was silence on the line. "Detective?"

"I'm here."

"Is there any chance you could assign a detail to her? To keep an eye on her, I mean."

"In case she's a killer, or in case she's going to be a victim?"

"Yes, to both," Hal answered after a missed beat. She wondered if the pause was because he and Anna were close, if his hesitation was reluctance to say anything that could be damaging to a friend.

Either way, she respected that about Harris, too. Information left unsaid was often more valuable than what was put out there. He was on Schwartzman's side. That much she could tell. And it helped her gauge where her allegiances would fall, too.

"No problem. I'll get someone out there after we hang up."

"Thank you."

"No need to thank me, Inspector. I need a break in these murders as bad as anyone." Harper paused. "You think he'll hurt her?"

"I don't think he'll kill her," Hal answered. "From what I can gather, he doesn't want her dead; he wants her back."

"And how the hell does he think he's going to accomplish that?" she asked.

"That's the million-dollar question."

After they'd hung up, Harper pressed her finger against the inside of the bowl to pick up the last remainder of the chips. She'd seen plenty of jilted exes over the years. Many got drunk and disorderly, a few got violent. One drove his car through the front window of the house belonging to his girlfriend's new boyfriend and killed a cat. She'd been a police officer long enough to know people in general were capable of some crazy stuff.

But if what Harris said was true, this one took it to a whole new level of crazy. She phoned Dispatch to get someone out to Ava's house ASAP. As the phone rang, she reached for the chips and was disappointed to find the bag was empty.

MacDonald murdered two women to get Anna Schwartzman back to South Carolina?

Now what?

31

Charleston, South Carolina

Schwartzman woke to the soft hush of rain outside. A sharp pain throbbed behind her left eye. Even with her eyes closed, she could sense darkness in the room. The smell of paint. Ava's garage. She studied the silence. Spencer was gone. She was alive. Alone and alive. Was it possible?

She lay on her left side, the center of her back stiff and sore. Her hands tingled slightly, the blood supply cut off from being pinned. She studied the sensations in her body. Tenderness in her left shoulder and elbow. Her knees, no pain. Her thighs, also nothing. Her breath as she moved upward. She had been unconscious with Spencer. Would he have touched her or . . . worse? She pushed the thought away.

She tried to draw a full breath, but her hands were tied behind her. Pinned to her sides, her arms prevented her chest from expanding fully. She yanked her hands apart, twisting and pulling until the burn of the rope made her stop. Her left shoulder was pressed into the cement floor, the bone tender from rubbing against the hard surface.

She gathered her courage to open her eyes, squinting against the pain in her head, a piercing jab behind her eyes. A single light shone from a bare bulb overhead. Her fingers found the bottom edge of her hoodie, the waist of her athletic pants. She was dressed. She closed her eyes, blinked away the stains of the yellow light.

Behind her back, she wiggled her fingers and discovered something soft and flannel beneath her. An old blanket. A metal ridge dug into her right shin. She shifted and saw the zipper. A sleeping bag. She smelled smoke and something that stung in her nose. It made her think of rubbing alcohol. Spencer had pressed a cloth to her face, acrid with the smell of chloroform.

Eyes adjusting to the light, she searched the corners of the room slowly. She hadn't been moved. She craned her neck to search for Spencer. Waited for his shadow to emerge from the corner. He would relish her renewed terror. But nothing appeared. It took several minutes to be convinced that she was truly alone.

Her cheek itched, and she tried to scratch it against her shoulder but couldn't reach. She screamed and thrashed, struggling to pull her hands apart until she was breathless and the skin on her wrists torn and bleeding.

"Help me," she called out. "Please, God. Help me." She started to sob in huge, hiccupping breaths.

She stopped, imagined him watching. How much pleasure he would gain from her struggle. She refused to give him that pleasure.

Be calm. Think it through. She had to maneuver the rope so it was in front of her. There she could untie the knot with her teeth.

She edged the rope down her back and tried to reach her hands around her bottom. She got maybe halfway when something pulled taut against her belly. The rope was tied to her waist. Ava had been tied to her bedposts. Schwartzman cried out. Then clamped her mouth shut, expecting to hear his laugh. She was helpless. Trapped. Again.

Their entire marriage, she'd felt under his thumb. He'd wanted to know where she was going, who she would see. But now he had truly captured her, drugged her, bound her.

Worse, she had made it easy for him. She'd played right into his hands.

She pulled her knees up, formed a tight ball. He wasn't done. It was too easy. All those years, he had waited . . . only to leave her there alone? This was not the end of it, not by a long shot. But she wasn't done either. She rocked up onto her knees to get a better view of the room.

Lying on the concrete floor, maybe five feet away, was her cell phone. Placed perfectly out of reach. He knew the phone was there. He had left it for her.

She imagined plunging her hands into icy water, fought to ignore the burning in her wrists. She shuffled forward on her knees. The pain was sharp when she moved. She smothered her frustration. Took three breaths and imagined ice water again. The pain subsided slightly. The throb in her head dulled the slightest bit. She shuffled forward, closing the distance to the phone.

He told her he wouldn't let her go. He told her the cancer would kill her like he controlled the disease and would let it loose on her if she didn't stay with him. The notion made it clear how delusional he was. He was normally so calculating. How she wished he didn't know about the cancer. Worse that he was the only one who did. *Move forward,* she told herself. *Take the next step. Be strong.*

She filled her lungs and focused on the center of her body. She could fill her lungs, move. She scooted until she was within reach of the phone. Turned slowly around and leaned backward to grab it in both hands. She worked her hands to the left side of her back, craned her neck to see the screen at her waist. It worked. She could do it. Before she called the police, she wanted to see the recording. She took deep breaths and entered her passcode. She had recorded him. The screen came up. She saw her background picture of the ocean overlook from her favorite hiking trail. She swiped the screen with her thumb, found the camera icon. The video would be there. It had to be there.

But it wasn't. The last picture in her photo stream was the drawing the police artist had done of Terri Stein. She scrolled back, then forward again, her shoulder aching from the contorted position. The phone slipped from her hands and clattered on the cement floor. A sob caught in her throat, and she swallowed it down, wincing at the pain as she leaned back to pick up the phone again. She checked the camera images one more time, willing the video to appear. There was no video at all.

Sobbing, she curled forward and lowered her head to the cement floor, squeezed her eyes closed against the onslaught of tears. *Hold it together.* She took a deep breath and sat up again. On her knees, she aimed her phone's flashlight from her waist, illuminating the space in front of her and scanning the room in more detail. She searched the walls and across the floor. She expected a message, but there was nothing. The time read 8:57. She peered at the garage door, checking for light beneath. It was night. When had she come down to the garage? How long was she out?

Spencer had held her in a sleeper hold, his arm encircling her neck, then grabbing hold of his own bicep with the other arm. She could tell by how easy it was to tighten the hold. But a simple sleeper hold should not have caused her to lose consciousness for so long. He must have used more chloroform or something else.

She thought about calling the police or Harper.

She didn't want to be found like this. She wanted to free herself before she called the police.

Get out. She had to get the rope undone. That meant finding a tool to cut it. There would be something here. *Surely. Okay. Time to stand up.* She tucked her toes under and tried to roll herself back onto her feet. She got partway but didn't make it. Unable to catch herself, she fell hard on her left side. She bit back a cry and set her forehead on the edge of the sleeping bag, just within reach. Then she leaned forward and worked her feet beneath her to try again to stand. This time she pushed harder and made it onto her feet.

Guided by the flashlight, she made her way to the workbench. Somewhere there had to be a tool she could use to cut the rope. She would not give Spencer the satisfaction of her being found like this, like a helpless victim. She was not helpless.

What she found in the garage was a random collection of old extension and phone cords, nails, a tire iron. She turned her back to the bench and blindly pulled open the top drawer in awkward jerking motions, the ancient wood fighting her efforts. The drawer was full of twine, glue, paintbrushes, an ancient-looking drill, and a stack of old hangers from a local dry cleaner.

The second drawer was too low to reach without getting back on her knees, so she worked her toe under the handle and pulled. Paint rollers and brushes and stir sticks. A single hammer, several screwdrivers, every one of them a Phillips-head. She moved around the room, kicking things aside, scanning for anything that would work on the ropes.

Mounted on the edge of one cabinet was a large clamp. She tried to cut through the rope's fibers with the rough metal edge. She moved in a steady rhythm, pressing the rope into the metal until she was breathless. Then she pulled her arms to one side and looked at her progress. The rope showed no signs of wear.

She continued her search, moving along the garage surfaces. Nothing sharp. No hedge trimmers, no scissors, not even the most basic blade. Then, she remembered. Ava's broken lamp. *Thank God.* Gripping the flashlight, she crossed the garage, scanning the floor for the shards.

After two passes, she located the spot where the lamp had broken. The lighting components, attached to a long gold cord, lay on the concrete floor just inches from the pool of drying paint. Only a foot away was a handheld broom and a dustpan.

But the shards from the broken porcelain lamp were gone.

She had no choice but to call for help.

32

Charleston, South Carolina

Harper fought to swallow the gasp that lodged in her throat when she saw Anna Schwartzman. Seated cross-legged on a sleeping bag in the center of the garage, she might have been imprisoned for days or weeks rather than hours. Her hands were behind her back, her head down. If she hadn't looked up, Harper might not have recognized her at all.

The strong, straight spine was now hunched, broken. A patrol officer shined a flashlight directly at her. Anna kept her head down, the dark hair hiding her face.

"Christ," Harper shouted back at the officer. "Don't shine the light in her eyes."

The beam of light shifted to the far wall.

Had she been raped? She ran to Anna and dropped to her knees. "It's me," she said. "Harper. The detective from earlier. Okay?"

As Anna lifted her chin, Harper saw angry red marks across her neck as though the seams of a shirt or jacket had scratched violently across the skin.

"The police are here with me," Harper said. "You're okay now. You're safe." Harper saw ropes bound Anna's wrists and circled around her waist. Dried blood marked the lacerations on her wrists. "Was it him? Spencer MacDonald?"

"How do you know—"

"I talked to Hal Harris," Harper said, cutting her off so she didn't have to mention him again. "It was him?"

"Yes."

"You're certain?" Harper pressed.

"One hundred percent. Will you please untie the rope?" she added, nodding to her hands.

"Of course." Harper watched her. "Did he sexually assault you?"

"No."

Harper reached for the ropes and hesitated. "Was he wearing gloves?"

"No," Anna said, again pushing her hands toward Harper. "Please untie these."

"I need you to hang on just a minute, Anna. There may be evidence on the ropes." Harper pushed herself back to her feet. "Andy, call down to the Greenville police and get one of their detectives on the line. I don't care that it's ten o'clock at night—I need his help with this one. They've got to get someone out to MacDonald's house. No way he made it home already."

"Absolutely."

"Then get the crime scene team out here. Tell them to put a rush on it. I need them five minutes ago. And get the latex gloves and evidence bags out of my trunk so I can get these damn ropes untied."

Anna's shoulders trembled as she cried.

Harper touched her shoulder. "I need to get some gloves before I touch anything."

Anna shook her head. "No. He wouldn't have left anything. It's all clean. He didn't leave any trace. He's too careful."

"We don't know that, Anna."

"I do." Anna blinked back tears, but they escaped her eyes and tracked down her cheeks. "He kissed my face, my neck. I promise you—he didn't leave any evidence. Please," she added, spurring Harper into motion.

"I have to try," Harper said. She turned to shout at Andy; then she saw him appear with her box of gloves.

"Waiting for a call back from Greenville," he said with a glance toward Anna.

"Thanks," she said and nodded him toward the door. As soon as he turned away, Harper sank down beside Anna and pulled two gloves from the box. "Did he say anything about how long he's been in Charleston?"

"No."

"How long have you been down here?"

Anna shook her head. "I don't know. I just woke up."

Harper smoothed the gloves over her hands and started to work on the knots.

"He had me in a sleeper hold," Anna said, voice shaking. "He was taunting me. Tightening it, then letting go just before I passed out. Then finally he just held it."

The knot loosened, and Harper was able to help free Anna's left arm. Anna pulled it to her chest, cupping it against her. Harper worked at the other one.

"I don't know how long I was unconscious," Anna said, and Harper couldn't miss the vulnerability in her voice. The fear. If what Inspector Harris said was true, then it was there for her always. Had been for years. Harper tried to imagine living that way. She couldn't.

"I was only at the house maybe ten or fifteen minutes when I heard cats fighting," Anna began. "I knew it might be a trick. I thought I was ready for him. I really thought I was . . ."

Anna wore the same clothes she'd had on earlier. "You came straight here from the mortuary?"

Anna nodded.

Harper did a quick calculation. She'd left the mortuary just after four. That was more than five hours ago. Could Anna have been here for five hours? Harper freed her other arm. Greenville was just over three hours away, plenty of time for Spencer to get home again.

Anna pulled her hands close and rubbed gently at the lacerations. "When one of the cats ran out of the garage, I let my guard down. I was righting the can of spilled paint when he came from behind me." She tilted her head to the ceiling, fighting back her emotions. "He put me in a choke hold. I tried to fight."

"And you're sure it was him?"

"I would swear on my life."

Andy ran back into the garage with evidence bags. "Okay to collect the ropes?"

"Yes," Harper said. "If he was in here, Anna, he left something behind. His DNA has to be here. We'll collect the evidence and prove it was him."

"You won't find anything," Anna said, staring at the wounds on her wrists.

"There's always some trace evidence," Harper said. She thought about the running shoes in the entryway of Frances Pinckney's house. "Do you know Spencer's shoe size?"

"Ten, ten and a half. Why?"

The treads were men's size eleven. He could have worn larger shoes. That would have been easy. Too easy. "We'll check for footprints, too."

Anna looked so much younger than the medical examiner who had been in the morgue with Ava's body earlier. "I was recording . . . on my phone."

Harper glanced around for the phone, excitement tingling in her fingertips.

"He erased it. There's nothing there now." Anna motioned behind her, toward the back of the garage. "A lamp broke. He cleaned up the pieces."

Harper waited, sensing what Anna was going to say.

"He would never leave DNA behind." Tears streamed down Anna's cheeks as her shoulders shook.

"We don't know that," Harper said, trying to inspire confidence that she didn't feel.

"I do," Anna said. "I know it. He's on my skin, my clothes. Everything he touched. I want to scratch it off. But he won't leave a trace. Not a single trace."

"You have to hang on, Anna," Harper said softly, touching Anna's arm. The first rape victim Harper had encountered said the same thing. She had described an urgent desire to wash, to scrub every inch of skin, as if by removing any remnants of his DNA, she might also erase the memory of his touch, etched in her memory.

Anna pulled her hands into the sleeves of her jacket, clenched them into fists.

Andy jogged through the garage door. "Crime scene team's en route. Seven to ten minutes out."

"Mrs. Schwartzman was going back to the Embassy Suites from the funeral home. Call over there and make sure she's okay."

"Will do," Andy said.

Harper kept hold of Anna's arm as the flow of her tears slowed, then stopped, as her stature slowly shifted from victim back to the woman Harper had first seen at the mortuary.

—

Greenville police confirmed Spencer MacDonald was home, where he said he'd been all evening. MacDonald was an upstanding citizen. The police had no reason to doubt his story, and an ex-wife wasn't considered a reliable witness. That left Harper with no recourse to push them. At least Captain Brown agreed to put a rush on the evidence. Everyone was motivated to tie someone to the attack. If they were successful with that, it increased the odds of linking that same someone to the murders. For that, Harper had risked calling her captain at home in the middle of the night, and she'd been rewarded for her effort. The lab was already checking for the presence of saliva and other biologicals.

Harper spent an hour in the hospital room with Anna before going to the waiting room to make some calls. Standing in the corridor, she couldn't help but feel some excitement as the lab technician appeared.

Every investigator worth her salt knew Locard's principle, which held that the perpetrator of a crime would both bring something to the crime scene and leave with something from it. Harper had faith in the science. She believed in the exchange principle. She'd studied it for her undergraduate thesis and had seen it play out in every crime scene she'd ever investigated.

Not that it always led to a suspect.

What made Harper doubt herself was the look on the tech's face, the little shake of her head as she got closer.

"You found something," Harper said out loud, willing it into reality.

"No," the tech responded in a flat voice. "We found no presence of foreign biologicals on the victim. Nothing at all."

Harper stared through the exam room window, to where Anna sat on the exam table, wearing the hospital gown. She wore Harper's jacket over the top of it and a thin cotton blanket pulled over her legs. Her clothes had been entered into evidence. Except her underwear. Anna had been confident that there had been no sexual assault.

"Detective?" the lab tech prompted.

Harper sighed. "Nothing at all?"

"I'm afraid not, ma'am."

"She was sure he kissed her face," Harper said.

"If that was the case, we should have found something," the tech said pointedly.

"Or there is something we're overlooking," Harper returned, her tone a warning.

The lab tech opened a file. "The skin on her face shows the presence of dimethicone and lanolin."

Poisons? Drugs? They were words that meant nothing to her. "What are those?"

"Ingredients commonly found in moisturizer." The tech paused a beat. "And nothing else."

Harper replayed Anna's account in her head. He had kissed her. He'd choked her. "No foreign fibers?"

"We are just starting to sort through the fibers. The sleeping bag alone is like a bird's nest."

Harper opened her mouth.

"But no biologicals. None."

She exhaled a long, slow breath. She wanted to strike out. To scream. How could she go back in there and tell Anna they had nothing?

Anna had known he would be too careful to leave trace evidence, but Harper had been so certain that she would be wrong. "How in the hell is that even possible?"

"We scraped her fingernails, swabbed her face and neck, her ears. We checked her clothes for hair. All we found were several cat hairs. Two different types. I've got the details on those. They match the descriptions she gave." The tech opened her file.

Harper waved her hand. "I don't care about the cat hair . . ."

"There is literally nothing to indicate that someone else was in that garage with her."

The tech waited patiently. Harper couldn't believe he hadn't left any evidence. It was impossible. There was always something. But they didn't always find it. She hated that this might be one of those times. "Can you get me a copy of your findings?"

"We're dusting for prints. I'll let you know if we find anything."

"And keep me posted on the fibers," Harper added, praying something would come of this.

As Harper gathered herself to face Anna, her phone buzzed in her side pocket. She lifted it out, expecting Jed but seeing the number was from San Francisco. *Inspector Harris.*

"This is Detective Leighton."

"Harper? It's Hal."

"Hi."

"How is she?" Hal asked.

Harper recalled how shaken and small she had seemed in the garage. "Better than she was."

"The bastard kissed her," Hal said, repeating what she'd told him in her message. The anger hissed in his tone. "So we've got him."

"No."

"What do you mean no?"

Harper explained what the tech had told her.

Hal growled long and deep. She could imagine his teeth bared in frustration.

"I haven't told her yet."

"Christ," he muttered. "So what do you think happened? He kissed her, and then, once she was passed out, he cleaned her face?" A beat passed. "She said he was meticulous, that he never made a mistake, but that is just insane."

Harper felt a wave of nausea. "The trace they found was from some sort of moisturizer." She followed the thought through. "Oh, God. You think he cleaned her face while she was unconscious, then put moisturizer on her?"

Another beat passed while Harper considered the idea. She imagined Anna passed out, her attacker lovingly washing and moisturizing her face, a perverse facial.

Hal spoke first. "Yeah. I'm beginning to think that's exactly what that bastard would do."

Harper sent Andy to retrieve a bag of pajamas and extra clothes Jed had packed up from Lucy's closet as well as some toiletries from their guest bathroom. She took Anna to the Embassy Suites herself and refused to leave until she was showered, fed, and ready for sleep. Only when Harper was confident that she had done everything she could did she leave the room, pausing outside the door until the dead bolt slid into place and the locking bar clacked against the door frame.

It was almost one in the morning by the time Harper got back in her cruiser to head home. As her mind began to settle, her stomach growled. The bowl of chips she'd polished off as a dinnertime snack wouldn't hold her till morning. And morning was almost here. The smart thing was to drive straight home, eat a banana, and go to bed.

But Harper was a little too angry for that tonight.

Instead of heading home, she turned down Calhoun and headed toward the river. It was ten, maybe twelve, minutes to Krispy Kreme.

33

Charleston, South Carolina

Schwartzman woke in a strange bed, dreaming of cancer. But in her dream, the disease was Spencer's creation. He stood over her and touched her skin, a tumor growing under his fingers. In the dream, the cancer was just another way to control her. She pushed herself up in the hotel room bed and studied the bright sunlight that cut through the gap in the shades.

Instead of being disturbed, the dream left her with hope.

And an idea.

The clock on the bedside table read 7:47 a.m. She dialed the front desk from the hotel phone and requested her mother's room.

"I'm afraid she's already checked out," the clerk said.

Schwartzman set the receiver back in its cradle and slid her cell phone off the table. No missed calls, no texts. Had her mother waited for her in the restaurant last night? She dialed the hotel operator and requested the restaurant.

"I'm wondering if my mother might be down there," she told the hostess who answered. "She's sixty, about five four with blondish-gray hair cut in a bob."

The hostess put her on hold for several moments. "I'm afraid not," she said when she came back on the line. "I don't think we've seen her yet today."

Schwartzman was not surprised. Her mother was certainly already on her way back to Greenville. To be safe, she dialed her mother's number.

"Good morning, Annabelle," she answered as though this was just a regular check-in call.

"I just wanted to make sure you got home safely," Schwartzman said.

"That's very considerate of you. I'm just passing through Columbia." Her mother sounded the same as she always did on the phone. She might have been talking to the housekeeper or making a tee time. Polite, brief.

Schwartzman sighed. Some tiny part of her had hoped that maybe her mother had stayed. There was the familiar weight of disappointment. She knew enough not to tell her mother about Spencer. She would never believe Schwartzman—had never believed her before. Spencer would always be a prince in her mother's eyes. Nothing Schwartzman said would change that. "Will you text me when you get home?"

"Yes, dear. If I remember, but you don't need to worry about me." With that, her mother rang off.

Schwartzman washed her face and dressed again in the leggings and a volleyball sweatshirt that Harper had brought her. Today she would find new clothes. But first she had a call to make.

At a few minutes after eight, the phone rang in Melanie O'Connell's office, and Schwartzman prayed that Melanie was in the office today. And when the receptionist confirmed that she was, Schwartzman prayed that she could convince the nurse that she was an old friend dropping in for a surprise, that they would find an open appointment time to slide her into so that she could be sitting in one of the rooms, just like a normal patient, when Melanie walked in. And didn't Melanie love surprises? Wasn't she the same as she had been in medical school? Always one for an impromptu night out or a drink after the longest, hardest of days. Always bringing a light to the darkness of things.

Had it really been seven years ago that they'd met?

Melanie had been a fourth-year med student in Seattle; Schwartzman had been making the awkward transition of coming into a new medical school after three years at Duke and hiding from a crazy husband.

Her prayers were answered. A cancellation late in the day had opened up a slot. That the appointment was late in the day gave Schwartzman time to find a rental car. Time to stop by Ava's for some clothes. Time to get to Savannah.

She wondered if there was a way she could have convinced her mother to stay. Perhaps if she knew about the cancer. Or about the attack. But no. That was impossible. Her mother would never believe that Spencer was capable of something like that.

Schwartzman left through the side door of the hotel and crossed the park to King Street, where she caught a cab toward Ava's. She had the driver drop her at Tradd and Church, a block and a half from Ava's. From there, she could approach the house without drawing attention.

Ava's house looked exactly as she'd left it. Schwartzman used her key to enter and pushed open the front door wide as though to declare she wasn't going to be afraid. Surely Spencer wasn't here.

She entered Ava's bedroom, intent on not looking at the place where Ava had been killed. Caught sight of an evidence marker on the floor and rushed into the closet, closed the door behind her.

She would not look at the crime scene, not now.

Instead she moved quickly, rummaging through the closet drawers for something inconspicuous. She left Ava's house ten minutes later with sunglasses and a scarf to hide her hair. She wore a light jacket and khaki slacks of Ava's.

Again she saw no one. To be sure she wasn't followed, she walked for blocks and blocks in no particular direction.

As she walked, she took out her phone to call Hal. Fifty-some hours since she'd left that hospital room.

Before deciding she had to come here. Before her mother told her she wasn't staying. Before seeing Ava's body. Before the cats and the crash of breaking glass. Before being tricked.

Licked.

Strangled.

Another hospital, the opposite coast.

Was she a suspect in Macy's attack? Did Hal tell them she wasn't his attacker? *Could* he tell them? She was seized with the desire to sink down to the ground, huddle in a ball. Instead she marched on. Tensed up as she pressed the callback number.

Hal answered on the first ring. "Schwartzman," he said, the word coming out like some combination of a curse word and a great rush of relief.

"Macy?" she asked in a whispered voice.

"He's going to be okay."

A sound escaped her lips. A cry of relief, of pent-up fear. Pent-up terror.

"He lost a lot of blood, but you saved him, Schwartzman. If you hadn't stopped the bleeding when you did . . ."

But she had also put him in danger. She was sorry. It was the first thing to come to mind, but she couldn't say it out loud.

Sorry to Macy.

To Hal. For putting Macy in danger. For leaving.

For being stupid enough to think Spencer wouldn't go so far as to hurt someone else.

For Ava.

For . . . "He's awake?"

"We talked to him."

He was talking. He could speak. Her heart paddled against her sternum. "And?"

"He confirmed that your door was ajar, so he came into the apartment. Someone jabbed him in the neck. Some sort of drug. He turned and saw someone wearing a gas mask."

Schwartzman imagined herself in the next room, sleeping. Passed out. Had she fought at all? Had the intruder touched her? Watched her while she slept? She shook off the images. *Focus on what Macy saw.* "Could he tell who it was?"

"No. He said he was dizzy almost immediately."

"So, he thought it could have been me?"

"No."

She bit back a cry. She needed to hear that Ken knew she didn't stab him. She had to hear the words. "Hal. Tell me what he said! How does he know it wasn't me?"

"The eyes," Hal said. "He said his attacker definitely wasn't you."

Macy had seen the face. That was something. Surely he could remember another detail. "A man? A woman?"

"We don't have any more."

Why didn't they have more? Why couldn't they ask him who he saw? She imagined Macy lying in a hospital room, surrounded by tubes. God, what if he didn't make it?

She was afraid to ask.

"Not yet, anyway," Hal added. "He needs to rest."

Rest. Yes. If he was stable, rest was all he could do. Rest and gain his strength back.

But she had so many questions. She wanted answers. "Did he say why he was there in the first place? He'd never been to my place before."

"You texted him," Hal said softly.

"What? I never—"

"I saw the conversation," Hal confirmed. "Whoever did this, they lured Ken to your house on purpose."

Spencer had set Ken up. Had he intended to kill him? And why Ken? Why not just some stranger off the street? Could Spencer have known that she and Ken were friends, that they had bumped into each other one night and had dinner? She felt queasy.

She pictured Ken in her bed, the blood . . . shivered. "You promise he's okay? You're not lying to me."

"He is okay," Hal repeated. "He's weak, and he's sleeping a lot. We're going to try to talk to him again tomorrow."

Working to loosen her fists, she realized how scared she'd been.

"I want to talk about you," Hal said.

"I can't. I'm dealing with the stuff with my aunt. I need some time." She held her breath, waiting for his reply.

When nothing came, she started to panic. Even if he believed she didn't stab Macy, it didn't mean that the department did. Was she out of a job? Was she under arrest? She fought to control the waves of panic. "Am I a suspect?"

"No. Macy cleared you."

She kneaded a gentle pulsing above her right temple. *You're okay. They know you didn't stab Macy.* Hal was there, but she was here. She was the one who Spencer wanted. She was the one at risk.

But first she was the one who might have cancer, and she needed an answer to that. "Then you need to give me some time."

"How much time, Schwartzman? If what you say is true, that guy's a sociopath. He's not going to give up until you're chained in some room or dead."

"There's something I have to deal with first."

"Schwartzman, I'm in touch with the detective down there—Leighton—but we've got to work together on this. We didn't get anything from the box you gave me. Roger's team has been through all of it. And the flowers are clean, too. There's nothing to connect to Spencer. I need your help. I need to know everything there is to know about MacDonald, so I can work it from out here. A list of his friends, work buddies . . ."

"He's too careful, Hal. You won't find anything."

"Schwartzman. I'm not giving up on this. But I can't do it without you."

"I'll call you later today."

Hal started to say her name, but she didn't hear him finish it. She'd already ended the call and was heading to the old slave market to catch a cab to the rental car company.

—

She drove a full loop on the 526 before taking the ramp onto the freeway toward Savannah. Once in Savannah, she spent an hour driving along random streets, back and forth across town. She parked four blocks from Melanie's office and kept her head down, her scarf and sunglasses firmly in place until she reached the waiting room. All of it made her feel like an undiagnosed schizophrenic.

But she wasn't insane. Spencer wasn't crazy. He was incredibly calculating. Brilliantly so. Even she could admit that. Under different circumstances, Spencer might have been considered a genius. But she refused to believe that. He was sick. Twisted. But human. Which meant he was fallible. She clung to that idea with nothing short of desperation.

How could Hal—and Harper—link a murder in San Francisco to the ones in Charleston? There were no commonalities in the MOs. No proof that Spencer had left Greenville at all. Worse, proof that he hadn't. And no trace of him in any of the crime scenes. Even hers.

Which was why she'd come to Melanie. Since waking, she'd been haunted by the cancer. The cancer Spencer had discovered. Almost before she knew herself. And what if he had? What if the cancer was actually his doing?

It wasn't a thought she could share out loud. If she couldn't link the murders to Spencer, how did she expect to link a medical diagnosis to him? How preposterous to assert that someone three thousand miles away, not in any medical-related field, could have accessed her records. Let alone changed them.

They would say that she was in denial. Cancer was terrifying. Of course she wanted to believe the diagnosis wasn't true. It was natural to look for the possibility that cancer was another invention of Spencer's sick mind. She had been telling herself this exact thing since the idea first occurred to her.

Don't get your hopes up, Schwartzman.

Yet it was that slim chance that had brought her here and also why she had gone through every imaginable hoop to ensure that nothing about this visit to Melanie was traceable. Using a fake name to get a fresh read so she could be sure that Spencer wasn't fixing the results. How she prayed he was. For once she hoped Spencer was more evil than she imagined.

Slowly, though, as her stay in the exam room had gone from thirty minutes to forty-five, Schwartzman no longer wanted to be anonymous.

She wanted to see Melanie O'Connell as herself. Sit in a coffee shop or over a bottle of wine and share what had happened. Because Melanie was the only one aside from Ava who knew what Spencer had done to her, the only one she'd let in all of those years ago. The one who sat with Schwartzman long enough that it all came out. Who told her that she would always be there if she needed a friend.

So here she was—needing Melanie not only as a friend but as a doctor. *Maybe,* a voice told her. *Maybe,* she echoed.

Schwartzman sat in a chair against the wall of the exam room. She did not change into the gown or use the fabric to go over her waist. She did not get up on the table. Other than that, she acted like a normal patient. She waited, said nothing.

That was what she had wanted. A regular appointment with Melanie O'Connell.

Melanie had chosen oncology when Schwartzman chose pathology, and so the two of them had stayed close while their classmates wondered why on earth they wanted to face cancer and dead people when there were choices like pediatrics and family medicine or big-money options like orthopedics or plastic surgery.

When Melanie O'Connell walked through the door, she looked exactly as Schwartzman remembered her. Trim, petite, freckled, with brilliant red hair always in a ponytail. Like a grown-up orphan Annie. Only the new wrinkles around her hazel eyes belied her youthful appearance to suggest the passage of time.

"Hi," she said with Schwartzman's chart in front of her. The one with almost no true information. "I'm Dr. O'Connell." She glanced up to shake hands and stopped. Looked back down at the chart and then up again. She laughed. "Kate Victor. Our bitchy senior resident." The name Schwartzman used on her paperwork.

Melanie flipped the chart closed and set it on the counter. "Jesus Christ. Schwartzman!"

Schwartzman stood from the chair as Melanie moved across the room to hug her. "Hi," she whispered when they embraced. Tears welled, and Schwartzman fought them.

Melanie pulled her back, held her shoulders. "I can't believe it. Did Karl put you up to this?"

Schwartzman shook her head. "Karl?"

The smile disappeared. She waved a hand. "My husband. He's always trying to surprise me on my birthday."

"It's your birthday." Schwartzman remembered when they had celebrated Melanie's thirtieth birthday together on a private cruise in Elliott Bay with a group of graduating med students. One of their classmates had access to an incredible yacht. They'd had champagne and watched the sunset, one of those times when it felt as if everything would be fine.

"Forget it. Please. It's so great to see you. You look amazing. As tall and tiny as ever."

Schwartzman forced a smile. "Happy birthday."

Without letting go of Schwartzman's hand, Melanie grabbed the rolling stool from across the room and brought it over, nodding for Schwartzman to sit again. Her friend studied her face, and Schwartzman knew that she'd already figured out that something was wrong. Melanie was always like that. Able to read her body language, call her bluff. "What's going on?" she asked. She paused only a beat before adding, "Still him?"

Schwartzman exhaled. "Yes and no. Yes. But that's not why I'm here." Again Schwartzman had a fleeting thought—maybe more of a hope. "Or it might be."

"Explain."

"I've been diagnosed with breast cancer." It was the first time she'd said the words out loud. Like a gauntlet falling, like a death sentence, they felt so final. She wanted to stand up to it, to be strong, but the weight of the diagnosis was so overwhelming.

Melanie's expression didn't change. No reaction. No nonsense, no pity. Not like that sickening cheerleader in Dr. Fraser's office. "Do you have details?" Melanie asked.

"Invasive lobular cancer, right breast. Slow growing. Grade one. Less than two centimeters." As she spoke, Schwartzman reached into her purse and pulled out the reports she'd gotten from Dr. Fraser.

Melanie studied them, flipping through the pages and back again a couple of times.

"Does the cancer look real?" Schwartzman asked.

Melanie frowned. "Real? What do you mean?"

"I mean, is it possible that this isn't right?"

She read over the pages. "The reports look normal." Her eyes widened. "You think he could have . . ."

Schwartzman said nothing.

"How could he have accessed your medical records?"

"How did he find me in that bar in Seattle?"

"I don't know . . . faking the record would mean switching out the records with someone else's mammogram and biopsy. It doesn't seem possible." Melanie spread the photocopies across her desk. "But maybe." She studied the scans. "I can do a mammogram. The biopsy is a little trickier. We can compare these images to your breast tissue. Breasts are like fingerprints. No two are alike. I just don't know if we'll be able to make a good comparison using these printouts."

Schwartzman reached into her purse and found the thumb drive with the digital images. "The images are here."

Melanie swiveled the chair toward the door and stood, crossing quickly. She cracked it and stepped out for a second. "Angela, will you ask Dr. Thomas to check on room four? He said he had a cancellation. Then I need you to do a scan on a new patient. And will you please have Patty bring me my computer from my desk?"

Schwartzman exhaled as Melanie turned back into the room, grabbing the chart off the counter where she'd left it. Sitting again, she flipped it open, pulled the pen from her coat pocket, and began to write in the familiar backward left-hand scrawl. Watching her made Schwartzman tired. How many years had passed since she'd first made fun of Melanie for the strange way she held her pen?

In all those years, how little in her own life had changed?

Melanie rolled over to her. "Okay, I've got to check on a couple of patients. In the meantime, I'm going to have Angela do a new mammogram. First off, we'll confirm that the breast with the mass is, in fact, your breast."

"Thanks, Mel."

She nodded as if it were nothing, as if friends reemerged after seven years to check on falsified mammograms all the time. "I'm entering them under the name you left—Kate Victor—so when Angela asks you to confirm your name, use that one. Also, your birthday is today, 1979. I'll be back as soon as I can get away again."

Schwartzman closed her eyes during the mammogram. She didn't want to be tempted to look at the images. Maybe she could compare them herself, but she didn't want to guess. She didn't want to spend these last minutes worrying.

Here, with Melanie, she could relinquish responsibility.

She was safe here.

Almost two hours passed before Angela retrieved Schwartzman from the exam room and led her to Melanie's office. Before she sat, she studied the pictures on her desk. Two little towheaded toddlers—boys—and a girl who was maybe four with red hair and freckles. Another picture with a tall blond man. Karl, she guessed. Beside that was a picture of the whole family in a canoe, on a lake, the kids in bulky life vests.

The kind of life Schwartzman might have dreamed of once but had not dared to dream of in years.

Schwartzman knew the answer when she saw Melanie's eyes. Knew it as her old friend slid off her doctor's coat and displayed the gorgeous red blouse and black skirt beneath. Was certain as Melanie pulled her chair out and sat down.

"I've got breast cancer," Schwartzman said to save her the need.

"Yes." Melanie hit a button on her keyboard and spun the monitor so Schwartzman could see. Two scans, side by side. "This is the scan from your doctor's office—Dr. Khan." She pointed to the left. "This one is from today."

Other than a small section that Schwartzman knew was the biopsy, the two scans were identical.

"So, maybe he just switched the results on the biopsy. Maybe I have something benign."

"I called Dr. Fraser."

"What?"

"You signed the waiver to let me talk to him," Melanie said, laying her hand flat on the file on her desk. "I didn't want to come in here until I was sure."

"And?"

"You have to know what you're dealing with," Melanie continued. "If it's him or if it's real, so I called."

Schwartzman exhaled. "And you know for sure?"

Melanie stood and walked around her desk, sat in the chair next to Schwartzman. "He checked the sample images he took with those he got back from the lab. They're identical. These are your results." Melanie reached out to touch her hand. "You have cancer."

All the energy she'd expended to stay strong, to hang tightly to the hope, all of that was gone. All that remained was an empty husk. As she had all those years ago, Melanie sensed it. She put her arms around Schwartzman, and she, in turn, let herself lean into her old friend and confidante.

She did not think about next steps, about getting away, about the cancer, or about Spencer. For these minutes, Schwartzman allowed herself to simply fall apart.

34

San Francisco, California

Hal kept his phone in his back pocket, willing it to ring. All morning he experienced phantom vibrations and pulled the phone free only to find there was no call, no text. No word from Schwartzman or from the hospital about Macy. He'd been up since five, reviewing all his case notes over three cups of coffee and making the last of the phone calls to Sarah Feld's high school friends.

Her friends agreed that Sarah was different when she was home for Christmas. She had money, nicer clothes. She seemed happy. But she was also secretive. No one knew where the money and clothes had come from. Several suggested she had a married boyfriend. An ex-boyfriend suggested maybe she was into high-price prostitution. She hadn't even told them about the TV show.

With no leads left to follow, Hal had released the scene of her murder. He would have loved to find a way to preserve it, but nothing in his notes gave him cause to fight to hold the scene. Especially not when the building's management company was threatening a lawsuit. It came down to money. The apartment was too pricey to remain vacant.

Knowing it was his last visit, Hal took his time in the building where Sarah Feld was murdered. He went back through the rooms in her apartment, first without referring to his notes and then with them. He walked the corridors of the other floors, the stairs, and into the basement to the laundry and the trash room. He walked the stairs, twice. Sometimes this kind of exercise proved enough to pull something loose, to fire some piston in his brain, connect some wire that would illuminate the whole thing. Today he got nothing.

Standing back in the foyer in front of the victim's door, he studied the crime scene tape. He could pull it down. It would probably be a nice gesture. He wasn't feeling very nice. Instead he crossed the foyer to Carol Fletcher's door and rang the bell.

"Who is it?" came her voice from inside.

"Inspector Hal Harris. We talked the other day."

There was the sound of locks turning, and the door cracked open.

"Oh, sorry," she said, opening the door as she worked to tie her sweater closed. "I wasn't expecting anyone."

"I'm sorry to come by unannounced," he said. "I came back to release the crime scene and was hoping to ask you one more question."

"Sure. Of course." She hesitated, then let the door fall open. The dining room table was covered in papers. She motioned to them. "Sorry for the mess. I'm working on a deadline."

"I'll get out of your hair, then. I just wanted to ask about your interactions with your neighbor's sister. Had you met her before?"

"No. I'd never met her."

"Had Ms. Fe—" He caught himself before he called her by her real name. "Had Ms. Stein mentioned a sister?"

"Maybe. I knew she had a sister, but I don't know if Victoria ever told me anything about her. I'd seen the pictures of the two of them—the ones Victoria had in her place."

Carol glanced over his shoulder at the other apartment. As she did, the entry light shifted on her face, and the dark circles under her eyes were more pronounced.

"I appreciate your help. Are you doing okay?" he asked.

She looked a bit startled. "Having a little trouble sleeping," she admitted, motioning into the living room. "Plus the deadline."

"There are some good local support groups if you want to talk to someone," Hal offered. "I can send over some information."

"Thank you," she said. "I appreciate that. And I'll be in touch if I think of anything useful about Terri."

Hal thanked her and left her apartment. Maybe he looked as bad as she did. He wouldn't be surprised. He felt like shit. Across the foyer, the yellow tape on the victim's door caught his eye again.

"Ah, damn it all," he muttered and crossed the foyer to tear the crime scene tape down.

—

Hal waited for Roger in the small interview room. The plan was to outline everything they had on the whiteboard to try to pull the case together. Hal could buy himself only another day or two on this case before he would need to shift it off his priority list and get caught up on the new ones. Hailey and Naomi joined them in an effort to make it happen quickly.

Hal had drawn in the timeline for the San Francisco events in black. In green he added the events in South Carolina, though there was no evidence to link the deaths. Beside him, Hailey posted the images of the victims—bios, possible connections, dates and causes of death. Roger and Naomi filled in columns beside each victim with the key evidence they had collected.

Written next to Sarah Feld, the first item was "pendant." It was not identical to Schwartzman's. The variations suggested the two were crafted by different jewelers. The police had yet to trace either to a source. Line one amounted to nothing.

Next there were prints. Macy's print on the napkin led nowhere. The prints on the glasses and the bottle in the kitchen were the victim's, so nothing from them either.

Three, the lavender seeds from Feld's lungs. No good lead from those.

Four was the BOLO out on the woman posing as Terri Stein. Again, nothing yet.

Five, the security system failure at Sarah Feld's apartment was the result of a virus. The IP address came back to Feld's own apartment, which gave them nothing either.

Hailey stood beside him as he rubbed his head. "Not a lot to go on," she commented.

"Nothing to go on."

"We've got some traffic cam images of the person who entered Schwartzman's apartment before Macy was attacked," Naomi offered. "I think you saw these—right, Hal?"

"Roger sent me one."

"Let me take a look," Hailey said. She took the tablet and held it so Hal could see over her shoulder. The time stamp on the first was 11:09 p.m. The woman in the photograph had wavy, dark hair, shoulder length, partially hidden under a plain black baseball cap. She wore a black coat, tied at the waist. Black pants, but it was hard to tell if they were real slacks or the yoga kind women loved so much. Tennis shoes. She carried a black bag in her right hand, like a small duffel bag. Hal felt the same way as when he first saw the picture. It could be Schwartzman, or it could be someone else.

Hailey skipped to the next image, then the next. They all showed more or less the same thing. The woman never looked up. The cap covered her face in every shot. Her hands were under the coat sleeves. They literally had no clear image of her.

"What do you think? Is it her?" Hal asked Hailey.

"I can't tell," Hailey admitted.

"Not likely," Roger answered, walking through the door with a cup of coffee in hand.

"Why do you say that?" Hal asked. The hat was wrong for Schwartzman, but that wasn't enough. Roger would have another, more substantial reason.

Roger set his coffee down and pulled his phone from his pocket, handed it to Hailey. The image was a clear shot of Schwartzman's face behind the windshield of her car. "We have her entering the garage at 6:52," Roger explained. "She checks her mail at 6:56 and lets herself into her apartment at 6:59. She doesn't emerge again. The cameras inside the building are functional until 11:17 p.m. By that time, we've got this other person on the traffic cam."

"So no way it can be Schwartzman," Hailey said.

"Right," Roger agreed.

Hal studied the image. With the hat, the coat, the person might have been a man or a woman. There had to be something in these films to help them. He couldn't believe anyone could be that careful.

Somewhere there had to be a mistake. Find it. "Can we trace her back to where she starts walking?" Hal asked.

"We tried," Roger said. "She comes from somewhere down by the water. We pick her up about eight blocks from Schwartzman's apartment."

"If it's a 'she,'" Hailey said.

"That's what I was thinking," Naomi agreed.

"How tall is she/he?" Hal asked.

"We estimated somewhere between five eight and five ten."

"Could be a man or a woman," Roger said.

Hal turned his attention to the board. *Go through the timeline again; review what you know.* He felt so close to some realization, some clue that would break this thing open. He just had to knock it loose. "So there's an alarm in the basement at 11:39 p.m. Desk clerk follows procedure and locks the front door and goes to check the alarm. Comes back three minutes later and clears the code. What happened in that three minutes?"

"That's where we have a problem," Roger admitted. "From the desk, everything was working, but the system stopped recording, so nothing was captured. The guard didn't see anyone go by him, so our best guess is that the person posing as Schwartzman entered the building while the front desk clerk was in the basement."

"How did they get in the building?"

"That's the clever part," Roger said.

"I don't like clever," Hal said.

"Explain," Hailey told him.

Roger nodded to Naomi. "The alarm code in the alarm was for the exterior door. Shutting off the alarm requires a system reboot. The whole system goes down for about twenty seconds," Naomi explained. "There's no built-in redundancy to cover that time."

"Wow," Hailey said. "So the whole thing was planned to the second."

"Not necessarily," Roger countered. "It looks like the person on the street is holding a smartphone." Roger took the iPad and scanned through the images, pointing out a black blob that might or might not have been a phone. "The way she's got it in her hand, I'd guess it's a phone."

"And if it is? How's that help?" Hal asked.

"She—or he—could have set off the alarm from the phone. Easily."

"What about Schwartzman? She was inside the apartment." He could not stop thinking about her. Down in South Carolina . . . where was she this minute? Where was Spencer? Was she safe? Was Harper watching out for her?

Damn this whole thing.

"Halothane," Roger explained. "It's a general anesthesia, pretty readily available."

"Like laughing gas?" Hailey asked.

"Right. The gas was piped into her bedroom through the vent. There was a pressurized tank in the wall at the back of her closet.

Controlled remotely. We don't know how long the tank has been there. The gas would have knocked her out pretty quickly."

"A tank in the closet? How the hell is that even possible?" Hailey asked.

"We think it happened from the neighbor's apartment," Roger explained. "That unit was rented about two months after Schwartzman's was. Security deposit was put down, lease signed, but then the rental fell through about a week later. It could have been done then."

"I'd like to see a copy of the lease," Hal said.

"Sure."

"Also," Hailey asked, "do we have security footage?"

"No. We don't have anything," Hal said, cutting them off. "Even if Schwartzman is passed out, doesn't explain how they got into her apartment."

Hailey nodded. "And Macy? How did they get him to Schwartzman's place?"

"Text message," Hal said, hearing his own frustration. He already knew this. They were literally following this thing in circles. Every clue led to a dead end.

"Schwartzman sent Macy a couple of texts. Around ten fifty p.m.," Roger explained.

"How did this person know that Macy would even get those?" Naomi asked. "Someone texts me that late on a workday, and my phone's on silent. I don't hear a thing."

"Who the hell cares?" Hal said, his voice exploding off the walls of the small room. "It was a text. Macy got the text. He showed up there. He got stabbed eighteen damn times."

He crossed the room to the table and pulled out a chair, slammed his body into it. "Sorry." He was so angry, so frustrated. Terrified. The thing that made him angriest was the fear. He had no idea what she'd be facing down in South Carolina, how dangerous it was. If Spencer could manage to stab Ken Macy eighteen times without leaving South

Carolina, Hal didn't want to imagine what he could do with her right around the corner. How had he let Schwartzman leave this town? How was it possible that they had nothing at all on Spencer MacDonald?

There was a knock, and the interview room door cracked open. Another inspector in Homicide poked his head in. "Harris, there's someone here I think you're going to want to talk to."

"We're sort of busy—" Hal stopped when he caught sight of the woman standing behind the inspector. Her short red hair threw him off, but the rounded nose, the wide-set eyes—they were the same ones in the artist sketch Macy had done of the woman posing as Terri Stein. "You—"

The woman tried to shrink back, but the other inspector stood behind her, leaving her no way to escape.

Hal felt a surge of anger, the rush of relief. "We've been looking for you."

"I know," she said quickly. "I came as soon as I found out that Sarah was really dead."

"What do you mean when you found out she was dead? You were the one who found the body," Hal charged.

"Why don't we let her come in," Hailey suggested, pulling gently on Hal's arm before reaching out her hand and introducing herself. "I'm Inspector Hailey Wyatt."

"Stephanie. Stephanie O'Malley." She stepped into the room, and her gaze found its way to the whiteboard.

Hal motioned to Roger, who pulled the screen down to cover their notes and the images. "Naomi and I are going to grab a bite. We'll check back in an hour."

"Perfect," Hal told him.

Terri Stein aka Stephanie O'Malley watched nervously as Naomi and Roger left the room. When Hailey went to set up the video recording and get a waiver for the witness to sign, she looked as if she might cry. Hal didn't say a thing. The more terrified she was, the better it was for him.

Within five minutes of the knock on the door, Hailey, Hal, and Ms. O'Malley were seated at the table, and O'Malley had signed away her rights. Too easy.

The witness shifted in her chair as Hal leaned in. "You said that you came in as soon as you heard Sarah was dead. You didn't realize she was dead when you found her?"

"No," she said emphatically, glancing between them. "God, no. That was all supposed to be part of the show."

"What show?" Hailey asked.

"The reality show we were working on."

"Reality show," Hal repeated.

She nodded, looking back and forth between them before settling on Hailey. "*The Biggest Fright,*" she said. "That's what they were calling the show last I heard."

"They?" Hal asked.

"The studio, the director."

"What were their names?" Hailey asked.

O'Malley shook her head, sliding one foot under her. "It was all done online. I never met with anyone. Neither did Sarah."

"You knew Sarah before this?"

She nodded, licking her lips in a way that Hal associated with fear. "We knew each other from LA. We had auditioned for some of the same scripts."

"Where exactly did you and Sarah meet?" Hailey pressed.

Her eyes widened. "God, I don't even know. It's probably been two years ago, maybe three by now. People think LA is this huge place, but it sort of just happens. You start to recognize people from the circuit. Similar age, similar style, we ended up going for a lot of the same stuff."

"And this new show," Hal continued. "You were approached?"

"I wasn't. I don't know if Sarah was. I found the job posted on this online actors' board. Like a job board."

Hal raised his pencil.

"It's called the Cutting Board." She shrugged. "No idea why. Maybe like the cutting room floor where they edit a movie or 'cut' for the end of a scene . . ." Her voice trailed off.

"So acting jobs are posted on the board," Hailey said.

"Usually they're audition notifications, but sometimes they post for smaller gigs," O'Malley said. "This looked more like one of those. The posting was linked to a separate website where you entered all your information. I remember it was really specific. The listing was for two women. Midthirties, dark hair, prominent nose. The listing said to send head shots." She motioned to herself. "That's obviously not me, but I threw my stuff in there just for the heck of it. Sometimes a director thinks he knows what he wants, but he really doesn't."

"What happened next?" Hailey asked.

"I got a request back for some additional pictures with longer hair, darker hair, so I had a friend take a few with a wig. Then there were questions about how long I could be away, what kind of flexibility did I have."

"And that didn't strike you as odd?" Hal asked.

O'Malley rose in the chair to slide her foot out from under her and set both feet on the floor. "Not really," she said when she stopped fidgeting. "A lot of gigs require time away from home. And this was a reality show. I knew that much." She licked her lips again.

Hal recognized fear in the way she fidgeted, unable to sit still, but she presented none of the classic signs of lying. She didn't cross her arms over her body and avert her eyes, touch her face or neck. It seemed as if she was telling the truth.

"Plus, the pay was great," she added.

"How great?"

"Five thousand a week."

That was great. He barely cleared that in a month. "So how did they get in touch with you after you were hired?"

"It was all through the site. Details about where to go, what to expect. I just followed the directions, exactly like it said. I was to go and find the body. Scream and make a scene. Then go to the hospital for shock. Leave exactly forty minutes after I'd arrived, take a cab back to my car. They had a hotel for me. I was instructed to change my appearance and lay low for two days, then go visit the medical examiner. There was a guideline script for that. I was supposed to say how much they looked alike. They really did look sort of alike. It was weird."

"And after that?" Hal asked.

"Go home. Just drive back to LA."

"What was the address of the website?" Hailey asked. "Where you got your instructions?"

She stared at her phone. "Actually, I tried to get on the site today, and I couldn't. The site is gone."

Hal watched her. "You and Ms. Feld competed for jobs?"

"Compete?" she repeated.

Hailey met his eye. He didn't buy her as a killer either, but he had to ask. "Was there a rivalry between you?"

"God, no." Her eyes widened. "Absolutely not. We were totally different looks. She's so much more sophisticated, edgier. I'm so—" She motioned to herself, her round cheeks and ruddy complexion. "Me."

"Is there any other reason why you'd want to hurt her?"

"I didn't hurt her. I would never." She flattened her palms on the table. "I didn't even know the other actor was Sarah until I walked into that bedroom. I had no idea she was going to play the—" She covered her mouth. "You have to believe me. I would never hurt anyone."

"You stopped for gas? On the drive up from LA?"

The wide eyes returned. It read like genuine shock. "Yes," she said. "Right. I stopped for gas. That was part of the directions. I gave that officer my receipt. He said that was a strong alibi. He said I couldn't have killed her because I was on the road when she—" Again she stopped.

When she didn't continue, Hal asked, "And why didn't you answer my calls?"

"Right," she said. "That was in the directions, too. I was told to text or exchange messages—like phone tag or whatever—but not to actually sit down with the police."

Hal wasn't going to be able to press charges against O'Malley. She was obviously an unwitting participant, but maybe she could help him find the killer. He set his pen on the notepad and pushed it toward her. "We need that website and every detail about this job. What they told you to do, the directions. Every last thing you can think of."

"Of course. Absolutely."

"Start with your full name and contact info," Hailey told O'Malley.

Hal tried to move the pieces around. All of it done through the web, a specific site, no interactions. He'd have to get the tech guys in on this. He watched her. "The money was good, but did you get paid?"

She nodded, but something in her body language made him pause.

"What?" he asked.

She licked her lips again, standing up enough to slide her foot back beneath her. "It was actually the getting paid that made me start to wonder about Sarah."

Hal leaned in. "Explain."

"The check I got was from her . . ."

"From her?" Hal repeated.

"Yes. It showed up as a check written by her."

"Where is that check now?"

"I deposited it," she said, looking a little chagrined. "I had to," she added. "But wait. I took a picture." She rummaged through her purse for her phone.

She showed them an image of a check. Handwritten. Made out to Stephanie O'Malley. Five thousand dollars. Dated and signed by Sarah Feld, it was a personal check.

The only problem was that on the date that check was written, Sarah Feld had already been dead for three days.

35

Charleston, South Carolina

Schwartzman parked along the curb in front of Ava's house. She'd never seen the house totally dark before. Ava always left on the upstairs bathroom light to filter through the small hallway and into the two front bedrooms.

Was it off the night Ava died? Had someone else turned that light off? Was it on when she was there yesterday?

Beyond the house, the sky was the deep blue of nightfall. There were maybe ten or fifteen more minutes before it would be dark. She should go inside, take a look around before everything was pitched in black. She could have stayed in Savannah with Melanie for the night or gone back to the hotel, but she had driven here.

She had come back to Ava's. This was where she needed to be.

Here, where she could feel Ava and her father, and, hopefully, some strength to fight.

Cancer. Spencer. To figure out a next step.

She gripped the steering wheel. *Go inside.*

Her phone buzzed again on the passenger seat beside her as it had been doing all day. Messages from Hal, from Harper. She felt terrible not answering. She owed Hal more than the silent treatment. But she couldn't face him now. Ava's house already felt like too much.

Tomorrow. She would call him tomorrow.

The curtain in the bedroom moved. She stared at the window. No motion at all. It had to be a trick of the light. She cracked the car door and put one foot on the asphalt. She took a deep breath. What choice did she have? She wasn't going to sleep in the car. She stood and let the door close behind her.

"Dr. Schwartzman?"

She yelped, spun toward the voice. Adrenaline rushed through her limbs, her pulse an angry thumping.

A man stood on the sidewalk.

She froze, eyes adjusting to the dim light.

"I didn't mean to startle you," he said,

Her fingers cupped the car's door handle.

He wore a police uniform. Hands raised, palms out, he moved slowly toward her.

"Stop right there," she commanded. Her fingers slipped off the handle before regaining her grip. She cranked the handle up, pulled the door open.

"I'm Officer Sam Pearson," he said, stopped in the street. "Detective Leighton asked me to keep an eye on your aunt's house tonight."

Harper had mentioned parking a car in front of Ava's. Schwartzman scanned the street. "Where's your cruiser?"

"Just there, ma'am," he said, pointing one raised hand across the street.

The cruiser was parked on the far side of the street. "Okay," she said, not convinced. "Thanks."

"You're welcome, ma'am. I've been here since about two. Haven't seen anything suspicious."

She stood between the door and the car. "Okay, then. You can go. I'll take it from here."

Sam raised his brows. "Actually, the detective instructed me to go through the house when you came home."

If Spencer had never left Greenville and still managed to kill Sarah Feld and stab Macy, she had no reason to think he couldn't buy his way into the police department. "I'm afraid you're going to have to go."

"Excuse me, Dr. Schwartzman?"

"No way you're coming in that house," Schwartzman said.

Sam looked stunned.

"Are you alone?"

"Yes, ma'am." He touched his breast pocket. "How about if I call the detective? You can talk to her yourself."

There was a chill in the air. Ava's coat was in the backseat. She shivered. "All right. I'll be in the car."

She got back in the car and locked the doors.

Through the windshield she saw Sam on the phone, and she kept an eye on the gun in his holster. If he pulled a gun, could she drive away fast enough? He'd have to shoot her. She wasn't going anywhere with him willingly.

He scratched his head, motioned to her car. Who was he talking to? Harper? Or Spencer? She started the car.

Sam pointed to the phone in his opposite hand. He was coming closer. Too close. She put the car in reverse, backed up a few feet.

"The detective wants to talk to you," the officer yelled.

She cracked the window. "Have her call me, then." With that, she pulled into the street and drove away from Ava's house. She was not playing into any more of his traps. She would take nothing for granted. Her phone rang only seconds later. She hit the "Talk" button, took an involuntary breath of air, and said nothing.

"Anna?" Harper's voice.

"I'm here," Schwartzman said, her pulse slowing from its gallop. She could trust Harper. God, couldn't she trust Harper? She kept driving. *You have to trust someone.*

"Are you okay? I've had someone at the house all day."

She eyed the rearview mirror. No one in sight. "I had to take care of some things."

"Okay," Harper said. "But you're all right?"

Schwartzman said nothing. She was tired, on edge, and wary. She needed to go to bed but wanted nothing to do with going inside that house. Taking a left at the corner, she considered going back to the hotel.

"Anna?"

She did trust Harper. This wasn't a trap. Harper had a patrol car parked at the house for protection. To protect her from Spencer. "I'm here."

"Okay. Listen, I've got another patrol car headed your way. It's Andy, the officer from the garage yesterday."

At the mention of the garage, Spencer's warm, wet tongue was again on her face. Her stomach rolled. She pulled to the curb and opened the window all the way. *Breathe.*

"I want Andy and Sam to go through the house before you go inside."

Schwartzman clenched the steering wheel. She was letting the fear take over. *Pull it together. Inhale. Exhale. Breathe. Slowly.*

"Anna!" Harper's voice was sharp.

"Okay," she conceded.

"Sam said you were driving away. Where are you going?"

She exhaled. Harper had talked to the patrol officer. He was with Harper. They were not with Spencer. This was not like the times in Seattle, when the police didn't believe her. These officers were on her side. *You are okay.* "I'll go back. I didn't know who he was—I didn't know if he was really . . ."

"He's one of the good guys, Anna. Promise." There was a pause before Harper said, "I'm at my daughter's volleyball game, but I could come meet you."

"No," Schwartzman said. She had to pull it together. It was okay to be vigilant. But not crazy. *You cannot let him make you crazy.* "You stay with your daughter. I'm sure Sam and . . ." She couldn't recall the other name.

"Andy," Harper supplied.

"Right. I'm sure they will call if they find anything." And she had Harper's number. She could reach out. *He's not coming back, not so soon.* But she didn't know that. Not really. Spencer was nothing if not unpredictable.

"I'm going to leave a patrol car there tonight."

"It's not—" She stopped. But it was necessary, wasn't it? So she could sleep through the night?

"Just tonight," Harper pressed. "You sound like you could use a good night's rest. You're heading back to the house?"

"Yes."

"I've got my phone if you need me."

Schwartzman exhaled. The police were there to keep Spencer away. Harper was keeping the house protected, keeping her safe. "Okay. Thanks."

Schwartzman returned to Ava's. A second patrol car was parked out front, another officer standing beside Sam Pearson. The second officer offered his hand as Schwartzman approached. "Dr. Schwartzman, I'm Andy Hill."

Schwartzman dug into her pocket for Ava's house key, offered it.

"We'll take a look around and be right back."

The two men started up the stairs.

"Officer Hill," Schwartzman called after them.

Andy turned back.

"Would you turn on some lights upstairs?" She pointed up to the house. "Maybe the one in the bathroom . . . so it's not . . ."

"Sure thing."

Schwartzman retreated to the rental car and waited. The men reappeared a few minutes later, Andy leading the way. He gave her a thumbs-up. She met him on the curb, where he returned Ava's key.

"You're all set. Doors and windows are locked up, and the house is empty." He motioned to the other officer. "Sam will be here all night, and I'll be back in the morning."

She thanked them both and climbed the stairs to Ava's house, noticing the light in the upstairs bedroom windows. Despite the light, the two bedroom windows seemed to stare into the darkness like a blind man.

Inside, she locked the door behind her. For several minutes, she stood in the entryway, listening to the sounds of the house. There was a light wind, which made the windows on the south side chatter. She would sleep in the den. But first she had to take a look at the place where Ava died. Her medical examiner instincts forced her up there.

She couldn't stay in the house without seeing where Ava had died.

She walked up the stairs with purpose, but froze halfway up. Covering her nose, she stumbled backward, barely caught herself from falling.

Gucci cologne.

Was he here? The police had just checked the house.

She scrambled downstairs to the kitchen, checked the back door, the windows. The front door was locked. The patrol car sat on the street. The officer sat up front. He turned his head.

Alive, alert.

"Damn it." She stomped back up the stairs. This had to end. The fear, the cowering.

"You drown not by falling into a river, but by staying submerged in it," Ava used to say, quoting Coelho.

Now was Schwartzman's time to rise to the surface and swim.

At Ava's room, she gripped the knob, turned it slowly, and pushed the door open without moving into the room. She was sure she would see him standing there, his taunting smile, or hiding behind the door, waiting for her to close it. Her heart raced. Would he tie her up the way he had Ava? She waited. Three beats, five, and stepped into the room.

Smelled gardenias, rosewater, death . . . grooves were scratched into the footboard of Ava's bed where the ligatures were secured. The headboard, too.

She had fought.

Schwartzman retrieved the small orange evidence marker that had fallen under the bed, turned it in her hand. The residue of powder remained where they had tried to retrieve the assailant's fingerprints and found none. The sheets had been removed as evidence, the quilt thrown back over the bed. She pulled it down, saw the stains on the mattress pad where Ava had lain. The acrid smell of urine, sweat. Fear.

She yanked the comforter up over the bed.

On the bureau was a picture of Ava and her father as children. On the dressing table lay her grandmother's silver mirror and brush, the ornate monogram engraved on the silver. *E* for Esther. She touched the cool metal, fingered the etched letter.

Her family home was tainted, forever connected with him.

He had stolen her future, but he had her past, too. He'd left her with nothing.

She could not escape him.

As long as he was alive, she would live in fear.

36

Charleston, South Carolina

Schwartzman slept fitfully and was up well before the sun. She cleaned the kitchen, tossing out the perishables and fighting the memories of that room. Ava still kept buttermilk in the refrigerator for pancakes, still filled the little jar on the counter with Fig Newtons, something Schwartzman thought she'd only done for her visits. The smell of her favorite citrus dish soap. The peach tea she'd always brewed in the summer sun.

She ran the dishwasher and wiped down the countertops before going through Ava's closet. This time she moved slowly, searching for something that Ava could be buried in. She found a simple green dress that she'd seen her aunt wear. Chose an outfit for herself to wear to the attorney's office, black slacks and a cream sweater. The sweater with the slacks was dull, something Ava herself likely wouldn't pair together. Finally, she chose a simple black dress and laid it across the bed to wear to Ava's funeral.

She arrived at the attorney's office five minutes late. Ava's attorney was a man not much older than Schwartzman.

"Colin Glazier." He shook her hand and invited her to sit. He motioned to the green dress Schwartzman had brought with her to take to the mortuary after her meeting. "She liked that one," Colin said. "She wore it to a fund-raiser for the museum back in January."

Schwartzman wanted to know about the fund-raiser, to hear about Ava in the context of something so normal. January was months ago. He'd likely seen her since then. He would have seen her regularly.

Ava had come to her graduation from medical school. That was the last time she'd seen her aunt, more than seven years ago.

"Would you like us to deliver it to Woodward's for you? The dress, I mean," he added when she gave him a puzzled look. Polite, straightforward, it wasn't hard to imagine why Ava had selected him.

"Yes. Thank you."

He buzzed his assistant, who came to take it, and Schwartzman watched the dress go in a new wave of loss.

"You are the sole beneficiary of her entire estate," the attorney told her when she'd taken the seat across from his desk.

Schwartzman said nothing. Her mother had told her as much.

"Would you like to go through the assets now? Or would you prefer I put you in touch with her investment adviser?"

Schwartzman sat up in the chair. "Was there a letter or anything?"

"Yes. Of course." He passed her a sealed envelope.

Schwartzman opened it and pulled out a piece of heavy stock paper. Let out a shaky breath. The letter was typewritten. How she longed to see Ava's narrow handwriting.

> My dear Annabelle,
> I'm afraid I've left you quite a list, so don't hesitate to get help from Colin or his staff with all these old-lady details. Just because I lived in that house my whole life doesn't mean you

should. I know it will always find a wonderful family like ours if you should decide to sell.

Some things to remember, though:

Light fixtures in the entryway and den are original. If you sell the house, those should go to Christie's Auction first. Colin will have the number . . .

Schwartzman stopped reading, scanned the page, flipped to the end. It was nothing more than a how-to guide to taking the house apart. The second page was a list of people who could care for the house if Schwartzman wasn't ready to sell.

Where was the personal note?

She saw the letter was dated February, only a few months before. "Did she update her will recently?"

"The will itself hasn't been updated in more than a decade," he said. "But Ava tended to rewrite that letter to you every few months."

"Was there another version?"

"Ava always took the last letter with her and replaced it with the new one. She was very meticulous that way."

She wondered if something had happened in February, something that would make her draft this version. Had the earlier ones been more emotional? Or had those feelings Ava once had toward her niece simply dried up over the years? *Stop,* she told herself. Of course Ava loved her. She didn't need a letter to tell her that. But how she wanted one.

She blinked back tears and glanced down at the letter again. A full household, assets, investments. All of it coming to her. She folded the note and returned it to the envelope. She couldn't do this now.

"Thank you," she told Colin, standing.

"I know it's overwhelming."

She nodded.

He handed her a business card. "Let me know how we can help."

As Schwartzman started to turn for the door, Colin added, "She was really proud of you. She talked about you all the time."

"I appreciate that, thank you," she said, tears threatening to fall. She reached out to shake his hand.

He held on to hers. "One more thing. I know you'll be going through the house a little at a time. She didn't put anything about this in writing, but your aunt often mentioned that she had saved a whole shelf full of books that she wanted you to have."

Schwartzman ignored the tears that trailed over her cheeks. "Books?"

"Yes. She knew how much you loved books."

Ava's house was full of books. The library had somewhere close to a thousand volumes, and there were random stacks piled in each room. What did Ava mean?

As if reading her mind, Colin said, "The ones in the white bookcase in her bedroom. She was particularly keen that you should have those. They meant so much to her."

Schwartzman left the office, trying to remember if she and Ava have ever talked about books. Ava had been a huge fan of music, playing every type for her niece on the old phonograph in the living room when Schwartzman was young and, later, on a sound system that she'd had installed when Schwartzman was in high school.

Of course, Schwartzman had seen Ava reading—the house was full of books—but the idea that Ava had wanted her to pay attention to her books was a surprise. That they were in a case that Schwartzman had never even noticed was more surprising.

Schwartzman drove directly back to Ava's house without stopping to eat. The police cruiser was on the opposite side of the street now, and she recognized Officer Hill.

He rolled the window down. "Morning."

She waved hello.

"We just checked the perimeter, and everything is clear. As long as you're okay, I'm going to take off. We'll have someone back tonight."

She waved again and watched the cruiser drive away.

She let herself in and checked the downstairs before going up to the bedrooms. No smell of cologne. Despite her excitement, she moved cautiously, slowly.

She stepped into Ava's bedroom and looked for the bookcase. She found it in the corner of the room, tucked between the window and the dressing table. Compared with many of the antique pieces in the room—and the house—the bookcase was nothing special. It stood maybe four feet tall with simple whitewashed shelves, the finish worn along the edges.

Schwartzman drew the curtains and flipped on the light. The room was bathed in the warm, amber light of the old ceiling fixture.

Standing in front of the bookcase, she studied the titles. On the top shelf, Allende, Kingsolver, Oates, Walker, Angelou. Books Schwartzman had, of course, read. But none of the titles conjured memories of her aunt. She knelt on the floor and pulled out the copy of *I Know Why the Caged Bird Sings*. The binding was creased in several places. She flipped through the pages, but there were no markings, no turned-down corners. She replaced it and scanned the line of books, all paperbacks. They appeared to be lined up from shortest to tallest in no particular order. Would she need to go through each book page by page? Looking for what? Or perhaps it meant nothing at all.

But she didn't believe that.

"What were you trying to tell me, Ava?"

She ran her fingers along the spines. Books Ava had touched. Her long, lean fingers, fingers like her father's had been, like her own, their tips curved in just slightly, making them appear slightly arthritic. The clinical term was clinodactyly, a condition that caused a curvature of the digits, though theirs was mild enough to go unnoticed unless one knew to look. To Schwartzman, they were fingers that always looked old beyond their years.

The book heights grew steadily taller along the shelf up to a hardbound copy of *The Red Tent*. Tucked behind it was a short, narrow paperback. Out of place. She pulled the book out and turned it in her hands. *The Handmaid's Tale* by Margaret Atwood.

The edges of the pages were yellowed as if it had spent a great deal of time in the sun. Schwartzman remembered the story. Girls who lived to give birth, without love, without companionship. She flipped the book open and fanned the pages. Maybe a third of the way through, a folded note fluttered out. Lined paper, one end was fringed where it had been pulled free from a small notebook.

Her heart thudded in her chest as the paper fell to the floor.

She jumped up at a noise from the closet.

She flung open the door, yanked the chain to flood the tiny space with light, then kicked the hanging clothes, prepared for someone to leap out. The dresses swayed lightly, plastic and paper hangers from the dry cleaner whispering to one another.

She shut the door firmly, locked the bedroom door, and stared at the page lying folded on the rug.

She lifted the note.

Ava's neat cursive writing was visible through the back of the page. With a heavy breath, Schwartzman opened the note with trembling fingers.

At the top, PROPERTY OF ANNABELLE SCHWARTZMAN was written in capital printed letters.

My dear Annabelle,

It is my greatest hope that I am seated beside you as you read this, perhaps sipping on a glass of Evan Williams (an old one) that we bought to celebrate this newly hatched plan, a way to truly be free of your *past. Or, if you have planned an escape without me, that we are toasting to your present—or future—success.*

Though I know your mother wouldn't approve, spinsterhood has its benefits. You deserve better. Perhaps a little light reading will help. P. D. James was always one of my favorites. Or maybe your tastes take more after your father . . .

You have my eternal love,

Ava

Schwartzman let the letter fall to the hardwood floor and covered her mouth with her hands. The sobs shook through her sternum and rattled in her gut. Ava had been there when she first left Spencer, and she'd been preparing for Schwartzman's future.

How had Ava known that Spencer wouldn't give up?

Had Schwartzman given something away in those few conversations they had? Something that tipped Ava off to the ways he continued to torture her?

How long had she been waiting for Schwartzman to come back for her help?

She swiped the tears off her face and scanned the shelves for P. D. James. Found *Unnatural Causes* and pulled it out. Tears blurred her vision as she flipped through the pages.

There was nothing.

She found another James. Again nothing. And then a third.

Nothing.

She returned to the first and went through the book page by page. Then the second and the third. Through the windows, the sky darkened as the sun slipped behind a cloud. A gust of wind made the windows shudder in their panes.

Shivers rolled across her shoulders and down her arms.

After your father.

Her memories of him reading included law journals and the *New Yorker*, the local papers. Her eye caught a Clive Cussler novel on the bottom shelf. Unlike the others, this was a hardback. She pulled the book out and turned it in her hands, skimmed the back cover blurb—"a deadly game of hunter and hunted." When she tried to open the book, the pages were glued together. She tested the cover of the book, then the back, but both were sealed.

The spine was solid. When she flipped it upside down, she saw what looked like a drawer set into the book. She pried it loose. It came out only a half inch or so before it stuck on something. Schwartzman slid a finger into the opening and worked the drawer out of the book.

"Ava," she whispered as the drawer came loose.

The small cardboard drawer was filled with cash. Three separate stacks of bills. Schwartzman pulled the wedged bills out of the compartment and flipped through them. All hundreds. Easily two inches of $100 bills. How many bills in two inches? Three hundred? More? A single stack might be $30,000.

In the drawer was a second stack of hundreds as thick as the first. The third stack was fifties. Under them a note.

Be free, Annabelle. Love, Ava

Beside the word *love* was the sign for infinity. Love to infinity. It was what her father used to say to her.

She laughed through sobs.

With this much money, she could truly vanish. Live in Europe or South America. Never worry about Spencer again.

She felt slightly panicked. How could she leave everything?

What everything?

She had so few friends, and most of them acquaintances because she never felt truly rooted to a place, the shadow of Spencer always just over her shoulder. There was no family other than her mother, who she had seen for ninety minutes in the past three years.

Her career. That was what she had. It would mean leaving her career. Giving up her work.

No. That wasn't necessarily true. They had medical examiners in other places. It just meant starting again. More schooling, exams, licenses.

It could be done.

She stared down at the stacks of cash. How long had this money been hidden here, waiting for her?

She recalled those two weeks she'd spent with Ava, their correspondence in the months when she first moved to Seattle. Encouragement about finishing medical school. Ava had been the one to recommend the University of Washington in Seattle. She put Schwartzman in contact with someone in admissions. The woman who provided Schwartzman with a list of potential scholarships, who had called her four weeks later to inform her that she was the sole recipient of a generous scholarship. Schwartzman tried to remember the name of it.

Something clicked. That scholarship had covered her tuition, her books. Meanwhile, Ava had insisted Schwartzman let her pay for living expenses.

"You can pay me back when you're a doctor," she'd said, but she hadn't allowed that either.

Every December, Ava had sent a check with ample money for room and board. Surely it was no coincidence that Schwartzman had gotten that scholarship. If there even was a scholarship. Ava had put her through medical school.

Ava had sent her something each birthday, notes and a gift at Hanukkah, at Rosh Hashanah. Schwartzman had responded with quick phone calls and the rare note, always pressed for time with school and work. Ava always respectful of the crazy schedule.

On the shelf was another hardback book that looked out of place. This one was James Patterson. Hesitant, she reached out and touched the top of the book. When she pressed down, she felt the same hard material where the pages didn't give. "Oh, God."

She slid the book out and turned it over. Another drawer. She was afraid to look.

Maybe it was a note, something else from Ava.

But this one, too, was filled with cash. More hundreds, fifties, some twenties. She returned the drawer to the book and turned it over in her lap, read the book's description. "On the run from a dangerous criminal . . ."

Schwartzman held the book to her chest and let her tears fall.

It was too much.

How would she have reacted if Ava had given this to her in person? What could she possibly have said? How could you thank someone for this?

Ava knew.

She wouldn't have been able to accept the gift. She would have told herself there was another way.

Ava was dead now. Spencer had left Schwartzman with no choice but to accept the gift just as her aunt had wanted.

She stacked the two books and tried to think what to do with them before deciding that they were safest back on the shelf. She spread them out, moving other books in between, and then picked up Ava's note.

Through the paper, she saw writing on the back side.

P.S. I didn't forget your mother was a reader, too.

God, was there more?

Her mother really wasn't a reader. Schwartzman took books off the shelf, one at a time, thumbed through them for notes or another secret compartment until she had run out of books. The library was filled with law volumes.

Her mother would not have read those.

The only things Schwartzman recalled her mother reading were gardening magazines and cookbooks. She straightened the books on the shelves and went downstairs. The kitchen light was gray, the sun's light muted by storm clouds. The house creaked above her, and she paused to listen.

The wind. It had to be.

Cookbooks. She opened cabinets until she found two cookbooks above the microwave. She couldn't recall if Ava used cookbooks, but the two books were ancient. *The Joy of Cooking* was as old as she was or older. The other was called *The Busy Woman's Cookbook*, and it couldn't have been much newer.

Schwartzman set *The Joy of Cooking* on the countertop, expecting more cash. She flipped open the book.

Gasping, she slammed the cover closed and checked over her shoulder.

Ava had hidden a gun in the cookbook. This was what Ava meant by the book her mother read. It had to be. Cash, a gun. All for Schwartzman. All to help her deal with Spencer. The cash might buy her freedom and time, but the gun implied something altogether different.

An end to the running and hiding.

Schwartzman pulled down the second cookbook and opened it. Inside was an unopened cardboard box, not much larger than a pack of playing cards. Ammunition.

Schwartzman closed the book and reopened the first, sneaking another peek at the gun. The book in her arms, she sank onto the floor of the kitchen. The hard kitchen cabinets pressed into her spine as a reminder that this was not a dream. This was real. She had everything she needed to be rid of Spencer MacDonald once and for all.

Had Ava expected Spencer to come after her? She couldn't have. While Ava understood the depth of Spencer's depravity, even she had underestimated how far he would go to get Schwartzman back.

If Ava kept a gun for self-defense, certainly she would have kept it in her bedroom. Or at least somewhere more accessible than inside a gun-shaped cutout in a cookbook on a shelf in the kitchen.

Schwartzman closed her eyes.

Why hadn't she ever come back? She might have saved Ava from Spencer.

Instead she'd let this happen. Even if she had nothing to do with Ava's death, she'd allowed it to occur. Spencer was too clever to get caught by the police. Even if Hal and Harper believed her, how could they catch him? How could they stop him?

They couldn't. She squeezed the cookbook tightly against her chest. But she could. She could stop him. She imagined holding the gun to his head. Pictured the head wounds she'd seen in the morgue. She shuddered. The damage to the brain and skull. Right-handed, her bullet would more likely strike the left hemisphere of his brain. The center for language, for logic.

He would be dead.

She pictured the blood splatter from a head wound.

No. She couldn't imagine pulling the trigger.

Maybe there was a way to find something in his house, some evidence to prove that he was responsible for Ava's death. Surely something there would prove his guilt. She could find it.

And if she couldn't?

She lowered the cookbook, cracked the spine, and let the gun fall into her lap. It was murder. Premeditated murder. She touched the gun, fingered the ridges on the grip. A flash of heat, excitement, adrenaline. It would mean the rest of her life in prison. But where was she now, if not in prison? Spencer's prison. South Carolina had capital punishment. Death?

You're not living.

She lifted the gun and extended her arm. Imagined lining up the sight on the flesh between Spencer's eyes. She would make certain that Ava was Spencer's last victim.

She would finally be free of the fear.

37

Charleston, South Carolina

Schwartzman locked herself in the downstairs den, the only room on the main floor without windows other than the tiny powder room. She debated using her phone to do research. Her search history could be used against her if she was caught, but what choice did she have? She could go to the library or a public café, but not with the gun. In the end, urgency won out. Her first search request was for the date the last person was killed by capital punishment in South Carolina: 2011. That was promising. Only forty-three total since 1985. Surely, then, odds of a life in prison were higher than getting death. Lethal injection was the method used most recently. That would be preferable to electrocution.

It took almost no time to confirm her suspicions about Ava's gun. She recognized it as a revolver and from its size, guessed it was a .38 special. She'd seen enough of them in the files of cases she worked. The .38 had been the standard service weapon for most police departments from the 1920s to the 1990s. Even after departments replaced the .38 with pistols—San Francisco used the Sig Sauer P226, New York a Glock model—the .38 remained the most used backup weapon for police officers. Dating back to 1898, the revolver was favored for its small size—it could easily be concealed in an ankle holster under a pant leg—and for its reliability.

Unlike pistols, revolvers almost never jammed.

With newspaper spread across the rug, Schwartzman followed the instructions from a YouTube video to clean the gun, substituting the WD-40 for gun oil. The gun only had to work once, and everything she read online suggested that WD-40 was used extensively in the firearms industry. When that was done, she burned the paper in the fireplace, packed the gun back into the book, and replaced the book on the shelf in the kitchen while she worked her way through the rest of the house.

Other than the gun and the ammo, there was no sign that Ava ever owned a weapon. No paperwork in her files, no cleaning supplies anywhere, nothing with the NRA logo on it. The model number on the .38 dated it back to the mid-1940s, decades before gun registry laws were introduced in 1968.

Even if the gun was registered, matching ballistics required the gun and the bullet. That was easy to fix; Schwartzman would simply dump the gun. As her final act, Schwartzman took pictures of everything in Ava's house with her phone. She hoped to come back, but if she couldn't, she wanted to know what was there, exactly as she'd found it.

Using a duffel bag from under Ava's bed, Schwartzman packed up a change of clothes, the two hardback books from the bedroom, and the two cookbooks from the kitchen. The only other thing she took was the black-and-white photograph of her grandparents, her father, and Ava when Ava was maybe five or six and her father eight or nine.

It was nearly two when she left the house, loading the duffel into the trunk. She wondered if Spencer was watching, but it made no difference at that point. She drove straight to the gas station, filled the tank of the rental car, and stopped at a gourmet deli for a baguette and cheese, grapes and almonds, a bottle of pinot noir, and two bottles of water. It could as easily pass for a single woman's grocery list as sustenance for a road trip.

The pinot was for courage or maybe to celebrate.

She paid cash.

She headed north on Interstate 26 toward Greenville. It was just past five when she arrived at Sumter National Forest. As she drove, she tried to recall the campground where she and her father had pitched their small brown dome tent. She had only camped twice in her young life, both times here with her father.

Though she was a teenager and might have been helpful, she and her father were awkward campers. Setting up the tent took forever, the fire made with a log starter never burned longer than it took to make s'mores. One night was all they lasted, even though they'd originally set out for two.

What she remembered was that the spot where they camped was mossy and lush, hidden under a canopy of trees so thick that the morning sun hit the ground only in thin wisps of light. She wanted to find that place. There, she could practice shooting the gun without the risk of being seen or, worse, hitting a camper or hiker.

As she drove in, nothing looked familiar. It wouldn't be dusk for another couple of hours, but the clouds above her were dark, making it seem later than it was. She consulted the screenshot of the map on her phone, located the Horn Creek trailhead, and tried to orient herself. Horn Creek was far enough back in the forest and away from the campgrounds that she was unlikely to run into campers. She turned down one road but reached a dead end. With no room to turn around, she had to reverse straight out. She doubled back to the main road and set out again.

It took two more tries to find Horn Creek Trail. She pulled down the dirt road until it ended at the trailhead. There, not ten feet off the trail, was a small red tent. *Damn. What now?* She turned around and retraced her path, checking the map for another trail that looked smaller, more secluded. She did not want to see anyone out here, but the map offered no insight into which were the most popular trails.

The only other trail nearby was one that led to a lake called Lick Fork. Schwartzman made her way down the bumpy dirt road, praying there weren't campers there, too.

The parking area came into sight. Empty. The first drops of rain fell as she opened the windows and listened for sounds. Human sounds. There was always the risk of animals. Someone else might have been frightened, but there was nothing Schwartzman feared out here. Being killed by a mountain lion didn't scare her. That would make her death a fluke, the unlucky winner of nature's odds.

Being killed by Spencer. Being held by him. Being owned by him.

These were the fears that kept her awake at night and caused her to wake in a cold sweat. Sitting in the quiet car, she surveyed her surroundings again, then got out and went to the trunk for the satchel. Unzipped it slowly and studied the gun, the ammo.

She opened the box of ammo and put a fistful of bullets in her pocket.

She closed the trunk door quietly and, while the car light was on, thumbed the release to open the cylinder. Six slugs. Six chances. She remembered the one time she had shot a gun. She'd been maybe eleven or twelve and they were at a reunion of her mother's family. Some cousins she barely knew were shooting a 0.22 rifle at cans lined along the fence. Mostly boys, they taunted her until she tried.

That day, she lay on the grass with total focus, lined the sights on the can, exhaled, and pulled the trigger. Knocked the can right off the fence, got up, and walked away.

She only hoped she was still that good.

She drew three bullets from her pocket and slid them into the chambers. The car light clicked off. She stood, surrounded by quiet, and closed the cylinder, felt it lock. Careful not to drop anything, she walked up a short hill toward a patch of trees maybe sixty yards from the car.

The loblolly pines stood high over the cluster, their treetops swallowed by the low-lying cloud cover. Among the pines were bushes and other trees—sycamore, sweet gum, and elm. Standing in their midst, she could hear the rain hit their high branches, but the drops didn't reach the forest floor. Ghost-like tendrils of the clouds swirled through the high branches.

She blinked multiple times, urging her eyes to adjust to the dim lighting. She chose one of the loblolly pines, maybe three feet in diameter, and studied the bark, searching for a good target. Schwartzman settled on a knot oozing sap.

A little above his chest level, she estimated.

The perfect shot would be maybe two or three inches lower and an inch to the right. Hitting the cardiac notch of the left lung was ideal. Puncture the lung and the heart in a single shot.

Death would be fast. Not entirely painless but shock would likely dull his senses quickly.

She turned and took five long strides. Turned around. Raised the gun. Right hand wrapped on the grip, left hand cradling the right. There was no safety. Just cock it and shoot. She widened her stance, lowered her shoulders, imagined Spencer in front of her. That tree. Felt his kiss on her face, her lips.

The sound was deafening. The barrel kicked upward. Not as bad as she'd expected. She lowered the gun again. Pulled the trigger once, twice in quick succession. A little breathless, she moved to the tree, stared at the knot. Searched the surface. Nothing. She ran her fingers over the bark, searching for metal. Nothing. She'd missed. All three times.

She opened the chamber and turned the gun upside down, releasing the empty shells into her left hand. Three of them. Put them in her left pocket, zipped it close. Reloaded. Moved back again. Loaded four more. Took two steps closer this time, telling herself that she would be able to get close to Spencer when the time came.

Again she drew back the hammer and aimed. Fired. Twice. Three times. Four. Returned to the tree and saw nothing.

Who was she kidding? She couldn't do this. She would end up dead.

She sank down and pressed her forehead to the rough tree bark. *Damn.* What was she thinking? She should ditch the gun and go home, she told herself. Stop wasting time. As she rose to her feet, a glint of metal caught her eye. Her pulse steadied to a strong, clear drum. She touched the slug. How had she missed it?

The metal was maybe two or three inches from the knot. The same distance between the center of an average adult male's lung to the lung's edge. Four inches below the first, perhaps an inch to the right, was another. Maybe the spleen or the liver. Not as good as hitting the heart, but it would kill him.

She'd hit two for seven. Not terrible.

A moment later, she saw two more bullets side by side, maybe six inches lower. That would be his thigh, perhaps a knee. Better than 50 percent. She would have six chances. She could do this. Schwartzman could kill Spencer MacDonald. Six tries, she might even be able to kill him twice.

She pushed her finger into the hard wood, following the grooves created by the bullet. How deep the bullet had drilled into the wood. She pictured Spencer's chest. An easy through-and-through. Maybe the bullet would catch a rib and ricochet. She remembered a victim where a single bullet had created three separate wounds on the heart, all by ricochet. A small-caliber gun. The wife had shot him. She recalled the bitter woman who'd sat hunched down in her chair at the defense table when Schwartzman had testified in the trial.

How many bullets had she pulled out of victims? Her chest grew heavy. Fear and disappointment mixed into something with a nasty taste. The gun in her hand, she sank onto the soft, marshy ground, pressing her back into the tree's hard trunk. *Oh, God.* She could not kill Spencer. Not even once.

She dropped her head and let the gun slip from her hands. She was not a killer.

There was no question that Spencer MacDonald deserved to die. Perhaps she had even earned some cosmic right to be his executioner, but she wouldn't. Because that was a reality she would have to live with.

Wake with every day and lay down with at night.

She was a physician. She had taken the Hippocratic oath to do no harm. Even if her patients were dead people, she had vowed to take care of them in that death, to prove what had happened, how and by whom.

She was also part of the judicial system.

How could she continue to do her job and fight for justice after she'd committed murder? And she couldn't believe Ava had left that gun for Schwartzman to murder Spencer.

For self-protection, maybe, but not for murder.

She pressed the heels of her hands into her eyes. She would have to find another way to solve the problem of Spencer MacDonald. She rose slowly, picked up the gun gingerly, and released the cylinder, dropping the remaining bullets into her hand. She had decided that she would dispose of the gun on the way back to Charleston.

Keeping the gun only invited trouble.

Back at the car, she opened the passenger side door and knelt down to tuck the gun under the seat. She noticed a long hair on the barrel—hers, most likely. She pulled the hair free and studied the tiny white bulb on one end. The root.

Staring at the strand of hair, Schwartzman knew exactly what she had to do.

38

Charleston, South Carolina

As Schwartzman drove back toward Charleston, her mind weaved the tiny idea into a plan. She was disappointed she hadn't thought of it sooner. If she had, he might already be behind bars. The miles ticked by, and she made a mental list of all the pieces she would need. Others that would be helpful if she could get them.

Ava was easy. Frances Pinckney would be tougher.

It would mean calling Harper Leighton.

Schwartzman hesitated. She didn't want to bother the detective until she knew exactly what she was asking for, and how she was going to explain her reasons for needing it.

She stopped only once on the way back to Charleston, pulling off near the tiny town of Harleyville to dump the gun and the remaining ammunition in a small tributary off 7 Mile Road. Instead of dinner, she ate the food she'd bought earlier in the day—part of a baguette, grapes, and almonds. She was too excited to be hungry. Only as she was pulling into Charleston did Schwartzman contact the detective. She needed two things. One she might get. The other she likely would not.

"Anna?" Harper said in lieu of a greeting.

"Yes," Schwartzman said. "I hope I'm not calling during dinner."

"No," the detective assured her. "Not at all. Jed and Lucy aren't even home yet. She's got volleyball practice, and Jed's picking her up. Is everything okay? Someone's at the house, right?"

"I've been out for a bit, but I'm sure someone is there. It's not really necessary." She didn't want someone at the house. She couldn't anticipate Spencer's next move, but she suspected it wouldn't happen in these next few days. He'd made quite a splash, and he had to know he was being watched. Better to lay low.

Then again, Spencer had his own way of seeing things.

"No. It's absolutely necessary," Harper countered. "There will be someone on that house, at least through Ava's service."

That gave her two more nights to make this happen. She wanted this done before then. She wanted to stand at Ava's coffin and know that justice was being served. She had a lot to do.

"But you didn't call about the patrol car," Harper said.

"No," Schwartzman agreed.

"What can I do for you?"

Schwartzman drew a quick breath. "I'd like to see Frances Pinckney."

Harper remained silent.

"Examine her, I mean," Schwartzman clarified.

"She's been released for burial," Harper said. "The services are tomorrow."

Schwartzman swallowed. She pictured Frances Pinckney at the mortuary, dressed and ready for service. Or maybe she'd been cremated. Harper said burial, not cremation. "Is she at the same place Ava is?"

"She's not. If she were at Woodward's, I could call T. J., but I don't know these folks. Is everything okay, Anna? Is there something we should be looking into?"

"No," Schwartzman said. No arousing suspicion. "I guess I just wanted to see his other victim. That probably sounds weird . . ."

Harper didn't answer right away. "I don't think anything about grief is weird," she said. "Everyone does it differently."

Schwartzman felt tears burn her eyelids.

"Why don't you come to the service tomorrow?" Harper suggested. "I suspect it will be closed casket, so you wouldn't get to see her, but maybe being there would help."

Schwartzman considered the offer. Of course she would go. "That would be great," she said. Wings batted against the inside of her belly. Fear and excitement, possibility.

"Of course," Harper said. "She was a good friend of your aunt's. I'm sure the family would welcome you."

Harper was giving her access to Frances Pinckney's DNA. "Thank you." She thought of Roger. He would know the best places to isolate a home owner's DNA. She'd never thought to ask him. For her purposes, hair would be the easiest to obtain.

"It's at two in the afternoon. I'll text you the address."

She could pull this off. She could put Spencer behind bars. "Thanks again, Harper. There is one more thing," Schwartzman said.

"Sure."

"I'd like to go over the images in Ava's file."

"You mean the crime scene photos?"

"Actually, I'd like to see the coroner's pictures," Schwartzman said.

"Is there something specific you want to see?" Harper asked.

She thought about the images of the bruising on Ava's chest. She could not give away what she needed. She could not take the risk that Harper would take notice, that it would come out later.

"No." She spoke the word firmly. "I don't know what I'm looking for. I just want to look again, just in case."

"Burl's been over the body, Anna," Harper said. "He's good. I don't think looking at those images again is going to get us anywhere."

"I have to try," Schwartzman said. "You understand, don't you?"

A beat passed. "Of course."

"If I could just see them one more time." She held her breath, prepared to beg. She needed access to those images. It was the only way. "Please."

"They're uploaded into secure storage," Harper told her. "I can share the file with you electronically. The link will only be good for twenty-four hours. Is that enough time?"

"Yes," she said quickly, trying to imagine where she would go to view them. She didn't have a computer with her, and she needed an anonymous place where she could search the Internet without it being traced back to her.

"I'll text a secure log-on and password to your phone," Harper said. "Probably take me about thirty minutes."

"That's fine. Thank you, Harper."

"This is between you and me, okay?"

"Absolutely," Schwartzman agreed. "My lips are sealed."

"Get some sleep, Anna. I'll see you at the service tomorrow."

Schwartzman pulled to the curb on the next block and used her phone to search for an Internet café with computers for rent. They were harder to come by these days. She didn't want to wait until tomorrow. Farther down the screen, she found a place listed as Concierge Café, computers and concierge office space for rent, hourly. She dialed the number.

"Concierge Café," said a young man's voice.

"I'm in town for business, and my computer won't boot. I need to rent a computer for about an hour. You have computers for rent?"

"We do. We're open at seven tomorrow morning."

"And what time do you close tonight?"

"Nine o'clock."

Schwartzman glanced at the clock on the dash—seven forty-five. "Nine tonight?"

"Monday through Saturday," he said with the brusque shortness of young people. "Sundays we close at six."

Schwartzman thanked him and disconnected the call as she pulled from the curb in the direction of town. The address was close, traffic light, and she was in front of the café in six minutes. She parked, locked the rental car, and went inside, where she signed up for computer time and a cup of coffee. She took her cup of black coffee and went to the farthest cubicle. She'd paid for ninety minutes of computer time even though the coffee shop closed in just over an hour.

She'd take what she could get.

Evidence was not her forte, and she wished she could call Roger. He would have been able to enhance the pattern of the injuries to Ava's chest to identify the knee pads. She would be working in the dark.

You can do this.

The link from Harper had dropped into her text messages, and she found the site easily. Setting down the steaming cup, Schwartzman scanned through the thumbnails. Grief struck her midsection, rattling her spine. She pressed her fist under her rib cage and started to click through the images. Finally, she narrowed on the ones of the body preautopsy.

The head, arms, fingers, and then chest. There were several of the entire torso, but she chose one with a close-up of the pattern in the skin. One side. Ava's right breast.

She studied the perimortem bruising. Some sort of diamond pattern across the oval of the knee pad, but only the very center of the pattern was discernible. The bruises would continue to develop for several days after death, but the coroner had taken only one set of images. She considered returning to the mortuary, seeing Ava again. The idea made her feel empty, slightly nauseous. Zooming in on the pattern on the skin, Schwartzman launched a new browser and ran a search for carpentry knee pads. She clicked on "Images": 173,000 results.

She scanned the first pages, moving deliberately across each row. Clicked to the next. Scanned. She lifted the coffee mug and took a long drink. Searched the rows for the diamond shape. Every few lines, she returned to the image of the bruising for comparison.

"We're closing in ten minutes," the barista said, and, when Schwartzman didn't answer, he rapped his knuckles on the edge of the cubicle.

"Okay," she told him without taking her eyes off the screen.

She'd been through hundreds of images of knee pads, and none of them was quite right for the patterns in Ava's skin. Ava was approximately five eight, which put her chin at about five feet high and her breasts at approximately four feet. The bruising ran from the bottom of her breasts, which was probably three foot nine or ten when accounting for her age, and reached almost to the manubrial-sternal joint. The joint was approximately eight inches below the chin. Schwartzman jotted down the numbers. It meant the knee pads were approximately six inches long.

She stared at the number she'd written. He didn't make the knee pads. He was too arrogant for that. He had simply purchased a pair at a hardware store. In their old neighborhood in Greenville, there were a few Home Depots, an Ace, and a McKinney Lumber.

He preferred McKinney, which was smaller than the Home Depots. He always said the people were smarter there, not just a bunch of high school or college kids working for ten bucks an hour. But he wouldn't want to be remembered. That made Home Depot the safer bet.

She scanned through the first page, then the second. More of the same ones she'd seen.

She clicked again, and her eye was drawn to one in the center of the page. Frozen, she glanced between the image of Ava's injuries and the knee pads. *No.* It wasn't quite right. The pattern was close, though. The right design, but this one had more lines in the pattern. Was it possible they didn't show up in the skin? Could these be the right kind? *Damn it.*

If she went to Greenville, she could go to the local hardware stores. He wouldn't have driven out of state to buy them. But there were a dozen hardware stores in Greenville, not including the specialty ones. She didn't have time to look at all of them. She scanned the rest of the page.

"Five minutes," the barista called out as though making an announcement to a room full of people, although Schwartzman was the only one left.

She clicked forward, feeling desperation mount. What would she do if she couldn't find them? She could plant gloves. She would need to get his epithelial cells inside, which would be trickier. She made her way down the page.

Then she saw them.

She let out a little laugh. They were perfect. The same diamond pattern. Six inches. The appropriate oval shape and size. She went back and forth between the picture of Ava and the knee pads. These were definitely the right ones.

She clicked on the image. Tough Freight X was the brand. Style 8020.

She wrote it down on a piece of paper. Tempted to take a picture with her phone, she hesitated. There could be nothing to trace back to her.

Now she just needed to find them. They were offered at Lowe's, True Value, and Home Depot.

"I'm afraid I'm closing up, ma'am," the barista said.

She nodded. "I just need a couple more minutes."

"It's nine o'clock, ma'am," he said with a little huff. "That's the time we close."

"My uncle is very sick, and I need to let my family know. Five minutes." She met his gaze. "Please."

"I'm real sorry about your uncle, but I've got a lot of schoolwork left to do and I need to—"

"Fifty bucks," she said, cutting him off.

His mouth dropped open. "What?"

"I'll give you fifty dollars for five more minutes."

"Okay." He turned to head back to the counter. "You can have ten if you need it."

Schwartzman didn't respond but returned to the computer. She started to type in a search for hardware stores in Charleston but stopped.

No. She couldn't buy them here. And she wasn't going to Greenville.

She stared at the ceiling, thinking. Savannah, Georgia, was the closest large city. A couple of hours away. In Savannah there were at least two Home Depots. She clicked on the links. They opened at six.

She could be there and back before Frances Pinckney's service.

She took a long drink of the cold coffee and went into the search engine to clear her history. Then she logged out of the site with the autopsy photographs and took the single piece of paper she'd written her information on and folded it into her pocket. As an afterthought, she took the next three pages on the notepad, too, and folded them into her back pocket. Finally, she gathered her purse, went to the desk, counted out two twenties and a ten, and slid them across the desk.

"Thank you, ma'am."

"Appreciate the extra time," she said and turned for the door.

"No problem," he said as though it hadn't earned him fifty dollars.

Only then did she hear his accent. A damn Yankee.

A Southerner would have done it for free.

"I'm sorry about your uncle," he called as she reached the door.

Well, maybe he was learning something about Southern manners.

She stepped out into the night sky. It didn't matter. She got what she needed. And she could go to sleep tonight knowing that she was one step closer to putting Spencer MacDonald exactly where he belonged—behind bars.

39

Charleston, South Carolina

Schwartzman woke up at three and couldn't go back to sleep. Ava's burial was in thirty hours. Tomorrow.

Today was her last day to ensure Spencer was in jail when Ava went into the ground.

By four, Schwartzman had showered, eaten breakfast, and was standing in Ava's room, staring out the window. She held a cup of strong, black coffee—her second—and waited at Ava's bedroom window for the sun to banish the shadows from between the houses. She was ready to head to Savannah, but it was too early to leave. If she started for Savannah now, Home Depot would just be opening when she arrived. That wasn't the issue. The issue was the patrol car parked in front of Ava's house. Leaving at four in the morning was suspicious and, while there was a chance she could get out of the house without being seen, it was not a risk she was willing to take.

If she was going to pull this off, there was no room for error.

Cumulus clouds floated across the sky, taking shape as they moved. A rabbit, the left lobe of the brain, one in the shape of the appendix. A beautiful day, the winds were light. It would make for easy driving.

She took a long, deep breath and let the air slide out across her lips until her diaphragm was relaxed in an arch beneath her lungs. She gave a final exhale to push out the remaining air. It was impossible to empty the lungs fully. She drew the air back in, filled them again. Oxygen flowed into the bronchi, then into the smaller bronchioles and into the alveoli. Two adult lungs were the home to some three hundred million alveoli where the oxygen dissolved into the moisture-rich covering of the alveoli and diffused into the blood. She could feel the oxygen moving through her body as she worked to harness the terror into something productive.

Despite the breathing, she was both cold and hot at once, her body set in a constant series of shivers as though she were fighting the flu. This was the sensation she recalled when she lived with Spencer, days where every movement was in anticipation of a potential explosion. It was hard to focus, to think straight, and impossible to sleep.

It's almost over. Thirty hours and it will all be over. She had to believe it was possible.

She set the coffee cup down and went to Ava's bureau. Aside from finding Ava something to be buried in and borrowing clothes for her own purposes, Schwartzman had yet to go through Ava's dresser.

In a search of socks earlier, Schwartzman had seen the small boxes and glass dishes lining the center of Ava's top bureau drawer. She recognized earrings and rings, bangle bracelets, things she had seen on her aunt over the years. On the left side of the drawer, Ava's underwear and bras were neatly folded, on the right her socks were neatly matched and stacked. Without a second look, Schwartzman had grabbed a pair of socks and pushed the drawer closed.

Now she stood before the bureau and ran her fingers across the curved mahogany drawer. She slid the drawer open and stared down at the jewelry. She reached into the drawer and removed the first box. An aquamarine rhinestone necklace that looked to be from the 1920s. Too flashy. She dismissed several others that were too big. It had to be something that Ava might have worn under a sweater or her coat. Ideally, something that people who knew her might recognize. But Schwartzman didn't know which things Ava wore regularly.

She hadn't been around.

She stared down at the jewelry. If she planted a souvenir from Ava, then she'd need one for Frances Pinckney, as well. That meant stealing from a dead woman. She tried to imagine doing that. Her stomach tightened at the notion. What if she took something that Pinckney's kids had already seen? If they knew something was taken after their mother's death, the theft would point to Schwartzman. The whole thing would fall apart.

Or what if Pinckney's kids didn't recognize the necklace she planted? What if they told the police that the piece wasn't their mother's? That would be just as bad.

The evidence would be enough. DNA evidence was stronger anyway. Jewelry was circumstantial. But no one could deny DNA.

Focus on the science. She slid the bureau drawer closed.

She pulled on the pair of yellow cleaning gloves she had found under the kitchen sink and the box of Saran Wrap from the cupboard and crossed the room to Ava's bed. There, she stretched the plastic wrap about two feet across the floor, then stood to pull back the quilt and blanket, exposing the sheets.

The acrid scent of sweat and fear filled her nose, and she had to stop and slow her breath to keep going. She did not allow herself to avert her gaze. Every stain, every scent was a reminder of what Spencer had done, what he had to pay for. With clenched teeth, she tore off a strip from the roll of packing tape she'd found in the utility drawer and pressed it across Ava's pillow. Pulled the tape free and pressed it down again, lower across the pillow. Then a third time.

Lifting the tape toward the light, she saw the skin particles. Carefully she stretched the strip of tape across the Saran wrap, pressed lightly. She had tested to make sure the tape could be peeled back from the Saran Wrap. The process of laying the tape on the cotton sheets reduced the adhesive so it could be pulled back off the plastic wrap. Schwartzman repeated the process with four additional strips of packing tape, then used a baggie to collect strands of Ava's hair from the brush on her vanity.

Careful to return everything in the room to its place, Schwartzman packed a large Ziploc with the wrap with the strips of packing tape and the baggie of hair and slid it all under the mattress of Ava's bed.

At six fifteen, Schwartzman walked out of the house, stopping to say good morning to Andy, who sat in his patrol car on the curb. When she told him she was going for a walk, he didn't seem the least bit suspicious. She supposed she might have looked like the kind of woman who walked for exercise though she was not. She wore a baseball hat. A reasonable choice, to keep the sun off her face. Beneath her jacket, she wore yoga pants and a sweatshirt. Another hat in a different color was rolled into one pocket. Cash, credit card, license, keys to the rental car, she had everything she needed.

About a block from Ava's house, she turned back to see Andy's cruiser pull away from the curb. If all went well, she wouldn't see him again. After a quick stop in a coffee shop to grab a latte to go, she walked to the city parking lot where she had left her rental car. She arrived there before six thirty. Cell phone powered off, she drove out of Charleston.

She knew exactly where she was going. No navigation, no cell signal, no trace.

She set the radio to the 1950s station, drove at sixty-three miles per hour, and stayed in the slow lane except to pass and then only occasionally.

Along the way, she heard a couple of her father's favorites. Otis Redding sang "Sitting on the Dock of the Bay." Chubby Checker's "The Twist."

The drive took two hours and twelve minutes.

When she arrived at Home Depot on Pooler Parkway outside Savannah, there were easily thirty cars in the lot. She parked in the farthest row and tucked her hair up under the plain brown ball cap she'd found in the back of Ava's coat closet. An ugly thing, it had to be something she'd gotten as a giveaway. The hat had no visible logo, which made it perfect. She would leave it in a trash can on the ride home. She shrugged out of her coat and emerged from the car, wearing only her sweatshirt. The thin leather gloves covered her hands. It might have been a little strange, but she crossed her arms and pretended to be cold as she strode into Home Depot.

She walked with purpose, as though she knew exactly what she needed and where in the store to find it. Which she did not, but she wouldn't risk being remembered for asking a question. Her first stop was the tools department. If that failed, flooring. If they weren't there, she had two more Home Depots in the area. Failing that . . . *no.* That wasn't an option she would allow herself to consider.

When she had reached the middle aisle of the store, safe from view of the cashiers, she slowed down to read the signs. She passed power drills and a massive display of saws and found the knee pads on the bottom row beneath the electric sanders. She scanned the boxes, searching for Tough Freight X brand. Her pulse ricocheted unevenly in her throat.

"Can I help you find something?"

She jumped at the voice. She turned her head in the direction of the voice, careful to keep her chin down so that her face was hidden under the hat. "No, thanks."

He moved closer, his feet only a couple of feet away in her peripheral vision. "If you're in the market for a power sander, I think DeWALT is the best brand."

"Okay. Thanks," she said.

The crackling of his radio from his belt. "Customer service to flooring."

"Have a good one," he said and she watched his boots vanish around the aisle.

She turned back to the display and her eye caught the red *X* of the Tough Freight brand. She dropped to her knees and picked up the package, scanning for the style number. Flipped it over: 8020. She exhaled, closing her eyes. Held the box close. She'd found them.

Next she found a roll of plain gray duct tape.

On the way to the front of the store, she passed a display of blue latex gloves. As an afterthought, she picked up a box in medium.

Spencer was proud of his delicate hands. These would be useful.

As she approached the registers, she scanned the people working and veered toward the one farthest from the door, the youngest-looking cashier. Male. Early twenties. Someone who was not likely to pay her any attention. To him, she was another old woman. Perfect.

He barely looked up. "Sixty-seven ninety-eight."

She handed him seventy dollars in cash, took her change, and, wearing her gloves, she took her sack and walked out the front door. As she went, she balled the receipt in her hand and dropped it in the trash can. Next she threw away the handwritten note with the brand and the three blank pages she'd taken off the notepad in the café.

She kept the hat pulled low as she crossed the lot to the rental car and got inside. She started the engine, checked the area around the car carefully, and backed out of her spot. She drove straight back toward Interstate 95.

Thirty miles out of Savannah, she stopped at a gas station, put twenty dollars' worth in the car. Also paid in cash.

Then she drove to a strip mall that included a McDonald's, a gym, a nail place, and a video rental store and scanned the parking lot until she found what she was looking for—a spot far enough from the buildings to avoid any surveillance cameras.

Parked, she unwrapped the duct tape and pulled several feet of tape from the roll, balling it up. She opened the box of rubber gloves and pulled out two pairs. These she pushed into the bottom of the Home Depot sack. She removed the knee pads from their packaging and put them in the plastic sack with the extra gloves and added the roll of duct tape.

She gathered the trash—the balled-up duct tape, the box of gloves, and the packaging from the knee pads—and dropped the bundle into a trash can on the curb between the McDonald's and the gym. Glancing down, she saw the box of blue gloves was still visible, so she reached into the trash and lifted two discarded McDonald's sacks and laid them on top so the items could no longer be seen.

With one final look around, she returned to the car and started the drive back. It wasn't even ten o'clock.

Plenty of time to get home for Frances Pinckney's service.

40

Folsom, California

Visiting hours started at seven in the morning and ended at two, and it was already past noon. She could have been there already. Seen his big brown eyes in person instead of trying to zoom in on bad newspaper images from the trial.

She could have held his hands.

He had big hands. She could tell from the way they sat in front of him on the table in the courtroom. Big hands with thick fingers.

How long she had waited to touch those hands.

Up at six this morning, she had been absolutely positive he would call. She wouldn't even go out for coffee because she worried something would go wrong and she wouldn't hear her phone. Which was silly, of course. She could turn the volume as high as it went. She could put her little Bluetooth thing in. But she didn't want to be in a crowded coffee shop when he called. Or on the street. Or anywhere but a silent room where she could listen to his every word, savor it like caramel. Which was how his voice sounded to her.

She was absolutely positive he would call this morning, especially after missing their midweek call. He had promised they would talk before the weekend. It was Sunday. He'd never missed a call before. She could set her watch by their calls. That was how much she meant to him. How much they meant to each other.

It was one of the things she loved most about him. That he was so dependable. A sad statement for a woman to fall in love with a man for his reliability. But she had. Chuck never left her hanging. He always did what he said he would. In that way, he was unlike every other man she had ever dated. Certainly unlike her flaky father.

The traffic through Emeryville had been a mess, and now that she was past the Vallejo Bridge, traffic was starting to slow down again. She had to arrive at the prison by one thirty. They closed visiting hours to new guests thirty minutes before the hours ended. She shifted the Prius into third and cut into the slow lane to pass an idiot in a Beamer taking a casual drive in the fast line. Her ex had bought her the Prius. Light green. His new wife drove a black Porsche Cayenne. Of course she did. The bitch.

She sped around the Beamer, shifted into fourth, and cut back into the fast lane to avoid a truck in the slow one. The Beamer blared its horn. She gave the driver her middle finger. *As if.* It was his own damn fault, driving that slow.

The road widened into three lanes, and she was able to navigate around cars more easily. She sped past a highway patrol officer who was pulled off on the side of the road.

She hit the brakes. "Oh shit. Oh shit."

She glanced over her shoulder and saw his face. He had been watching. She checked that she'd slowed down to the speed limit and kept an eye on the rearview mirror. He was coming for her. *Please don't come get me.* Of course he would. Things never worked out for her. *Please. I don't have time for a speeding ticket today.*

The patrol car pulled into traffic. He was definitely coming for her. *God, why can't I be lucky just one time? I deserve this. I deserve to see Chuck after all I've gone through for him.*

The patrol car passed several cars, narrowing the distance between them to only three cars. No lights yet. She held her breath and clenched the steering wheel. The car behind her was right on her tail. She moved into the right lane. The Beamer flew past, slowing only long enough for the driver to wave his finger at her. A big smile on his ugly face. "Screw you, asshole," she mumbled.

The police car was two behind her. The lights went on. She collapsed into the seat. She was going to miss Chuck. There were tears in her eyes. She was going to lose it. She was going to fall into a puddle in front of a police officer and tell him what? That she was trying desperately to make visiting hours because her boyfriend, whom she'd never actually met, was in Folsom Prison. *No.* That wouldn't work. She let the sobs build up. She'd tell him another story. Use the sobs to her benefit. She calmed a little.

She had to think about missing Chuck.

She had to cry.

In the rearview mirror, the highway patrol car pulled into the fast lane and sped by. She exhaled and let out a cry. He wasn't after her. As the patrol car passed, she smiled at the officer through her tears, but he wasn't watching her. She wished he would pull over the jerk in the Beamer, but the patrol car passed that, too, heading fast up the left lane.

When the patrol car was out of view, she glanced at the clock on the dash: 12:34 and it was six minutes fast. She was only twenty minutes away. She'd be there by one o'clock, which would give her enough notice to have time with him.

She pulled down the vanity mirror and checked her eyes. She'd have to touch up her makeup when she got there. They had exchanged pictures, so he knew what she looked like. And she hadn't done some typically stupid thing like send a picture of herself when she was ten years younger or twenty pounds lighter. It was a picture of her. Not a bad one, of course, but realistic. She wanted to look her best today.

Even fifteen or twenty minutes together would be enough. That was all she needed. Maybe a shorter time would be better. He would be unhappy that she'd come. He was very clear that they shouldn't see each other. She wondered if he would recognize her. It was just the one picture. Maybe she could pretend she was from his attorney's office or something. She stared down at the clothes she'd thrown on. Yoga pants and a long zip-up. She didn't look like anyone from a law office, and it was Sunday.

If she were one of those skinny women with the expensive workout clothes, the kind with the high, perfect ponytail and the long, lean legs, then she could.

But that was not her.

She forced herself to take slow, steady breaths to wash out the adrenaline. She had worked herself into a lathered frenzy. She winced at the term. Her father's. That was what he called it when she got upset. As a child, she'd asked him what it meant, and he told her that lathered was what happened to horses after they ran.

In hindsight, it might have seemed like some sort of compliment to be compared to a stallion, but he quickly made it clear that the frenzy was a kind of madness, one she had inherited from her mother.

It was impressive the impact he'd had on her, considering she spent only a week or two a year with him throughout her childhood. It didn't take much to plant the seed of self-loathing in a child. She hated herself when she got upset like this, and it was always her father's voice in her head.

"Calm down," she commanded, remaining in the slow lane and keeping at least two car lengths from the car in front of her, a real challenge on a California freeway. But she put her will to it. She might have a frenzied side, but she was willful, too. Another compliment, care of her father.

Soon she was at the Folsom Boulevard exit ramp and turning on to Natoma. Prison Road was surrounded by grassy rolling hills and dotted with thick, old oak trees. As she crested the hill, she saw the prison grounds in the distance. The campus was larger than she'd expected. The parking lot itself might have belonged to a football stadium, though it was mostly empty.

While she'd anticipated the ugly, industrial-looking buildings, some of them actually looked okay, a bit like castles in Scotland might look. Something about coming down the road through the grassy hills toward the high metal fence filled her with giddy pleasure. And beneath that, something stronger, more profound.

This was the rising tide of her life's meaning.

After all the missteps, all the wrong turns and failures, she had finally met her match. And he was here—just beyond the guard's gate. He was inside these walls, but because of her efforts—her brilliance—he would be out soon. Within months. Her work was done, and his attorneys were beginning the appeals process.

She slowed at the gate and lowered her window. The guard stepped out of the small structure, clipboard in hand. "You here for visiting hours?"

"Yes, sir."

He glanced at his watch. "Processing ends in ten minutes, so make your way straight through the main doors. They won't accept any new visitors after one. No exceptions."

"I thought it was a half hour before."

"An hour, ma'am." He raised his hand, and the red-and-white gate rose. He waved her through, and she put the car into gear and drove on into the parking lot. According to the car clock, it was 12:53 when she shut the engine off. She had brought a bag of makeup to freshen up, but she wasn't going to miss the processing. Instead of fussing, she lowered the mirror, pinched her cheeks, gave them a couple of light slaps to work the color into them, and got out of the car.

Processing involved verifying her identity, filling out pages of paperwork about who she was and why she was there, then going through a metal detector and submitting her purse to X-ray. She was behind an angry Hispanic woman who was hugely pregnant. It took some effort not to stare at the huge tattoo that covered the large portion of exposed breasts before disappearing down into her tank top. It was one fifteen before she was inside.

"Wait here. We'll call you when it's your turn."

She wondered where Chuck was when he got the call. She was under the impression that he worked out quite a bit. During one call early in their relationship, he'd told her how much working out helped break up the monotony.

That and reading. He was always reading.

She had recommended *Unbroken* to him, and he'd told her where he was in the book when they talked. She remembered when he was reading about Zamperini's time in the Japanese concentration camp.

"It's a lot like that in here, Cici," he'd said, using his nickname for her the very first time. "You have to be able to take the punches to stay alive."

As she waited, she kept her head down and pretended to be reading something on her phone while she studied the people in the room. The visitors were almost exclusively women. A few older ones who might have been mothers or even grandmothers of inmates. The others looked younger, and she saw, with some remorse, that they were nicely dressed up for their visits. The woman two seats away had long orange nails with tiny jewels at their tips. She smelled strongly of a vanilla perfume and wore a low-cut black wrap dress that showed off her full figure. She drummed her fingernails on the armrest of her chair and swung one red-sandaled foot impatiently. On her right ankle was a tattoo that read KAMAL 2008.

The woman glanced her way and rolled her gum into a line between her front teeth before blowing a bubble and popping it with a little smack. Her eyes rested on Cici's hand, the one she had at her mouth. The woman's gaze was like a series of sharp punctures to the thin veneer of her confidence. Within seconds the doubt began to fill her like water into a punctured raft.

And then she heard her name. Once. Then again and she rose, wiped her hands on the side of her jeans, and hurried to the guard stand.

"Charles Bollardi. Booth nine." The guard pointed.

She moved down the line of divided glass cubbies, passing a crying woman and one whose body was pressed up against the glass.

She moved past booth six, then seven, and slowed as she came upon eight. Her stomach was in knots. What if he was angry that she'd come? What if she'd blown the whole thing for him? But surely he would have just sent her away . . .

"Move along, bitch," said the woman in booth eight. "You ain't part of this conversation."

She hurried past and found booth nine empty. Chuck wasn't there. The corridor on the other side of the glass was empty. She edged closer to the glass to see if someone was coming.

But there was no one. Only a guard, standing with his back to the white wall, hands behind him, eyes moving along the line of prisoners.

She sat down, set her purse on the shallow desk, and folded her hands in front of her. Then moved her purse to the floor and put her hands in her lap. Quickly she pinched her cheeks again. Slapped them until the heat flooded her skin, and, as she did, he came into view.

She gasped at his size as he sat across from her. He'd looked large from the courtroom pictures, but she hadn't expected him to be so tall. He was six two or three at least. She clasped her hands together as he pulled out the chair and fell into it. He lifted the receiver off the wall, and when she didn't move, he rapped it on the glass and motioned to hers. Her hands trembled as she reached for hers. An awkward laugh bubbled in her throat.

"He—" She cleared her throat. "Hello."

"Who the fuck are you?"

Her mouth dropped open, and spittle edged out the corner of her lips. She wiped it quickly and gave him a nervous smile. "I know you said not to come, but I had to."

He shifted in his chair uncomfortably and frowned.

"I hadn't heard from you in almost a week and I guess . . ." She waited for his expression to crack, for him to realize it was her. "I was going a little crazy, you know?"

"No. I don't know. I don't have a goddamn clue." His voice was different—he suddenly seemed so crass, so unsophisticated.

"I'm sorry, Chuck," she offered.

"Who sent you? Was this Carmen's idea? I'll kill that fucker."

Even his tone was wrong. On the phone, he'd always sounded husky and a little distorted, but she'd chalked it up to the connections, being inside the prison and on a cheap cell phone.

But the change was more than the voice.

His language was different. He was different.

"Chuck," she whispered.

He wiped the back of his hand across his mouth and squinted at her. She touched her own mouth as though he was telling her she had something on her face.

"I know I wasn't supposed to come," she whispered. "But aren't you even a little happy to see me?"

Chuck leaned into the glass and tapped, beckoning her closer to him. She moved in until their faces were separated by only the thin distance of bulletproof glass. She studied his lips as he spoke, anticipating his words.

"I've got no fucking clue who you are." Spittle flew from his lips and sprayed across the glass. "Tell whoever sent you to go to hell."

Chuck stood and slammed down the receiver. She could see that his lips were moving, but she couldn't make out his words. A moment later he was gone.

The receiver clenched tightly in her hand, she stood frozen, watching the door where Chuck had disappeared. She felt the stares of the other prisoners, the visitors. The woman in the next booth glared at her, whispering into the receiver. Behind the glass, the guard watched her.

How could he just leave?

Her heart felt as though it might burst from behind her lungs. Her pulse drilled into her temples.

It was hard to breathe. Her chest was so tight. She rose to her feet, shaking. After what she'd done for him. He could not just walk out on her. He loved her. He promised he loved her. Her fist gripped the receiver until it was painful. *No. No.* She slammed the receiver against the glass divider. "Chuck!" she shouted, her own spit spraying across the glass. "You get back here, Chuck!"

She slammed the phone again, then let it clatter to the desk as she pressed her fists on the glass. "You asshole. You can't just ignore me, Chuck. I'm not going away. You're not getting rid of me that easily. You get out here and face me like a man, Chuck!"

A firm hand latched on to her left arm. She spun, certain it was Chuck. She faced a guard, jerked her arm free as another clamped on the other side. She tried to free herself, thrashing in the arms of the two police officers. "Let's go, lady."

"Let go of me. I need to talk to Chuck. I need Charles Bollardi. It's important."

"Sure, lady," the other guard said. "Let's go find a place to cool off for a while."

She lifted her legs, made herself deadweight. As she hung between the two officers, they dragged her away. People began to clap. Someone howled. Pounding from behind the glass, muted whistles.

She stood on her feet then, straightened herself up. "You can't do this to me. You do not want to screw with me," she warned the police as they led her to a solid white door. A third officer held the door open. Inside was only a table and two chairs. A perfect place for her and Chuck to talk.

Because they had to talk.

41

Charleston, South Carolina

Fisted hands deep in her pockets, Schwartzman was trembling as she walked out of Frances Pinckney's service. The roll of tape in her pocket, the Ziploc bag, the thin leather gloves of Ava's, she hadn't used any of it.

The air felt unnaturally warm, wrong for how cold she was. The sunlight was blinding, and she stood on the concrete steps, blinking into the bright light.

She glanced back at the mortuary, unable to recall anything that was said about the deceased. She could conjure rough images of those people who were seated at the front of the room, standing in front of the closed casket. She could picture their mouths moving. Handkerchiefs clutched in tight fists. Halting, emotional speeches. The ceremony felt dream-like to her, seated in the last row. As far from the body as possible in the room.

She had nothing.

Schwartzman had failed to get within fifteen feet of the coffin, not that it would have mattered with a closed casket. She looked back at the building, imagining the morgue-like room below where Frances Pinckney had been prepped. Where strands of hair and skin cells would have been scattered across the floor like leaves in autumn. Schwartzman stood close but also infinitely far.

She had no way to get to that place. Even if the prep room hadn't already been cleaned, there was no way to positively identify which hair belonged to Frances. She could hardly plant just any hair. It had to be a match. And evidence of Ava wasn't enough without Frances. It would be too easy to point the finger at Schwartzman. *The accused was married to a medical examiner who wanted him behind bars. She was even at his home the night he was arrested.* Of course they would say she had planted the evidence. Her aunt's hair, her skin cells, they would be easy to come by.

It would never work unless she had something from Frances Pinckney.

She could go back inside. Perhaps she could ask about the mortuary prep rooms, as a sort of professional interest. Even if they let her in, they would certainly not leave her unattended. And even unattended, there remained the issue of cleanup, of identifying the right hair, the right skin.

She would have to think of another way.

An image of the cemetery came to mind. Digging up the body. Shudders coursed up her spine and rolled across her shoulders. She was not going to dig up a body.

"Anna."

She turned into the sun and shielded her eyes as Harper Leighton approached. Dressed in a skirt suit and low heels, she hardly looked like the same person as the woman in her uniform. Behind her was another woman dressed in black. Harper motioned to her. "I wanted you to meet Caroline Pinckney, Frances's daughter."

Schwartzman reached out her hand. "It's nice to meet you. I'm so sorry for your loss."

"Yours, as well. Mama talked about Ava all the time. She was a wonderful friend to her after Daddy passed."

Schwartzman swallowed. Ava might have told her about Frances, too, if they'd talked more often. She might have even met Frances, had she visited. Had she been in touch. Had she been more attentive.

Of course, if she'd done things right, they all might be sitting at lunch, Ava and Frances beside them.

"You should come back to the house," Caroline said, touching Schwartzman's arm. "You can meet my brothers. We're on Jasper Street near Radcliffe."

Caroline Pinckney excused herself, and Schwartzman watched her go. Only then did she realize what she'd been offered. The house. Frances Pinckney's house was perfect. Her DNA would be all over that house.

The sun warmed her.

"You doing okay? You look a little flushed."

Schwartzman felt the heat in her cheeks, the desperation of wanting so badly to collect something to use to frame Spencer. "I'm okay. I think it was just warm in there."

"A lot of folks," Harper agreed. "Don't feel like you need to come to the house if you don't want to. I know you've probably got a lot to do for tomorrow."

Schwartzman didn't want to admit that she'd already decided she would go straight to Pinckney's house. That she would find some way to collect hair. At the very least, she needed hair.

"I've got to go find my mom," Harper said. "I'll touch base later."

"Sure." Schwartzman watched her go. Then, making certain not to appear to be in a rush, she walked down the block to her car to head to Jasper Street.

Hand in her pocket, Schwartzman held on to the roll of tape as she stepped into Pinckney's house. Frances Pinckney's house was a traditional Charleston double like Ava's. As Schwartzman walked in, she saw the stairs straight ahead. The foyer was filled with people, the living room open to the left. It would be difficult to go up the stairs unnoticed. *No. Not difficult. Impossible.*

A man approached. "I'm David Pinckney, Frances's son."

"Annabelle Schwartzman," she said.

"Ava's niece," he said. "You lost your aunt, as well. I'm so sorry."

"Yes," she answered and found her eyes welling.

"Oh, I'm so sorry." He scanned the room. "Let me find a tissue." He patted his coat pocket. "I gave Caroline my handkerchief."

She pressed her fingers beneath her eyelids. "I'm fine. Really. It hits me sometimes."

He touched her shoulder. "Of course."

She looked around the house. "Did you grow up here?"

"Yes," he said. "Mom and Dad bought the house when Patrick was two, so I was born here."

"It's beautiful. My aunt's is a similar style, I think. Three bedrooms?"

"Four," he said.

"In Ava's, the master is on one side and two children's rooms on the other."

"Actually," he said, "Mom and Dad and Caroline were on that end." He pointed up the stairs to the south side of the house. "Rob, Patrick, and I were on the south side. It's two bedrooms with a Jack and Jill bathroom in between."

Schwartzman made a note of the layout. "Made sense to keep you boys together."

"I'm sure Caroline was happy to have her own bedroom. Teenage boys aren't the tidiest."

"I don't imagine." Schwartzman glanced at the door. She had the information she needed. Upstairs, south side. She wanted to go and be done. Particularly before Harper arrived. But she couldn't see a way to leave the conversation gracefully. "Are you all in the area?"

"None of us are, I'm afraid. Spread out all over. I'm in Chicago. Rob is down in Memphis, and Caroline's closest. She lives in Durham."

"I imagine that was tough on your mother."

"Yes. She would have liked us to be closer, especially after Dad died."

"Of course," she said.

"It's hard to stay here. Jobs are pretty limited."

"Sure." Schwartzman began to feel antsy. No sign of Harper. Yet. But she didn't have much time. Harper was on her way.

"Unless you're in tech or education," he continued. "I'm an engineer. Best offer came from Chicago, and I've been there ever since."

Schwartzman forced a smile, stole another look out the front. If Harper arrived, she'd have to slip to the back of the house, hide until she could get upstairs.

Just then someone called his name.

Schwartzman exhaled silently.

"You'll have to excuse me," he said. "My brother's calling me."

"Of course," she told him, gently squeezing his arm. "I appreciate the time."

"Okay, Rob," he called as he started across the room.

Schwartzman looked up the stairs, trying to decide how to get up there. She wanted to walk straight up. But she couldn't. Someone would surely stop her. Or at the very least follow her up.

She needed time in Frances's room. To collect hair and skin.

At least three or four minutes. And that was if nothing had been disturbed. If someone hadn't changed her sheets or cleaned the room.

If, if, if . . .

No. She could not go up those stairs.

Schwartzman saw Harper Leighton on the street. Before Harper saw her, Schwartzman turned away from the door and walked to the powder room. She ducked her head in. Empty. With a quick glance over her shoulder to ensure no one was watching, she pulled the door closed and continued to the back of the house. As she was turning the corner, she saw Harper being greeted by David Pinckney. On her arm was an older woman. From their similarities, Schwartzman guessed it was her mother.

Schwartzman turned the corner, expecting to find the kitchen.

Instead there was a second staircase. Back stairs. She started straight up the stairs.

"Excuse me," a woman called behind her.

Schwartzman turned around, trying to look as though she might cry. Her pulse trumpeted in her throat, and it was hard to believe the throbbing wasn't visible from even where the caterer stood four feet away. Schwartzman motioned up the stairs and ran her fingers under one eye. "David told me to use the upstairs bathroom because the one down here is occupied."

The caterer glanced toward the front of the house. "Okay, sure. We're just supposed to keep guests downstairs."

"Of course," Schwartzman agreed. "I won't be long," she added and walked up the stairs without looking back. It was all about looking like you belonged. Not hesitating. She reached the top of the stairs and turned toward the south side of the house. Pressed herself against the wall, squeezed her eyes closed.

This was a terrible idea. Sneaking into a dead woman's room to collect her DNA?

She had to convince the police. They had to believe Spencer was connected to both Ava's and Pinckney's deaths.

Schwartzman crept across the hall, staying close to the wall. She could just make out the tops of heads in the foyer below. She chose the first door on the south side of the house and found a small bedroom. Caroline's room. She pulled the door closed and quickly moved to the next door.

The master bedroom.

"Oh, God," she whispered, forcing herself to step inside.

The room was large and smelled of the sweet ripeness of the old. The sounds of the guests downstairs filtered through the door. She scanned the room quickly. The four-poster bed. Handmade quilt, the edges a little frayed. Someone had made the bed. Or perhaps Frances made it the day she died. Schwartzman pictured Ava's bed and forced the images away.

Hurry. She pressed the button to lock the door and moved directly to Frances's bed. She pulled the small roll of packing tape and the Ziploc bag from her pocket, put on the thin leather gloves, and pulled the quilt and sheet back to expose the fitted sheet pillows.

There was a sound at the door. She yanked off the gloves and threw the covers back over the pillows. Froze.

Scratching. She crossed the room quickly, shoving her gloves and the tape into her pocket before turning the knob just enough for the lock to pop from the knob. Listened. A whimper, a high-pitched bark. She cracked the door, and a small white dog ran into the room.

"No," she told the dog that stood in the center of the room, wagging his tail. The dog let out a playful bark.

"Shh," she whispered, returning to the bedroom door. She scanned the hall; seeing no one, she closed and locked the door again.

All she needed was Pinckney's brush to make sure she had sufficient DNA. Hair with follicles. She didn't have time to check the ones from the sheets.

She would collect extras and check them later.

The dog barked and scratched at her shoes, barked again. Panic filled her limbs until moving felt like shifting sandbags. She reached down and lifted him up.

"Shh," she said again, reached into her pocket for her gloves.

A creak.

The direction of the front stairs. She rushed back to the door. Popped the lock. Her breath like a windstorm in her ears. The sound like high heels on wood.

Close.

She stepped away from the door, holding the dog close.

The door opened, and Schwartzman stood, facing Caroline Pinckney. "What are you doing in Mom's room?"

Schwartzman felt the blood rush to her neck as she turned back. "I'm so sorry. I—"

Caroline's face hardened.

"I came up to use the bathroom," Schwartzman said. "When I came out, I heard this little guy, scratching."

"He was in Mom's room?" Caroline asked.

Schwartzman nodded, her throat too tight to form words.

"Cooper," Caroline said and reached for the dog, taking him from Schwartzman's clutches. "What are you doing in here?"

Schwartzman followed Caroline out of the bedroom. Took a last look at Frances Pinckney's bedroom as she closed the door. She hadn't retrieved any DNA. Not a single hair. The idea that she was leaving empty-handed left her feeling cold and sick to her stomach.

Caroline stopped at the top of the stairs to allow Schwartzman to join her. "You hear all those nightmare stories about people being robbed during their funerals."

Schwartzman swallowed the awkward lump in her throat. Was Caroline accusing her? Her original plan was to take a piece of jewelry. What if Caroline had walked in while Schwartzman was looking through her mother's things?

"That's awful," she offered. The idea of stealing from people who were already totally bereft was appalling. *You were almost that person.* How low would she stoop to be rid of Spencer? *You got rid of the gun.*

"I can't be in there."

"I understand," Schwartzman agreed. She had stood on the front porch of Ava's house, dreading the thought of entering the house. How she wished she had more memories of being in Ava's house, of their time together.

David Pinckney met them on the stairs. "One of the catering staff said someone was upstairs," he told his sister, glancing at Schwartzman.

"Just us girls," Caroline said.

David frowned. He seemed about to say more, but Caroline walked past him.

As the two women reached the bottom of the stairs, Schwartzman saw Harper Leighton in the living room. Schwartzman offered a small smile.

She turned to Caroline. "I wanted to say thank you," Schwartzman said. "For the things you said about Ava and for being so kind. I know this is a hard time."

Caroline reached out and squeezed Schwartzman's hand. "You're welcome." As she removed her hand, a small white puff of dog hair floated between them. "Oh, Cooper. You make such a mess."

"He sure is cute, though," Schwartzman said, reaching up to scratch the small dog behind the ears.

Removing her hand, she balled it into a fist and pushed it into her pocket, feeling the downy fluff of dog fur against her fingers.

As she walked out the front door, she saw Harper catch her eye. But she didn't stop.

She couldn't face Harper.

42

Greenville, South Carolina

Schwartzman stood in a cluster of dogwood bushes across the street from the house she had shared with Spencer.

The night was dark, the moon hidden behind storm clouds. Light from the street lamps cast eerie shadows along the street. She had parked at the end of the block. She wore a jacket and thin gloves, not unreasonable for a Southerner when the temperatures dropped and the rains fell. It might have been a little warm for it today, but not enough to arouse too much suspicion. The sack of supplies was tucked in her jacket, pinned down by her left arm. Everything else was in the pocket of her jacket.

She had been over the plan a dozen times in the past hour. Two dozen. Parked in a remote strip mall parking lot, Schwartzman created the evidence. She didn't let herself consider how quickly the police might dismiss it, wouldn't allow herself to think about how much better it would be if she had DNA evidence from Frances Pinckney. Used the Saran Wrap from Ava's room and applied her skin cells to the knee pads. She avoided pressing the tape to the knee pads directly so that there was no transfer of the adhesive residue. Instead she laid the knee pads faceup in a plastic sack and rubbed them with the Saran Wrap, then shook the tape out above them. Even in the dark, Schwartzman could see the bits of skin and dust float down onto the pads. As a final measure, she tucked two of Ava's long hairs where the Velcro straps were attached to the knee pads. An easy enough place for them to have been caught during the attack.

Next she unrolled the very end of the duct tape and pressed the adhesive side to the inside of the Ziploc bag containing dog fur from Frances Pinckney's home, the only thing she'd managed to get there. She dropped the roll of tape, the two knee pads, and two pairs of unused latex gloves into the sack and tied it closed.

She patted her pocket. Felt her phone. The phone was set to silent. She had ignored two calls from Harper, four from Hal. She would call as soon as it was over. She knew exactly where everything would go. All she needed was four minutes in the garage. She could probably do it in two. Then there was the matter of getting Spencer to confess. He wanted to. He would love to know how much pain he was responsible for, how much she had suffered. If he wasn't being recorded and he knew she couldn't use it to put him away . . . then just maybe she could get him to say the words. She needed to hear them. Her pulse was an even, quick drumbeat.

She felt fear, but beneath it was something else. Something Schwartzman found wholly unexpected. Something lighter and softer. Giddiness, she might call the sensation. A kind of electricity that was different from the fear. On the dark street, across from the home she had once shared with Spencer MacDonald, she was buoyed by possibility.

Hope.

Built just two years before they were married, Spencer had intended the house as a traditional colonial. Directly over the centered front door was a rounded terrace perched atop the second story, which Spencer called his tower.

Ironically, the tower was false, inaccessible from the house except by crawling out one of the small second-story bedroom windows and going across the roof. Something she'd never seen him do. The house had seemed grand when she first moved in, a starry-eyed new bride. Even then, there was something looming and dark about the house, but she'd convinced herself that moving directly from her parents' exquisite home into one of her own was a badge of honor. The longer she lived there, the smaller and less impressive the house became.

Standing on the street, she couldn't see the appeal of the house at all. The features were out of proportion—the rounded terrace cartoonishly large while the windows on the upper level were puny against the huge surface areas of plain white siding.

Schwartzman watched the dark house, washed again in the cold fear she'd felt living inside it. Spencer's anger was woven into the perfectly appointed couches and the carefully set pictures and vases. One incorrectly placed pillow or a picture hung slightly awry was enough to break the thin veneer of his self-control.

This was the house of her nightmares.

Same house. Different woman.

A woman with a way to put him behind bars.

The master bedroom was on the opposite side of the house from the garage. And unless something had changed, the garage wasn't included in the alarm system. She would go from the garage's side door, plant the evidence, and then leave again. From there, she would simply ring the front doorbell.

A loud mechanical click filled the night. The garage door rolled upward. She ducked, crouching behind a cluster of pink summersweet bushes. Spencer's gold Lexus backed out of the garage. The car turned out of the driveway and passed her on the street.

He was gone. Spencer was gone. That was too easy. She checked her watch. Nine fifteen. Where was he going? She stared down the street after he had disappeared around the corner, half expecting to see the headlights come back. The street remained quiet and dark.

This was so much better, she told herself, stepping out of the bushes and heading toward the house again. She'd wait for him inside. Throw him off guard. Unless it was a trap, somehow he knew she was here. Was it possible? The tissue in her lungs contracted. Breathing became harder. What did it matter?

Either way, you are going in there.

Schwartzman rounded the side of the house and passed the small shed where the garbage cans were housed. Beyond that was what Spencer had always termed the "maid's entrance," which was essentially a door into the garage. He refused to enter the house this way, just as he refused to take out the trash or clean. She tested the knob, careful to use her one gloved hand. Locked. She was almost relieved. Finding the door unlocked would have unnerved her, as though he were expecting her. She could always go through the window above the garage workbench, but maybe there was another way.

She crept down along the side of the house and peered into the formal living room, then into what Spencer called the family room, which was a smaller, cozier version of the living room. Nothing had changed. The same goldenrod couches. The same toile throw pillows. On the small table beside the couch was a picture of them on their honeymoon exactly where she'd last seen it.

Instead of an evil force, Spencer seemed pathetic. This grown man stuck in the past, loving a woman who despised him. Wasted years for both of them, and to what end? Where did he possibly imagine this would lead? Or was this his idea of entertainment? The on-again, off-again stalking a way to stay sharp, to avoid being bored by a life of golf and board meetings?

But Spencer was anything but pathetic. She knew it. Frances Pinckney knew it. Ava knew it.

This might have ended years ago. All she would have had to do was reach out to Ava. Ava with her plan. Resources that could have protected Ava, protected Schwartzman.

Remorse seared into anger, and the anger made her relive the memory.

She had just begun to feel the weight of the baby inside her, a small but constant pressure against her bladder. It was a weekend morning; only she and Spencer were in the house. It must have been the hottest part of the summer because the air-conditioning was blasting. She was forever wearing sweaters inside while Spencer complained about the heat and told her she was overreacting.

Still in her pajama bottoms and a tank top, she had come out to the garden to cut flowers for a vase in the living room. She had left the door open. Not all the way open but enough to let out some of Spencer's precious cold air. When she returned to the house with her flowers, the door was locked. Spencer stood behind the glass, smiling. She waved at him to let her in, but he ignored her.

They stood like that for a few minutes before he walked away. She made her way around the back of the house, tried those doors, then the maid's entrance, and finally the front door. All locked. She rang the bell, but Spencer didn't answer.

She had no phone, no car keys, no proper clothes. Determined not to give him the satisfaction of begging, she returned to the garden and settled into the dirt, using her bare fingers to weed around her flowers. But soon she had to use the bathroom. Again she tried the doors, rang the front bell, even checked a couple of the windows along the back of the house. Without success.

In the end, she urinated in the small back patch of their yard and spent the day outside, waiting for Spencer to unlock the door. It was some time after three when he finally did, calling out to her that he had invited her mother to an early dinner. She would be arriving at five thirty, he told Schwartzman, and she should make salmon.

Schwartzman returned to the house, filthy, sunburned, without the flowers she had picked, which had wilted and browned. She showered, went to the store, and fixed salmon for dinner, nodding politely while her mother told her how she ought to be careful about getting so much sun. "It will make you look old before your time."

"That's exactly what I told her," Spencer added, still wearing the morning's smirk. "She just insisted on spending the day outside. I don't even think she wore sunscreen."

And the two of them shook their heads at her, the little one unable to care for herself. Her mother reached across and patted her son-in-law's hand. "Well, thank goodness she has you, Spencer."

Sunburned and exhausted, Schwartzman felt overwhelming shame. Shame for leaving the door open, for getting herself locked out, for believing that his cruelty was her own fault.

That evening, after her mother was gone and Spencer had left the table and the dishes for her to clean up and settled into the den for his news program, she'd taken a spare house key outside and found a narrow slot between the cement foundation and the door frame at the maid's entrance.

Now, her pulse speeding, she crouched down in that same spot. She walked her gloved fingers along the base of the door's threshold, ignoring the bits of leaves and debris. She imagined spiders—brown recluses and black widows. She continued along the trim until she touched the hard edge of something metal. *The key.* She used the rental car key to pry it free and stood, cupping it in her hand.

She wiggled the key into the lock on the garage door and tested it. It caught. Nothing happened. It was rusted. Too old. He'd changed the locks. She tried again. And again. Bit her lip hard. Squeezed her eyes closed. "Come on." Used two hands to force it.

At last the key turned, and she pushed the door open a couple of inches. Froze. Waited. For alarms, noises. Nothing. Fear mixed with anticipation. She removed the key and returned it to its hiding spot, stepped inside, and closed the garage door behind her. She was in.

The motion sensor light on the garage door opener was still on, the space lit by the single bulb. She crossed to the large trash can and, with her hand tucked into her jacket, opened the lid. It was nearly full. The police would have to come tonight. She lay the top open against the garage door and pulled out two large kitchen-size trash bags. Beneath them were a handful of flattened cardboard boxes. She pushed the boxes aside and set the Home Depot sack on top of another white trash bag below. A length of rope on Spencer's workbench caught her eye. She added the rope to the sack and set the boxes flat again on top, then returned the last two trash bags to the can. She closed the top, looked around that she hadn't missed anything. It was done, the trap set.

Should she wait for him to return? She would have to. She needed to confront him, to convince him to tell her. She had to hear the truth from him.

The police would find the evidence. He was guilty. She wanted to hear it from him.

For Ava. For Frances Pinckney and Sarah Feld.

For herself.

The cold metal taste of fear filled her mouth. Ran down her throat.

What if the evidence wasn't enough? She didn't have anything from Frances Pinckney other than a little dog hair. What if the police didn't believe her?

She had to try.

Schwartzman put her hand on the door between the house and the garage and twisted the knob slowly. The alarm system made a double beeping sound and went quiet. He hadn't set it, which meant he wasn't going to be out long.

Or he knew you were coming.

It doesn't matter, she told herself.

Stepping slowly into the darkened hallway, she shivered in the cool air. Smelled lemon and lavender. She had forgotten how much Spencer loved lemon. How refreshing to think that some memories did fade.

As always, the house smelled clean. Beneath the clean smell, she detected the scent of moisture. Mold. Rooms closed up too much for too long. The stale mustiness she associated with air-conditioning after so many years of living without it.

In the darkness, she studied the sounds of the house. The air conditioner whirred noisily, and something else, water and glass maybe. The dishwasher? Nothing human. Spencer was gone, but for how long? She moved quickly through the hallway and paused at his office. The door was cracked open, and the memory of Ava's garage came back. She pressed her hand against the outside of her jacket, feeling the texture of the necklaces through the wool. His study. That was where he would keep souvenirs; she was certain.

She stopped, listened again. Not another sound. She nudged the study door open with her foot, kept her back to the wall as she rounded the doorjamb and entered the room. Silent. Empty. *Spencer isn't here. You watched him leave.*

But she knew better than to trust the obvious.

She crossed the room to the glass cabinet where Spencer kept his prized collections. A couple dozen pens—Montblanc, most of them, although there were Montegrappa and Waterman, as well. The collection hadn't changed much since they were married. With her to hunt, maybe collecting pens had lost its appeal.

On the shelf below the pens were about six or seven boxes. Wood, hand-carved, and made from exotic species. African teak and Brazilian rosewood. His favorite had always been the one in the back corner. Its surface was beautiful, the way the wood grain rolled across the top surface like rippling water.

"Please," a woman cried out.

Schwartzman froze, her pulse a drumbeat in her ears. Pushed the cabinet door closed. The hinges shrieked. Schwartzman jumped, held her breath, listening.

"Please!" The voice carried through the hall. The terror resonated like shock waves through Schwartzman's body.

It could be a trap. But Spencer was gone. She'd seen him leave.

"Please don't hurt me," the voice cried out, followed by sobs.

The sobs might have come from her own chest. Schwartzman drew slow, even breaths to calm her racing heart. Fought off the urge to sprint through the house and out the door. She imagined Sarah Feld. Schwartzman wanted to call out to her, held her silence. She cracked the office door, stepped into the hallway. Listened through the thumping of her pulse. Moved cautiously. She kept her back to the wall, listened with every step. Crying.

It came from the bedroom. Someone was here. She palmed the phone in her pocket and drew it out as she stepped into the hallway. She called 9-1-1. The screen didn't respond to her gloved finger. She yanked the glove off her right hand, shoved it into her jacket pocket.

The woman cried out again.

She could see into the bedroom at the end of the hall. The two doors along the hall were open—the first was the bathroom, the second the master closet. Both rooms were dark. Even without light, she could see the pillows on the made-up bed, the matching lamps on the bedside tables, a small stack of books on Spencer's side closest to the door.

Her back pressed to the hallway wall, she dialed 9-1-1 again. Nothing happened. A green circle appeared on the screen. *Call failed.*

"Help me," the voice cried out. The terror in the plea pulled Schwartzman forward.

Back against the wall, she crept down the hallway. Her breath felt shallow and painful in her lungs. The wall texture scratched her elbow through the thin jacket as she dug her toes into the carpet to propel herself forward.

"Please," the voice whispered again.

Schwartzman peered into the dark master closet but saw no one.

The voice was close. It had to be coming from the closet. Schwartzman dialed the emergency number again, gripped the phone, and watched the screen.

Again the call failed.

She froze just feet from the entrance to the closet. *Be smart.* Spencer kept a phone on his bedside table. She passed into the bedroom in the dark, moving heel to toe. Alert, upright, ready.

Still no sign of Spencer.

She put her cell phone in her pocket, lifted the house phone from its cradle. Held her breath as pushed the "Talk" button. Exhaled at the hum of the dial tone. She dialed 9-1-1. Put it to her ear. The phone went dead.

Fear gripped her neck and shoulders with cold, crushing fingers.

"Help me," the voice said.

She took two steps forward. Standing outside the closet, she reached in with her left hand, palmed the wall for the light switch, and flipped it on. The room was bathed in bright light. She blinked at the yellow spots in her vision, fought to banish them. Dark clothes lined two sides of the closet. On the third wall, she saw her own clothes. Bright yellows and soft pastels, still hanging where she had left them.

At the back of the closet was a new opening leading into another room. It hadn't been here before. A clean doorjamb, a sliding pocket door into the wall. The door height shorter than a normal door. Maybe five feet high.

She couldn't see into the darkened room. "Who's there?"

The crying started again.

"Who is in there?" she repeated, louder.

No answer.

She was cold to her bones. *Get out.* She turned to leave. A light cut through the darkness. A lone spotlight shone from high on the opposite wall. Below the spotlight on the blank wall, Schwartzman saw her. A woman was huddled on a dark floor. Dark, wavy hair hung to her shoulders. The narrow hips and back reminded Schwartzman of Sarah Feld. *Oh, God.* She was right. Another one.

"Let me help you," Schwartzman whispered, moving toward her.

"No," the woman cried, sobbing.

"Come on," Schwartzman said as she reached the opening.

The woman's head dropped down. She wore the cheetah hoodie. The one Schwartzman had bought in San Francisco, the one she'd been wearing in the garage.

He'd taken it—what—to put on his next victim? No. The hoodie had been taken into evidence along with her other clothes. How did Spencer get it?

She blinked into the darkened room. The floor was covered in a dark tile, the walls almost black, and something about the lighting made the woman appear partially obscured, as if she were separated from Schwartzman by a cloud.

A mechanical hissing filled the room. Schwartzman reeled backward, the phone trembling in her grip. The room was booby-trapped. The woman turned toward her. Even with her hair obscuring her face, Schwartzman knew her. She let out a cry. Her knees buckled.

The woman was her.

43

Greenville, South Carolina

It was a projection.

Images of her lying on the floor of Ava's garage. Behind her head, she could see the splintered pieces of the porcelain lamp. The video overlaid with her voice.

He had filmed her in Ava's garage.

"Please," her own voice cried out, the sound echoing in the small room.

The fear choked her. Unable to breathe, she pedaled away. Her head struck a shelf, and she cried out as she dropped to her knees. She dropped the phone to cup the throbbing in the back of her head. *Get up. Get away.* The picture changed. A video of their wedding day appeared. Her mother walking her down the aisle. Her mother's proud smile, her own more tentative, excited and nervous. So naive, so young. So close she could reach out and touch herself.

She grabbed the phone off the carpet. The image switched to her unborn baby. The ultrasound image of the head and rounded spine, the little fists tight balls. Ready to fight but too young. The sound of the tiny heartbeat thundered against the walls. Schwartzman pressed her hand to her mouth, closed her eyes against the sound, then opened them again, unable to look away from the tiny fluttery heart. Her baby. Her daughter. She reached out to touch the image. It vanished in her hand.

Just then the dark room lit up. The large wall became a thousand tiny rectangular screens, each the size of a subway tile. Solid light. Blinding. Lines raced across the screens. A series of flashes followed, and the wall became Spencer's face.

She gasped. His head was immense. Twenty times its normal size. More. She could see the small mole on his left cheek, the tiny scar above his right eye where he fell off his bike as a child.

"So lovely to see you, Bella," Spencer thundered.

Below him the film of her unborn child played on.

She spun away. Sprinted for the dark hallway, tripped, and caught herself. Her pulse bored through her eardrums. Blinded by the bright images, she palmed the wall, found the edge of the door. Her vision was filled with Spencer's giant face. The room went dark, the screen black again. She tore out of the closet and into the hall, slamming into Spencer, who stood like a concrete wall. He didn't even flinch.

She cried out.

His expression split into a grimace as he laughed.

She slammed backward, striking the wall. A picture dropped to the floor. Glass shattered. She swiped at her face with the back of her hand and felt the wetness of her tears. Why hadn't she kept Ava's gun? She would pull the trigger. She would.

"You like my new project?" he said, closing the bedroom door behind him. He crept toward her until his features were visible in the dim light. His eyes were darker and wider than she remembered. Empty and flat. How had she ever imagined they were warm?

"Stay away from me," she warned, her hands up as though she could fight him.

"But surely you'll tell me what you think? I spent months on that room."

Oh, God. He'd planned this for months. The murders, to bring her to this. What was this?

His teeth flashed in his mouth as he clenched his jaw. "You don't remember."

She froze, said nothing.

"You have no idea why I made this room," he said, the words little bullets firing from his lips.

She sucked in a breath. Was this where it ended? Had she been naive to think he wanted her alive?

"It's the old pantry and half bath," he said, his voice calm again, deliberate though she could tell he was fighting anger.

She scanned the closet for something she could use as a weapon.

"Do you remember?" he pressed.

Shoes, hangers, clothes. His wallet on the bureau. Nothing.

Spencer's lips split into a wide, ugly sneer. "Well, you'll know soon enough. Now that you're home again, Bella." He lifted his hand. She saw something small and black. A gun.

She raised her hands to cover her face, stepped backward as Spencer pointed it to the closet. The room was bathed in light.

Her heart raced. Hot nausea rose between her lungs, welled in her throat.

He held a remote control. "Come see." He moved past her.

As soon as he was past, she ran. Down the short hallway. Grabbed hold of the doorknob. It wouldn't turn. She shook it. Pounded on the door. She was trapped.

"Come now, Bella." His voice directly behind her.

She spun around, pressed herself into the corner between the wall and the door. "Let me out of here."

"But you haven't had the tour," he said.

"Stay away from me."

He grabbed hold of her arm, spun her to face him. "Do. Not," he spat, raising his palm to strike her. "Ever. Tell me," he continued, drawing out each word. "To stay away from *my* wife." His palm slowly morphed into a fist as he lowered it again. "You are my wife, Bella," he said, his voice almost a whisper. "I made you an anniversary present. Our twelfth anniversary . . . you do remember the importance of our twelfth year, don't you?"

Pressed to the door, she couldn't think what he was talking about. She had to get out. Stole a glance over his shoulder. He jabbed his hand out. Like he was thrusting a knife. A rapid clicking sound and the angry buzzing of electricity. Searing heat punctured her middle. She cried out. Fire spread across her limbs. Every muscle contracted. Then it ended, and her legs collapsed. She dropped to the ground. She pushed herself off the floor, arms shaking.

Spencer stood above her, the stun gun aimed at her. "It does hurt, doesn't it? I rather like it," he said. "This, the cell phone jammer, I'm just full of surprises, aren't I?" Grinning, he pressed the button again. She started at the buzzing sound of the weapon. "You're full of surprises, too, Bella." He shook his head and made a tsking sound. "Not good ones, though. You've forgotten quite a lot in your time away."

There had to be another way out. The sliding glass door in the bedroom. A window.

"Now, come see the room I made for you," Spencer said firmly. His jaw tightened, and she saw the shift of the stun gun.

Get up. Do what he says. Stall. She eased herself onto her knees, tears in her eyes.

He reached a hand out, but she stood on her own. Took a step. He shoved her hard. She saw the sliding door on the far side of the bedroom. It would take too long to open.

He pressed her into the closet. The room beyond it was tiny. Painted dark gray. A twin bed along one wall. Small bookcase, black. Gray rug. No color at all.

"You look so surprised." His lips curled into a smile. "I wanted you to feel at home. I know you're not a fan of color anymore, Bella."

She hesitated, bending her knees to run.

Spencer grabbed her by the arm, threw her toward the space.

She caught herself, ducked under his arm. He was faster. Shoved her into the wall and slapped her hard across the face. She dropped to her knees. Gasped. Tasted blood in her mouth. An angry pulsing in her lip.

"I warned you, Bella. I've had enough."

She remained on the floor. "What do you want?" she screamed at him.

He cocked his head sideways, his eyes narrowed. Insane. "What every good husband wants . . . to make my wife happy."

"You killed Ava to make me happy?" she spat at him.

"You made—" He caught himself and closed his mouth, shook his head.

He did it. Of course he did it. She wanted to hear it. "Say it, Spencer. Say you killed her."

Spencer held the stun gun high in his right hand. Moved toward her.

She scrambled backward, but he caught her leg, held her. His grip too tight. The stun gun. He clamped a knee on either side of her waist until she was forced onto her back.

Pulse throbbing in her neck. Every cell screaming no. She tried to twist free.

He pinned her hips, leaned down across her.

She shoved his chest. "Get off me!"

The stun gun touching her cheek, she froze. Waited for the clicking sound that didn't come.

He patted down her jacket. Removed her cell phone from her pocket.

"Let me guess. One zero two zero." He typed in her passcode, grinning.

He knew her passcode. Ava's birthday. Of course he did.

He held the "Power" button, shut the phone down. "No recording in here, darling." He tossed the phone over his shoulder. It bounced across the closet carpeting. She lost sight of it.

"Now, let's take your jacket off," he said, pushing the jacket down off her shoulder.

Panic lodged in her chest, her throat. She couldn't breathe.

The stun gun made a buzzing sound. She flinched.

"Hush," he responded. Calm. The stun gun so close to her face.

He grabbed hold of the jacket's sleeve, yanked it down off her hand. Shoved her to one side, pinning her hips, and jerked the other sleeve free. Patted the jacket until he was satisfied it held no wire. Tossed it, too. She gasped at the feeling of his hand on her shoulder. Clenched every muscle against his touch. His palm moved down her arms. Across her legs and hips, up to her crotch; he let his hand rest there.

"I don't feel a wire," he said. "That's good."

She squeezed her eyes closed. He palmed her breasts, cupped them and squeezed hard. She gritted her teeth against the pain. He could not hold her. They would find her. Harper or Hal. Someone would come here. Wouldn't they? She would die first. He could not keep her alive here.

He rolled her over, clutched her backside. His weight lifted, and she drove onto her hands and knees, scrambled away from him.

"You're clean. I'm so relieved," he said with an exaggerated exhalation. "I want to trust you, Bella. We have to have trust in our marriage."

"You want trust? Then, tell me," she said, her breath heavy with fear. "Tell me you killed Frances Pinckney. That you killed—" Her voice broke.

She couldn't say Ava's name.

Then he was on top of her, his hot mouth at her ear. "Yes, Bella. I killed her. Because of you, Bella," he whispered. "Because you wouldn't come home to me. But I knew how to get you here, didn't I?" And then he shifted away, his voice returned to normal volume. "Come see your anniversary present, Bella. This is the year we make our son. Just like my parents did. A beautiful, healthy boy."

How could he say those words, not twenty feet from where he'd killed her baby girl?

The hideous smile grew until it consumed his face.

"Come on," he said. "Don't you want to experience it fully?"

When she hesitated, he reached down and grabbed her arm. Yanked her upright.

She twisted her hand from his grip. "I'll never have your baby," she seethed. "We will never be together."

He laughed. "I like this new you, Bella. This strength suits you." He moved forward again, the stun gun coming toward her.

She stumbled back, struck the bureau. Reached to catch herself. Her fingers brushed something hard, metal. She eased her hand toward it, felt the thin metal. One of Spencer's pens. She wrapped her fingers around it, pulling it into her fist. The pen hidden at her side, she shifted away from the bureau as he closed in again. She took another step backward, desperate to be angry and not afraid. To feel fury. It had been there.

"Your father would be proud."

The words were as sharp as a scalpel. She moved away, stumbling.

Suddenly she was in the tiny room. Her prison. Darkness surrounding her, the baby's heartbeat pounded in her ears. Spencer blocked the doorway, huge and too close.

The baby's ultrasound filled the screen again. *Thu-thump, thu-thump* . . .

As she fought to look away, Spencer's face filled the screen. Her baby's heartbeat echoing off the walls.

Images flashed around her.

The wedding, herself huddled on the ground in Ava's garage, her baby . . .

And then Spencer was beside her. Gucci cologne filled her nose. He drew in a deep breath, inhaling her scent as if she was prey. His tongue on her cheek, his mouth on hers.

The walls closed in. She couldn't breathe. Her fingers tightened on the pen.

He lifted the stun gun to her cheek. "I won't let you leave again, Bella," he said through gritted teeth.

She raised her left arm against the stun gun and swung her right, using all her power to drive the point of the pen into his arm. Spencer cried out, dropped to his knees. The stun gun slipped from his hand as he reached for the pen that stuck straight out from his shoulder. He jerked it free.

"You bitch!" He launched toward her, his eyes bright as a caged lion's.

She stumbled toward the hallway. He yanked her down.

"You fucking bitch," he shouted. His hand clawed at her arm, his fingers tightening on her neck. "You're not going anywhere, Bella." He bashed her against the wall. She struck her temple, saw black.

She screamed and kicked. Swung her elbow at his head, missed. Felt his grip loosen. She stretched her fingers toward the stun gun.

His fist struck down on her back, and she collapsed into the ground. The carpet stung her face as she gasped for breath. Rage built inside her, and she rose, swinging her fist backward. She connected with his groin. He doubled over, and she launched her foot into his chin. Kicked her other foot into his chest.

He groaned.

She bucked herself across the carpet until her fingers gripped the stun gun. Rolled onto her back and moved away. He was huddled, cupping his bleeding arm. Blood pooled beneath him. His eyes were hooded, narrow. His teeth bared like an animal's.

She stood, aimed the stun gun. Lunged at him and pressed the button. Electricity crackled. Spencer didn't react.

She'd missed.

He rose slowly, pushing his back up the wall. His face shone with perspiration. A line of spittle marked his chin. He stepped forward. Closer. The stench of his sweat in her nose.

She buzzed the stun gun again.

He took another step. He was only a couple of feet away. She willed him to stop.

He smiled. And kept on coming. He wouldn't give up.

She launched herself at him and connected the stun gun to the wound on his shoulder. Pressed the trigger and held it.

Spencer let out a piercing scream and collapsed.

Schwartzman sprinted through the bedroom to the sliding glass door. Unlocked it and yanked on the door. It didn't open.

Glassy-eyed and panting, Spencer filled the closet doorway. "You should have stayed, Bella," he growled.

"Never." She grabbed the antique marble-top bedside table that had been hers. She tilted the table, dumping the light onto the floor.

The bulb exploded.

The table was bulky, awkward to lift, but she heaved it into the air. Clutched the top to her chest, the legs aimed at the glass door.

"No!" he shouted.

She closed her eyes and charged through the door. Glass exploded, raining down small, tempered bits. She crashed onto the porch, fell across the table, landed hard on her hip. Scrambled up. Fighting to draw breath, she ran into the street.

"Call nine-one-one!" she screamed. "Someone call nine-one-one." Her cries were answered by the wail of sirens.

Two squad cars screeched to a stop in front of her, their lights swinging through the night air. She bent down, holding her stomach with both arms and fought not to cry.

44

Greenville, South Carolina

Schwartzman pressed the back of her hand to her bleeding lip. She didn't take her eyes off Spencer's house.

He was inside.

A third car tore up to the curb, and Harper Leighton jumped out. "You guys make sure MacDonald doesn't go anywhere," she shouted to patrol.

The officers started for Spencer's door.

Then Harper was beside her. "Are you okay?" the detective asked.

"How in the world are you here?" Schwartzman responded.

"I called in a favor from a friend down here. He works for a local security firm. I asked him to do a drive-by for your car." Harper motioned to Schwartzman's face. "He hit you?"

Schwartzman touched her lip, saw blood on her fingers. "A few times." She wiped it on her pants, looked back at the detective, who still wore the dress from Frances Pinckney's service. "I've only been here twenty minutes, maybe a half hour. It's a three-hour drive from Charleston."

"I had a hunch you were coming here."

"So you drove three hours?" Schwartzman asked. Was she worried that Schwartzman had planned to kill Spencer? Or was she worried that Spencer might hurt her? It didn't matter. Either way, that was going way beyond the job. Schwartzman felt a deep surge of gratitude. Instead of facing a group of strangers, she had an ally.

"There was something about the way you were at the Pinckneys' house." The detective paused. "That and Hal Harris wouldn't stop calling me." Harper nodded to the house. "MacDonald inside?"

"Yes," Schwartzman said, shuddering at the memory. "He recorded me in Ava's garage. Not the attack itself, but he's got video of me in the garage. Can we use that?"

"Yes. Proves he was there."

Unless he has another explanation. Which he would. Spencer would have a story about how he'd found her there. He had admitted to her that he had killed Ava. No one would ever hear it, but she had. She knew.

Let him try to explain the evidence she had planted.

Tightness in her gut. Planted evidence.

She didn't make him kill.

She flinched at something touching her.

"You're shaking," Harper said, wrapping a jacket across Schwartzman's shoulders. Harper waved to a man in a suit. "Tom."

"Harper," he said, raising his hand to her. "Long time."

"This is Annabelle Schwartzman," Harper said when the man joined them. She turned to Schwartzman. "This is Tom Overby. He's a detective with the Greenville PD."

Overby motioned to the house. "You want to tell me what happened in there?" he asked Schwartzman.

Schwartzman drew a shaky breath. She wanted to leave, to be as far from here as possible. *Soon,* she told herself. "Spencer was—is my husband. We've been separated for seven years. He killed my aunt Ava and another woman in Charleston. And I'm pretty sure he was involved in a death in San Francisco. The lead detective out there is Hal Harris."

Overby nodded to Harper. "Detective Leighton caught me up on the theory."

Schwartzman was keenly aware of the intensity of Harper's gaze. She kept her eye on the Greenville detective. A man she didn't know. Would never know. "I wanted him to tell me he did it. I wanted to hear him say he killed them. And I thought there was a chance that I could find some piece of evidence to link him to their murders."

"So you decided to drive up to Greenville from Charleston and show up at his house?" Overby flipped open his notepad. "This man you suspect murdered your aunt and two other women?"

Schwartzman risked a glance at Harper. "We're burying Ava tomorrow." She looked back at Overby. "Ava is my aunt. I had to try. We know how she died, but I thought maybe I could discover something more, something I could tie back to evidence on her body. Some evidence to prove it was Spencer. Before we buried her, I had to know I hadn't missed something."

Schwartzman felt the fear settle lower in her chest. She could do this. There was no doubt between her and God that Spencer was a murderer. That he'd killed them. All she was doing was making the justice happen.

"And did he confess?" Overby asked.

"Would it make a difference?"

"Not unless it's recorded," Overby said.

She shook her head. It was not recorded. "He has video footage of me in the garage of my aunt's home, where I was attacked."

"He showed you this film?" Overby asked.

She cleared her throat, pushed past the sound of the baby's beating heart. "Yes."

The detective looked at the house. "We need probable cause to go in."

"Look at my face," Schwartzman says. "He hit me. He was holding me against my will. I had to throw a table through the sliding glass door to get out," she said, hearing her voice rise. "And he used a stun gun." She pulled up her shirtsleeve to show him the mark. Two small red burns. She ran her finger over them, grateful for their presence. They would probably scar. She would have a lot of scars. She took a deep breath. "He locked the bedroom door from the inside. He's added this area by the closet—it's like a kind of prison." And there the fear rose again, into her throat.

Overby nodded. To Harper, he said, "It's enough to hold him for a few hours, take a look around the house. But I don't know how much more—"

"It's enough," Harper said as though she knew what was inside. Could she know? Schwartzman glanced at the detective. She had faith.

Schwartzman had lost that. Overby instructed one of the patrol officers to go in for Spencer. "Tell him he's being held on assault and battery and unlawful imprisonment. And read him his rights."

Schwartzman watched the officer walk to Spencer's door.

"Will you excuse us for a minute?" Overby asked Schwartzman as he pulled Harper to the side.

Schwartzman watched the backs of the two detectives, wished she could hear them. Overby motioned to the house, to the street. Was he changing his mind?

Would they let Spencer go?

"I'll have your badges for this!" Spencer's voice.

Schwartzman jumped at the sound.

"This is private property. She's the one you should arrest. Her! Right there!"

Schwartzman wanted to look away. She forced herself to look at him, to watch as the officers led him to the patrol car. His eyes narrowed on her, but they weren't frightening. She held her chin up, her eyes steady.

I'm not afraid of you. Not anymore.

The officer opened the door to the patrol car, put his hand on Spencer's head as he was lowered into the car. The door closed behind him. Schwartzman watched every second of it.

Harper returned to Schwartzman, put an arm around her shoulders. "The paramedics are here, Detective Overby. If there's nothing else you need, I'd like to get her checked out."

"Go ahead," Overby said. "I'll call out the Crime Scene Unit, and we'll see what we can find."

Harper led Schwartzman away from the detective. They made a loop around to avoid walking by the patrol car where Spencer sat shouting. Schwartzman wanted to ask what the detective had said. At the same time, she didn't want to know.

"You should have told me you were coming," Harper said.

"I know. I wanted to see if I could find anything. I—" She stopped. She wanted to curl into a ball. It was almost over. Wasn't it? She stood straight and wiped her hands across her pants. She turned to Harper, who waited patiently. "How did you get the police to come? I tried to call them from inside the house, but he had a jammer. The calls never went through."

"I got nervous," Harper admitted, then lowered her voice. "In the end, I told them that you had called me for help. That was enough to get them over here."

"I was . . . he has this room—" Schwartzman felt the throbbing pulse of her baby's heart. The sobs just broke free, and she struggled to contain them in her belly and chest, to hold them back.

Harper wrapped her arms around Schwartzman and led her past the ambulance, out of view of the patrol car.

"He told me," Schwartzman said. "He told me that he killed them—that he had to because I wouldn't come back to him."

Harper exhaled and pulled her into a hug. Schwartzman didn't fight. She rested her head on the detective's shoulder and let the tears come. "We're going to get him," Harper said. "We are."

Schwartzman didn't answer. What more could she say?

As the tears slowed, Harper moved her ever so gently to the ambulance. A paramedic helped her sit on the wide bumper. The adrenaline fading, she began to shiver in earnest. A second paramedic wrapped a blanket over her shoulders while the first started to clean up her lip. They put ointment on the burn from the stun gun. "You've got a nasty bruise up here, too," he said, grazing her temple.

She flinched at the pain. Was that where he'd hit her? Or where she struck the wall? It all ran together. *It's over,* she told herself. Pressed her eyes closed to let that sink in.

"We're going to want to photograph those injuries," Harper told them. She touched Schwartzman's arm. "Hang tight while we get someone to do that."

Schwartzman wondered if the police would find the other evidence linking Spencer to the crimes—the knee pads, Ava's hair, the fur from Pinckney's dog. The film from Ava's garage connected him to her attack but not necessarily to the murders. She wasn't counting on it, but it would be nice if he'd slipped up somewhere along the way.

But he *had* slipped up.

He had slipped up by thinking he could get away with murder, that he was somehow above the rules.

"I'm not going to bandage anything until we get those photos," the paramedic said. "Can you hold on awhile?"

Schwartzman nodded. The paramedic joined his colleague and the two began packing up their supplies. Her jacket and phone were still inside. The glove was in the jacket pocket. She had to go back. She looked back at the house, hesitating. It was just a house. The paramedics were talking as she slid the blanket off her shoulders and walked toward the house. Head back, shoulders up, a last good-bye.

She would never come here again.

She hesitated at the porch. Glass strewn across the concrete pad, sprinkled over the lawn furniture, the chaise lounge where she used to sometimes sit and read while Spencer was at work.

An escape to all of this.

The patrol officers had Spencer outside. The crime scene team had yet to arrive. Without being seen, Schwartzman stepped back through the broken glass door and across the carpet in the bedroom. Saw the picture of them as newlyweds on the bureau.

She reached out to touch the marble edge where she'd lost her baby. Held her hand back. Pressed it instead to her belly. Felt the grief tug at her spine.

She flipped on the light and banished the shadows from the room. It was still yellow.

She would always hate yellow.

The brightly lit closet was just a closet again. He'd kept her clothes to make it look whole. It was too empty, half lived in. She picked up her jacket, checked that the glove was still in the pocket, then bent down to look for her phone. Pushed aside the long dresses that had been hers in another life. Dust floated into the air as they swayed. She found her phone and glanced in the direction of the prison Spencer had built for her. Fought not to turn away. *It's just a room.*

She forced herself to step across the threshold, found the light switch, and turned it on. Three white walls, blank. Sad-looking without the terrifying projections. One wall was painted dark gray. A twin-size bed stood along the gray wall. The bed linens in lighter grays and whites. A small black bookcase, lined with books. She didn't look closely enough to tell which ones. The throw rug. A well-appointed prison. What would the crime scene team make of this?

Closing her eyes, she could hear the baby's heartbeat. It would always be there. She let out her breath, released everything she could from the room, and turned away again. Back down the hall, through the bedroom, out through the broken glass door.

Lying on its side was her bedside table. The marble was cracked, and one piece had rolled into the grass. One of the legs was in two pieces. The drawer had fallen free, and its contents were scattered. Pens and a familiar notepad, one she'd kept by the bed. A bottle of Advil. Probably also hers from all those years ago.

He had tried to preserve her in these things.

Failed.

As she moved past, she spotted something on the bottom side of the drawer. Clear and silver, it might have been a sticker of some sort. She used her toe to turn the drawer upside down, leaned in.

"Anna," Harper called.

"I'm here," she responded as Harper came into view.

"What are you doing?" the detective asked.

Schwartzman pointed at the bottom of the bedside table. "Look."

Harper crouched beside her. "What is it?"

A small bag was taped to the bottom of the wooden drawer. Through the clear plastic Schwartzman could see a thin silver chain with a pendant. "It's a turtle," she said, her whole chest welling with the words. "A sea turtle."

"You recognize it?" Harper asked.

Schwartzman's eyes filled with tears. "Ava."

Harper stood and called out, "Overby!" She put her hand out to Schwartzman. "Don't touch it. I want to preserve any prints." Harper's phone rang on her belt.

Schwartzman took a last look at the necklace. Of course it would be the turtle. She had shared that story with Spencer—she and Ava and their matching sea turtles. She stood and turned toward the street, ready to leave this place behind her. To leave Spencer behind her.

"She's right here," Harper said, handing the phone to Schwartzman. "It's Hal," she added. "He's been a little worried."

Schwartzman took the phone and brought it to her ear as she walked toward the street. "Hi, Hal."

There was an audible breath. "You scared the crap out of me, Schwartzman."

She couldn't help but smile. "I'm sorry."

His voice dropped. "You're okay?"

"Now I am." She saw Spencer in the back of the patrol car. His face red, his mouth moving though she couldn't hear him anymore. "Actually I'm better than okay, I think."

"Sounds like they've got enough to hold him, at least for a while."

She imagined the sea turtle necklace. It was enough, wasn't it? "I hope so," she said, the safest answer.

"We got a lead out here, too," Hal said.

"You did?"

"Sarah Feld's neighbor, Carol Fletcher, has a thing for guys doing hard time," Hal said.

Schwartzman walked past the ambulance, away from the patrol cars and sat on the curb. "What do you mean?"

"Fletcher dates men who are incarcerated," Hal continued. "She hooks up with them online. She's had three or four long relationships like that—over messaging and the occasional phone call. We're talking about relationships that have lasted years."

"So Spencer pretended to be a prisoner," Schwartzman guessed. "It worked because they'd never met."

"We think so," Hal confirmed. "She was at Folsom yesterday to visit a particularly nasty criminal named Charles Bollardi. Mr. Bollardi said he'd never seen her before, told her to get lost."

"And Fletcher didn't appreciate that?" Schwartzman asked.

"No she did not," Hal said. "In fact, she pitched quite a fit. They called in Sacramento PD. Guy there thought it was pretty suspicious when Fletcher's home address matched the address where Rebecca Feld's daughter was murdered. He suspected there might be a connection, so he called us."

"You think Carol Fletcher was Spencer's accomplice?"

"Seems like a real possibility," Hal said. "She lived across the hall from Feld. Would have made it easy to kill her. And to pretend to be you the night Macy was stabbed."

Schwartzman exhaled. "Is she talking?"

"She's in holding," Hal said. "Hailey and I are going over there now, but I wanted to talk to you first."

"Thanks, Hal. I almost can't believe it could be over," she admitted.

More than seven years she had waited.

"Yeah. Me, too." There was a moment of silence before he asked, "What now?"

She watched Overby and Harper walk out to meet a crime scene van that was pulling to the curb. "What do you mean?" she asked Hal.

"What will you do?" Hal asked.

First she would take care of Ava. "My aunt's service is in the morning."

"And then?" he asked.

"Then I'm coming home," she told him.

He exhaled. Relief. "I was thinking I was going to have to come down there and get you. Truth is, I'm a little afraid of the South."

Schwartzman laughed, wincing at the pain in her temple. "A lot of people are."

"But I don't need to come down there because you're coming home?" There was a question in his voice.

She smiled.

"Yes, Hal," she told him. "I'm coming home."

EPILOGUE

Three Weeks Later

Schwartzman stood in front of Ken Macy's house. The house was a pale blue, the third in a line of identical homes with rounded terracotta roofs that looked like Chinese hats and front windows divided into five equal panes over a narrow, single-car garage.

She walked up the steps and took a full breath before ringing the bell. The house was quiet, and she felt sharp disappointment that no one was home. She shifted the box to her other arm and looked around for a spot where she might leave it. There were no plants or decorations on the porch, which was visible from the street.

It would probably be stolen.

But then the door swung open, and intense fluttering filled her gut. She had worried about how he would react to seeing her, but when he saw it was her, Ken smiled.

"I hope I'm not bothering you," she said.

"Not at all." He stepped back. "Please come in."

"Thank you." She walked into the foyer as he closed the door behind them. He motioned to the front room. "Sit in here?"

"Sure." It was tidy, simply decorated but stylish. The rugs in the entryway and the living room had large geometric patterns like something Native American. He crossed the room slowly but without limping or favoring one part of his body.

Did he have pain? Eighteen stab wounds in all. Because of her.

She started to sit and realized she was still holding the box. "I brought this for you."

"You didn't have to do that."

She held the box out. "Please."

He took the box and sat down, turning the plain black box in his hands. He smiled and let out a low chuckle. "What is the appropriate gift to give the guy almost killed by your ex-husband?"

She gasped and pushed her hand to her mouth. "Oh, Ken. That's so awful."

"I'm teasing, Anna."

"I am so sorry. I didn't know he would go that far, that he would—"

Ken moved to sit beside her, set his hand on hers. "I'm serious, Anna. It wasn't your fault. I'm alive. I'm going to be able to go back to work . . ." He hesitated. "I'm going to be okay."

His eyes were sincere, open.

She pulled her hand slowly from his, returned it to her lap. "I can't express how awful I feel for what happened."

"I heard about your aunt."

Schwartzman blinked against the tears.

"I am so sorry."

She swiped her cheeks. "Open it," she said, nodding to the present.

He drew out the bottle of Evan Williams. "Bourbon."

"It was my father's favorite." She had inherited eleven bottles when her father died. It was one of her pleasures, sitting in her apartment with a glass of bourbon and a book or an old movie. Those bottles were gone. The one for Ken was the first bottle of Evan Williams she'd ever bought.

"Would you like a glass?" he asked.

"I don't think so."

"Another time, then."

"Yes," she agreed. A moment of silence passed between them; then Schwartzman rose. "I should be going."

Ken remained seated. "I am grateful, you know."

"Grateful?" she echoed.

"The doctors said I was very lucky that you woke up when you did."

"I was lucky," she said, thinking luck was a ridiculous notion to apply to her recent past. But that night, she woke before Ken died. She liked to think that her father and Ava helped her wake up.

"Well, I'm grateful."

He was the same Ken, despite what he had been through—kind, caring. She hoped they would be friends. It would be a rough few months for them both.

Her mastectomy was scheduled, and she would have her own healing to do.

But maybe after that.

Hopefully.

"I can let myself out." She wanted to ask him when he'd be back at work, but she was afraid to hear the answer. It had already been a month since the attack. How much longer would he have to wait?

Ken stood. "I hope I'll see you soon."

"I'd like that," she said and knew it was the truth.

Walking down Ken Macy's front steps, she was relieved. He was walking. There was no medical equipment in view in the apartment. He obviously made it up and down his own stairs. Maybe he really would be okay.

Would she forgive herself then?

As she got into her car, her cell phone rang. She expected Hal. He would be getting off work soon, and they planned to meet for dinner. But looking at the phone, she saw the 864 area code. Greenville. *Spencer.*

She didn't have to answer. But she did.

No more running from her fears.

"Schwartzman," she said and held her breath, expecting his low raspy voice.

"Annabelle Schwartzman?" said a female voice.

"Speaking," she confirmed. Her fingers found the "Lock" button on the car door, pressed down.

"I'm Laura Patchett, the assistant district attorney for Greenville and Pickens Counties." The voice was succinct, no nonsense. Professional. Schwartzman was wary. "I wanted to talk to you about Spencer MacDonald. Or more specifically, the case against MacDonald."

Against Spencer. The case for keeping him in prison forever.

Schwartzman pressed her eyes closed, leaned hard into the seat behind her. She fought to control her breathing, her pulse. Just his name sent her into fight or flight. "Yes," she said, drawing slow breaths. *In. Out.*

"We'd like you to testify in the preliminary hearing."

She replayed the words in her head, listened to the response of her body. Absent was the clenched gut that came with thinking of Spencer. He was behind bars. He was going to jail. Forever. Her mother had been shocked at the news that Spencer had been arrested. Schwartzman heard the denial in her mother's responses. Even when Schwartzman recounted the details of what he had done. The same as it had always been. Would her mother believe he was evil when he was convicted of killing Ava? Maybe. But maybe not. Schwartzman's pulse slowed. She opened her eyes. Watched a jogger pass with a dog.

"Dr. Schwartzman?"

"Yes."

"I was asking if you'd be willing to—"

"Yes," Schwartzman interrupted. "I'll testify."

"Wonderful," Patchett said, and Schwartzman could hear the relief in her voice. "We are looking at setting a date for two weeks from Wednesday."

"Let me give you my e-mail address, and you can send me the dates so I can arrange my travel and get coverage at work." Schwartzman recited her e-mail address, and Patchett thanked her again before signing off.

Schwartzman glanced at the dash clock. It was almost six fifteen. After nine in Greenville. Patchett was working late. *Good.* Putting Spencer away was a priority. *He's never coming back. He can't hurt you anymore.* Her shoulders relaxed and she started the car, felt her phone buzz. *Hal.*

"I'm over in the Sunset, heading your way," she told him.

"Great," he said. "I'm about ten minutes away. I'll get us a table. You want wine?"

"Actually, will you see if they've got Evan Williams bourbon? I think I've seen it behind the bar. If it's there, I'll take it neat." The DA was building a case against Spencer. While he sat in jail, she was on her way to dinner with a friend. Reason to celebrate. *No. Reasons* to celebrate.

"Bourbon? I've never seen you order bourbon."

"I'll tell you the story when I get there."

"Look forward to it. Hey, and drive safe, Schwartzman."

"Promise," she told him.

Safe. She did feel safe. *You are safe.*

Finally.

She turned on the radio and pulled into traffic.

ACKNOWLEDGMENTS

I am incredibly grateful for the generosity of those who helped make this book possible. I take full responsibility for whatever errors remain and for occasionally bending the truth to fit the story.

For research, I am forever indebted to the invaluable resources at SFPD who have been answering questions since book one. Thank you also to Jacqueline Perkins, medical examiner, Guilford, Rockingham, Alamance, and Caswell Counties, North Carolina; Alison Hutchens, forensic services supervisor; and D. P. Lyle, MD.

A gigantic thank you to Meg Ruley, this writer's dream agent, and to the team at JRA, who have offered me such an enthusiastic welcome. Thank you also to the extraordinary JoVon Sotak, who fell in love with Schwartzman, and to Sarah Shaw and the incredible team at Thomas & Mercer. I am so grateful to the phenomenal Mallory Braus, who pushed Schwartzman and me to be our very best.

I am endlessly appreciative of those who support the process of writing a book—my first reader, Randle Bitnar, who keeps me aimed in the right direction from page 1; Dani Wanderer, my star proofreader; and the friends and family who let me be reclusive when I need to write and who know to have wine at the ready when I emerge. Mom, Nicole, Steve, Tom, and Dad, I am so grateful, never more than this past year and a half.

To Chris, whose love and partnership make this life such a splendid adventure. And for Claire and Jack, always for you guys.

ABOUT THE AUTHOR

Photo © 2012 Janie Osborne

Danielle Girard is the author of nine previous novels, including *Chasing Darkness* and *Savage Art*, as well as The Rookie Club series. Her books have won the Barry Award and the RT Reviewers' Choice Award, and two of her titles have been optioned for movies.

A graduate of Cornell University, Danielle received her MFA at Queens University in Charlotte, North Carolina. She, her husband, and their two children split their time between San Francisco and the Northern Rockies.